CW00864633

ONLY
BLOOD

LEO HOFFORD

ONLY BLOOD

Leo Hofford was born in Singapore. He is a Queen's Counsel at the Scottish Bar, married with three children. He lives, works and writes in Edinburgh

~~~~

Copyright Leo Hofford 2015
Leo Hofford has asserted his right under the
Copyright, Designs and Patents Act 1988 to be
identified as the author of this work

All rights are reserved. This book is sold subject to
the condition that it shall not by way of trade or
otherwise, be lent, resold, hired out or otherwise
circulated without the publisher's prior consent in any
form of binding or cover other than that in which it is
published and without a similar condition, including
this condition, being imposed on the subsequent
purchaser

ISBN 978 1 326 42333 9

To my wife, Jackie, for her forbearance over long nights spent by me in my study, and to my three children, Oliver, Sophie and Phoebe, for their enduring questions and support. Also, to David Scott for his friendship as the story unfolded and to Paul Bartlett for his inspiration to persevere. Finally, to Alison Craig whose selfless encouragement started me off and drove me on.

CHAPTER 1

"I'm surprised at you, Wilson. That's all I'm saying. I didn't think you were such a purry kind of pussy." It was an irritating, awkward pitch of a voice, sort of stetched like a thin reed, full of nasal tone.

Calum turned to see who was there speaking at him. He half-knew the strangled voice and he recognized the skinny-butted figure seated like a bag of useless bones at the back of the shop, rolling a cigarette between his fingers, one boot lazily on the chair in front of him, smirking quietly. "Oh my dear," Calum said slowly. "Joey, Joey. Look at you. Look what was scraped off the top of the bog." He stepped towards Joey and scrutinized him.
"What are you staring at, Wilson?" drawled Joey.
"Well, you got so boney," Calum said. "You still got worms?"
"I've no' got worms," he said, licking the paper and rolling the tobacco tighter than he meant. "That's unfriendly."
"Well, you're skinny as fuck," Calum said. "Must have some intestinal shit, cancer thing, that makes you look like that."
"Like what?" he said.
"Like spit on a stick."

Joey lit the wodge of tobacco that hung limp from the cigarette and the end ignited, growling red, as he sucked the smoke into his chest. Next to him a man of similar age with a soft, puffy nose, small eyes and thick eyebrows, breathed open-mouthed with a heavy, rasping sound. "Maybe it's not my health you should worry about," said Joey.

"Why's that?" he asked.

"Oh, just rumours, you know. I been hearing things," said Joey, looking up. "Little bird's been talking in my ear."

"Is that so?" said Calum. "And was the bird a tit? Because that would stand to reason."

Joey did not say anything but you could tell he was unhappy to have Wilson make jokes about him. He took another deep draw on the tobacco, as if to give him courage, releasing a plume of smoke that drifted across Calum like street fog.

"Nobody tell you that stuff's bad for you?"

"It keeps me calm," he said.

"You want me to help you with that?"

"You being funny?" asked Joey. In the silence, the young, fat, overgrown boy on the bench close by him, leaned up hard against the wall and let out a further rasp of air from his throat.

"What's wrong with your fat friend? Why's he breathing like he's going to die?"

"Never mind him," said Joey. "He had an accident. Made him appreciate the sensation."

"The sensation of what?"

"The sensation of breathing."

Calum smiled. "He *sounds* like a pervert." The young man started to raise himself but Joey laid a hand on his arm and he settled back down. "Well?" said Calum, sounding bored.

"Well what?"

"What is it that you're so keen to tell me about?" He looked around. "Surprise me. Your mother's name?" He laughed and behind him, Finnie, the shopkeeper stood to one side, looking down at his black shoes

6

bought from Barga. He wished he was there now, in the *Grotta del Vento*, counting stalactites.

"I'm just saying," said Joey, when Calum's laughter subsided. "If you had heard the rumours, I'm not so sure you would be picking through all that woman's stuff and the like."

"Why do you say that Joey? Your boyfriend there not like perfume? Does he not look *nice* in the red panties?"

Tom stood up, kicking a chair to one side. "Hu thwink hamma fwaggot?" he said, threatening to drool. Calum could see the scar looping down from his mouth across his throat, joining together like two bits of string that do not exactly meet. Mr Finnie moved towards him and caught the chair as it slid across the floor. He looked pale. He took a handkerchief from his pocket and dabbed perspiration off his forehead. He was tempted to say something but knew that would be foolish. He put a finger and thumb on either side of his moustache and smoothed it with a downward, parting motion.

"Why does he speak funny like that?" said Calum. "Is he a sick boy?"

Joey shook his head and moved between Tom and Calum. "Alright," said Joey, pressing his arm back against Tom's chest. "Neither Tom nor I are looking for a fight."

"Well," said Calum. "I'm pleased to hear that. Nobody wants to see kids gettin' hurt." He picked the underwear off the counter and inspected the gusset with an unblinking eye.

Joey felt drawn towards the same spot. "I just asked myself why you were looking at all that stuff." He looked from side to side and smiled. "That's all. Just speaking aloud."

7

"Well, you see Joey. I forget how young you are. You're still shittin' your pants, aren't you? Do you know anything *at all* about relationships?"

"Relationships?" said Joey.

"The love between a man and a woman." Calum combed a thumb and forefinger through his wild beard. "It's a very sacred thing, Joey. When a man's been away it's hard on his wife. She has to get by on her own with no man there to please her. Her man is, as you will know, her tower of strength." He stepped close to Joey and sunk himself into his ratty eyes. "You know what? If the man's not there, he cannot satisfy her needs, can he?" Joey nodded. "Some of those needs are spiritual, some are physical." Tom smirked but was forced to look away. "You amused by that fat boy?" Calum asked, touching his own forehead with the side of his finger. "If you want to jerk off you might go elsewhere."

"Come on, Wilson. Are you serious about this?" said Joey.

"Clearly I am."

There was a moment's silence, then Joey said: "I don't think you need to worry too much about satisfying those special needs she has." He lowered his face, glancing sideways at Tom. He looked up again. "At least, by that I mean her physical needs, if you know what I mean."

"What are you saying?"

"Just seems they may already be pretty good satisfied just at the moment."

Calum frowned, stepping closer. "What the hell are you on about, you little shit?"

"Oh," said Joey, drawing again on the cigarette and easing the smoke out between his teeth. "Guess I touched a nerve."

"Explain yourself, Joey, before I rip your balls off."

"I'm sorry," said Joey, a light smile tugging at his lips. "I thought you knew. You knowing about *love* and all that sort of stuff."

"Knew what, you damn fool?"

He smiled. "Logan," he said. "Sean Logan. Seems strange, all us fools here knowing about it. And you? Well..." He threw an arm and gestured towards the small number of folk still in the room, merged in the shadows. "Are you telling me you really didn't know?"

"*Sean* Logan?"

"That's what I heard," said Joey.

"How do you know? Where did you get all this shit from?"

"Tom here, happened to be sitting right outside the party when it happened." Tom nodded wisely.

"Logan's still in school," said Calum.

"I don't think so," said Joey. "He wears long pants now." He paused. "When he wears pants at all."

CHAPTER 2

Tom breathed heavily and noisily, his face dressed in a broad grin like sunlight finally shafted between the clouds. Calum looked at Tom like he had never seen anything so disgusting. He pulled up the collar on his coat and realised he was still holding the panties. He threw them on the counter, next to the perfume, and left the post office. Mr Finnie lifted the panties and folded them symmetrically across the gusset. By the time Calum had mounted his horse, Joey and Tom had followed him out and were standing in the doorway, unable to peel the look of wry amusement from their faces. Mr Finnie stood behind them in the doorway, a light sheen of sweat still reflecting on his forehead.

"This Logan a friend of yours, Joey?" he asked, as he gripped both reins in his right hand, resting a palm on the pommel.

Joey crushed his cigarette under the toe of a holed left boot with no heel and then kicked the butt to one side. "Put it this way," he said. "If he was on fire, I wouldn't waste too much piss on him."

"You look like you need some new boots."

"So?"

"Boots cost money."

"That is probably true."

"Well," said Calum, containing his impatience. "You may want to earn some, to pay for the new boots."

"I might," said Joey. "I didn't know you were interested in footwear."

Calum sat in silence. He stared with cold edginess down at Joey. "You may need time to think about it. Shoes are a serious business. We can talk later when the heel comes off your other boot."

10

"Fair enough," he said. "These boots aren't going anywhere."

"That's the truest thing you said."

"My office is always open."

Calum lifted the reins with one hand and pulled the horse harshly round to the left. He kicked hard behind the girth and cantered along by the low wall, then filtered into nothing through a gap in the hedge. As he rode home, he thought of his wife. He had the feeling in his gut that he might have got the balance very wrong this time.

CHAPTER 3

It was raining steadily, relentlessly, if anything a little harder now, as they squatted low in the cloak of darkness, behind the old hawthorn hedge that weaved a leafless slice along the edge of a potato field. It was not that heavy kind of rain that comes and goes. This was rain that came in a billion tiny droplets, soaking every inch as it landed, audibly raking the ground as it dripped from the canopy of trees around them. It seemed to land and trickle down the back of the neck like a slow-poured basin of tepid water. Everything they touched was wet and every leaf and blade of grass only served to make them wetter as they brushed past the foliage towards the house beyond them. It seemed a good plan to wait until now, with darkness hiding their movements, but the sky was a heavy black sheet and it was not the easiest thing to know where to put your feet in this field. Tom was thinking they should have taken the roadway up; it would have been a sight easier and who was going to see them? It was nighttime and nobody was going to hear them either, not with the wind whipping a gusting breeze around their ears. Instead of which they were plodding up a potato field in the pitch dark with enough rainwater in their boots to float a boat. Tom could feel his tummy rumble because he had not eaten since breakfast and he dribbled lightly from the corner of his mouth. He could hear Joey not far away, moving more lightly across the ruts.

When they got to the top of the field, bathed in blackness, they could just make out the old cattle pen, the barn and another outbuilding and a coop that would house the chickens. There was an old stable at one end of the barn where any horses there might be would be pulling dry grass from haynets. Any cows or sheep would be out in the field, but they could neither see nor hear them. All was quiet, just the sound of light rain coming down on their heads, the occasional gust of wind through the trees and the burn flowing higher and faster than usual at the far end of the field. Calum took the Spencer rifle off his shoulder, pulled down the lever on the underside of the stock and released a new rimfire cartridge into the chamber. He looked at Tom and Joey who had heard the lever and who were thinking for the first time that this was real and that shortly they would be killing someone. Yes, *killing* someone. Together, they each took a cap and ball revolver from their pockets and, at the same time, they cocked the hammers, their thumbs slippery on the metal. Tom seemed to be pointing the barrel straight at Calum who pushed his arm away with a combination of irritation and anxiety. Fucking boys dressed up as men, he thought. They climbed over the wooden gate, making very little sound, but it was a high one, designed to keep people out, and it was awkward to swing your leg over and still hold a cocked gun in your free hand. Beyond the gate, they made their way across the short stretch of stone ground between them and the house, treading as softly as was possible to silence the noise beneath their boots. Calum followed the length of the building and looked in at the far window, but could see nothing. Joey felt the water in his boots and cursed. Tom breathed heavily against the quiet that engulfed him and his growing fear. The wind whipped at them in the darkness. Calum went to the nearer window, stood on his toes and he peered in. There was a pull drawn across the opening to keep the draught out but through

the crack at the top he could see the back of a woman.
Calum allowed himself a smile. He could see little of
her, but he imagined that would be the old woman,
the one Joey told him about. He knew she lived here
with Logan. He did not have any argument with her
or the daughter. There was no point in shooting the
women too. On the other hand, if they got in the way
and they chose to be awkward, then he would know
how to deal with them, he had no doubts about that.
He had shot bigger, uglier animals than women in his
time. He looked again but could see only one. Maybe
there was just the one; they would take her. Where
was Logan? That was what troubled him. He had
asked around and he had been told that Logan stayed
on the farm mostly, so he would be there. So where
was he? One way of finding out was to take hold of
the women. If anyone knew where Logan was, they
would. The three men went from the window along
the mud border, up on the porch to the main door.
Joey raised his boot as if to kick the door down but
Calum stopped him with a light hand on the front of
his shoulder and then gestured. Joey felt the door
handle in his wet hand, squeezed the cold metal and
turned. The door eased open and they entered.

CHAPTER 4

Lizzie was at the kitchen, to one side of the oak-beamed room in which they were standing. Calum glanced at the petulant flicker of the fire; it was smoking like someone had put on some wet coal or peat not so long ago, spitting and cracking loud puffs against the steel grate. Yet the room was warm and in a way it was welcoming; he could smell cooking, some biscuits or a cake. There was no sign of Logan. He put his muddied finger to his lips or what seemed the likely repository of his lips, since all three had heavy wet hats on their heads and their faces were covered by damp, cotton bags with small holes cut out for the nose and the eyes. Tom glanced nervously around the room, saw nothing and breathed heavily against the cotton. He did not like this cloth over his face, constricting the breathing. He could not really see the point of it. They would kill whoever was here any road, so why waste time making the job uncomfortable?

The three of them moved quietly, fanlike, towards the kitchen where Lizzie was scraping burnt treacle off a pan with a small knife. Joey was a man blessed with a pointed nose, and it picked its way through the material covering his face, emerging on the surface like a small thorn or a young rosebud or, strangely, a little like a pale nipple. When Tom saw the pseudo-nipple it made him want to laugh and he was glad now he had the cloth on his face to hide his features. He had learned one sure thing in his life: Joey did not like to be laughed at. However, the face bag did not hide his shoulders; they were shaking and lifting up and down. He was not sure if he was seriously laughing; it may have been his fear escaping. Calum was not looking at Tom, but moved on ahead and looked through the open door to the kitchen; he was satisfied that the woman in there did not appear to have any sense of their approach. He signaled to Joey with his finger, first pointing at him and then jabbing towards the woman's back. Joey swallowed as if he had a hard pea caught in his gullet. His throat was dry. He stepped very slowly forward through the open doorway. He had taken only a few ginger steps when he became aware of the squelch of water in his boots. Lizzie must have heard something too, for she spun round, immediately holding the knife out in front of her. Her eyes were wide and fired up as she took in the company. She quickly edged around the table, taking small steps backwards towards the far wall. She said nothing to them, but waved the knife about in a circular motion, her face flushed and a wild, terrified look in her large, flashing eyes. The men came fully into the room and stood pointing their guns at her. Calum lowered his rifle so that it was aimed at her wool-slippered feet. He raised the palm of his hand to silence her in case she intended shouting or bringing the house down with some misguided idea that she would raise the alarm.

"Where is he?" Calum said, his voice calm, quiet and without emotion. When she failed to respond, he repeated a little louder the same question: "Where is he? And where's your mother?" When she said nothing, he stepped forward a pace. "It's not that I want to," he said. "After all, you're a pretty girl, you've got your future to think about." Still Lizzie said nothing, but her arm was shaking though she tried to keep the knife steady between her fingers.

"The thing is," he said. "If you don't want to tell me then I've not got much choice, have I?"

"What do you mean?" she said finally. "I've done nothing."

"If you don't tell me…"

"I don't even know you."

"I'm looking for Sean Logan," he said. "Where is he?"

"He's not here. He's gone."

"Where?" She did not answer. "Come on now," he said. "I'll beat it out of you."

"I don't think so," she said. "I don't think so at all."

There was a click immediately behind them. They instinctively turned to look. "Don't turn around!" They stopped their uniform movement in its tracks. "Or the next noise you hear will be a bullet entering your head." Aunt Marion emerged from the small doorway opening onto the pantry to one side of the kitchen. In two hands, she was holding a four-barrelled Reicher. I had told her before I left that it was a joker's gun and she should not waste her time on such an unreliable tool. You could fire it just once, releasing all four barrels simultaneously. If you were very accurate you might kill four people. If you had no luck or skill at such things you might kill nobody but give yourself a nasty bruise from the recoil and break a finger. You might have the barrel insignia printed on your forehead for the rest of your natural life. Or it might even blow up in your face, invert your two front teeth and turn your nasal cavity inside out.

"It's not a proper gun," I had told her. "Please, will you take the Webley? It's good and easy to handle. It shoots very well with just one hand."

17

"I'm not planning to use it," she had said. "You may need a little gun like that, so you hang on to it." She picked up the Reicher again. "This will be fine," she had said. The discussion was over.

"Now," she said, holding the gun tightly, and speaking to the three men in front of her. "I don't pretend to be the world's best shot but I'm willing to bet that from here, in this small room, with this gun of German design and Austrian manufacture, I should be able to remove at least one of your three heads, if I have to." She paused. "Which one, I don't know, but if you fancy your chances, go right on and be my guest, turn your head and I will do my certain best to blow it clean away." Nobody leaked so much as an ounce of breath or a sideburn hair in her direction. "The law's on my side. You broke into my house."
"Don't make things worse for yourself," Calum said, out of the silence. "You must know why we're here."
She moved a few steps closer. "You think it's okay to walk in my house and threaten to shoot us women?" Tom began to shake, just a little at first and then uncontrollably. Joey kicked him with the side of his boot. The tip of Joey's nose still peeped from his facemask and Tom took one look and began to shake again. "Let's drop the guns," she said. "Let's take our time. Nice and slowly because we don't want any misunderstandings, people getting shot and dying. You with the whiskers can start off," she said.
"How do you know I got whiskers?" asked Calum eventually.
"I can see them," she said. "Poking out the side of that bag on your head, like dandelion weed in a herbaceous border." He hesitated and then, bending his knees, he gently dropped the Spencer rifle to the

18

floor and it made a clatter as he did so. Joey and Tom took their cue, leaned down and put their revolvers on the floor in front of them.

Marion remained where she was, close behind. "Think I should shoot them, Lizzie?" she asked.

"No," she said. "But I can't see the harm in doing them with this knife. I could circumcise them first."

"That won't be necessary, Miss," said Joey.

"Well hold on now, just a minute," said Aunt Marion. "My daughter Lizzie wishes to rearrange your genitals. You came in here pointing guns at us. So, we've got to give that due consideration."

"It's important to set an example," said Lizzie. "And I'm not always clumsy. I'd make a good job."

"What if we was circumcised already?" asked Joey. The other two looked at him, quizzical beneath their masks.

"We do have to behave civilized, Lizzie." Aunt Marion said, "I'm not sure we can go around just mutilating."

"They came in here with the guns. You said it yourself. Bags on their heads and looking for a fight."

"My daughter has a very straightforward view towards violence," Marion explained patiently. "But still, this is doing my nerves no good at all." She looked at Calum again. "I'm not expecting three beauties, but I want to see your faces before I make a final decision." She shifted slightly and moved her legs an inch or two further apart, as if she were securing her position to fire the gun by pushing her soles into soft mud. "Now, let's take off our hats, shall we? No need to be formal. And let's remove the bags too."

The three men, one after the other, removed their wet hats. They threw them on the table in front of them. Tom and Joey pulled off their face bags. The tip of Joey's nose was contoured by a ring where the bag had restrained three-quarters of his nose. A second or two later, Calum followed and removed his. "Ah-ha," she said. "So now we know who is who round here."

"I didn't come here to bother you," said Calum.

"That's strange, I had the impression you came here to kill us."

"I'm here for Logan. My business is with Logan."

"What do you want with him?"

"There's a score to settle. It's a private matter," he said. "But in the end I want to kill him. Or hurt him so badly he won't walk again."

"Well, it's not a private matter any more," Aunt Marion said. "You just broke into my house, waving guns about and that takes it from the private domain to the public." She did not take her eyes off him. "So, I'll ask you again: what business have you got with Sean?"

"Well, I may as well tell you then," he said. "Irrespective of what you decide to do with that museum piece, Sean Logan interfered with my wife." He turned his head fully towards her. "There's a price you pay when you do such things. Every man knows that."

"I see," she said. "A man tips his cap at Mrs Wilson and you go around shooting people?"

"We're not talking caps here," he said. "Tipped or otherwise."

"Even so," said Marion.

"Even so nothing!" he shouted back. "He has to pay for dishonouring my wife."

"Why don't you speak to your wife about it?"

20

"I already did," he said. "She now understands my point of view."

"In that case, why are you here, waving your guns at me and my daughter?"

"Sean Logan insulted her. He's insulted me too. My wife has learnt her lesson. Your nephew needs a lesson too."

"You think killing or maiming him will improve his table manners?"

"The etiquette has to be followed. He needs to be taught how to behave. He needs to learn to respect the property of others," he answered.

"It won't do him much good if he's dead."

"Well, he shouldn't have disrespected."

"I should shoot you now," she said.

"With that?" he said, indicating the Reicher. He had turned around completely. "It'll probably blow your head off before any bullet comes near mine."

She held the gun more firmly and bit her lip. "If you're a gambling man," she said. "You might want to take that risk and find out." He had that look in his eyes: he wanted to take the bet but there was an outside chance she would fire that thing. "Or you could leave whilst your head is still on your shoulders." He looked at her, down the four barrels of the Reicher, then reached carefully over to the table and picked up his hat. He placed it firmly on his head. "And take the terrible twins with you," she said. Joey looked at his revolver on the floor by his feet. "Don't even think about the guns, boys, because I am really losing my patience here."

"I need that gun," said Joey.

"Lizzie," said Aunt Marion. "Take the bullets out of the guns, would you?"

Lizzie leaned over the table, took each gun in turn, including Calum's rifle, emptying the chamber and pocketing the contents. Aunt Marion waved the Reicher at Joey and Tom. "Now get out before I tickle my own trigger." Calum picked up his rifle and walked to the door, He gave her one last, uncertain look. Aunt Marion kept her eyes on Joey and Tom. "I hope you two realise how close you came to losing your testicles," she said. "Next time you go to the toilet, thank God that you still can. Now, as I said, get out."

From the doorway, Calum said: "Tell your nephew I was sorry I missed him." He opened the door but a thought occurred to him. "It won't happen next time." He moved half out the door and then stepped back in again. "The thing is he decided he could piss me off. He chose to insult me. He thought he could just do what he wanted and walk away." He touched his whiskers. "Now that's just not right. We have to behave like civilized, human beings. You don't play with another man's things. It's not gentlemanly." He smiled at her. Her hand tightened on the breech. He slipped through the door and was gone. The other two scuttled sideways, like crabs on a changing tide, facing into the room, following quickly behind and out the open door. When she looked out of the window, she saw the shapes of the three men already moving in the wet, dreary darkness towards the lane, beyond the gate. She slammed the door shut hard and slid the metal bolt, top and bottom. She looked at Lizzie and Lizzie looked at her. "Shit," she said. "I forgot the bullets for this thing."

"My god," said Lizzie. "That could have been embarrassing."

CHAPTER 5

Three sides water and shaped like the head and shoulders of a Highland Terrier with the Isle of May puffed out like a fleck of silver spit. This is Fife, where the smell of wet, brown forest soil hangs in the air, testifying to its love affair with farming and what comes off the earth. Connected by land and sea, by fish and fowl, one can look on any map and see the small tick-like villages along its neck – Methil, Buckhaven and Wemyss are just a few. Beneath the snout, squeezed below the windpipe, you might find Dysart, a place of no interest, but take the road north as I myself had done, step out of Fife in all its rolling, craggy beauty, and you will fall upon Montrose, on the eastern seaboard. Further west by the old roman road and you reach Buckstone, a place that had featured centrally in my most recent activities.

So much for geography. I was riding home in a dead man's cart, dried blood under my nails and the stink of whale oil on my coat. On this occasion I had no cause to meditate on the Montrose wading bird, hosteled in its mud lagoon. I was headed for Tullis, my village, nestling some way across the River Tay, still a good distance to the south, deep in the eastern heart of Fife. Even this far north, spring was approaching early with all its pink and white blossom and the greenery was marking out its speckled space in the hedgerows. As I drove the cart towards Tullis my tongue was dry in my mouth. The events of the night had taken something out of me. I was bruised, battered, ribs had been cracked and maybe broken and I smelled of smoke and spermaceti. What I had considered important, those dreadful lifetime demons, what I had always thought required to be addressed, had been confronted and yet, here I was, in its aftermath, broken and sore and I had to confess, feeling little better for it. Would that come later? Where was the satisfying glow that should follow retribution? The heat had gone out of me and there was little left but coldness within and a slow, dancing breeze that whispered like a prickly reminder across my skin.

When I arrived at the farm, I realised then the importance of keeping my gun beside me. Surely it was the first rule of gunfighting: to get off the starting block you had to have a gun. I knew where my rifle *was*. It was neatly holstered, hanging to the right hand side of the saddle on my horse, Master Henry. In normal circumstances, I could access my rifle pretty quickly. There was a knack to it and it was a skill I had perfected. I could have the Lee-Enfield out of the saddle and in my hand, firing at whatever, in less time than it took a man to blow the snot from his nose. However, when I heard the click-click-click (yes, there were three) to one side of my head and a little behind, I knew that the holstered rifle hanging off my saddle may as well have been on a tea plantation in China for all the good it would do me. I was rooted to the earth like an ancient tree, hard by the gate to my yard, ten feet from my horse, Master Henry and a million miles from salvation.

CHAPTER 6

Earlier that day, when I had finally reached Tullis after a long ride, the sun was up and had given way to a grey and overbearing sky. I had brought the cart down between the ash trees, brushing shoulders against the small spear-shaped leaves with their toothy edges. I chose not to look to my right, that gap in the trees and the broken stones that marked the track. I knew full well what lay up there. My memory was good of an old path that wound along the side of a grazing field, leading to the place that was her home. The thought of her up there gave me warmth in the coolness of the morning. I longed for her now. Still, that all seemed prehistoric after the events over the previous few days. Her green eyes came to mind like they were there to torment me. She had said that from the house you could see the Logan farm or at the very least you might spot the fire smoke. She said that if the air was damp you could taste the peat on the tip of your tongue, you could smell it when you breathed.

Sometimes, with all the tree growth, it was hard to see the smoke going anywhere. It was not so easy to see beyond your own fields, filled with grass, barley, potato shoots, trees and broken weeds. I certainly had no memory of being able to see Tullis from her house, let alone having sight of the Logan farm. However, memory is an unreliable friend. If I shoot a man, do I remember the look of terror in his eyes, the blood on his shirt? My memory is coloured by circumstances. It will not be his death I remember; it will be my memory of his death that I may have inadequately remembered. I had often thought that the truth may

25

be just one man's version of another man's poor memory.

The track was wider then as I manoeuvred the cart along the edge of the village, having emerged from the trees. My horse, Master Henry, tied to the back fender, a striking, characterful, chestnut, who seemed reluctant, full of hesitation, perhaps tired by the journey, wishing it was over. We entered the main street of Tullis. I took in its understated buildings, houses mainly, some wood, some stone and earth, some held up with cow shit or hen goo. Three homes on the one side and four on the other, some more just behind, some thatched and mossed over, damp on the outside walls and no doubt running water on the inside. The road ran on to the east across a square and more houses. The square may have been a small common green, but nobody stood on it now, so early in the day. We rode on towards that patch of green, more brown than green, more circle than square, feeling the regular, stiffening breeze blow across the rough path to the side, as it did most months of the year. I knew, without looking, where the old church was hidden, almost overwhelmed by its cemetery, but I doubted that too much had changed there in the short time I had been away. The post office store was three hundred yards further along; nothing good ever went in there and the same came out. The church had a heavy door and a tower to one side, like a large, upward pointing finger. The rusted, metal bell and the chipped, stone cross were obvious clues that this was God's house, the bodies stacked like plates to one side and underground. There had always been a gold-painted fish on the roof. This was the one day I noticed it. There was a shop or two with the occasional swinging sign that offered supplies and services: *Cobblers* and *Victuals*. *Hardware* tucked in along at the end. Mr Hamilton's house too, the big one behind, boasting all his oil paintings and Alsace drinking wine. There were people about now. A head with wet hair shining, the smell of damp cloth, three Belted Galloway cows herded along the street by a young boy who looked at me like I was dressed back to front. A white goat and a black-shawled woman. The rough road stretching on, past a grey-skinned house and other sober homes and rusted sheds, leading to a fork in the road, where left took you to the sea where I knew from bitter experience that the water was cold as the brow of my dead mother. To the right, you were on the road to Cupar or Stirling. The better roads, with their raised spines, ready to drain off the early spots of rain, undulating like coiled rope, trailing down to the boats that ferried passengers across the Firth.

I pushed on through the village, turned to the left and followed the track on up to the Logan farm. I had no idea what I would find there. This side of Tullis you could almost smell the sea air and you could hear the yap of the gulls as they bleated overhead. The narrower path up to the farm was bordered on each side by a brown and green hawthorn hedge, occasional rocks of varying size creating a wall and the odd rowan tree lazing its trunk, snakelike against the stone. I stopped the cart and touched the moss-topped wall. The old woman by my side stared at my hand vacantly; she had not spoken the entire journey. I could see the chipped stone pieces along the floor of the track, and I remembered all too well the work laying that surface. The sky looked less threatening now, a lighter, whiter sheet, broken by the occasional patch of almost blue sky. There was a growing suggestion, in case anyone missed it, that we should not lose heart, that spring was really coming.

As I turned the last bend, I raised my head and and took in the view. I picked out the farm that housed all my long cherished memories. A part of me wondered if I would find it burnt to the ground, but that was the doom and gloom in me, the cup half empty, never full. I twisted round on the hard bench and I could see that the gate off the field that led to the cattle pen lay open, yawning its muddy lip towards the descending hills and the distant volcanic island of Inchkeith. I cast my eyes to the south, the old view, the sweep of my childhood. I could see the rough path cut through the side of a pasture field, its borders pitted with earth scoops, the work of moles or brown hares. Beyond the track, across the grey canopy of treetops, I could sense the water's edge and I could see the Firth, its shores jagged with rocky spurs, then a yellow sand, blown in a dust and a heap towards the piling dunes. I could see the golden green of the marram grass, stringy and dry, its roots in creeping, bindweed tourniquets, above which broad, aquamarine straws rose and slumped. Stiff, sycamore, leafless saplings spiked the surface and there were patches of early, yellow-flowering, poisonous ragwort, tucked along the lower edges. I remembered a boy pressing on down to swim one day in May, a foot in the blue-brown water, the tide spuming up the beach as high as late spring would allow, the wave tops spitting spray beneath the rising wind. To one side lay the Bombo Burn, a stream of water relentlessly whispering, meandering in small swirls and slurps along a tight

28

ditch, edges forever crumbling, down by the hawthorn hedge, the polka dot, red, bird-berries alive in summer, and another light path cut with horses' hooves through the crust of winters gone and cattle tracks too, leading again to the shore. This was Fife and everything led to and from the water. Carving east, it flowed by the length of the pitted, stone, wall with its round, black coping and broken filling. I had mended that wall. More back-breaking work, it was a wonder I could walk. I looked on past the closed, wooden gate where the plough and other farmyard tackle would always lean rust-bound against the whinstone gable. Going beyond, the green field with its anonymous sheep's wool tagged on the wooden fence and tacked again by the prickly thistles.

I turned again to look up at the house. I dismounted from the cart, stepped forward several paces and attempted to throw up the metal latch. The latch was stiff and unyielding, its surface pitted by time and weather. With two hands and some persuasion it shifted and I was then able to open the wooden gate onto the yard. I remembered now those old roof joists that made the gate, how I cut them up, sized and treated them, then fitted the pieces together, to create a gate that had swung open without a squeak or a squeal, without anything to remind me of when my mother died and my world ended. I thought I heard some hens from round the side of the house. I looked up at the rusted iron fish on the roof gable, still twisting in the breeze like it had been hooked and announcing the wind's current direction.

Aunt Marion and Lizzie appeared on the doorstep, waving their arms at me, Lizzie stepping out from the shadows ahead of her mother, emerging into the yard. I waved back. Suddenly they stopped in their tracks and at that exact point I heard the sharp click. It was a noise I had heard before; it was a sound like a heavy key turning in a stiff lock. It reminded me of the lock to my father's cell. I greeted it with respect and total stillness. There were two further clicks, neither of which lessened my concern. Click-click-click could mean only one thing. Shit, three guns.

CHAPTER 7

As I stood by the grey-black, splintered, wooden gate nervously considering why this man with the voice I thought I recognized, and two others along for the ride, had chosen to point an 1860 Colt army hand gun .44 caliber cap and ball straight at my brain, I had a sense of my father returning, as I too had returned. I could see his figure standing over by the slatted door, or at least I had the ghost image of him inside my head. Behind my glazed eyes, he still wore his heavy over-jacket and an old grey tunic taken from another great Afghan war.

It was barely autumn when my father, Horatio Logan, had begun his long walk home after the second Afghan war was over, following a route that took in northern Iran, Turkey and Bulgaria, before entering Romania, passing through the Slovak Republic and other principalities. Then on into Germany. We all come back to somewhere, sometime, is what Horatio figured. Usually the place we started out from. It was the close of the war and he was none too sure if they had won or lost. He only knew that he had had enough. With all the bribes and the treachery, it was the tribal chiefs who looked to have taken most of the spoils. He had been an infantryman, part of the British force under Major General Roberts in the attack on Ayub Khan. He swung his sword and discharged his powder with the best of them, killing some and injuring many, particularly at Kandahar where Khan had finally been defeated. My father was not apparently inclined to reminisce over all that useless, wasted blood. He had seen death amongst those he knew. Some had been close friends. War had a rotten stink about it. Aunt Marion said he told her that a leg cut from a body left him unmoved. Ask him to smell it and that was a different matter. Not just the smell of death or hideous infection; not just the rations that rotted and grew woolly beneath a film of mould. It was all these things and more. It was the place itself, the warm fug, the dust, the dry wind, the decay of people and their unholy environment. The smell clung to him like sticky resin, on his hair, his skin and his clothes, and still there long after he had left it all behind. He could smell it and he could taste it and all heaven's water would never wash it away.

He survived with his life and had avoided capture by the Afghans. Not everyone was so lucky; some within his own regiment had been captured, killed or mutilated. He knew what the Afghans could do to a man. His bad dreams left him drenched. He knew a captive would be staked to the ground. They would hammer a plug into his mouth to gag his swallow and the sweet little Pathan women would squat over him and pee until the poor soul drowned in the urine. His dreams were full of such images.

Horatio started home with some thick, leather soles on his military boots, comfortable square toes with snug, rather than tight, heels. Proper calf skin boots had always been important to him: in any war, you had to look after your feet. Without your feet you were nothing. He was not totally destitute. He had some semi-precious stones in his pocket – a small quantity of amber, a green garnet tsavorite, two pink stones, a colourless goshenite and a lump of aquamarine. He also had some rough gold that he kept wrapped in a soft, pigskin bladder sewn into his inside pocket, and a knife in his shirt, sheathed in embroidered leather against his chest. This makes him sound like a better miner than a soldier. Wherever he picked them up, these were most of what he had, with breath in his body and blood in his veins, carrying all the oxygen he needed to fight the infections that tend to blight a ramble through Western Asia.

The fact is that, when the Afghan war more or less ended at Kandahar in September 1880, my father put his things in a large canvas bag and started walking. I say more or less ended because that war never did end: it surged like tidal water and then sloped away; forward and then back through the years before and after, like a horse endlessly spooked by its own shadow. October 1880 was a quiet time and for him, if not everybody else, the war was over. He drank an extra cup of Darjeeling tea that morning, then headed up the goat paths that trailed across the hills to the west, steered himself into Iran and began the journey home.

In Mashhad he was bitten on the penis by a tik-tik fly. I say penis, but to be precise it was a hairless patch on the underside of the left gonad. There are twenty-three species of tik-tik fly, each one of them completely bloody useless. I have nothing but respect for the bee, the slug, the wood louse and the butterfly but the tik-tik fly makes me want to pee all over it. Which is probably what my father was doing when it bit him. In any event, it is my belief that they serve little purpose. I read somewhere in Mr Shifner's library that they kill up to three hundred thousand people worldwide every year. Mind-boggling numbers but precision is hard to come by. In fact it may be more; if I was trying to be funny I might say that was just the tik of the iceberg. For a bug with a three week life cycle that is a level of physical harm the Emperor Caligula could only dream of.

Tik-tik flies do not normally leave the Kalahari desert, so it was no doubt something of a surprise for Horatio to find one attached to the underside of his cock / gonad in this particular part of Iran. Anyhow, he lay there in a Pashtun woman's hut, on a camp bed made of green tree limbs and thick leaves culled from I do not know where, a place in which he fully expected to die and out of which she, equally, fully expected to inherit the pig skin bladder full of gold, not to mention those other charms he kept in the leather pouch. Sadly for her, the brown paste she spooned down his throat did not kill him and nor did the tik-tik fly. There may be good reason for that: after all the tik-tik had flown all the way from the Kalahari; it may have been tired. My father hallucinated for more than a week, did not know who he was or where he was, yelled and cursed, but made little sense to anyone who could understand. He thought and the Pashtun woman also thought - and the goat at the door had a suspicion - that he was going to make use of that hole she had dug for him; he had no pretentions that he was anything but very sick and in his more lucid moments he realised his prospect of seeing Fife or the Logan Farm ever again was dissipating like the haar that pushed in from the sea and laid a cold shroud across that distant place. Yet, it is never over until it is over, and he turned the corner on the twelfth day and thereafter commenced a slow, ratcheting recovery. Nevertheless, he still looked a lot like a bag of skin on a clothes hanger. He gave the old lady half of what was in his leather pouch and, to his surprise, she waved her hands at him and indicated that she had no need for his thanks. She was probably annoyed by her own success. He took no notice and gave her half the gold as well. He had some more tea, spooning the sugared dregs into his mouth, gathered up his things and headed out into the bright, unyielding light of northern Iran for the first time in seventeen days.

For reasons unknown to me, my father Horatio took a diversion through Romania – a country of two principalities that had only properly come to exist some twenty years earlier. The streets were notoriously dangerous and still full of heavily-armed soldiers from the Turkish-Russian war, bands of military thugs who were consistently free with the use of their guns, fueled by consumption of a white spirit, not unlike vodka – distilled from something close to a potato but in essence no more than the kind of alcohol you might use to dress a bad cut.

It was in Romania that he came upon Tatiana, a dark skinned, black-haired woman in her mid to late twenties. The details are sketchy. The story goes that he had heard shouts coming from a single storey house, situated on the outskirts of a small town. I do not know its exact name. I once tried to find it on a map, but there were many possibilities and they all sounded much the same. My father's inherent curiosity led him to investigate the shouts and general kerfuffle. Had he kept walking I would have no tale to tell and the world would have been a quieter place without my interventions. I may have been someone else, ignorant of what else might have been and none of what happened needed to happen and other things might have happened. These are the tricks life plays on us. When he approached the house he came upon two men holding this woman by the arms; she was agitated and struggling. Some of her clothing was torn and hung from her shoulder and she was doing all she could to shake free. They wore Romanian army uniforms that were filthy and stained with some kind of grease or maybe fire ash or tar. She could smell gun oil on the back of one man's tunic that bore no indication of rank. A third man in a Russian army coat shouted at the young woman in a language Horatio could not follow and hurled his flat hand against her uncovered face. There was an old man, cowering in the corner by the wall, clutching an old woman in black clothing. They cried smothered screams through the cloths they held to their mouths. This was the moment Horatio's story truly began and in a sense, where it ended.

He yelled at them to get their filthy hands off her. In the circumstances, it seemed to him a modest, reasonable request. It was totally absurd. They turned their heads towards him as if he were mad or had grown wings. The two men holding the woman threw her to the ground and swore at her. Then they stood straight, glowered and swore at him. She had become even less relevant than before. Two of them reached for the swords that hung from their waists. Beheading was a popular sport in Romania at the time. At the same moment, the Russian officer pulled a pistol from the dark leather holster on his hip. All this happened in less time than it takes a tik-tik fly to bite a man's penis, but already Horatio had raised his Snider-Enfield and fired off three quick shots. Each of the men fell to the ground and within seven and a half seconds (approximately) not one of them was still breathing. They were dead, each with a blink of red drilled through the forehead.

It was a strange and impetuous thing to do, to fix upon this dark-skinned woman, to put his life at risk for someone he had never known. Yet, instinct had come to play an important role in his life. Instinct had drawn him into Romania, this broken principality, to this remote unknown lawless village, far from the capital. Instinct had drawn him to this half-derelict house where the young woman was the subject of this assault. Horatio lived by what his guts told him and a sense of what felt right and proper. Even the day he started walking home had been a day driven by instinct – why else would a man embark on such a journey across the barren terrain of Afghanistan and Iran without even taking leave of his commanding officer? They might come after him, he knew that. Anyway, he shot these men and that was all there was to it. And it had been fine shooting too and the slaughter was not entirely undeserved.

Yet the woman, it seemed, was driven by instinct too. She followed him out of Romania, deciding with very little deliberation that she would leave everything she had ever known behind her, including the impotent old man with thin lips and white stubble on his chin and the sobbing woman who had now finally removed the cloth from her mouth. Whatever instinct told her, she said farewell to the old folk and followed Horatio away from the town. She bobbed along behind him, layered by many skins of clothing to keep off the day's heat and ease the night's cold, but carrying precious little else.

Over the days that followed, he grew to know Tatiana better and he surprised himself: he enjoyed looking back to see whether she was still there. She was. Small details at first, larger ones followed. She was a woman who kept her face lowered, like she was embarrassed about something, but if you scrutinised the deep pockets of her eyes, ringed in black charcoal as they were, you would know they had seen much. The eyes almost spoke to you, something that was accentuated by the way she hid the rest of her face and concealed her hair. She wore a silver-threaded, silk shawl across her head. You could be fooled into thinking she was one of those odd religious types, although Horatio doubted that. He never saw her pray. He never saw her on her knees. This was modern day Romania. Up close you could smell a perfume, at first not so unpleasant but, nevertheless, quite overpowering. My father liked the perfume, he had no issue with that. They spoke little on the journey, but she attached herself to him and gradually insinuated herself directly into his company. She began by boiling water, then moved on to cooking small plates of food and over time they grew closer, exchanged occasional words or expressions or a movement of the hand to signify by a gesture that he did not mind her presence there. Eventually they shared some of their experiences, tentative at first but growing in boldness. They spoke largely in broken English, bad French and tortured Spanish, but they used the movement of hands and expression to signal to each other when their linguistic talents fell short. Without the need for deep discussion, he thought she understood him. She understood too what a harsh place a war could become. She had seen that barbarism in her own country. When the walk was finally over, having carved a route up as far as Tilbury, along the muddy Thames estuary, they took a boat up the east coast to Scotland, landing at the small port of Leith, north of Edinburgh and then, oddly, endured the worst, most turbulent part of the voyage: a short ferry ride through a gusting, swirling easterly wind, over the water to Burntisland in Fife. It was cold when they arrived, a long way from the heat, dust and flies of Afghanistan. The hedgerows still carried the stubborn snow that would not melt. They took a horse trap to Tullis to complete a journey that had taken four months and nineteen days.

CHAPTER 8

Tatiana became Horatio's wife. Plainly it was a role that was alien to her: she cut an enigmatic figure around the Logan farm. She was foreign and she had those unusual characteristics that tended to ruffle feathers amongst the indigent population, people who viewed Edinburgh and Glasgow as exotic destinations. My Aunt Marion (about whom I will tell you much more later) said Tatiana had a habit of clicking her fingers when she wished to make a point. She wiped her nose with the open palm of her hand. She put her fork to the right of the plate and held it in a gripping paw as if she might stab your face and drag it through the gravy. She peed whilst doing the squat, in the Pashtun manner. She ate all types of nuts if she could lay hands on them; she would sell her soul for a pistachio. She threw salt across her shoulder (rather than over). She wore a jangly glass bead on her ankle. It was believed that she coloured her hair, for in bright light its long, shiny coils betrayed some trace of henna with a hint of aubergine. She was a woman who spoke very little but what she said in English was crucified by her Romanian accent. Even the most benign comment when crushed by her accent sounded hostile and aggressive or even haughty. To her, none of this was important. She was an orthodox Christian. She recognized the resurrection of Jesus. She had a blue crucifix tattooed on her shoulder. She understood my father and what he was about and, to her, that was enough. She could read his thoughts before he opened his mouth to speak. Whilst anyone could tell he was in love with her (Aunt Marion said he was in a *swoon* whenever he laid foggy eyes on Tatiana) there was not much about her that the Tullis town folk could ever find to like. Even her name excited animosity, a prickly hostility, an unquenchable suspicion. She never understood why they did not like her.

"They don't know you," said my father.

"Yes?"

"They fear you." She made a face at him. "When you do that with your eyebrow you can be very frightening."

My grandfather lived with them. He had become Horatio's father late in life, long after he had given up all hope of ever having a child. His wife was dead now having died of tuberculosis, a slow death of blood-tinged sputum, night sweats and plummeting weight loss. He had a square head that was virtually toothless, had warts on his yellowed fingers and a long, hooked nose protruded from a position too close to his eyes. When the good looks were handed out he was in the wrong queue. Still, to my grandfather's credit, even at his advanced age he clung to a reasonable head of dull, grey hair. Nobody could say that he did not make the most of this asset for he caked it in duck fat and in his pocket he carried a comb allowing him to drag regular lines through its syrupy surface. For whose benefit? Good question. Aided by a diminutive growth gene, he was kept in a lumpy bed recess just under five foot long, positioned at one end of the old kitchen. When he became noisy or unruly a heavy curtain could be drawn across him. This would smother the sound rather than silence him altogether; apparently, words came to him readily and he could bark them quite audibly from behind a drawn drape. He had a mouth shaped like a dark slit and when he spoke it was like a window snapping open and shut ninety times to the minute. He did not shave his beard more than once per week, lending him a ragged, scrappy kind of look that matched his rough, abrasive character. He too was suspicious of his son's Romanian wife and he rarely spoke directly to her – not that she would have understood anything he said. When he did speak to her she stood puzzled and uncomprehending – her accent and his absent dentistry strangled meaningful conversation. The three of them rubbed along together but Tatiana and my grandfather shared little love for each other. They lived at a distance, in a perpetual state of mutual suspicion and unease.

Tatiana's tears were of the quick-drying variety when my grandfather's life expired earlier than expected on the back of a pickle and ham lunch less than a year after Horatio and Tatiana returned from the Afghan war. Pickle and ham, pounded by compromised dentures can be cataclysmic to an octogenarian experiencing reflux oesophagitis and tongue dehydration. To some extent he was the author of his own misfortune: he choked to death when he failed to cut the large sandwich pickle to a readily edible size before squeezing it into his mouth.

After his death, Horatio and Tatiana lived a quiet existence for the most part, the two of them together and largely inseparable, but always busy and working hard, with cattle, sheep, hens, potatoes, spinach, asparagus during the spring, and all the weight of working life that grips a farm. In general, they stayed away from the village and the simmering hostility of its people. As time went by any desire for social contact diminished further and they became like islands in their own river. It was not just Tatiana who sensed this isolation from those around them. Something had changed in Horatio too. Perhaps he was not the man he had been before he went to war. War changes a man. It seems to me it took him deeper into himself, making him less comfortable with all those ordinary aspects of life and people that he used to take for granted.

Hindsight is an annoying thing. Hindsight can only give you a red face. With hindsight it may be that the cruel events that followed were fuelled by precisely that lack of interaction between the Logans and the villagers in whose midst they chose to live. Out of sight, buried up at the farm, never could mean out of mind. Of course, if they had to speak to those who lived in and around Tullis then they would – or at least my father would. He was not an island. Some take the view that all people are individuals and they are entitled to act in any way that most accords with their principles. Of course, I agree with that in the broadest sense but I also recognise that if you swim against the tide you run the risk of drowning. When people withdraw into themselves; when they pull away and button up their tongues, others round about do not always respond with charity. They take personal withdrawal as an extraordinary insult, more provocative and contemptuous than mere words.

I know now that there were occasions when they were seen to be going about their silent business and the villagers asked themselves why they would bury themselves away like that. Did they think they were better than the rest? Their treasured isolation encouraged the spread of repeated stories and rumours. Extraordinary imaginings grew up all around them. One story had them bowing before Cailleach, a one-eyed witch with decayed teeth, foot-rot and knotted hair. You have got to remember, these were not sophisticated times. There were tales of dancing Celtic jigs before a smoking, green wood fire behind the house. For God's sake! They got diseases; they spread diseases; they even invented unknown diseases and put them into their blood with brown eggs and black pudding for breakfast. They ate rice for the carbohydrate and sheep testicles for the protein. The testicles had a light down of lamb's hair. If there were no testicles they used goat's tongue. They ate berries from the wood and they laid ragwort poison in the trees for the birds. The grey plover flew no more in these parts, killed off by the Logans. Even dead Sanderling were said to have been hung on red strings, swinging from the wooden fence that abutted the track close by the Logan farm.

Some spoke of Tatiana as a great beauty with dark, flashing eyes, her pupils black and large, glinting like sparks off a sharp axe. Yet nobody had seen much beneath the purple shawl she often fixed around her head that rarely slipped across her shoulders, so such stories of great beauty were not easily verified. Others tagged her an evil, tea-faced, witch, with one side scarred by the whip of her previous husband, believed to be a Romanian Commissar. Now dead, no thanks to her. These were rumours and wild tales that shared one common value: they had no truth. Indeed, many years later, Aunt Marion used to laugh at the absurdity of all this nonsense, discussed at a time when I was trying to unravel what had occurred. She laughed, like my father did before her, but the way it all ended was far from funny.

Men from the village heard the stories, mulled them over like they were pulling fleas and nodded their heads like they were not surprised to see so many. They all resented the isolation the two Logans imposed upon themselves. They resented the isolation the Logans imposed upon them. The situation created a festering mistrust that bloomed into hatred. Some things you cannot adequately explain.

Some discussions were overheard and reported back. Others repeated what they said and what others said to them. No doubt not all of it is true, but these are the snippets that emerged:
"She's got an odd smell"
"Heavy and putrid, like a cave with no air"
"Not the sweetest perfume, I grant you"
"Pretty, if you don't mind your eyes crossed"
"Pretty, if you don't mind scars"
"Pretty, if you don't mind moles"
"A mole as big as a heifer's arse"
"A blanket on her head"
"She believes in Jesus"
"She believes in the Resurrection"
"She's a heathen"
"There are better looking women"
"Face like a bent shovel"
"Seen too much digging"

This was the shape of the conversation, so Aunt Marion told me many years later. She had heard it herself and heard others describe it. They perceived her as a threat although nobody could explain exactly what she threatened them with or what they had to be afraid of. The mood was interchangeably subdued and angry. They discussed her odd clothes ("Romanian rags") and her unusual appearance, the dark pencil around her black eyes, bare skin around her ankles. They said she had a chain on one, made from silver balls and blue glass. Her face, they said, was thin, foreign, silent, full of bewitching lines. It was a different colour, or at least, a different *tone*; it was not *their* sort of face; it came from the Black Sea and defied ethnic comprehension.

They wanted to send her home. Home they said was Romania. Resentment, anger, even fury at her and the place Tatiana had taken in their society was not sufficient to lead to the events that followed. It took a small number of relatively minor episodes to move the crisis to the next level. It began with sixteen head of cattle dying for no obvious reason at the wet end of Hograt field, where the grass dipped into a large trough. There was a south-westerly wind prevalent at the time and it left a bad smell to permeate the village. Some said, more reasonably: hold up and think on it. Was it not the rain that did for those cows? The field was like a bog, poor beasts must have drowned. Logic would blame the farmer – a dozy drunk, they said - for his reluctance to face the great outdoors and mind his cattle without a warming whisky. Such was the voice of moderation, but others sparked different rumours. It was Logan and his weird, black-eyed woman who had brought all this upon them. Foreign down to the metal rings on her Carpathian fingers. To these people, there had to be a responsible party: there had to be a face on which to pin the brouhaha of blame. Next, the broccoli crop wilted and slumped lower than a pig's belly, oozing a foul-stenching fungus up its sticky, wilting shaft. This and the many other disasters seemed to be turning Tullis on its head. Could she be responsible? It all changed when she came. Next, Mrs Hodgart at Smithston Farm lost twenty-seven Scots Greys, a number of top Bantams and a prize sow called Master Ham in just one night, the coop awash with blood and feathers, the sty the colour of Russian soup. People were crying out for illumination, whilst the chickens only wanted their heads. Everyone, from churchmen to cobblers, wanted an answer and they were prepared to look in some strange places. Master Ham and all the hens were dead, the two hind legs and half the belly absolutely missing. Legless, chopless. Would a fox eat twenty-seven heads of chicken? A fox with an appetite, but took nothing but the heads. Then, seven toads were discovered, each staked to the ground with the knife-sharpened point of a thick bamboo cane. The locals were looking for someone to point the finger at and the foreigner – though not an obvious toad-hater – had a case to answer. When the hay in one of the old barns close to Tullis spontaneously combusted, burning to ash not just the winter feed but the building with it, the time for a reckoning had arrived. There had to be more to it all than the whimsicality of God and the arbitrary weave of nature, far more than too much rain, hungry foxes and headless Bantams. It was clear that toads did not easily stake themselves to the ground; the hind legs and belly of a sow would not, of their own accord, mysteriously part company from the trunk. There had to be someone to blame.

CHAPTER 9

The time came. She was a fat old cow – a Galloway beef – that lay dead by the shoreline where the Bombo Burn spread its flow past the Logan farm and eased out towards the waiting sea. She was just one dead cow amongst seven. Together, they gave off a putrid stench but nobody was inclined to move them. When the gas inside the dead guts finally leaked out, the flatulent blast caught the gentlest breeze and once more hung like a heavy cloak across the village. It had been warm weather for the time of year, and the stench never seemed to clear. That stench was so close to the Logan farm that it seemed to many to be the source. When they did get enough men together to move the carcases, they were rotted to the consistency of a French cheese, the limbs pulling apart like torn bread. Strong farmers emptied their stomachs at the side of the field. It reinforced the view that Romanian magic was at work somewhere here. Tatiana was never far from the sneers and accusations. Who else to point the finger at? To blame God would provide no satisfaction at all; to blame nature was like blowing warm breath up a penguin's *orificium venti*. People discussed these vexatious issues up against the damp moss of falling dykes, behind closed bedroom doors, under the sticky boughs of sycamore leaves, above the mole holes that coned the undulating fields and behind the wettening udders of milking, Ayrshire cattle. It was noted that the Logan church attendance had been poor and remained to this day singularly unimpressive. Even the minister, his finger hooked behind his collar, expressed sheepish concern.

There was a rising clamour for some unarticulated act of revenge. Something had to be done. The thought polluted the minds and reason of individuals and their households. All too quickly, they acted on their prejudice and hatred.

CHAPTER 10

8 years later

It is no part of my business to keep secrets here. That is not the point. That is why I must tell a story that does not always cover me in glory. Then again, I am not that man we read about in the magazines – Charles Dickens in a kilt, all thistles and heather and a Dundonian bunnet. I am not a professional in the writing business – a fact you may well have guessed already. You may or may not wish to know a little about me since I am the penny whistle through which this tale finds its sound and it is my shadow you see cast across it.

I was brought up by my Aunt Marion and her daughter, dear sweet, undeniably clumsy, Lizzie. I plodded merrily through my early years, submissive to their devotions and directions. It was they who dressed me in clothes cut from an old, crushed, embroidered, velvet curtain stumbled upon in my father's Afghan journeybag. I had no objection: it was a fabric that kept me warm. Furthermore, there is no doubting I looked good dressed in my brown curtain, if just a little weirdly Pashtun for conservative Fife, and it lasted a long while, being cut from a large spread and making more than one outfit. I believed I presented something of a dash round about the Tullis medina, but my skin at that time was fortunately thicker than a pig's arse and I was mostly insensitive to the perpetual sniggers that snorted all around me.

Not only was I a sartorial picture of brushed velvet elegance in a fecal shade of golden brown, Aunt Marion and sweet, but clumsy, Lizzie saw to it that my brain was given some passing stimulation; between them they decided that I was to have a proper school education. They pushed and prodded at the burgh authorities to allow me to see the inside of their teaching establishment. Once those in charge of such matters had relented, as they were obliged to do by virtue of the Education (Scotland) Act of 1873, I quickly learned to read a book and hold a pen, to add, subtract and make the occasional, inspired, long division. To be honest, I know now that it was not the least bit easy for Aunt Marion to take me down to the Tullis Board School to enrol me, a place with crumbled lime-plaster walls, the flaked paint floating to the floor that always echoed back at my feet like a final reprimand. It had a tall, black, whinstone chimney and a solid, studded, oak front door that threatened to close forever behind me.

I was initially oblivious to it all, no doubt too preoccupied with myself to be too concerned about those who pinched their noses at the name Sean Logan. Memories of those things that had occurred and whose ripples had broken the water in all directions were still not far from people's minds. They were all too aware of what had passed at the Logan farm and the horrors that had been sown there. Fair to say, not everyone blamed my father for what had happened but nevertheless not too many were prepared to own up to that heresy.

As for school, whilst I had no time for my fellow students (and they had no time for me), nevertheless I took a deep, enduring shine to the education I was offered. It drew me in like a warm fire on a cold night and I was without doubt the top pupil amongst those desperate, big-eared goons. It has to be said that I was, in so many ways, the totally deserving author of my own good fortune. When others put their grey jotters away, I sat until Mr Shifner, a stern, skinny schoolmaster in a dark tweed jacket, leather-patched elbows and black worsted trousers, tugged at his curly sideburns and said "Logan, have you not got a kennel to go to?" That was Mr Shifner's sense of humour at full stretch. The thing was I always wanted to finish that work before I left. I do not know where this came from, this ridiculous thirst for knowledge, but there is no doubt I had it in buckets and spades. I had a simple, unquenchable curiosity about the way things worked. My mind seemed always full of brilliant questions and was never short of dazzling answers. If I heard my cousin, Lizzie, make noises in the toilet I would ask questions about the source of the noise, the length of the noise, the constituent parts of the noise and whether there was any mathematically calculable pleasure to be derived from the noise – such as volume and velocity and, later, issues relating to the coefficient of expansion. Clearly, some questions were not always designed to be useful but they intrigued me nonetheless. Bowel movements were not my only intellectual intrigue. Why is it that when a fat man on a moving vehicle jumps in the air he stays in the same place? This was the source of constant wonder to me. Have you ever thought to consider what would be left if you poisoned your tweed-jacketed, black-trousered teacher, put him in a six foot coffin, but then chopped off one third of his legs to fit him in a freshly dug hole in the ground? I did and I expressed my result as a fraction, a percentage and, to fill time, I togged it up as an algebraic equation so that anyone could work out in an instant what percentage of legs might be removed in order to fit any teacher of varying length into a regular grave.

Such exquisite curiosities smouldered red like hot ash in the fire basket of my child's mind. As a distraction, I buried my small head in a book about a girl called Alice who fell down a rabbit hole only to come face to face with a warren of anthropomorphic beasts. That story I found silly at times but dear God, it was strangely chilling and I read it to the end. It was called *Alice in Wonderland*. Fractions, multiplication, syntax, grammar, even the construction of the Latin gerundive sentence, held no fear for me. I was never afraid of facts, figures or anything else that came out of a book from Mr Shifner's library.

All this maybe could explain to some small degree why I grew up without friends. Friends were poor cohabitants of my curious world. It never occurred to me that they might be a necessary part of the human condition. It goes without saying that I do not wish you or anyone else to feel sorry for me, since I was quite happy with the friendless nature of my situation. I shed no tears over having had no friends and it never did bother me in the slightest. To my understanding, it was a perfectly natural state of affairs and I would not have had it any other way. Besides, I *had* plenty of friends. My friends were on the pages of the book I was reading; they were amongst the integers that formed part of the equation I was intent on solving with such precocious, startling aptitude. They were amongst the syllable-stunted pronouns I slotted alongside my ever conjugating verbs.

Albeit I was like an Irish lurcher on heat over any book I could lay my hands on, I grew up, nevertheless, aware that there was a gap in my life created by the ghosts of two souls who would ever be strangers to me. My parents were spiritual wisp, the invisible spray that rises off the broken wave. Whilst they had no corporeal presence I still had the feeling they were in and around me, pushing and pulling and directing my decisions and thoughts. Of course, that was the truth of it: I was just a boy but sometimes I sensed I was acting a story in which I had been given the part of a fully grown man, a role for which I was nowhere near ready and of which I had absolutely no experience. I stood apart with my shiny, dark hair, my imperceptibly hooked nose, my crushed velvet, Afghan journeybag curtain clothing and my open, sometimes impertinent, demeanour. I carried in my heart a huge hole, a deep yearning for the mother I had never known and the father I could never have. It ached badly and often, filling me like empty hunger, to feel that absence. It welled up inside me and choked me with a rising nausea, deep in my guts. It was like a stone in my undersized shoe, something I could never forget and never get rid of. It may explain why I did not smile much and I frowned a lot. When Lizzie used her hairdressing skills to cut a straight line across my fringe I might have killed her with just one, accidental look.

One final curiosity about me was that I did not speak. I could not speak. I had never spoken. I was, as my classmates endlessly pointed out, JUST A DUMB FEKKIN' MUTE.

CHAPTER 11

We share the same ignorance as to why, in the common parlance, I was a *dumb fekkin mute*. Was this connected to the dreadful events at the Logan farm on the night before my birth? I do not know, ask Hippocrates, ask the writers of the *Corpus*. Psychoanalyse our old friend Freud, free associate until your balls drop. I ask questions and I have a lot of the answers; but I do not profess to have any ready answer as to why I should have been born dumb. Maybe I am a quizmaster with only half a game. Still, I will say in my defence that I am not a stupid man and I was not an idiot boy: I knew pretty early on that something awful happened at the Logan farm the night I was born and I have spent most of my life reassembling the pieces. The fact is, I was an anxious little cunt and the reason is obvious: I had a sense of the connection between the moment I became the celebrated mute and the violence of my mother's mutilation, within a heartbeat of where I lay inside her. In a sense, her violation was mine too.

Whatever the reasons for it, I was always anxious around people. To me, people were a curiosity that made me nervous. As a young boy, I always had a problem making and maintaining eye contact. Of course, when it came to the gruesome detail, the blood and guts of what occurred, Aunt Marion was not the kind of person to keep these things back. She thought it better the innocent child should know and if necessary, make the appropriate adjustment. She told me about it so often, I might just as well have been there, Rubens-like, painting an oil canvas of the family slaughter, my very own *Massacre of the*

Innocents. I could have had somewhat clumsy Lizzie do me a tapestry, if she could sew without smearing blood on the thread. Then again, blood on the thread might have added authenticity. I could almost visualise a tattoo on a shoulder or an arm, but where that memory came from I could never tell you. Was it my mother and her shoulder tattoo? Was it one of her assailants? Was it a memory at all? Memory has a habit of falling between stools. Who would have told me, after all? Maybe Aunt Marion – *probably* Aunt Marion - for she had no scruples about painting a portrait in rich colour tones of my father's bone-handled fish-knife that he was not afraid to use. She would tell me these things when I was in my crib, when I was just a toddler, when I was bouncing off the kitchen hearth and eating lumps from the rope-handled peat bucket, before I could even walk, certainly before I could understand the barbarity of what had occurred. She told me the story of that night repeatedly – or at least what she knew of it and the snippets she thought I could just about digest without gagging on my pureed supper. She had a way of gesticulating with a flat, vertical hand, a whole twisting right arm and a straight finger with an arthritic knuckle that made me know too well how my father filleted old Ben Mercer with that Afghan fish knife. Mad Bob too was a regular constituent of our conversation. I could see the daylight through Mad Bob's pepper-shot belly and I could almost smell his Callander pigs as the finely sliced Mr. Mercer exhaled his last, undeserved, wretched puff.

But when I was still five, Lizzie was reporting that I was a consummate failure at speech development. "He's not talking," was her robust conclusion. "Is he

56

ever going to speak?" She would poke me with a sharp finger in the hope that with some momentary discomfort I might break the silence and make a potent sound. Did she really expect me to tell her to fuck off? I do not think so. Whether she expected it or not, she never gave up trying.

"Maybe he has nothing to say." Aunt Marion countered. "We could all learn a lesson from that," she said, raising an eyebrow at Lizzie.
"He's five," said Lizzie, as if she needed to say no more. The water came out the top of her cup because she was intent on swirling it around the rim. Before it spilt, she said: "He should be talking."
"He may not want to."
"It's not entirely natural," she said. "Maybe you're giving him the wrong food or something."
"He may have good reasons for not talking." She looked up. "And there's nothing wrong with my food."
"He's got a tongue in his head, so why's he not using it? It's not normal being like that."
"Nobody said he had to use it."
"He's like a bloody monk." Lizzie understood Aunt Marion's view that if people spoke less the world would be a better place. In any event, it might be a quieter place. Silence to Aunt Marion was no bad thing. "A very silent monk." Lizzie touched me on the chin and tried to force a finger between my teeth. "Have you looked in his mouth?" she said. "I did because I thought there might be a blockage."
"That wouldn't stop him talking," said Aunt Marion.
"Might stop him breathing."

"Mind," Lizzie said. "He is reading now. He's not completely stupid. Did you see him read? And I think he understood what he was reading too."

"There's no law against that. You might enjoy a book yourself."

"Well..."

"It wouldn't kill you," she said, "once your body got used to the shock."

"If he can read, why can't he speak?" Lizzie leaned back on her chair, tipping the front legs off the ground. "He's got teeth inside his lips."

"Teeth of all things."

"Inside those lips."

Aunt Marion looked over at Lizzie, a blend of irritation and amusement marked on her brow. "I wouldn't do that if I were you."

"Do what?"

"Tip back on your chair like that." The chair went back a little further and the legs slipped out from under her. Lizzie found herself on the floor. "I was going to say, it's not safe."

Lizzie uprighted the chair and sat down again, rubbing the side of her leg. "He should be using his tongue on his teeth to make proper sounds. You know, speech," she said.

"It's not what you've got between your tongue and teeth that matters," said Aunt Marion.

"I wouldn't know about that."

"Maybe you wouldn't."

Lizzie looked down at her hands. She looked a simple girl in the dull light but she knew her own mind. True, she was clumsy. She did not give the impression that she had attended a smart finishing school for ladies. There was a roughness to her but then again, there was sincerity and there was an instinctive intelligence. "I do know that you're nothing much if you can't talk," she said. As she turned away to stack the plates by the old sink, a knife clattered off the top plate and landed between her feet. "Oh," she said. "That always blooming happens."

I could hear them over the top of me, like a strong draught blowing through the gaps around the kitchen door. I knew what they were saying but that did not awaken any desire on my part to share the medium of language with them. I was happy to move my lips and bash my young molars together but could I make a noise? I suppose I liked the way they talked about me. Better that than to be ignored. After all, I could understand most of what they said. Maybe it made me feel more important than I was.

Yet, burgeoning self-importance was not the only reason why I might have been a mute. It was not specifically that I did not want to talk; it was just that I had no mechanism in my head prompting me to articulate words and interact with those around me. There was nothing within that compelled me to talk, nothing that worked like a vocal trigger. I lacked the motivation to speak and, to my mind, there did not seem too much point to it. There must have been good and wholesome reasons why a clever boy, as I undoubtedly was, would keep things clammed up on the inside. In a sense I was like my father in that both our worlds were surrounded by walls: his were hewn from stone, but mine were no less impregnable for being invisible. The effect of not speaking is that everything stayed in that small cell, somewhere inside me. I had conversations, of course, just like any other, but they were interactions that took place inside my head and it was I who controlled them. The four walls of my skull became an alternative space inhabited by people who spoke and acted in any way demanded of them - by me. Inside the bone of my head there was a place that I could inhabit whenever it suited. I soaked up the life around me and I spewed it up all over my brain. It was a place where my mother and father could infuse, breathe, sleep and share a conversation. My mother would smile, curling her front hair darkly between her fingers. She would eat an apple from that old orchard on the green slope to the other side of Tullis. Always rosy on one side only, where the apple might have caught the sun. She would hold her bottom lip between her teeth and my father would look back at her with that deep fondness in his liquid eyes. In a *swoon*. My mother would hug me close to her, I could smell her pungent scent, and my father would put his strong soldier-farmer hand on my skinny shoulder, and I would feel the tips of his fingers through my cotton shirt against the bone. He would say.... well, he would say most things I wanted him to say. In my head I even had a bedroom with bookshelves wall to wall, a slate with a fresh box of white and yellow chalk and a silk Afghan rug on the floor, its pink and burgundy petals swirling around the aqua-blue, like thick-skinned flowers on water. I could look out the sloping window of my bedroom and see only the things that I wanted to see. When I was a little older I could see Ben Mercer getting gutted, his spine yawning pink bloody lips to either side. I could see Mad Bob picking gunshot from a big hole through his thick, leaky gut. I could sometimes see out of the hole in his back if Mad Bob stood against the light and puffed up his chest. I could lock the door without lifting a finger or a foot. I did not have to move a muscle. That is the good thing about a bedroom and general living accommodation inside your head. That is the reward for being so close I could see the pain in their teary eyes, I could touch their blood and feel their breath against my cheek. None of it was real in the accepted sense, but to me it was more vivid than life or death or ash from a hot fire.

CHAPTER 12

At the beginning, when I was a young, smooth-chinned boy and I ventured into the village, people in Tullis would speak to me and expect to have an answer. I am sure it occurred to my simple mind, what right do they have to expect an answer? I do not know whether consciously I chose not to answer or if I could not physically articulate the words. I am not so sure, but I am certain that often enough, even if I could have spoken I would not have breathed an undertaker's whisper because, as I have said, the real conversations were going on inside my head. They looked at me as if I was not exactly all four legs on a pit pony. As if, because I had no tongue, I must have no pulse in my heart, no brain inside my head, as if all the cerebrospinal fluid had flooded down the ventricles and swamped sweetly odorous chloroform on my ability to think or talk. They might even have thought that I was contaminating them with some of my mother's Romanian magic life force.

There were occasions when, as a young boy, I was sent down to the village and at such times, I was forced to confront others with my blank inability to speak. Once I went to pick up some steel nails and wire wool from Mr Fawcett's, a shop that also sold cooking pots, wood glue, set-squares and other hardware but with a new line in two grades of wire wool: coarse and not so coarse. It was a shit shop with nothing in it that ever amused me, but it had a rusty, tin roof and I loved to be there when it rained because of the thunderous noise, like a thousand steel tacks banging against your skull, drowning out the voices. On this particular occasion it was not raining at all, so

I had no interest whatsoever in being in Mr Fawcett's shop other than to fetch half a dozen masonry nails and the wire wool (not so coarse). I was waiting for Mr Fawcett to put them in a bag for me, a bag that I had brought with me for just this purpose, when I was approached by an old lady (she seemed old to me) in a big, flat, crinoline hat containing two goose feathers and a floppy bow and a canary yellow dress with a lace collar bucketing up her neck. Her appearance was unusual for Tullis, with its dull greys and browns. The toes of her shiny, black shoes peered out beneath the hem. She held a white lace handkerchief and she patted me on the head with the papery palm of her boney hand. There were freckles on her fingers but the skin was dry. I suppose I must have looked at her as if she had kicked my testicles during a pleasant dream. My startled reaction to being manhandled may have betrayed the belief that I took offence at the old coupon who had taken the liberty of patting my head without invitation, something I did not encourage. Of course, she did not see the inside of me and was too steeped in personal decay to know what I was thinking. She did not know I had a head that contained the other world, where I had a bedroom with bookshelves and parents and Ben Mercer getting gutted and Mad Bob with his daylight hole. She pressed me for my name as if it were a key that would open a locked door. She asked questions about my school and whether I could read. Had I read the *New England Primer*? Did I not know that it was full of useful phrases: *A Dog will bite A thief at Night* and *The idle Fool Is whipped at School*. She asked about my awkward velvet clothing, which she commented was vulgar and faintly Persian. She asked about my mother and father and where, who and what they were. And every other useless geriatric enquiry you could think of before you expired with suicidal ideation. As I say, I had never before seen this old pike's frontage in all my sweet and pleasant existence, so I stared back at her, with vacant eyes that rose above the saucer hat, its feathers and floppy bow, but made no contact with anything larger than a fly on the window, without a single word from my mouth to break the shrill little silence she had created by her own inquisition.

"Where is your talkative nature child?" she persisted, an edginess growing in her voice. "I have asked you many questions, and yet you do not answer. What is it with you? Everybody's got a thing or two to say. Even a Persian bird sings in April."

I looked at her and she looked at me. We connected in a solidarity of silent enmity. I wanted to take the pencil from behind Mr Fawcett's ear and spear each of her eyeballs. I would have drawn black charcoal lines on the whites. I would have gladly hung the eyeballs over a fire and barbecued them to a crispy skin. I might even have smeared the eyeballs in a carmelised onion sauce and scoffed them with cow's milk. Or would that have been going too far?

"It is irritating when a child fails to converse," she said finally, as I wallowed in my ocular fantasy. "It's very irritating to me that when civil words are addressed to you, you are not in the least concerned to respond with anything more than vacant stares. You seem to be an assertively annoying young boy. Believe me, there is nothing to be gained in life by staring and squinting and eating the air." Then she smiled a twin strip of thin, puce lips like two skinny threads. "After all, you're not a fish."

"He doesn't speak," said Mr Fawcett helpfully, if a little late to recover the situation.

"Nonsense" she said. "All boys speak. Even the stupid ones speak." She looked down at me. "Come now. Ignorance at this level is inexcusable. Don't worry if it makes no sense. Just move your jaw and adjust the slackness of your lips. Like so." At which point she demonstrated her skill at moving jaw and lips, teeth and tongue in some insane pattern so as to produce speech. "Let's-hear-you," she instructed emphatically.

I continued to stare at the yellowing whites of her wrinkled eyes. The bags beneath sagged like they were full of coins. I stood motionless as a stone pillar.

"Infuriating," she said eventually. "Quite infuriating," she repeated. Once more, she bent her face towards me but was met by a distance, deep and impenetrable as a Rocky Mountain canyon. She looked away from me and up once more at Mr Fawcett, who was wiping his damp palms against a green pinny, and who then raised both eyebrows and both hands simultaneously, as if joined by a thread.

"He doesn't speak," echoed Mr Fawcett. I noticed he had teeth that I had not seen before. "Never has done, I'm told, and that's the truth."

"Well, I suppose that's a relief," the old lady said. "That there are medical reasons behind this disappointing phenomenon. I'm so glad it is not just me he gawps at."

I took my bag of nails and wire wool (not so coarse) and left Mr Fawcett's shop, my chin set firm against my chest, and not a second too soon or I might have laid my clenched fist on her. As it was, there were bloody half moons surfacing on the white pads below my thumbs. I did not know who she was. I had no reason to know that many years later I would point a gun in her vicinity and use it too.

Having no voice in the classroom only served to spread distance between me and the other children. At first they would observe the crackling eccentricity. Then they would pick on it, like children do, until it bled a small, unbroken trickle. They chanted "fekkin' dumb mute!" at me like I was deaf not dumb. They goaded me with provocations and did the best they could to tease me out of what was to them, undoubtedly, a hostile and threatening tranquility. I could have been a Zulu speaking Swahili or some other Bantu tongue and they would have been all smiles. Just like the old lady with the eyeballs and the lace neck bucket in Mr Fawcett's shop, silence to them felt like a defence they had no means to understand or undermine.

If, some years later, Lloyd George had puffed himself up and leaned across the Berlin peace table to address the Kaiser, and if he had simply confronted him with a solid, frozen whiskery silence, my belief is there might never have been a Great War. The terrified Kaiser would have been off to change his red-stripe trousers within the hour. Silence is a weapon. These boys never came close to drawing the voice out of me. As time went on, their endless jibes, like tiny broken fires, sparked and petered out. They abandoned the niggling torture they sought to inflict and they left me alone. I suppose they thought where was the pleasure when the beetle whose legs you are pulling off fails to adopt a limp, or even do the courtesy of telling you to absolutely fuck right off. After a while they forgot about me, like I was a bee sting they once had, nothing more than a burst of apitoxin that they were now well and truly over. Like all the others, they talked over and around me, as if I was the grey mist, invisible, vaporous or not even there at all. I was a disappeared child, just a faint shadow woven into the country colours of a background canvas. They could speak about anything and never think that I had ears on each side of my head. If they noticed the ears at all, which is doubtful, to them their purpose was no more than elaborate decoration on a strange bone. They were unable to acknowledge that those translucent tissue flaps were proper listening devices, connected to the billions of neurons in my cerebral cortex. To me, they were the one-way conduit from the outside world. They drew in the life and tempo of the other existence and fed the complex sponge inside my head; they made the presence in there one that I could bear.

I have to confess, that is all a long belt on a short pair of pants. It is what I have told you already: I lived in a private world with no friends at all, and in all truth I did not care two figs about it. It seems to me I did not very much deserve to have friends.

CHAPTER 13

9 years later

It was only a matter of time before I started on the guns. Without a doubt, my father had no gun cupboard, no shiny hook at the jail to hang his Snider-Enfield rifle from and nobody had thought to remove it from the house. Mad Bob maybe remembered that loaded firearm better than anybody. Every time he used the toilet would be an easy reminder. I knew it was there in my father's room, on top of that old oak wardrobe that smelled faintly of fungus and stale breadcrumbs and old cloth and leather boots.

It took me a while to get it down off the top ledge and have a good look. I waited until Aunt Marion and Lizzie were out of the house, collecting something or other from Tullis. In I went, stood on a farm chair from the kitchen table and felt the dusty top of the wardrobe underneath my fingers. I gripped the cold barrel and slid it slowly across. I took it down, the silence all around me, like a choirboy showing reverence at the altar. The chair was shoogly, made the rifle slip in my hand as I held it, all of a sudden, so that I nearly dropped it. Having recovered my balance, I was pleased to discover that, whilst I had very limited experience on the subject, it seemed to me that this was a seriously good gun, with a long barrel and a sleek, shiny, rosewood grip. I put my finger against the trigger, felt the zingy, cold metal against my skin, aimed at the black raven on the wall beyond the window and pulled the trigger, mouthing an explosion as I did. In my head I saw a small Afghan take the bullet and flop softly against the wall.

When I looked again I saw there was no Afghan and no raven either, nothing.

I read a book about rifles that I found in the Modern Warfare section of Mr Shifner's library. Mr Shifner had always encouraged my reading (largely, I fear, as a means to discourage my intrusions on his personal time) and slowly I had come to enjoy the free use of his books. Still, my sense was that he also derived some small pleasure from seeing my figure hunched over an open book with a fierce concentration etched across my face. He was not used to his pupils taking such an obvious interest. It may have been quite gratifying. I suppose the one thing he liked about me was that as a mute, I had no choice but to live in a world of total silence and he was happy enough to see me in there, on my leper's island, foraging quietly for knowledge amongst the books like I was a pig hunting truffles. For me, it was a logical next step to start stealing those books.

The first book I stole was called the *Nuttall Encyclopoedia* and it was reasonably informative to a boy with an interest in guns and small explosions who theorized on the release of inflammable oils and gases at high temperature. By way of background to the more scientific aspects of the book, it even told me the story of Jacob Snider, the American inventor who was buried at Kensal Green Cemetery in London. It did not give the full facts of his life and death and that was a disappointment to me. It told me nothing of his parentage and precious little about his long journey to London, but I was able to learn that the Snider-Enfield rifle, derived at least in part from his name, had gone from firing three rounds per minute with the muzzle-loader to ten rounds per minute with the breech-loader. That was Snider's doing, converting the old muzzle-loader into a breech-loader. At a single stroke, he changed the world, allowing users to take ten lives per minute whereas before they took a paltry three. That is the inflationary world we sometimes inhabit.

My father had been a good storeman with the cartridges too, keeping a plentiful stock on the shelf at the back of the wardrobe, wrapped in greasepaper, safe from the fungus and breadcrumbs and occasional moths. There were fourteen packets with the rifle, of what they called a "Boxer" which was a new type of metal cartridge. All you had to do with the Snider-Enfield was cock the hammer, yank the breech block lever and fire. Boom! Say your prayers! A deadly shot through the heart, my Afghan friend!

It was an easy gun, the Snider-Enfield, and I spent plenty of time with it doing target practice on the beach. You could have a lot of fun shooting at bottles and apples. When apples were out of season and the bottles were all finished, I had to improvise. I found a dead basking shark washed up on the shoreline. I took some limewash we had used on the inside wall of the old barn and I painted a target on the shark's soggy flesh. I held a cloth to my nose but the limewash helped smother the rotten smell. I wrote the word "Mad Bob" splash bang in the middle of the target. There were maggots already leaping in the shark's belly and they moved a thousand tiny wiggles as I jabbed the paint onto the target. I stepped back, looking at my handiwork. I walked away a good distance along the beach and lay down against the marram grass. I prepared myself and got my breathing just so. Then I must have filled the shark with twenty-five or thirty cartridges, each one getting closer to the centre. Clearly, it was not much fun for the maggots but, having pulled back a further distance from the target, I could even get a hit at five hundred yards. There were times when I got lucky at a thousand yards, and that is a very long way to travel to hit the shit out of a maggot. Most were safe at that distance. The shark looked like egg nog by the time I finished, but I was pleased. The Snider-Enfield had proved it was a good gun and I was a not-too-bad shot. How many poets write about good guns? Well, since you ask, it is well known that Kipling did:

> *A Snider squibbed in the jungle -*
> *Somebody laughed and fled,*
> *And the men of the First Shikaris*
> *Picked up their Subaltern dead,*
> *With a big blue mark in his forehead*
> *And the back blown out of his head.*

That's how the heavily moustached, bespectacled Mr Kipling saw the Snider and he was pretty well right on the money. He was on the big fat bullseye there. It was a meaningful gun in anyone's lexicon and it killed a lot of people, not least the Fenian Brotherhood who were stirring up a lot of trouble over in Canada at the time, so I recall. How Canada got mixed up with the Fenian Brotherhood, I do not know. There is some limit to my very extensive knowledge of domestic and international affairs. But I knew how to shoot, that was the thing for me, and my long-term targets were becoming more clearly defined.

CHAPTER 14

1 month later

There are defining moments in every life, whether your journey is that of an ant, a leather army boot, a philosophising drunkard or a hot shave Turkish barber (of which I knew there was one in Blantyre). These are moments that set you off on a particular course you might not otherwise have taken. You may choose the route inadvertently and some thing or some force will get hold of you and propel you like weightless fluff to where it wants you to go, whether you like it or not. The bird's feather falls to earth but could land just about anywhere. Of course, it may be just a small tilt on the rudder or something more powerful and deliberate that turns the boat around and sends the sailor on his way, cutting through a new ridge of ocean waves, the sun flipped from one shoulder to the other. Small or large, whatever your actions may be, they may steer you in a direction over which you have no control, taken away from the comfort and certainty of those reassuring voices that dwell inside your head.

I was still just thirteen years ten months and three days old. It was May and we were outside in the Tullis Board schoolyard, breathing the crisp morning air. There was a suggestion of soft prickles and green shoots thinly pushing out from the raggedy, hawthorn hedges; the sycamores were showing tight, little buds along their boughs and the pale yellow daffodils grew with peeping, half-hidden heads along the earth banks outside the school's iron gate. The sky was predominantly blue and there was no more breeze than usual. The mild warmth of the sun was on our faces. Mr Shifner was having a migraine for which he took a spoon of syrupy medicine from a green, unlabeled bottle and sent us outside to consider the proper use of verbs, adjectives and pronouns. Most of the goons in my class were beyond educating in such esoteric matters but since the General Education Act of 1870 every gormless Jim in the country was expected to succumb to a small infusion of education. I was leaning against the sill of a ground floor window, in the company of these simian impostors, wishing the migraine break was over and we could get back into the classroom for a bit more of *William Pearson* and *The Self-Help Grammar of the English Language*.

Weary of the ease of English grammar, I amused myself by conjugating Latin verbs, two at a time, third person plural to first person singular, reeling them off in my head as I stood by one of the front windows to the school. I sound like I was just being clever: I probably was. Momentarily, I was distracted from my conjugations by the stonework around the mullions, noting that it was poor and broken and in need of pointing. You could pull stones out from the crumbling mortar. If Mr Shifner had seen me doing that he would have given me extra work detention after school. Extra work detention after school did not bother me one bit. So, I pulled a large lump of hard stone from the mortar and weighed it in the palm of my curled hand.

There were three other boys close by and I sensed them as they insinuated their loathsome presence. In my life then and the life that was to follow, these boys came to assume some importance and influence. Forgive me if I sometimes grimace when I mention

74

their names but their sobriquets did not always fill me with a warm, affectionate glow. I will attempt a formal introduction. There was Tom Burns, the son of a farmer with just enough brain, potted like dry compost in a shaven head, to half fill his old man's miniature clay pipe. The shortness of his hair served only to accentuate the bulbous nose on his pudding bowl face. Beside him, sitting with his trousered bum on a wooden log, was Joey Sharpe, another farmer's boy. He had none of the round, over-fed look favoured by Tom. He was grey-skinned, thin-lipped, already topped with a light growth of soft hair – of which he was seemingly very proud - on the slim ledge beneath his nose. There was a smear of meanness that hung from his pores like sweat or damp. Then there was Rory Turner, squatting on his worn heels, fair hair on his head, blue eyes looking out, skilled in the art of projectile spitting, forever sniffing up the liquid trails that leaked from his fine young nose. He had large ears that lunged forward like clam shells and his eyes were unusually shiny. Of the three at that time, I suppose he was arguably the least repellent, but you would not bet your house on it. I was there, or nearby, but I thought I was quite invisible to them. Usually I was just a thing at the back of the room or a chameleon that suggested its presence but was never really there. A silent, sombre, useless shadow of a ghost. On this occasion, however, these boys had time on their hands to fix their focus more steadily on my unnecessary existence. Alive to their own boredom, they had become strangely aware of, and irritated by, my presence and by my ability to keep breathing.

Joey rose off his log like an extending toad and moved a series of small, unambiguous steps in my direction. He leaned forward and insinuated himself in my space. "The old man still in the pokey, Seany?" he asked.

Tom raised his soft head and shelled a nostril with his thumb. "His dad's in the pokey for sure."

"Got a bad attitude," said Rory, sniffing, like he was consuming a hearty meal.

"Knives is very sharp, Seany. Didn't you know that? Did no one tell your dad that you have got to be careful with knives?"

I looked at them but my eyes were soulless, empty rooms.

"Knives are very dangerous, Sean," said Joey, sneering over his thin slice of lip.

"Not advisable to play with the knives, Sean," squeaked Tom. "Not really sensible. He looked at his friend. "Shouldn't do that, should he, Joey?"

"Shouldn't do what, you dopey bugger?" asked Joey.

"Play with knives. People – should – not – play – with – *knives*."

I could feel their squeezing little eyeballs upon me. They wanted me to react and I was happy for the price of two specks of farmyard cow dung on my Afghan velvet curtain pants to deny them that pleasure. I maintained a look of bland congeniality. If they had looked into my own limpid eyes they would have seen nothing more than their own blurred reflections.

Slowly, each of them edged towards me. Small twists and moves into my space that were designed to intimidate me. "Ma dad says your old man got twenty-five years."

"Fuckin' deserved it," said Joey. "He used a blade."

"That's what I was saying, Joey. Knives are dangerous toys," said Tom.

"Not very civilized though, is it Seany? Killing that guy Mercer I mean," said Rory. "Skinned him with a knife no less. The man's a fuckin' animal for doing that." They still looked at me. Rory was the least animated. He turned away and gazed back at me across his shoulder, sly as four eyes on a fox. Joey looked straight through me with his knife-gash eyeslits. Tom forced a smile from his overfed mouth, wrinkling his soft nose and exposing his grey-brown teeth. There was a long period of silence but maybe it was just five seconds.

"Fucked his mum," said Joey. "So my dad says." He looked at me. "The cunt's got no fuckin' manners, I suppose," he said.

"You'd give her a poke, wouldn't you Joey?" said Tom.

"Just like your dad," said Rory.

Joey looked at Rory and then looked away. He moved a step closer to me. I could see his yellowed, pitted skin now. "Not me," he said, jutting his face straight at me. "I wouldn't touch her with fuckin' gloves on." He waited a moment and then turned and tossed a stone into the ploughed field beyond the fence. The dry earth threw up some dust. "She was a gypsy fuck, mate." He threw another stone that clipped the fence. "No dogs, no fucking gypsies, those are my rules." Rory spat a gob of mucus. Joey crabbed back over to me by the window. He held his face unnecessarily close to mine and I could see again the open pores of his skin. "Peg on nose time, I'm thinking."

"Think she enjoyed it?" asked Tom, still smiling, his disembodied voice sweeping in from behind.

Joey insinuated himself closer still, his breath quick and stale against my face. "She was a passionate woman," he said. I did not like the sensation of Joey's breath against my skin. It was almost sticky. "Matter of fact," he said, glancing at his fingernails. "There's a reason why gypsies are born with their legs apart." He looked over at Tom who still smiled widely. He was relaxed and once again curled his thumb into his nose. He clicked his tongue. "Did you know, Tom, Sean here's mum was known as Noah?"

"I didn't know that Joey," he answered. "For what reason was she known as Noah?"

"Because," he said, now very pleased with himself, pausing for effect. "Because she liked to take them up her two at a time." They laughed so loudly that other kids by the wall craned their necks and looked over at us.

"What do you fucking expect?" said Rory. "But my dad's horse would have taken advice before he fucked her."

"Stands to reason," said Joey. "A horse is a valuable and discriminating creature."

I will not bore you with the odorous charms of these conversing pygmies. Suffice to say that the fizzy cup of bonhomie towards my dead mother did not run over for very much longer. That was just about as far as Joey got with his eulogy to her memory. A black cloud, full of Helman ghosts and forgotten grief, had imbued itself within me and for the next thirty-seven seconds I became mightily unhinged. For the first time in as many years, I had left the room inside my head and I entered the battle zone. I was on Flodden

Field or Waterloo. I was my father at Kandahar meting out the slaughter. I was a urinating Pashtun woman. I was not wholly in charge of who I was or where I was or what I had become. The deeply bedded control system was debilitated to the point of total malfunction. Had I been inside my head, I would have lived behind a heavy locked door with shackles on my legs and arms. Maybe I still had one foot in each world. By the end of thirty-seven seconds, Joey had two broken ribs and a tooth hanging out of his skinny mouth on a bloody thread. Tom had a lip thick as a sea mussel, an index finger bent ninety degrees to the left, with a dislocated crack along the shaft and a high pitched ring in his right ear where my fist had exploded the pressure in his eardrum. Rory never left his wooden seat; he did nothing at all, other than land a gob on the left side of my head that caused a slick of momentary wetness. Most of the damage was inflicted with the stone I had pulled from the pointing beneath the window sill. It happened to be flint or some such variety of sedimentary chert. It acted as a crude knuckle-duster but almost broke my own fingers in the process.

I noticed later that I had blood on my skinned hands and I was not at all sure it was mine. I dabbed at it with my pinkie finger and touched my tongue with the tip. The taste was like sweet metal with a bitter salty finish. I wiped my hand on my sleeve and reflected on this uncharacteristic physical outburst. I had shown that I was capable of volcanic violence. I had tasted my enemy's blood. Surely this was a fine catalyst for change?

The worst of it was that they kept me out of school for that expression of filial indignation, but it had provided a solid enough indication to those who dared hover in my proximity of my passably psychotic nature. On the whole I did not have too much trouble after that. It taught me something too. It taught me what could be achieved with a fist thrown well with conviction and clear intent and a big stone wedged between your fingers. It taught me about playing fair: on the whole, do not entertain the idea. There was no use fighting on an equal footing: Marquess of Queensberry rules and all that fair play bullshit were an unnecessary luxury.

CHAPTER 15

So, my fists had done some fast-talking for me and I
did not feel two penny's worth sorry about it. Of
course, I would like to think I was better than just a
blossoming psychopath mapping out a future life in
the art of assassination. After all, I had a beating brain
on my shoulders that told me I had the flower of
intellectual promise. Then again, neither do I want
anybody thinking I had nothing on my mind but
reading and crunching numbers and working
algorithms. Now I think about it, I know that I *was* an
impossibly complicated character. I had a real love for
books and there were times you could not thread skin
between myself and the page I was reading. People
could find that annoying and my Aunt Marion was a
case in point. Not unreasonably, she expected me to
pull some serious weight around the farm – after all I
was the only man right there, with the rest of the
family in the jail or sleeping with the worms. There
was many a time when I could see Aunt Marion
wanted to bawl me out for not chopping cut logs, not
cleaning out the klinkers from the old fire grate or not
doing a proper job of mending a broken wattle fence
so a goat got out and ate the small saplings at the end
of Hograt field.

She would yell at me to pull my weight when she had
lost the will to cope or things were getting her down.
"You're the man here," she would say and I would
look at her vacantly. "Lizzie and I, we need you to do
the things that a man can do." My eyes dipped. And
I *was* the man, even aged thirteen years and ten
months and three days.

I will grant you I was sometimes lazy, but is there a growing boy alive who is not just occasionally a little bit awed by the prospect of a whole twenty-four hours in any one day? That was a lot of time to get through. Or maybe it was not laziness. Maybe it was the selfishness of youth, that unassailable belief that my young life was designed to stand foremost and eclipse every other. I knew there was more to me than splitting logs, sweeping shit and hoeing weeds. I had a good pair of hands and I knew they were for more than pulling teats in the milk parlour. At the same time I was well aware that Aunt Marion took some pride in the fact that I could read quicker than her. She took pleasure from knowing that I could explain the meaning of a binary numeral system by a simple note on a piece of paper, without a word from my silent lips and without drawing one vaporous drop of sweat off my blackening temples. She knew that as well as skinned knuckles I had live wires and electricity between my ears.

People think that a man of few words is a man of even fewer brains. I call that pure ignorance. It seems to me that a man who flaps and wags his tongue wastes his energy. The man who speaks less has more time to think. He is not wasting precious moments articulating with his pretty, pink lips the sparks that fly around his brain. He has spare capacity to ponder targets, strategy and resolution. He sees the wider picture, untramelled by the drowning pull of words. On the other hand, I was increasingly aware that one did not always have to be dumb to play dumb. A man could live a life with few words, speaking only when it suited. He could speak a little but he could wear a distant gaze and relax his jaw and let his facial muscles slump. He could get close to his prey without raising a suspicion because he was commonly supposed to be just a little bit dumb.

Nevertheless, whilst being dumb – or even playing dumb - had its up side, it also had a down side. There was a lot of times I felt like I was trapped inside myself. I felt like someday I would have to talk and I would have to scream, yell or roar out loud or else I was going to explode. At times it felt like I had my head in a bottle and the air was being sucked out. These times I felt like I was experiencing death by a thousand suffocations. I was a bee in that bottle and I was using up all my air.

Maybe it all started with the battering I gave those boys behind the hawthorn hedge in the Tullis Board schoolyard. A flint stone that travelled up from some distant chalky ground (not Fife, but elsewhere), ending up in my clenched fist. Breaking those ribs and spilling that blood seemed a surprisingly satisfactory way to get these snakes off my back. Those boys immediately found they warmed to the inclination to keep a little more distance between us. I found myself a sight less anxious when I came to be around them. I looked them in the eye and, to my surprise, it was sometimes they who looked away first.

If my fists were in good shape, I was becoming a sharp shot with the rifle too. With a little more practice, I could pick off a flea on a pig's arse when I had the desire for it and got my range just right. Lizzie and Aunt Marion knew that I was using the rifle now, but then we lived on a farm and it would have been unusual not to get involved with rifles. Killing is what farming is all about. There were rats in the barn and you had to shoot them to keep the numbers down. Good practice too. Rabbits were good for the pot, particularly if taken with a good, clean blast from the Snider-Enfield. I could skin a rabbit in less than a minute, like I was peeling fruit.

Yet, at first, the shots fired around the farm got Lizzie all shaken up and excited. "What's all that banging going on?" I heard her ask.
"I don't know," said Aunt Marion. "Maybe it's the sound of you dropping stuff."

CHAPTER 16
1 ½ years later

Young people often make the mistake of thinking that when something is done, it is done. Like fights in playgrounds. When I was 15.3 years old, I learned how things are not always entirely finished when you thought they were finished. My enlightenment came at a time when my feet were planted knee high in slithery, mud water flowing through the Bombo Burn.

There was a field running west from the house at Logan farm. We did not tend to keep anything much on it. The ground nearest the house was fertile enough and with a bit of work it could have been productive. Sometimes you have to decide if the drop of sweat you earn is worth as much as the bucket of sweat you expend in achieving that result. Balance is the critical issue, albeit sometimes you cannot help but lose your balance and all the decisions that follow are skewed by that lack of equilibrium. With this particular field, as the grass swept down to the burn, you got the feeling the brown soil would be richer, more sympathetic to the vagaries of growing a successful crop, easier to squeeze out some half-decent grazing for the sheep. In fact, the truth is the earth grew sandy and dry and nothing much would grow there. We had tried year on year, but it stubbornly refused to yield anything particularly edible. More sweat went into that earth than ever came out of it - and still nothing much would grow.

I was down at the end of that stubborn old cunt of a field, behind the prickly sow-thistle, where the Bombo Burn snaked past, winding up to the next open ground where it grew to a modest flow, gassing up in a bubbly gush, carrying the rain off the hills beyond, all the way to the firth and the open sea. I was in the cold, muddy water, and as I say, it was up to my knees and seeping in through the loose stitching of my boots. Where I was stood, there was as much mud as there was water. The banks on either side of me were made up of the same dry, sandy earth as the field itself and they were crumbling and breaking down into the burn. There were rocks too that had rolled off the top and into the water and, together with the sand and the earth, they were closing off the passage of water. I was digging out a deeper channel, like a human dredger, using a pick and mostly a scooping spade, in an effort to restore the flow.

I had been so lost in my own thoughts, so intent on completing the sedimentary excavation, I neither saw nor heard them coming. The first thing I knew about it was when I felt a large gob hit the back of my neck, almost at the same time as I heard it leave his mouth. I ran my fingers over it, thinking that maybe it was a seagull or a puffin that had struck lucky. I looked up to see not the bird loosening its bowels, but Rory Turner, smacking his lips with two straight fingers, blue eyes big as plates on the wall.

Joey, his skin cast grey as the overcast sky, was at his side. "Nice one," he said.
"Thanks Joey." Rory was pleased, inwardly triumphant. It clearly meant something to him to hit the target.
"Not seen you in school for a while, Logan," said Joey. "You're neglecting your education." I looked up from the water and there did not seem too much

point in responding, even if I could. What was I to do? Write him a note, explaining that sometimes work on the farm had to come first?

"Not good Seany," said Joey, smoothing the light, furry growth above his lip with a skinny hand, avoiding the spots that pitted his chin. I had time to think that the down of hair above Joey's lip was a growth without ambition, a frustrated, pointless work in progress. It was wispy like a girl's. I would have liked to have pulled it if I had been close enough or it had been long enough.

"Anyone fucked your mother recently?" said Tom, and he laughed so loud you would think the world's best comedian just walked into Tullis. Slowly his laughter subsided. "That was funny," said Tom, in case we had not got it.

"We have unfinished business with you, haven't we?" said Joey, getting serious. "Of course, we're better prepared this time." He pulled an object from his pocket, flicked his arm out to his side, and I watched a clean blade unfold with a sharp, ugly point. It was what they called a flick-knife, something I had not seen before.

I leaned on my spade and pushed the sweat-soaked hat back on my head. Given the weakness of my position numerically, I had an urge to reason, but for that I required words. If I had had words, I would have asked them what it was about my mother that so intrigued them. They bleated on, but did they know the first thing about her? Did they know one thing about my father for that matter? Every word they uttered was a poop born out of ignorance.

Not surprisingly, I did have some concern that things might end up much the same as last time in the Tullis Board schoolyard, except it would be *my* ribs pointing the wrong way and *my* teeth floating in the water. The knife would be sticking out of *my* gut and that would be a bad – maybe deadly - development. I wondered if that was the kind of balanced outcome we look for in life. But, in the same breath, I knew they had pigs' balls for brains. They wanted revenge? Because *Seany* had hurt the little boys? Was it an eye for an eye they were after? Even if I could speak, could I have ever found the words to persuade them that they were stupid and wrong? That revenge was a tasteless, pointless syrup?

"That Lizzie of yours," said Joey. I looked at him, holding his eyes.
"She's just your type, Joey. You know, on the big side," said Tom.
"But a nice nature, Tom. She's got a nice nature." He looked back at me. "We might be very good together. There might be some poetry between us. I might be interested in giving her some poetry of my own." I was mildly irritated, rather than angry. Some anger, touched with despair. I would have told him that the day she looked at him was the day he was stuck in hell and she and all the other angels were resisting the urge to reveal their Pashtun heritage. "I've been thinking about her a lot," Joey persisted. "She's got potential." Rory smiled at that and Tom chuckled and wiped his mouth. To Tom, this was better than the clowns he had studied pictures of, at Chipperfield's Circus. He liked it when Joey spoke like that. I wanted to tell him that if he so much as wished her good morning, it would be the last

greeting he ever slotted from that weasel mouth. However, I could tell that for once he was focused on the arithmetic. In other circumstances that might have been good news, but the calculation here was relatively elementary: there were three of them and just the one of me. There were no witnesses. He was smug, his smile so wide, I could see his stained molars between the thin lips, the same teeth I had sought to rearrange at our last thirty-seven second meeting. He still had the open blade in his right hand.

At that moment Tom took it upon himself to launch the attack by jumping off the sandy bank. All this intellectual jousting was beginning to pall on him. He had appreciated Joey's sense of humour, his genius at setting the tone, but he was impatient to get to the point. It was time for the punch line. He wanted to sort me out with his fist before the clock ticked off another wasted minute. Joey could stab me later.

Had he landed on me with his full weight, I would have gone down like a boxer with jelly legs. Luckily for me the sand crumbled under his feet and he was a fraction slow or sluggish with his elevation off the bank. I had just enough time to pull the spade from the water and swing it against his chest. Doubtless, I am to be congratulated on the zip and speed of my immediate response. That in itself would have been quite satisfactory – another couple of ribs would have popped, a small amount of blood may have been spilt and it would have been over. The other two might have taken fright at the sight of all that gore on my shovel. Nothing to write to the Marquess of Queensberry about. I might have made a run for it. Unfortunately, the spade was a heavy, sharp-edged old bastard and when I dragged it up it was slow coming out of the water. Tom was slow to elevate because of the soft, sandy terrain and he sank into a position of mortal danger. When the jagged top edge of my spade connected with the unfortunate Tom, instead of breaking his ribs it caught his pink neck and ripped the most outrageous hole in it. He lay beached on his back to one side of the burn, the soupy water swirling over his cotton drill thighs and tugging at his feet, the blood gushing from his neck and left shoulder and slicking red across the stones. The spade had left a hanging flap that would have folded neatly back against his Adam's apple and all sorts of anatomy was visible, hovering inside the butchered flesh.

Joey and Rory jumped down off the bank themselves, one after the other, their faces all of a sudden cast greyer than wet ash. They stood on either side of Tom, not knowing what to do. You could see what looked like Tom's windpipe through the hole in his neck, but there was a lot of blood and it was flowing freely down across his shirt, obscuring the view.

"You've killed him!" yelled Joey, waving the knife at Tom then me. "Ma gawd, you've fucking killed him!"

My own thought was that it would take more than a spade in the neck to kill a slob like Tom, but in truth my confidence was not so great and I worried in that moment that I had inflicted a potentially mortal injury. I walked a few steps back and demonstrated a movement against my neck and then I raised my thumb and pointed at Tom. I wished to convey to the imbeciles that they should push a finger or two into the massive open wound since in my opinion that might be the best way to stop the flow of blood. I stood there quite calm. I could have been demonstrating how a man would mend a fence. I was extremely cool: if I had raised a hand I swear it would have been as steady as the horizon behind it.

"Rory!" shouted Joey. "For fuck's sake, he's meaning put your finger in his neck! Put it in the fuckin' hole in his neck, will you!"
"I'm not putting my finger in no fuckin' hole!" Rory froze. "You put *your* fuckin' finger in the hole!"
"*My* finger's not big enough to go in the hole!" Joey yelled.
"You saying I've got fat fingers now?"

I raised my palms, as if it was obvious that this was the best, indeed the only, way to stop the bleeding. I lifted two fingers and gripped them with my other hand, in an attempt to signify that the efficient use of the two digits was highly desirable should the aim be to stem the flow – a technique supported by even a rudimentary study of *Gray's Anatomy*. With some difficulty, I climbed up onto the sandy bank. They had to stop the hole, that was the main thing, but thus far they seemed paralysed with fear or a deep revulsion at the sight of a throat that opened in the wrong place.

"Anyway," shouted Rory. "You may not have noticed, but I've got a ring on my finger!"
"Well?" said Joey.
"Well, my finger won't go in the fuckin' hole! Not with a bloody ring on it!"

Tom gurgled a noise with small, oxygenated bubbles and blood still flowing from his wound.

"I'll hold your ring!" shouted Joey. "Give me your fuckin' ring and I'll hold it," he said encouragingly.

Rory stood back. "This was my grandma's ring!" he shouted. "It never leaves my finger! Third from the right! It never leaves my fuckin' finger! It's a bad omen to take it off my finger!"

"Aw Christ," said Joey. "Aw Christ! Fuck your grandma! It'll be a bad omen if Tom's dead an' all!"

"Hey!" said Rory. "That's my fuckin' grandma you're talking about!"

CHAPTER 17

There was another gurgling, gasping pitch, followed by a gentle fizz from Tom's throat as the air escaped. I stood on the bank and I was looking down at the pair of them, pointing at each other, jabbing fingers at the body below their feet, shouting profanities across the mud and water between them. I could feel a smear of sweat spread across my forehead. It crossed my mind for the first time that Tom might die and my life could very well die with him. I was not sure I was ready for my life to die. Not just yet. The whole idea made me very nervous. I had done some interesting chemistry and some elementary human biology. I had also recently obtained that copy of *Gray's Anatomy* from Mr Shifner's library (which he was not getting back). Therefore, I recognized the importance of the thyroid cartilage. It crossed my mind that the spade may well have cut the thyrohyoid muscle and even split the cartilage itself. Or worse, the *brachial plexus*. I felt a sense of rising panic that began in the pit of my stomach, scaling the insides of my torso and sending a light tingle through my pectorals before it launched a flush of greater warmth to my already overheated head. Tom gasped and gurgled. Joey and Rory shouted at one another, gesticulating, saying they would not put their fuckin' fingers in the fuckin' hole. Jabbing the knife for emphasis. And then it happened, something that was propelled, switched on and empowered. It rose from somewhere and, amidst the trickling of the burn and the splashing of the mud, it emerged between my teeth and across my tongue, threading through those half-open lips, bursting from my mouth like air from a cave or light through a window.

"I never did much chemistry," I said. I peered at Tom and I stepped a pace towards him and looked over at Rory and Joey. "Something tells me it's all over unless you stop the bleeding." It was a strange sound to hear these words come from my mouth. It was distant in my ears and sounded like it came from somewhere else. The tone of the voice was neither high nor low. I sounded like a boxer after a long fight. There was more air to the voice than proper volume, but I recognized it as a satisfactory and surprising first step. I was not yet ready for a public oration but I had said my first words. I looked at Tom and back again at Joey who stared at me with a deep puzzlement etched upon his features. He dropped the knife and it clattered against the rock at his side. Rory looked up from Tom, his blond hair blowing across his face, his eyebrows curled into a question. "That's just my opinion," I said and I coughed. Still they said nothing in response. "I'm not qualified in medical matters, but that's how it looks," I said and almost smiled. I took a towel out of the bag I had left on the grass mound close to the water, screwed it into a ball and tossed it towards them. Rory caught it with his right hand. I was still outwardly calm but, if truth be known, I too was beginning to lose it. I was becoming deeply concerned about Tom's ongoing prospects in the full panoply of life and meaningful existence. "Hold it to his neck Rory," I rasped. "Hold it hard against his neck." Rory kneeled down on the bank and pressed the towel against the wound. I scratched the hair on my head. "That's a lot of blood in the burn," I said. "I might boil my water tonight." I walked a short distance up the overgrown field, dragging the bloody spade through the sow-thistle weeds. "He'll need stitches," I called out over my shoulder.

"You need to help us!" shouted Joey.

I turned. "I don't think so," I said.

"You can speak?" said Joey.

"So it seems," I said. I began to move away once more. "I've told you what you need to do."

"You just going to leave us here?"

"He's your friend."

"You can't just go," shouted Rory.

"I can," I said. "Just watch."

I arrived back at the house. I had a strange sensation in my throat. I coughed a few times and that seemed to help. There was nobody home, as I expected, so I took the kettle off the stove and poured myself a cup of tea using the leaves from a wooden box in the wall cupboard. The tea was soothing as I sat there thinking about what had occurred. Something had switched itself on, after all these years. What it was, I did not know. All I knew was that something had come out of my mouth and it had sounded pretty good. It was well articulated and it came out free of saliva or unwanted pauses. Words, for god's sake! They were genuine words with proper syllables, the type found in the *Oxford English Dictionary*! They just fell out of my head.

Yet I was concerned about Tom. I hated the fat fool but I did not plan on being responsible for his death. I have to admit I thought to myself, here we go again: if he dies I may find myself choosing paint for a new cell. Well, it happens. My father would be so proud, what with taking after him, a stella career in criminology, going straight from the classroom to the jail cell. I drank the tea in the deepening gloom. I picked a *Darjeeling* leaf from my tongue and wiped it against my leg. I poured a second cup and then stepped out into the yard. I cleared my throat and said the word 'beautiful' and it came out, a little husky, but it was there, resonating in my ears. Another word, another milestone. I had not imagined it. I looked down the field towards the Bombo Burn. "Beautiful," I repeated, and it was still there. I felt another flutter of anxiety but if you had looked in my eyes you would have seen nothing but flint and dark liquid pools. "Beautiful," I said again, with a more syllabic intonation. Music never sounded better. Even though the early evening was cool, I felt a light sweat beading on my temples. I looked again towards the burn. There was no sound and no sign of any movement. Surely they were gone?

An hour later, I did not notice Lizzie as she climbed over the gate and playfully threw a stick at me to get my attention. "Hey!" I shouted. "No need for that!"

Her knees just went from under her.

CHAPTER 18

1 year later

Nothing had changed physically. I had power in my lungs, vibration through my voice box and a resonator by means of my throat, nose and sinuses. I was doing nothing different: the air stream poured from my lungs through the vocal folds of my larynx, perched bird-like atop my windpipe, just as it always had done. Except now it produced sound. Now the parts all worked together in harmony to provide an effortless voice. Now that I had found that voice, I could speak and articulate the thoughts in my head to those on the outside and, after 15.3 years of silence, I had things of importance I very much needed to talk about. Finding my voice was one thing, but there were all kinds of pressures still driving the air out of the bottle and suffocating the life out of me.

Lizzie thought I should be a little more grateful. Aunt Marion asked if I might wish to pay a visit to the Church, find a pew and say my thanks to He who had brought about this fabulous healing. I did not see for one minute why *He* should take the credit. I never blamed Him for the affliction so I would no more blame Him for its passing.

As I say, I was troubled by the intrusive questions that kept pressing in on me, breaking up the night and darkening my spirits through the day. I could not stop these overpowering thoughts, piled ten high like towers of gambling chips at a blackjack table. I could not stop myself from asking many of the same questions, over and over. In my head I sounded like a squealing pig repeatedly honking at a turnip that had no clear answers. Questions that racked me from my earliest days, when I knew I would in all likelihood never see either of my parents again. Questions that were so basic they scraped the barrel, like who had done it? Why had they done it? For what had they done it? My dear mother. They good as snuffed out my father. They changed my life. But who were they? If I were a man, would I go looking for them? How could I find them? Was that it, forming from the miasma of loss, a desire to find and obliterate those responsible? Were the questions no more than small steps, foothills only, in the quest for my own personal justice? With increasing clarity, I could see formulating in my mind, a process which had begun the day I was born. It was the search for retribution and my own personal equilibrium.

Retribution is, of course, an ugly word and an even uglier motivation, but that is what it was. It sounded better than revenge. I vowed to myself, something that I had long felt my life was leading towards, that I would find someone and I would hurt them for what they had done. I would balance their pain with my pain. It was not a particularly laudable, sophisticated or intellectual response. It was raw, it was animal. Just now, it was little more than an aspiration. I needed to put some skin and muscle over it. Then again, I thought, aspiration and lofty ambition is all very well; I did not yet know who the perpetrators were or where I could find them. Then again, they only had to give me the chance. There would be a time when they would think themselves happy these criminals. Would they have wives, I wondered. Would they have parents, brothers, sisters around them? Would I strike at the very heart of them and would all the joy turn to grief? The taste of fruit in their mouths would osmose into ashy pulp. My sorrow and revenge would lever tears from their eyes. Only then would they know that the debt was paid. Perhaps the bigger man would offer forgiveness. That, to my mind, was a Jesuit philosophy that I would have no part of. It was a humiliating placebo for an illness that demanded a more direct remedy.

As I sat, quiet is the truth but by no means dumb, I pondered heavily on the who and the why. I had small grains of knowledge on the subject but they were stretched very thin. Sometimes, when there is something out there you do not know, and you want to know, it is best to sit back and think about the things you do know. When you know what it is that you do know you can then perhaps work out what it is that you do not know. It is a process of deductive reasoning by inference. I knew well enough the hand that was dealt my mother. We still ate off the same kitchen table in the same room where it happened. Yet I would not get rid of that table, not for all the philosophical books in Mr Shifner's rosewood library. Each time you sat at the table you dined with the dead. You put your hands where it was done. Then again, you need that sometimes because the brain is very protective; all too quick the grey cells will draw a greasy film across those experiences it does not want you to know or remember. To my mind, it was important to hold onto these things.

Yet, given I had the raw facts, what else did I know? I pursued my line of investigation with the person who I considered knew the most and who I felt could assist me in my quest. I told Aunt Marion I was trying to organise my thoughts.

"Your thoughts?" she said. "I still can't believe I am hearing your voice, let alone your thoughts."

"Well, you are."

"I'm not sure I'll ever get used to it," she said.

There was a silence and then I picked up the loose thread. "I have to understand more about what happened."

"What happened?" she said.

"About what happened to my mother. And what happened to my father too."

"Well, I can see that, but I thought you knew all there was."

"I have the bare facts. There's lots I don't know."

"You're intelligent, Sean."

"I am."

"So work it out."

"I will work it out."

"You know what happened. Put the pieces together."

"I'm trying."

"You're analytical too."

"I believe I am."

"So, analyse."

She was right about my kind of intelligence, my gift of analysis. I had the ability to keep ten thoughts on ten levels in my head all at the same time. That would tend to confuse most people. The trouble with speaking is that you cannot articulate ten separate thoughts all at the same time. In that sense, thinking is in a different league to talking. I said: "What I'm trying to do is piece the events together."

"The events?"

"Yes."

"You don't want to let these things go?"

100

"How can I let them go?"

"People have to move on."

"I don't want to do that," I said. I rose to my feet and stood by the fire. I noticed the grey in her hair. "I would be turning my back on them."

"What do you want to do?" she asked. "Where will this take you?"

"I don't know."

There was a long silence. "Is it revenge?"

"Revenge sounds ugly," I said. "Justice is better."

"Semantics," she said.

"When you've had justice," I said, "semantics is all that's left."

"Revenge may not end happily."

"It has that reputation."

"It sounds a bit angry for you," she said.

"Which is why I call it justice." I turned away from the fire. "The thing is there is no equilibrium in my life. Everything is skewed around this one thing. I have to, somehow, find some balance."

"You know, digging graves is dangerous work," she said. "You can fall in."

I sat down again and sighed. "I will lay out my thinking to you," I said. "Small grains of rice, that's all they are."

"That sounds fine."

"But?"

"But when you put a seed in the ground you don't always know what will grow." She looked me in the eye.

"You are full of worthy homilies today," I said peevishly.

"I've got one more. Have you heard of this one? Before you embark on vengeance first dig two graves."

"Seeking justice is dangerous?"

"Perhaps."

"I must be careful of what I wish for?"

"That too."

"It's good advice," I said emptily, although I knew it was.

"You could leave it alone," she said.

"There are wounds that will not heal." I was becoming impatient. "They stay green forever."

"Seeking revenge is what keeps them green," she said.

"Anyway, after all these years," I said, "why are you trying to discourage me?"

"I'm not," she said. "I have told you everything. I have never kept from you what happened."

"Yet you're not convinced I should find those responsible."

"We have choices," she said. "You say you have no choice, but you do. A fool walks with his eyes closed."

"You think I'm a fool?"

"No."

"I don't know what I'm doing?"

"You don't know where it will lead."

"My eyes are open," I said. Aunt Marion said nothing, but looked straight ahead. "I can't see through walls but my eyes are open."

"Maybe I should have said nothing."

I came away from the fire and sat down beside her. I saw again the heavy grey lines that weaved through her hair. "I don't blame you," I said. "You *could* have said nothing."

"That might have been dishonest. That is what I thought at the time."

"You have been true to yourself."

"Your father might not thank me."

"Maybe not. But I am not my father."

We sat in silence for a while and then I leaned forward, elbows on my knees. "I have to work it out," I said.

"You already know everything."

"I'm just thinking."

"Go on then." I looked at Lizzie who was by the kitchen table. "Don't look at her," said Aunt Marion. "Lizzie knows as much as I do. She may be clumsy but her heart is in the right place and her head is straight." Lizzie smiled and lowered her face to the table.

CHAPTER 19

I began with the obvious. The night began with a lot
of men coming up the track, shouting, making a stink
and a whole lot of noise. It was not yet dark, but it
was afternoon and the sun was well down. My father
was not to be intimidated. He confronted them
outside the front of the house on the porch or by the
gate somewhere. My mother? She was inside. Was
she sick with fright? A little maybe, but she came
from a background steeped in fear and violence. She
almost died from it the day my father met her. How
many of them were there outside? I would come back
to that. Headcount later, but my father was on his
own, in the thick of it, not intimidated, confronting.
My mother was in the house. Let's say agitated, not
terrified, maybe shaking a little by the window. She
would not frighten easily. Then what? A bit of a
discussion with the men, pushing against the gate, a
few insults traded. Fingers pointing, jabbing and some
bad feeling. Drink had been taken. Tempers were
getting heated. Blame was being handed out with
stabbing fingers and spit and red ears. Then someone
maybe got hold of my father and he ended up face
down, maybe getting kicked, lying in the dirt,
wondering how did we get to this? One man against
how many? What did he think he was going to do?
Blow them away with words like he were Moses on
the Mount? I suppose then there was a scuffle, maybe
it turned into a bit of a fight. A lot of heat over
nothing. He was trying to stop them, but they pushed
on through and into the house, like they had a right to
be there. Windows were broken, easy throwing
stones. Suddenly, there was a shot, everyone stopped,
and out came Mad Bob with a hole in his stomach.

Mad Bob who? Just Mad Bob. Someone said he came from Dysart. Most bad stuff does. Montrose, thought Aunt Marion. She had heard that old bag Wallace, husband was a butcher or worked at Skene's abattoir, heard her mention it under her breath.

"So," said Aunt Marion. "It's Mad Bob from Montrose. Maybe."

"Or Dysart," I said. "In any event recognizable by the large amount of daylight passing through the hole in his belly."

"Can't be too many of them," said Aunt Marion.

"You ever been to Dysart? The place may be full of them."

"Montrose," she said.

"Whatever," I agreed. "Still not a lot there to go on."

"What else do you want?" she asked.

"A surname would be useful."

"Weir," she said. "Weir's the name. Didn't I mention it?"

"No, as a matter of fact you didn't."

"Well, it's Weir. Mad Bob Weir."

"How do you know that?"

"He spoke at the trial," she said. "He was the peacemaker, you see. Your mother shot the man who was waving the white flag."

"That's not true," I said.

"Well, that's neither here nor there. That's what he testified, I heard it with my own ears."

My father had then gone for his gun but that was never going to happen. As I said before, the first rule of gunfighting is make sure you have a gun. It was inside, so he ended up getting beaten, but not before he had given Ben Mercer the good old fishknife treatment. My father must have been pretty good with that knife. In a flash, Ben Mercer lay there, a man of perfect symmetry, a man of two disconnected halves: a fully balanced equation – something I found appealing.

"An edifying picture," said Aunt Marion.

My father had done all he could have done. It would never be enough. It must have nearly killed him to find no effort was sufficient to hold back the darkness these men brought into his house. He would have laid there, a big gash on his broad head, where the hair now would never grow on account of a Victorian mahogany table leg swung against his temple.

"It was not his natural parting," Aunt Marion said, and I heard Lizzie snort at the back of the kitchen.

"Then they…" I said but paused.

"Well, don't rush now, Sean. You know well enough before they got round to that bit they broke more bones in her body than was strictly necessary."

"I know that," I said. "You told me that already."

"It's part of the story."

"I was trying to be sensitive."

"I know."

"They beat her like bongo drums," I said. "It was only then, when they had finished…." We were silent for a minute. Then I asked: "How many are we looking for?"

"I don't know," said Aunt Marion, "how many *you're* looking for. But there were four. Maybe five? Nobody took a roll-call."

"Ben Mercer was dead, so take him out of it."

"Must have been three or four anyway," she said.

"Definitely three or four."

"Could be there was more, I don't know."

"But where were they from?"

"Hard to say," said Aunt Marion.

"There's Mad Bob from Dysart," I said.

"Montrose," she answered.

A thought intermittently crossed my mind, cutting in and out like a page that keeps dropping from a book. It gave me an uncomfortable feeling. "Do we live amongst these people?" I asked. That was a question that had picked and scratched at me for years. Were we the only ones who did not know?

"None of them came from round here," said Aunt Marion. "None directly from Tullis."

"Not that you know of."

"Not that *I* know of anyhow."

Then again, I was not so clear about that: some of them had faces that were known to my father, so it was likely they were native to or at least loosely acquainted with these parts. The one with the table leg skills on my father's head was portly, that's what my father had told Aunt Marion. Portly. "Had thin, fair - or even red - hair on his head, but it was a while ago. Hair may have gone by now."

"Men and their hair," said Aunt Marion, "are easily parted."

"Anyhow," I said. "He took charge. Where he led the way, others followed." I paused. "But that's all we know about him. There must be thousands close to that description."

"There's something else," said Lizzie moving towards them for the first time. "I was at Fawcett's shop and I overheard something."

"Yes?" I said. "When?"

"A while ago now. A few months. And it may be nothing."

"Tell us, Lizzie."

"I was outside Fawcett's. I wasn't doing very much, but I was just by the steps and I was sort of looking around at things. I think I'd forgotten something and I couldn't remember what I'd forgotten. Or maybe I'd dropped something, not too sure what though. So I was thinking about what...." She noticed Aunt Marion's withering look. "Anyway," she continued. "These two women come out and they don't see me because it was cold and I had my hood up and a scarf on my neck." Aunt Marion rolled her eyes. "Well, in any event, I heard them say something." At that point she paused.

I nodded her the encouragement to keep going. "Are you going to tell us what?"

"They said something like, I don't remember exactly, something like 'that one makes my skin creep, I don't like it'. Then the other one said something very strange. Well, it was strange to me."

"Which was?" I said.

"She said 'don't be surprised' or something, then, 'he was one of them that did Logan'."

"Anything else?"

"Well, that's all really," said Lizzie.

"He was in the shop," I said. "The person they were talking about?"

"Could be."

"He was in Fawcett's shop?"

"Maybe. I don't know. That's the impression I got though. Tea?"

"Aunt Marion, you said he was a redhead? And the hair was thin?"

"That's what your daddy told me. He didn't remember much on account of the table leg."

"But those were the words he used?"

"Yes I think they were the words he used. At least, thinning hair and redhead."

"He would not be young now, would he? He might have little hair and it could be red or fair or grey-fair."

"Maybe."

"And maybe that was him. In Fawcett's shop." I turned back to Lizzie. "Before that, had you been in the shop yourself?"

"Yes, I was. I had to buy a lathe stone for the knives."

"Did you see anyone in the shop?"

"No," said Lizzie.

"Could he have been?"

"Yes, and now I think on it, there was someone in there with Mr Fawcett, but I didn't see him. He was in the small room behind the counter."

"Who was?"

"Somebody was."

"How do you know?"

"Know what?"

"Know he was there?"

"Because Mr Fawcett carried on talking to him, even though he was serving me. I thought that was rude."

"You couldn't see this man?"

"No," Lizzie answered. "That's what I already said."

"But you heard him?" I persisted.

"Yes."

"And what did he say?"

"Just small stuff. I don't remember."

"Okay." I thought about this. "He may be from round here," I concluded. "Or why would he be there?"

"Oh, he's definitely from round here. He said it was a short ride from Buckhaven, even in this weather. He had a horse outside. Big chestnut mare with four white socks. I remember thinking it had been sweating a bit. A lot in fact. There was foam under its girth. I never like to see too much foam under the girth. "

"Anything else?" I said.

"No. I told you I didn't get a look at him. He was in the snug behind the counter."

"There's one other thing," Aunt Marion said.

"Yes?"

"Your daddy said he heard music." She stared at the fire.

"Not music, mum," interjected Lizzie. "Humming."

"Humming?" I said.

"She's right," said Aunt Marion. "It wasn't music. He thought it was music, but later he said it wasn't music at all. It was just a kind of humming."

"Yes," I said. "But he'd been hit on the head."

"With a table leg," said Lizzie.

"Mahogany," said Aunt Marion.

"He *would* hear music," I said. "Or humming."

"Yes, but your daddy could hold a note. He could sing quite well and he knew about music. He said he recognized the tune. It was a piano tune. He could play the piano, at least when he was a boy. Never had a lesson, but just seemed to know which keys he should hit. He never had a piano himself. I was quite different. I had two left hands."

"So, he said he heard a piano tune," I said.

"A piano tune, yes. But the man was humming it," said Aunt Marion.

"I need to think about that," I said.

Who could hum the music of a piano? Was this a recognized skill? The answers raised only more questions. My mother took Mad Bob to task with the Enfield rifle of course. Nice shooting. Good

110

ventilation. Alas, it had to lead to a mild escalation of events. Where was Mad Bob now? Mad Bob Weir. What was he doing? Maybe, if he was still alive I would find him and give him the second barrel. And then there would be balance and a satisfactory symmetry. I love symmetry. There was the other guy too. A friend of Mr Fawcett? He let him sit in the snug behind the counter. That had the feel of a friendship or a degree of proximity beyond the paying customer. Could be from Buckhaven? There was a Buckhaven in Fife. Not far on a horse, but distance enough to work up a sweat. Particularly if you were carrying a portly man.

"Is there anything else?" I asked. "Anything else at all?"

"Just one small thing," said Aunt Marion. "In fact two small things."

"Yes?"

"One was very tall. One of the attackers. Your daddy said he towered above the rest."

"Okay," I said. "And the other?"

"One of them had the tip of his finger missing. His index or his pinkie, I'm not sure."

"Was he the hummer?" I asked.

"Might have been. Who knows?"

"Can't be too many people without a pinkie," I ventured.

"Does anyone want tea?" asked Lizzie.

"It makes me want to cut the whole bloody hand off," I said.

"I haven't got any hands," said Lizzie. "It's tea or nothing."

CHAPTER 20

Some while later I was sitting by the fire. It had been raining outside and I had been out, checking the sheep and putting feed in the hen coop. I had been thinking about foxes biting the heads off the hens. Sometimes they took the hearts from the lambs. Give them half a chance and that was what they would do. They never ate the carcase. With the hens, they never did anything but bite the head off in a kind of frenzied blood-lust. With the lambs, just steal the heart. Was it revenge? Or was it justice? Did the snooty hen give the grumpy fox a rude gesture from inside the coop? Is that what revenge or justice was, just taking off the head, stealing the heart and leaving the body?

I had come into the house, sat myself down on the wooden farm chair in which I had always been told my father used to sit, and I lodged my boots on the fender. The steam was coming off in tight, twisting swirls. Aunt Marion was applying her sewing skills to an old shirt of mine with more holes than a pea colander. Lizzie was by the oven, stirring a pot of parsnip soup. I suppose it *could* have been parsnip soup but I would not necessarily have bet my darned shirt on it. I picked up a beaten copy of some poems I had diverted into my possession from Mr Shifner's library and I browsed the middle section. The page was dirty and the light was dim there by the fire, but I knew the words well enough.

"What's that you're reading?" Aunt Marion asked, but I think she knew.
"Poems," I said.
"Poems?"

"Yes, rhyming things."

"Well, Lord Byron, why don't you read me one?"

"Poems, I always think, you should keep in your head," I answered.

"Why's that?"

"They lose something when you take them outside."

"Is that what's troubling you?" She asked. "Taking things outside?" I looked at her and said nothing. My voice had been in my head all these years. It was not exactly surprising that I would keep my poetry there too. "Anyway," she said. "Just read me a poem, like I asked you."

"You heard of Landon?" I asked.

"Landon on the moon?"

"No. The poet," I said. "You don't seem to be taking this seriously, Aunt Marion." Sometimes she made a joke of everything.

"Oh?" she said. "It's just I'm not sure I asked for a biography."

"Well, poetry is a serious matter."

"I never heard of him."

"Her," I said. "Landon was a her."

"Well?" said Aunt Marion. "Let her be heard." By the stove, Lizzie looked up and then back down at the soup which she stirred with a regular scraping motion. It was like having your cochlea stroked with an iron pipe. Aunt Marion placed the old shirt on her knees and rolled her eyes.

"Just two verses," I said. "Break you in gently."

"Should suffice," she answered. "I'd like to survive the night."

So, I read the first two verses to her:

Ay, now by all the bitter tears

113

That I have shed for thee
The racking doubts, the burning fears, -
Avenged they well may be –

By the nights pass'd in sleepless care,
The days of endless woe;
All that you taught my heart to bear,
All that yourself will know

I stopped. "You might as well finish it," she said.

I would not wish to see you laid
Within an early tomb;
I should forget how you betray'd
And only weep your doom:

"I'm not sure what it means," she said eventually.

"Well, it's quietly angry," I said.

"Yes, I think I hear that."

"It tells me that people get their just deserts," I said. "If they wait long enough."

"Why doesn't she just say so?"

"It wouldn't be a poem."

We did not speak for a while. Just the sound of sparks cracking and spitting off the fire, the tough scrape of Lizzie's spoon in the soup pot, and the clicking of Aunt Marion's tongue as she pulled on the darning thread at the back of my shirt.

Eventually, I pulled my boots in from the edge of the fire. Aunt Marion put her needle down by the green thread on the wobbly, wooden table at her side. "I heard you shooting your daddy's rifle."

"Just rats," I said. "It needed oiled. You got to work a gun to keep it in condition."

I could hear Lizzie once more stir the pot. Aunt Marion turned towards her daughter with an eyebrow raised somewhere near the rafters. Lizzie stared back at her and dropped the spoon in the soup. She bravely fished it out with her fingers but yelped like a burnt cat when she felt the heat. Once her fingers had cooled she licked the spoon and burnt her tongue. The cloth that held her hair in place was smeared with parsnip. She licked her slightly burnt, parsnip index finger and exhaled noisily.

"Are you sharing the soup with us or are you just drilling a hole in the pot?" said Aunt Marion, sighing deeply, rolling the whites of her eyes. For a moment she looked like a dead fish, her lids wide open and unblinking.

No tale about Fife can ignore the fish that swim in silver shoals along her shores. Of those fish, the *clupea harengus* is a smooth, slender, aquatic craniate with a white, lustrous sheen of a skin, speckled on its upper body. It holds a hint of bottle green and cobalt blue. The snout is a smear of black slate. The lower jaw protrudes to give the fish the scowling look of an old man with big gums and no teeth. There are many names for this slippery fellow: some call it the 'torn belly' or the 'wine drinker' and I knew it as the herring - in those days there were plenty spilling night and day off the rocky promontories along the coast of Fife.

From time to time we fished the herring. It was popular and a good price could be had for an aquatic netted from the grey-green sea without a prohibitive primary cost. The herring could then be salted, vinegared and smoked all in the pursuit of a modest profit. Somebody would surely have carnalised it if they could see a return on their investment. In any event, a spate of herring taken at the right time – just before they swam north to the Faroes – was a chance to lay down some fat for the lean winter months.

It was early, the sun invisible, when Lizzie put out a breakfast of sourdough bread and cooked ham on a stone plate, a pie disgorging a boiled egg like a dead eye and a pot of strawberry jam with lumps that might have been fruit one time before Napoleon met his mother. I helped myself to the pie, the egg and the jam and I slurped loudly at the black tea. I enjoyed it all so much and, like a fool, I used my voice to tell Lizzie that I loved her and that she could bear my children. It was a stupid thing to say and, on reflection, I am not sure that is the kind of thing you should say to your elder cousin, but she smiled kindly nonetheless and dropped the butter dish.

When it comes to fishing for herring, you need a boat and you need plenty of hands to work the boat and pull the fish out of the sea. The water is often rough and cold and you have to respect that. The closest farm to us on the Logan steading belonged to a man named Harcourt, a gruff man of few words, but to me he seemed decent enough, although he liked to spit. I do not generally like the type of person who spits all the time. It seems very unnecessary. The mucus is a slippery secretion but it is useful and protects the body from infection, the kind of thing you see in fungi, bacteria and viruses. Your average body produces about one and three-quarter pints of mucus per day and, to my mind, it is not desirable that we all go around spitting out one and three-quarter pints of mucus per day. The streets would soon become unwalkable.

As for Mr Harcourt, he was the type who might speak a few choice words to you if pressed with something designed to cause immediate pain, but for the most part he preferred to use two and a half words even if there were twenty going free. The two and a half words would, of course, be punctuated by a sly spit. You could see Mr Harcourt's farm if you walked to the high field some six or seven hundred yards up from our own. He had some Blackface sheep, some wheat and a plague of weeds in a stony field and a strip of broccoli that never amounted to much more than promising shoots that never delivered. He had too much sand in his soil. He had nothing much to speak of, but then there was just him and his son Duncan to provide for. Mr Harcourt's wife was long since dead, buried and topped with a coarse *poa annua* meadow grass in the cemetery. Hers was one of the tidier stones complete with inscription, standing straight in death as she stood in life. Father and son had no need for much else to see them through, but they always did the fishing since they had the boat and it had proved it could be the source of reasonable profit. As I said earlier, you cannot run a fishing boat on just two pairs of hands and a gutting knife, and old Mr Harcourt, off his own bat or because his son Duncan had persuaded him, sent a message down to Aunt Marion that if I was willing, I should join the fishing party. I was guaranteed a share of the catch and if there was money made he would see me right. Aunt Marion accepted those terms on my behalf, had Lizzie fill me with pie, egg and the enigmatic jam impression and sent me on my way, like a crusty seadog, to join the crew.

Before I could leave the yard, the sun was already up but issued no more than a diffuse, pale grey light across the fields. I looked at the sky and there was a heaviness there. The shadows would not be here for long and the black clouds were already blowing in from Yellowcraigs and further east.

My instructions from Aunt Marion were to drop by at a house some way across the village, a spot well removed and a distance up the other side, at the end of three rough sheep-grazing fields. It was a house that had the benefit of a decent view down to the sea. It was windy up there and was a spot quick to pick the worst of any bad weather that was coming through. The house belonged to a fellow called Calum Wilson. I had heard of him and I knew him to look at – I had seen him come out of the post office from time to time and I noticed first the swagger he had about him, as if he had everything in the world to be confident about - but I had never exchanged a single look or word with him before. Aunt Marion said Mr Harcourt wanted me to drop by Wilson's place and make sure he joined the fishing trip. He was lazy, he said, but would be useful. The man was no saint, he knew little about fish, but he had undertaken to come on board. Mr Harcourt said we needed all the hands we could get but he had been let down by Wilson before, so why he trusted him I did not know. If he had taken a drink (which was entirely possible) I was told it was my job to persuade him the sea was leaping with fish and the air would do his sobriety a whole lot of good.

I was thinking, a little sulkily, this detour was out of my way and we could manage the boat and a net with just the three of us. Calum Wilson, as far as I knew, was something of an idle bastard even with a boot up his rear end; it was common knowledge that he did indeed like a drink and I felt we could do without his *bonhomie de la mer* on our particular fishing trip. In any case, it was a common myth that more hands made light work; it depended what the hands were doing. If the hand had a finger up its arse, it was likely to be doing nothing much more than tickling its prostate. Still, I was not in the mood to have my ears clipped, so I said nothing, just nodded with resignation at Aunt Marion and straightaway moved

119

down the track leading away from the Logan farm. Sometimes you had to bite your tongue or else it would go flapping all over and whack you in the gums. Yet, as I have said, I was sure in my own mind that we had no need for Calum Wilson on this happy sea trip. Even old Mr Harcourt knew he was a drinker and plenty others who drank with him would not argue. My impression was of a weak puff of wind at sunrise and not much blow by sunset. I did not relish the prospect of a day in the boat with him either: doubtless nothing but stench off his spirited breath.

I cut through the village that, at this time, was still quiet as a pauper's grave. The only person I saw was Mr Fawcett brushing the earth off the step to his shop. He shouted across a greeting at me and I looked up and nodded. I now had a voice but I chose to use it sparingly. I wondered who had been in his shop recently. There was plenty of time to work that one out. I had it in mind to pay Mr Fawcett a visit to discuss wispy redheaded visitors to his snug behind the counter, when the time was right. Through the other side of Tullis I walked along the church wall, then jumped down and cut between the trees. I threaded my way along an old goat path, dodging the squads of heavy, black droppings, and at the end I crossed over a broken wattle fence that hung down from a leaning post. I picked my way through the heavy brambles, scratching the backs of my hands. This, I thought with a thin mutter, was at least the quickest way to Wilson's place.

Indeed, it took twenty minutes to get there whereas it would have taken forty by the road, so I was pleased about that. It lightened my spirits a fraction. The route I had taken meant that I approached the house from the back, rather than the front. By this time the sun that had faintly risen with a pale chill in the east was already heavy and thickset in a solid blanket of grey cloud. There was a damp wash to the cold air and I could feel a light drizzle against my cheeks. That was how it could be round here, in these fields and woods we loved so much: one minute there was the threat of a little sunshine, face gently warming, the next you were wringing out the rain from a wet shirt.

Calum Wilson's place might have looked sweet enough on a dry, sunny day, its view caressing the green, leafy fields below, lightly skimming the Firth of Forth beyond. Today it was a depressing sight in the grey gloom. There was a back wall to the house ahead; the skim coat of lime plaster had parted company in many places and lay at the foot of the gable in broken, damp pieces, leaving the wall like a crumbly cheese. The rubble looked to have been there a while but nobody had thought to clear it away. It was like somebody puked and did not trouble themselves to brush down the lumps. The woodwork around the eaves was flaked and blistered and the wood itself was split, soaked and plainly rotting. It was easy to see you might push your finger all the way in like it was old Miss Havisham's wedding cake. The window sills were like a soft sponge and there was a yellow fungus like hard custard pasted on the uprights. Grey slates hung from the roof like stale biscuits. Some were broken or had disappeared altogether. Some leaned against the gutter, their ends poking out the front and scooping up the rain.

I walked close by the house. Wet logs lay beneath a leaky canopy and a coal box with a rotten, wooden lid that had been left open. It smelled of mould and sweating hay and fungus. The coarse grass at the back of the house had become a mud bowl where the rainwater was fast collecting in broken pools. I stood by the window towards the front of the house. I wanted to look in through the glass. It was smeared with a thick grime. I wet the window with the rough sleeve of my jacket and rubbed noiselessly. I have to say I did think to myself, what the hell here and now was I doing? Of course, that did not stop me, not one bit, not for one second. I was intent upon my task and pressed myself to do a better job of it. I took a rag from my pocket and cleared a small funneled circle in the glass. I was curious. Unfortunately, that was just the kind of person I was and the creature that I had become. If you had given me a riddle I would have chewed on it all night until my brain was sorely convulsed, by which time I would have solved it. Other times, I did things without a thought, as if instinct just took over and pushed me on in there. I am not sure it was the danger, but then again it might have been. Danger can make you do the stupidest things and, as I stood by the window with its clear, inviting, circle drawing my eyes through the grime, that day was no exception.

CHAPTER 22

Through the glass eye I had formed with my rag, I saw the end of a daybed and a blanket, some clothing and two male calf-high boots on the wooden floor, toe to toe like they were ballroom dancers picking out Polka steps. My eye was drawn further into the circle. I formed the impression I was looking at a naked leg, side on. It looked to be a pale leg with the slightest hint of creamy pinkness. Not a hair on it. Quite smooth. Quite beautiful. It was so soft you could picture the dimples. It was neither a fat leg nor a thin leg. It was a slim leg but with texture and contours. Not just a bone, as you sometimes might see, but a leg with character and fullness. It was robust and, with some growing excitement, I could imagine the taste of it, the sweet musky taste against the tip of my tongue. I could imagine running my hand from the calf and into that crevice behind the knee.

I have to confess my heart skipped as I thought about that leg. To this day it still does. Ridiculous, I know: it is, after all, only the lower limb and not uncommon so far as *Gray's Anatomy* is concerned. Nevertheless, it very nearly took away my power of breathing. A woman's leg was in front of me and I knew I had never seen anything so desirable and so worthy of serious attention. How had it taken this long? If the truth be known, I wanted to lick and drag my tongue from behind the knee, up across the thigh, and maybe enjoy the midlands before heading north, until my mouth ran dry as paper. I swallowed hard. I looked with my left eye and I felt something in both my balls. I experienced a tingle in my scrotum and a growing experience asserted itself inside my trousers. I made myself breathe because I was going blue. My lips were very dry and I could feel my tongue against the roof of my mouth, clicking just a little against the dryness. I could hear the catch in my throat as once again, I tried to swallow. I moved my head a little to the right and traced my eye down through the circular hole in the grey-brown dirt of the glass. I was looking once again upon the woman's leg, and how soft the skin appeared as it curved, pale as cow's cream, towards her naked bottom. Her arm lay across the man's chest, her face below his ribs and close against his side. Were they sleeping? I thought I could hear the man snore. It occurred to me that the last thing a man should do in the company of a leg like that was snore. The very last thing he should do was sleep. A fullness pushed hard against the front of my trousers. What would have happened had there not been a sudden, unexpected movement? I threw myself back against the side of the house.

I hugged the building and edged my way towards the rear door, then turned the iron handle. I could have knocked but even my own mother would have said I was acting strangely that morning. I entered.

I was in a hallway. It was a small house and there seemed to be no upstairs to it. I could see the bare rafters. The walls were dirty and unpainted and the floors were blackened timber. I saw no one and at first I could not hear a sound. I could see there were two rooms at the front of the house, one on the left and one on the right. The one on the left turned out to be nothing more than a boot room, with some game and tackle hanging from the cracked ceiling. The floor was blotted with clods of dry mud. Coats draped the steel hooks by the door. Three rabbits with staring eyes hung from a rope attached to a cupboard handle. A bundle of snares were wound around a flat-headed nail, jabbed in the wall. There was blood, stained on the mat that lay across the floor slabs. I looked towards the other door, the door leading to the room on the right. The room I had been looking into from outside the house. I steadied my breathing, tried to make it even and smooth like I was in control of myself. All I could hear was my own heart beating in my ears. I could smell damp woodsmoke hanging heavy in the air. I felt it was time I introduced myself.

"Calum Wilson, you there?" Immediately, I heard the scrape of a chairleg against the floor.
"A minute now!" a male voice barked. "Who the hell is it? I've got a gun here, I'll blow your fuckin' head off!"
"It's Sean Logan. Do not fire! I'm keeping the head."
"And?"
"I'm here about some fishing."
"Is that so?"
"It is so," I said.
Calum appeared in the doorway. He was a relatively short man with wild hair on his head, sideboards that ran from his ears to his chin, growing outways and joining together at the bottom. He had a pale, green-tinged skin. He had creamy puss in the corner of his left eye and he stood in his bare feet without any trousers. He had no gun. "What do you want, then?" he said.
"Fishing," I said. "You're supposed to be fishing."
He looked vacant.
"How old are you?" he said.

"Mr Harcourt sent me."

"And you are?"

"The larynx I understand to be a sensitive and useful organ that I have come to enjoy in recent years. Consequently, I say things only once, but I am not without heart and I do make exceptions for the slow-witted. For the second time, Sean Logan is my name."

I could see the woman a few feet behind him. She pulled her gown tight around her waist. She smiled at me. Her eyes momentarily stunned me, like they were shafts of brilliant green light. "I was told you were coming," I said.

"By the by," he answered. He looked at the woman and then back at me. "By the by."

"Well, you can suit yourself, " I said. "I've delivered the message and I have put myself to the inconvenience of repeating it."

"You're a cheeky fuckin' sod," he said.

I looked at him. "Really?" I said. "I never thought of myself that way. Anyway, I'm not waiting." And I took my leave.

The man annoyed me. He was that type, bordering on the slack. By which I mean he was not one who seemed to care much about anything; he did not appear to stand for anything. He was as limp as he was loose. Stood there in his pimpled bare legs, he was the very epitome of *slack*. Or so I thought. No matter what personal view I took of him, I had indeed delivered the message. The woman turned away, stifling a yawn, as if she was bored by it all. If Wilson chose not to turn up that was his call. I turned on my heel and made my way out through the back door of the house, the way I had come. I cut around the edge of the boggy field without a backward glance. If I had looked I might have seen the figure at the small scullery window, watching my retreat.

I did not think it likely that I would be followed and I had no regrets about that. I joined the old farm track that ran straight down to the shore between the twin spines of two moss-covered walls. I followed the path along the water's edge until eventually I came upon Mr Harcourt and his son Duncan at the small quayside. This quayside could take two small boats end to end but it was rarely used and almost never by two boats at the one time. The quay stones were breaking up with the persistent heavy swell and over time they were toppling piece by piece into the grey water. The waves and the rising, falling tide, continued to push into the fissures and split them wider apart. No matter how long you waited, one day the sea would have its way.

The wind had picked up. It had sent gusts to batter them as they worked to prepare the boat. Duncan was tarring a split in the side of the hull. It was amazing how these old cups stayed afloat. The rain came harder on the back of the wind. My jacket was already heavy with the wet and the spray I collected during the walk down from the Wilson farm. The boat itself was made of wood, perhaps twenty feet long, painted black with a white stripe along the top edge, two sails, one large with a box top and the other the size of a handkerchief, with a couple of good oars on board just in case someone messed up the navigation. On the port side was painted the boat's name, in black letters against a white background: *Firth Wind*.

The boat was done and ready to sail. They had stowed the oars and other equipment, fixed the net and stored it in the bow and finished off the tarring at the hull. By then the wind was creating a big squall and the tops of the waves were splashing hard and white against the boat's ribs.

"Take it he's not coming?" said Mr Harcourt to me as I had approached.
"Fresh air was not his priority," I said.
"Thought not." He said. "Lazy sack of shit." He spat against the quaystone.
I had looked at the boat. "Are we okay with three?" I asked.
"Four," he said. "Thought this might happen. Should be right with four though." At which point fair-haired, blue-eyed, projectile-spitting Rory Turner stepped out from behind the sail and grinned at me.
"Going to be some trip, Logan," he said. "Hope you can fuckin' swim."

CHAPTER 23

1897

There is that moment in a human life when an event occurs that stands every other in its wake. It is the big syntactic pivot, the word around which every sentence is formed, on which each existence will turn, changing what came before and transforming all that follows. It is the moment that will cast a conspicuous, indelible shadow, a grey unbroken wash, for good or bad, across the length of a person's life. It is the jump of a train from one set of tracks to another as those aboard head in a direction they had not foreseen, invited or anticipated.

Keira McLeod had that experience when she was seventeen years old. She was a woodland farmer's daughter from Blairgowrie, birthplace of the Scottish raspberry, a small Perthshire town at the foot of the highlands, where the Cairngorms flatten out from blue-grey mountains to green foothills. It is a wet place that feels as if all the rain off the hills had to go somewhere and it chose to come here and ease itself through a funnel into the River Ericht. Keira lived in a black, slate-roofed farmhouse on the southernmost edge of the Meiklour Wood, not so far from General Wade's post-Jacobite military road that carves its way through the highlands, to the northwest by Loch Ericht. Her brother Ian, lived across the landing in a room with a broken window latch, so that the case leaned to one side and the gap was filled with old paper and horsehair. The draught still found its way through and breezed lightly across his brow as he slept in the iron bed beneath. He was always getting colds. Her mother and father lived along the creaky landing. Her father slammed the bedroom door at night, when he was there. Sometimes she heard him pee in the outside toilet. Sometimes he farted and belched before he had finished the final drops. At the centre of the Meiklour Wood was a natural spring loch known as the Hare Myre. In the days that followed, Keira could not go back there because of what happened. Her brother Ian coped better by spending as much time as possible floating upon it in his simple, wooden boat. Somehow, by being on top of it he was able to keep the demons away. Sometimes he put a line out and took some fish and these he would bring back to the house. Their mother would cook them on the stove. Keira found them hard to swallow – the eyes always seemed to stare at her.

The house in which they lived was a wood frame, leaning shack of a place built along a low ditch into which it threatened to slide. It was built by a moron in the wrong stupid place, is what Keira's father always said, articulated in a tone of gruff petulance. It should have been built higher up where the earth and the grass were relatively dry, so you would not get all this damp, seeping into your bones. He had a point. The house had two floors. The roof had a dip half-way along the ridge as if it struggled to support its own weight. It had uninvited pigeons in the loft and a woodlice infestation around the front porch which had once been painted green, but which had no colour to it now. Keira thought that the pigeons maybe got in because they tore themselves a hole beneath a missing slate that nobody had bothered to replace. The woodlice got in because the front porch was a holy Mecca crying out to them like they were god's special children, drawing them into its darkness and ballooning moisture. Sometimes you thought you could actually hear them crawling beneath the hearth at the front door, like they were tiny soldiers on military manoeuvres. Her brother Ian used to eat them as a small boy and said they tasted like "strong urine". Keira loved her brother, with his pants hitched up halfway to his chest, but she had no urge to sample bodily fluids.

The house had a name: *Merrylees*. Merry means happy in my book and lees are the deposits of dead yeast that sink to the bottom of a beer vat. Whoever the idiot was to come up with that name had already spent too long with his head under the beer tap. In any event, in Keira's view, the house was closer to yeast dregs than genuine happiness. Their home was near to and over-shadowed by the dense, red-brown wood of pine trees that surrounded it, pushing in on it, like they were squeezing out its life with their roots. Whilst enjoying the heavy scent all around, still it was always damp, even midsummer. Damp from the moisture that dripped off the sweeping, evergreen needles whenever it rained. Theirs was a house that never had much warmth and the fire in the iron grate never did any more than spit out a small, petulant flame, as if it were saying, I am alight but under duress. The house smelled faintly of fungus and was usually cold, giving rise to intermittent hacking coughs, sore knees, wooden stairs that creaked under your weight and fires that never worked like they would out there in the ordinary world.

Keira's mother was Alice and she had her own way of dealing with the cold that covered their bones like frost on a gate: she moved around a lot. She was

131

always active, she never stopped working morning to dusk, all the while like a demented woodpecker. She made jam out of plums, raspberries and red berries that some people said were poison. She said she had never had a death yet. She swept the floors so hard you could see sparks fly off the brush. She hammered a nail in the wall and hung a coat off it. She banged it in so hard she could have hung a bridge off it. She scraped mould off the bedroom wall like she was dredging scum from a canal. She chopped dry kindling for the fire that refused to burn (because it was still green, she never gave it time to grow old and die), and she did not stop for tea, argument, urinary convenience or two civil words for fear of being accused of momentary indolence.

Keira's father, and the husband of her mother Alice, was Graham. He could make his gruff whinges but in reality he could have no real complaint because he contributed very little to the betterment of family life. He was a mean-spirited, uncharitable kind of man who felt that existence, in spite of all his blessed gifts, had dealt him an unfair hand. "Nobody gave to me a leg up," he would often say, the reason being he would have stolen the ladder. He liked to spit in the fire and watch it sizzle. "Don't look to me for nothing; nobody ever gave me nothing." He was a discontent with tiny, greedy thoughts that he wore in a miserly space he called a brain, squeezed beneath his filthy tweed cap.

To be fair to Keira's father, every man has aspirations. He had thought there would be more to his existence than was to be found at Merrylees, by Meiklour Wood, and he was disappointed. Every time he checked his cup, it was nearly bloody empty. He always reacted with surprise. In one sense he *was* generous: he liked to share his disappointment with those around him. As I say, he reacted with deep surprise at the evidence of his failure; his increasingly feeble mind was unable to comprehend this miserable lack of success at any venture he embarked upon, far less doing anything to change its course. He surrendered himself to it and lashed out against those who lived in his vicinity. To his edited reckoning, it was not he who was at fault. They – that is those around him - were all responsible for what had happened, or what had not happened in his life. His eyes were sharp drill holes, the type you might hammer in the ground with a thin peg. He had a level of insight into his condition: he recognized the cup was broken and beyond repair, even if he did not recognise that he was solely responsible. He worked hard to assuage the rising tide of personal negativity by consuming alcohol he expertly brewed in a lean-to, straw-covered shed at the back of the house. In here, he devised a giddying concoction, sweetened with a sugary sauce to make the alcoholic acid digestible. If anyone said he had few friends, that person would have to correct himself. He had no friends.

Keira was not particularly unhappy. That may surprise you, but if you think about it, most people discover that once there is recognition of a stone in your shoe then you come to live with it. You come to an arrangement or an accomodation. Sometimes, you even miss it when it is not there. That is not to say that Keira was entirely euphoric about her situation and indeed, she could remember much happier times. Merry moments when home-brewed whisky did not smear its blur across her father's life, when he had given some small pleasure to others, when he had worked to provide something for his family. Those were times Keira fondly remembered, even if the passage of time had exaggerated the warmth of her memory: those were brief times, when he had talked to her, looked at her with gentle, curious, eyes. Once he even played Whist with her, an English card game. With every trick he took he pulled the head off one of her dolls. He thought it would teach her something, but she did not remember what. She had two headless dolls that summer and she never found the heads that he had hidden. Keira remembered hide and seek with her brother. She could picture her mother smiling on the doorstep. They were specks of silver memory in the inky darkness. Those days slowly melted away and as her father's skin grew tight and yellow, his temper grew meaner. Too much drink played all hell with his constitution. He would get to his feet and bowl over in pain as some part of his body protested against the never yielding assault on his liver. He lived in a deadly cycle, his brain shrinking from the abuse, his guts straining with the poison. If he resembled anything good, paternal and human by the time Keira was seventeen, it was only ever because he wanted something. He hung around most of the day, doing nothing very useful, staring at his daughter to make her uncomfortable. He seemed to enjoy and delight in that, just looking, just making her feel awkward beneath his gaze. There were times when her mother, Alice, would try to control him, but he beat her hard with the back of his hand and sometimes a wooden paddle he kept in the brew house. There was no boat to accompany the paddle. He broke her mother's nose more than once: it had become genuinely three dimensional. It was always the door that did it, they were told, but Keira's mother must have forgotten they had rooms just down the landing. They could hear the hand when it hit her face or split her lip.

Keira's brother Ian, had sometimes tried to intervene with limited success. It was not his fault. When he was a young boy he was strong and determined and would push his father away so that his mother and sister might escape the full extent of his brutality. For his efforts he often had a fist plugged into his own face. Sometimes, it was a brick-like punch to the head and Ian would see the stars. If hit very hard, he would see the whole galaxy. Keira would bring him round with a cold towel on his head. Graham once slashed Ian's lip with a jagged ring and the wound bled for a whole day. Each time it stopped and he moved his mouth the blood started up again, dripping down his chin. He still had the scar along the strip beneath his bottom lip. Sometimes his father would have him on the floor and he would kick his ribs until the blood came out of his mouth. He would bite his own tongue. He was a young, modest boy though, and he never would have claimed he was given to huge acts of bravery. There were times when he was shameful that he had hung his head and turned away as the blows were coming down; sometimes he got on the floor and put his hands over his ears. You could not blame him for that but it caused him quiet guilt for the rest of his life. He never said as much but Keira knew it. They both remembered. Her father remembered nothing at all. All this led to the one moment I was talking of, the moment that changed their lives forever.

Keira was digging carrots in a field to the north of
Meiklour Wood. Through some rapturous quirk of
Paleozoic geology, the field stood in a rift valley
where the soil had turned light and sandy. Here the
thick, wet earth around most parts of Meiklour Wood
gave way to well-drained soil. That kind of rich,
almost dry soil had a fertility that seemed to suit the
carrots like no other place; they grew big as table legs
and tall too, virtually leaping out of the ground.

Keira had been out for an hour or two – she had lost
any idea of what time it was – and she had filled a
large, wooden basket with enough carrots to take back
to the house. She hummed as she went about her
work. She was taller than most, slim as a young tree,
and her arms ached from all the pulling. She had soil
marks on her skirt, but she didn't care too much. She
brushed the dirt with her hand and it never slowed
her down. She was seventeen years old, gone
February, her skin was good and her dark hair hung in
a flow of small curls, just loose to her shoulders. She
had what you might think were the greenest eyes, but
when you looked more closely at them you would see
that they were flecked with grey. That was what
made them so striking. They were set against the
clearest complexion. You found that your own eyes
were drawn to hers. You never knew if they were
green or grey or even blue. As she worked, from time
to time she would look up and see the red deer. There
were stags as well as hinds, the former distinguishable
by their size and the huge antlers they bore which
they would shed in the spring. Sometimes you would
not see them but you could hear the loud bark and
clatter of their antlers echoing through the woods as

they jousted with one another. Often they came down to take a look at her as if she were some curiosity they had to satisfy themselves upon. Sometimes she could not see them, but she could tell they were out there, gazing with their glistening, unblinking eyes. They might have thought she would have something for them. Maybe some carrots, because clearly she could spare a few. Still, Keira was not breaking her back in order to feed the deer; they could come along later and scavenge after she was gone. The carrots she gathered she placed in the large willow basket on the ground; they could be cleaned up and some would be put through to Perth market whilst others would be buried in the big old rusted tub of sand at the back of the house and kept for use, as and when.

The work was hard, doubled up as she was, and she could feel it either side of her spine. Yet, the sight of a basket growing heavier with the stacked carrots was satisfying. That was a good thing and she thought that she would work on a little longer but be careful not to overload the basket so much she could not get it home again. Sometimes she had to drag it on a rope. She might have to make two or three runs. The light was fading and it had begun to rain a little but not too much to trouble her. She had no fear of drizzle.

She had a basket close enough to full when she had a sense more than anything that she was not entirely alone. She did not know if she saw something move or heard the ground carry the weight of another person, but she sensed there was something or someone out there. It might have been a deer or some other animal. There were wild cats out here, at least that's what Ian had told her, and foxes too.

She stood up straight and looked across to her left, down towards the Hare Myre water but saw nothing. As she turned back, she glanced over her right shoulder. She saw her father standing there, leaning to one side, his face blue-grey in the early evening light, his chin unshaven, his big hands by his sides. She saw him and he saw her, but neither said one word to the other. There was nothing unusual in that. She had got used to his morose nature. Sometimes he said not a word for days, brooding over something that he chose not to share. However, today she felt that silence as he looked her over. He had on a long, black coat and some cord hung from his waist that was doing a poor job of holding up his trousers. Even from where she was stood, legs stretched across the ditch, albeit not a huge distance away, she could smell the staleness off his body and the drink coming away on his breath. It was like bad cheese or infected feet.

She shivered – not from the cold – when he said: "Put the fuckin' shovel down." She had a sense that something bad was about to unfold and she would have no power to stop it from happening. Still, she put the shovel down.

CHAPTER 24

When, some time later, Keira found her way back to Merrylees, she placed one hand on the door and leaned towards it. The snib was unrestrained and she fell in through the front door. Her mother Alice was making raspberry jam. She stood with some small pots by the kitchen table, some sugar, a can filled with cold water and a hot, red, sticky tar bubbling in the pot. Alice looked up, stopped what she was doing, dropping a pot that smashed against the stone floor. Looking at her daughter, it was as if Alice understood what had happened before Keira even spoke.

Her mother stood in a momentary daze, as if a strong light had been shone into her eyes, before she moved towards her daughter. "I've made too much," she said. "It's gone past the setting point. You try putting your finger in it, you'll see it doesn't wrinkle." Keira's brother, Ian, never light on his feet, moved hesitantly towards her. He had stood up from the soft chair by the fire, his face pale in the grey-orange light. He came over and stood by her side. His mother took Keira's other arm and together they brought her in and sat her down on the couch. She was trembling all over and they could feel it through her clothing like an electric charge. There was no hiding that her dress was torn all up one side. Ian had still not said anything, but looked at his mother, went to the big, metal urn by the sink, and filled a glass with milk. He brought the glass back over and put it in Keira's open hand. He did not touch her. "What's happened to you?" was all he said.

Keira told them everything, from the moment she had looked up to see her father in the carrot field. Her mother stared right back at her whilst Ian turned away, faced the window. When she had drunk half the milk, she put the glass on the table beside her, wiped her hands and continued with her account, recalling events as if she were recounting solid, historical facts. She was careful not to make judgments. She did not know why it had happened but she knew that she could not hope to repress telling what had occurred even if she had wanted to. It came out in a steady unbroken stream. She thought they might say something but they stayed quiet. Her mother had sat close to her on the couch and had put one hand on her shoulder. The hand was light against her, hardly touching. Ian did not move from the window, just his broad back to her and his head dipping down to look at his feet. As each word came she felt the better for it. She already knew that she and her life had changed. In the heavy silence after she was finished, it was in her mind that they might still blame her. She was confused but if she carried guilt for this, if she had brought this thing about by her own actions, she believed they would tell her so. If she had been at fault, they would tell her and it was only right that they should.

Ian took the iron poker from the coal scuttle next to the small fire in the grate that spilled a small glow but little flame. "I'm going to fix that chimney one day," he said. "Listen to what I'm saying. I'm going to fix it and make that fire really go." He jabbed at the small, damp log and the embers splintered into red sparks. "I'm going to make it go like it should go."

Alice told him to forget the bloody chimney. The bloody chimney was the least of their worries. She took her hand from Keira's shoulder, stood by the table and lit the kerosene lamp. She moved over and stood by Ian. Her face in the yellow light was anxious and strained. She looked at her son and he nodded. Without the need for words they knew what they would do. She turned her face, her tired eyes passing from him to Keira. "You'd better come with us," she said coldly.

Keira had no real understanding of where they intended to take her or what they planned to do. They had said nothing, passed no comment, articulated no judgments. Did they think she was responsible? Did they blame her for this? Had she brought this calamity upon her, upon them? It crossed her mind that they would take her out and punish her for an event that she should have prevented.

"Things," Alice said, "have to be brought now to a conclusion." She looked at Keira and again at Ian. "I'm having unchristian thoughts. Bring the poker," she said.

CHAPTER 25

They marched like pilgrims to Hare Myre water, in the middle of Meiklour Wood, at least in part their minds full of grim intent and their hearts as heavy and suffocating as the darkness that surrounded them. There they found Keira's father at the same old fir tree where she had left him, slumped like a bloated corn bag, not so long before. He was on his back still, his neck and head against the brown, sappy bark. They could see his wasted silhouette stretch from the base of the tree, his knees a little bent, the toes of each boot parted and pointing to either side. In the gloom, one could almost see the carrot basket, lying exactly where Keira had left it, a heap of green top shoots sprawling out one end, a small distance in from the edge of the field. Her father was half asleep in a whisky-laden stupor, exorcising demons through a deep strangled snore, the green bottle empty against his chest. Keira stepped back from her mother's side. She would not approach any further. Ian stood over his father and lay a hand on him, roughly shaking him by the coat. Her father's eyes flickered open and he saw Ian and also Alice, who stood behind him, and at first he had the look of somebody who might have been pleased to see them, like it was a nice surprise them turning up just at this juncture. He looked, of all things, to be smiling, but it was a nervous, devious smile. Then they shouted in his face, called him filthy, rotten, jabbed him with their fingers and Ian slapped him with his hands. As they did so, you could see the fear rising in his bloodshot eyes. Ian asked him a question. Then he asked again when his father slurred something incomprehensible back at him. The questions grew louder but their father did not have too many good answers. There was no exculpation, no plea in mitigation. Ian shouted at the older man and against the lamplight you could see the spray of saliva shower off his lips. You might have thought it would end there, but then Ian swung the iron poker and beat it hard against his father's head. He beat him with the poker, maybe seven or eight times, until his face was broken and pulpy and the flesh was torn off his nose and his teeth hung in bits from his jaw. The poker was now bent some two thirds of the way up its iron shaft. That showed how many years of hate he must have sucked up. Even then the old fool spat the blood from his mouth and tried to speak. Where was the point in that? Sometimes, the talking is over. In any event, he made no sense when he was drunk. He made even less sense when he was drunk with his head hollowed out on one side. Evidently, things had gone a long way but it was not yet over. Keira, lifting her head just a little, was hoping it might be. She had half-expected them to beat her on some notion that she may have shared some of the blame. Instead they were beating her father. He lay still on the ground, raising a hand up towards his wife. He looked at Alice as she came close. He expected mercy from her at least, but he could tell quickly from the wide eyes that she was not in the mood for pleasantries or reprimands. His expression implored her to look at him and recognise this was only who he was, the man she married. His eyes begged her to show some mercy even if forgiveness was beyond her. Forgiveness for what? Alice took the poker from Ian's hand, raised it above her head and drew it down hard against him, catching the square edge on the top of his left eyebrow. The side of his face peeled away like she was pulling back a prayer mat. Like her son,

143

she rained blow after blow upon the head and body, each met with a dull thud, and she went on until she was exhausted, until the man's eyes did not look back at her. Her husband lay flat now a few feet from the tree, his head battered, unrecognisable, pouring out its memories with broken thoughts weaving a slick in and out of the bone and the blood.

"There's your retribution," she said, shaking and gasping for breath. "I should have taken it sooner! God forgive me!" She dropped the poker, wiping the spray of blood from her cheek.

CHAPTER 26

1 hour later

Later that night, Ian came down to retrieve their father's body. There were no flies yet, but he kept swatting at them as if they were there, invisible but swarming. Ian was a strong man, his muscle hard from chopping wood and doing the physical things that go with farming trees. He had just a little difficulty raising his father and placing him on the floor of his barrow. They tell the truth when they speak of a dead weight and Ian understood that now; his father had become an inert lump that seemed to grip the ground, reluctant to budge. Once in the barrow, he trundled the small vehicle along and the vibrations caused an arm to fall out and it gently struck a tree-trunk. He wheeled him to the small wooden boat, with its paint broken and blistered and lifting, a boat that was berthed against the low jetty to one end of the Hare Myre water. It was a long way with a barrow on a steel wheel and the lifting grips carved heavy grooves into the palms of his hands. Of course, he knew it had to be done and it had to be done now. Leave it till morning and who knows what busybody would find him. He tipped the corpse onto the wood-planked jetty like bricks falling from a brickie's hod. He dragged the weight from the jetty and, with much pushing and shoving, cajoled the heavy bundle into the boat. Like a bag full of hammers, it fell stiffly with a clatter, its limbs twisting awkwardly.

As the body lay there, face up, stiffly gazing at the stars, the face of the old man in the increasing gloom was only recognizable in parts, with all that damage done by the poker, so it didn't hurt Ian too much to look at him. He recognized the shape of the small round jaw. Even the ear looked familiar, although partially detached from the skull. He looked at his father and felt no remorse. Nothing. He did not remember any good times and it is only the memory of good times that feeds remorse. He filled the black coat pockets with sand, pebbles and granite rocks that he picked off the shoreline. He lifted a large lump of stone and dropped it as gently as he could against the body in the boat. He rowed out to the middle of the cold water and watched and heard the ripple effect as they went. One time he thought he caught a noise from the old man, but he laughed at himself when he looked down to check. You fool. It was clear as day there was no life left in him. It must have been the oars grinding against the rollocks as he pulled the blades through the water.

The light rain had stopped by the time he took the rope from his pocket. He attached it to the large lump of rock as if he were tying a food parcel. He cursed himself for choosing a smooth rock; a jagged edge would have been better to make the rope stick and stop it from sliding left and right. Still he thought that it would do the job, once the tension was on the rope. He took the loose frayed end and pushed it round behind his father's stiff neck before tying a large granny knot just beneath the chin. He had thought he might do a cow hitch knot of some kind but concluded that a cow hitch might well slip, and out would pop the old man with all that gas in him like some freak at the fair. Instead he chose a reef knot, better than a granny knot, though often enough tying one produced the other accidentally. It was right, he thought, they called it a granny knot. After all, a granny knot got the name from being the rope they always tied around the neck of a grain sack. Tying this rope around his father's neck was just keeping up with agricultural tradition. This could be a daddy knot, he thought, and chuckled grimly. It was hard not to make small jokes: it kept him sane. He felt the old man's stubble brush against the back of his hand. He accidentally touched his adam's apple too, resting like a fat egg. One for the urn, as they say in Japan. Ian was amused by something he remembered: in Japan they said you could measure a boy's puberty by the size of his adam's apple. He took hold of his father's coat and lifted him to the edge of the boat, where he balanced him like a plank to one side of the splintered bow.

"Goodbye," he said. "Sleep well." Then he tipped the body and it slipped gracefully into the water with a quiet slurp. For a short while, it floated close to the surface, the toes up like a pair of fins. He could see his father's face lit by the kerosene lamp, rippling beneath the water, one eye just a little open and the other an empty hole. He threw the large rock into the water next to his father and he thought he would see him sink straightaway. When it did not go, he poked at the body with his oar but it resolutely bobbed on the surface like a half-sunk canoe. He was thinking hard what he could do to send the man to the bottom when, a second or two later, the body disgorged a large bubble of gas and then harpooned from sight. Minutes later, he had to believe that his father was now at the very bottom of the loch. Ian stared into the water for the best part of an hour, drifting only a little way to the east where the water fern spread its easy

147

growth. Then he picked up the oars, eased them noiselessly into the rollocks, and rowed back to the shore.

They said to anyone who asked – and in all honesty, there were not many - that the old man had finally taken himself off. It was not so unlikely. They confessed that they were not that sorry. They said they thought he had gone to Glasgow but they could not be sure. He had talked of London often enough. He had no close family to speak of - *they* were his close family. After a while if anyone really cared, they at least stopped asking. There was no great love for him in that stretch of Meiklour Wood and he did not offer the kind of company that anybody would miss.

CHAPTER 27

Ian took over the running of the farm and made an almighty good job of it. The death of his father liberated him, took a weight off his back and injected a new energy. It was in truth a strange kind of farm; the crop was the trees he harvested and he was know as a logger or more and more they called him a lumberjack. From year start to year end, he felled the trees, from birch to oak, in every type of weather. He immersed himself in the work; planting ever more saplings and making more efficient use of what he already had. He built a small one-storey woodshed to the north side of Meiklour Wood, on a spot cleared of shrubs and trees, with a pleasant raised view out over Hare Myre water. Sometimes he fetched his Tonkin bamboo rod from the rafters above the woodshed, dug up some fresh worms and oared the same old boat from its mooring out to the middle. There was freshwater trout here, spearing the water with their pale cream bellies and speckled backs, and they could be caught if you considered carefully your fishing strategy. Before putting two feet in the boat, Ian pinched a wedge of gritty dirt from the ground and rubbed it into his hands. He knew well enough that no fish came near a worm that harboured a whiff of humanity. For good reason, they were scared. A fish could recognise his assassin by the smell of his fingers. He sat on the middle seat of the boat, stretched a fat worm between two pre-tied gang hooks and presented his line to the water. He thought of his father, as the line sunk from view. On the whole, he liked to keep the line a little short.

Ian built up the timber business and, unlike his father,

he did not pour the profits directly into his liver. He had his own supplies of hardwood timber, including plentiful oak and elm, but he found ways of importing the same resources from elsewhere, the Scandinavian coastal conifer forest mostly (along the Norwegian coast from places like Lindesnes and Senja), and he developed good business contacts supplying, in particular, the growing demand there was for the wheels of horse-drawn vehicles. Still, the home-grown Scots elm was as native to Scotland as a flat bunnet to a Dundonian. Ian knew well enough that 'Loch Lomond' is *Lac Leaman* in the Gaelic vernacular, meaning 'Lake of the Elms'. The place was full of elms. Their slippery barked trunks could be cut into long, straight planks and it was not long before Ian had an additional shed with a small yard next door where he installed a power-driven saw to get through the work that bit quicker and to a better finish. After a year or two he had orders from all over the place - builders as well as farmers in the area - as far away as Cupar, Stirling and the cities of Glasgow and Edinburgh. He was making a success of the business his old father had started and taken nowhere. His father was lucky enough to have a prime view of that success through one hundred and twenty feet of Hare Myre water.

Yet of course, it had to be said, with success came other issues, not all of them welcome or expected. His own sister came to be of growing interest to families from Tillicoultry to Cardenden who had sons looking for wives who might provide. Sure enough, Keira was an attractive girl but any fool knows that looks fade but gold keeps its colour. One of those sons who took an interest was from a Fife family, living some

150

distance over the other side of Perth. Like himself, the family had a farm with a handful of acres, but if he was honest, this man's people were a hard bunch of grabbers and Ian did not particularly take to them. Those he had met were greedy, conceited. How the son came to know of Keira was not clear but he had a mother with ambition and it was more than likely her who set him on the scent. There are mothers who are good at that. Ian met the son a few times and there were moments of jocularity when he would perhaps grow upon him a little but, in his heart, he always sensed that the whiskered man pursuing his sister, whilst bright-eyed with a sharp, caustic tongue on him, was not in any sense being true to himself or anyone else. He was a man who might laugh the loudest but behind his eyes were glassy beads that moved furtively from one scheme to the next. He reminded him of his own father in the early days, now dead beneath the water. How often did a daughter choose a mate the mirror of her own father? Furthermore, it galled Ian to find this man was no worker. He had that look about him that exuded a kind of measured indolence, if only he could be bothered. It made you think he could turn to fat or drink or women or all three, but the effort would be too much. There was laziness in this man, but there was a wily deviousness too. Ian recalled too well that he had once said to this man of whiskers on the make, that he was welcome to take away a load of planks he had cut to build a new roof on his own byre. He did not expect to be paid but he might have expected the fellow to make some small offer that Ian could magnanimously decline. He just took the wood all the same. Looking back on it, as he sometimes did, this boy had never given any hint that he would not be

151

paying, and as it turned out he did not pay. Ian's view was that he had stolen it – which may have been harsh, since at best he had not been forthright – yet, in his more forgiving moments, he recognized that maybe he had not explained the situation. People said he had other attributes. He had some money, he had something that looked like a farm. He had the backing of his family. For some that was enough and some to spare. He and his family laid siege on Keira like bluebottles sucking juice from a cowpat.

If she was honest about it, Keira was more than ready to be taken away from this black, fir-side grave. She could not bear to look at Hare Myre water, its mirrored reflection above the frozen, hidden depths. She avoided passing by that way if at all possible. Her brother Ian, on the other hand, appeared not to share her sensitivity at all. He was happy to fish the loch from morning to dusk if work would allow. She had seen him feed the worms onto the hooks before he took to the boat.

It was two years since the night of her father's 'disappearance'. They had not spoken about it, neither what he had done to her or what they had done to him. Whatever happened to that old steel poker? Was it at the bottom of the loch with the other secret? They never saw it again but she noticed a new one behind the fender. It was as if the old man had indeed taken himself off to London. Sometimes, when you tell a story often enough and you tag on some mild embellishment, some little lie, you reach a point when you start to believe it yourself. The story becomes credible. For some people the truth disappears and the lies are all that remain and the lies become the imposters of the truth. So the story had become the truth and what had occurred could not be spoken of because in this cuckoo world these things had not happened at all. And yet, this was nonsense and Keira knew it, her brother knew it and her mother too. Yet, not one of them could acknowledge it. When she thought about these things, it made her angry and frustrated that she would never escape all the lies and pretence. These were ghosts she could not hide from and guilt that she could never outrun.

Keira knew that the only possibility of a true escape from the hell that was in her head was to leave all this behind and go some place else. It occurred to her often that maybe marriage held that prospect, however daunting it appeared. Besides, despite the fact that the timber business was working, even with all this activity in the woodshed, growing another besides, it still only provided a decent income for Ian and his mother. She felt like she was surplus. She knew little enough about timber and did not have a man's strength to climb a tree or swing an axe. What could she give to a business like that? She could sweep the woodshavings off the floor twice a day, but where was the reward in that? Besides, it brought on the bronchitis all that dust and mess. She knew that in time it was possible that the business would do a lot more, but just now there was not enough here for her and what there was, was no good for her.

Ian, at twenty-two years old, was himself ready to settle down. He was not entirely repelled by the sight of women and they did not find him extraordinarily obnoxious. He had grown up with two of the species sharing their attributes, and there was every prospect

153

that he would marry one day, particularly if the business continued to grow the way he intended. Why should he not? Nevertheless, Keira knew all too well that there was more to it than just the money. It was becoming obvious to her that every day she existed in their lives was another day to remind them of the fir tree at the edge of Meiklour Wood and the events that took place there. It seemed to Keira that Ian had largely come to terms. He could float on that loch for hours, a fly dancing on the water, or his line trailing out the stern. It did not appear to trouble him that his father was pegged to the bottom with a big rock on his chest. It did not bother Ian at all. Their mother was a different story. She soon took to speaking less and less and most of all, she did not speak a word to Keira unless it was torn from her. She turned in on herself and she spoke to God. She ate less. The skin sagged on her white-freckled arms. Always fidgety, she became fractious and prone to migraines and unable to sleep when she lay down at night. It was clear to Keira that the ghosts were tormenting her and every time she took a look at her daughter those ghosts glowed a little brighter.

Alice turned her back on Hare Myre Water and never set eyes upon it again.

CHAPTER 28

1900

In hindsight, when Calum Wilson asked her to marry him she did not take sufficient time to consider the sanctity of the vows, the financial wherewithal of the bridegroom or the relative appeal of his wit and general disposition. She had thought his caustic, bruising sense of humour was well crafted, if a little contained and sometimes a little superior that bordered upon bullying. She enjoyed some occasions when he gently sparred with Ian and left her brother looking just a little pompous or sanctimonious. She did not dislike him for it and she felt it would soften over time. She had not given a thought to his habits relating to hygiene, sexual experience or whether he wore his socks to bed. The facial hair did not repel her. After all, she grew up in the country with occasional pigs and ferrets. She had not reflected upon the physical and psychiatric health of his bloodline, the forbears to which she might tether her own progeny. She had not thought long on whether he was cruel or kind to his livestock, whether he knew his grazing from his silage, whether or not he could fix a fence, or whether he would chase women and drink himself to death like her father. She had thought of none of these things and, in hindsight, that was pretty much a mistake. The truth of the matter is she wanted to get on her way and he was the fastest route out of Meiklour Wood. Quickest is not always best. When she should have been looking beneath the whiskers at the man's temperament and other features, her desperation was such that she thought of little more than how soon they could read the wedding banns.

They were married in Kilconquhar Church at seven minutes past eleven on a Saturday morning in October, beneath an unusually crisp, blue sky, surrounded by gravestones and enclosed by a broken wall that stretched as far as the loch. Nevertheless, the days were cooler now and the sun would be gone by noon. To be late by seven minutes to her own wedding she had considered a useful ploy to signify to her new husband that whilst she intended to offer love, honour and obedience, she did not intend the traffic to be entirely one way. Seven minutes was the opening trade. Ian stood at the door to the church in the place of her dead father. He walked her up the aisle to stand beside Calum, who awaited her just below the altar. His hair hung down from his head untidily and his chin was rough with beard and whiskers. Ian thought of the unpaid for, semi-stolen timber in Calum's byre and then put the thought to one side – today was a day for celebration, not stolen wood. Alice sat in the front pew, her thin body pressed against the hard seat, her eyes full of fear and regrets, cursing the cold draught that slapped the tops of her shoulders.

"Will there be prayers?" she whispered to Ian, when he sat down beside her.

"Yes, I imagine," he answered.

"Very good," she said. "I like prayers and hymns. Something from the psalms." She bit her lower lip and looked away. These days she was given to this kind of strange religious enquiry. The remainder of the guests were broken parts of the Wilson family and those they called their friends. Mrs Wilson did not speak to Keira until later in the day, when the celebrations were under way. She was unsteady on her feet and her breath betrayed her intoxication. She put her hand on Keira's arm and gripped it hard.

"You better watch out, girl," she said. "You better watch him." She looked back over her own shoulder. "He can be... I mean, it's just that sometimes, he's got a mean streak."

"A mean streak?"

"Yes, yes." She drew her face closer to Keira's. "A mean streak."

"Why do you say that?"

"He's off my hands now," she said. "I can do that." She looked about her. "You should watch your back. Stir him up the wrong way and you're proper fucked." She put her hand to her mouth, as if concerned that she may have been overheard. "He'll fuckin' kill you if you cheat. Best not, if you're getting my message." She saw her son approaching and she dropped away out of sight.

The following night after the wedding - because it was a two day affair which Ian had paid for under no duress, albeit when drink had loosened his tongue, he released the occasional, modest grumble - Calum took Keira home to the house in Fife where they planned to begin their married life. It had been a rough, jolting journey up from Kilconquhar and she was cold and hungry when they arrived. As their cart drew up outside the house, she was alone in the quietness with her new husband. He had said nothing on the journey but she was not concerned. She had never wanted a man who mistook talk for action.

"This is it," he said. "For better or for worse."

She climbed down from the cart after him. In doing so, she caught her shoe on her dress and stumbled forward. She would have fallen but caught the wheel of the cart and remained upright. At that point he laughed at her and she wondered if he would have laughed more or less if she had landed on her knees. The strange, removed look in his eyes as he laughed and the dry tone of the laughter itself made her sense for the first time that their marriage might not be easy.

The house was cold and empty and there was filth on the floor. There was a smell of wet clothes. There was a pair of muddy boots in the hallway and the mud had dried and was breaking off. She looked around and then began to clear the mess. She looked for a cloth and wiped down the surfaces. She put her hair up in a small, neat bun. She found an old brush with broken bristles and swept down the floor into a small pile that her new husband walked through once and then disappeared. She found cups in a cupboard, some plates and cutlery and a teapot. There was no food anywhere. The water came from a pump at the back of the house. The windows were so dirty you did not need curtains.

Her husband came back into the kitchen. He waved his arm at her, as if she should follow him from the house into the old byre next door, across the small yard. The roof of the byre had fallen in some while back but on one side, collecting damp and the feathered droppings off the many pigeons, lay the pile of timber that Ian had gifted.

"Is that the timber," she said. "From Ian?"
"It was good of him, I'm sure," said Calum.

158

"It wouldn't harm anyone to thank him," she said.

"If it's thanks he's wanting he may as well whistle."

"Still, the timber will rebuild this, won't it?" she asked, waving a hand randomly about her. "It may give us a new roof in here?" she said.

"What do you know about it?" he said.

"Well, I don't know but..."

"Become the builder, have we?"

"No..." she started.

"Building the new roof, whatever next?"

"I just..."

He did not cut her off. Instead he looked straight through her and he said nothing, and that had the same effect. He stepped towards her and, as he did so, whilst his movement unnerved her, at the same time she had the unlikely thought that in the right light, and with a shave, he might have been handsome. The whiskers were too much but they softened the hardness that came from his eyes. It crossed her mind that he was going to kiss her and, in all truth, she was not indifferent to the prospect. She was now a married woman and she understood what might be expected of her. So when Calum approached her in the old roofless byre, she saw a curious, mischievous look in his eye and misconstrued it as the start of that marital process, the evolution that she imagined married life to be.

Once he was there, standing before her, without warning, the smile not moving from his lips, he beat her hard against the face with the back of his hand, first the left and then the right. He struck her a deep blow with a clenched fist in the soft hollow of her stomach beneath the rib-cage. The pain was the worst she had ever experienced. She had not known he was left-handed. He had long nails. The breath escaped her and she fell to the floor with a startling crash. She gasped for breath. He stood over her, but she was hardly there a moment before he bent down and gripped her by the front and pulled her back onto her feet.

"I want us," he said, breathing heavily in her face, "to start off as we mean to continue." He put his short fingers around her throat and held her hard against the wall and its rough, wooden slats. She could feel the broken mortar crumbling against the back of her head. She was winded and struggled to breathe. Her feet were barely touching the floor, just the tips of her toes. "It's a bad thing to start off badly," he said as the light began to fade from her eyes. She pulled at his hand around her neck. She tugged at his fingers and tried to tell him he was choking her, but she could hardly get the words out, so tight was his grip. He drew his face closer to hers and she could see every pore of his nose, every line across his forehead and all the angry fire in his brown eyes. "You're under my roof now," he said, blind to the irony of the roofless byre. "Decisions about what goes on around here are up to me. Do you understand?" She looked at him and felt a deep sense of terror, a blush of fear that rose and engulfed her. He smiled. "If you have received the message," he said. "Nod your head." She had little choice but to move her head. "Teamwork is what I'm after, see? We pull together and you do what I say. That way we get along fine. Are we clear? Mrs Wilson?" He dropped her and her legs folded beneath her as she slid back to the ground.

When he reached the open door to the byre, he stopped and turned to look at her. He could see that

she was coughing and weeping. He smiled at her, showing the tips of his teeth. "Don't go getting upset about this. I want things to be right between us," he said. "Come on. We'll go in now." He spat a lump of yellow phlegm against the doorpost and watched it slide. His eye was caught by the wooden planks.
"What the hell are we going to do with this lot?" he said.
She tried to speak but could not voice words. "Roof," she said eventually.
"Wood's no use to us," he said, ignoring her. "Somebody will pay something for it." He moved through the door, tossing over his shoulder as he went: "Come inside. I just got married, my girl. Let's celebrate."

CHAPTER 29

We were set for the high seas alright. Mr Harcourt was anxious about the weather. It was picking up, blustery, showery, filthy weather coming. There was just the three of us. And Rory. My thought was that Calum Wilson would have been a liability and I was happy he was nursing his hangover back on the daybed. Rory was also a liability and I would have to mind my footing. I will admit I had a picture of Calum's wife in my head and she was on the daybed too, wearing very little. As that thought slipped through my brain's connecting tissues, I pulled hard on a rope and the boat was dragged by the wind through the dull water. I looped it and flung the bundle to one side. I had more to think about than Calum Wilson's daybed. I knew I had to take heed that Rory was still with us and I had to keep one eye on him for fear of what stunt, salivitic projectiles or otherwise, he might wish to send in my direction. He would not have forgotten the mess I made of Tom's voice box when careless with a loose spade in the Bombo Burn. The wind had taken hold of the sails, and they bulged to the front, like a couple of fat boys with their tums out. The boat moved swiftly away from the quayside, drawn by the hard blow and already whipped by the lash of heavy rain.

Mr Harcourt called his boat a lugger. The pedantically disposed mariner would no doubt argue that the lugger was a small vessel with two sails on two masts or more commonly, three sails on three masts, and that old Harcourt's boat did not fit the bill. Whether the gruff old farmer's boat bore any kinship with a *bona fide* lugger was open to question: whilst it had two masts and two sails, one was large with a square top and one little bigger than a large pair of Tom Burns' underpants. The rust-red canvas sails had to be hauled up each of the masts by heaving hard on a halyard rope. *Firth Wind* had a halyard made from baling twine, plaited into something thicker than my forefinger. When I had pulled on the rope at the quayside I had already felt the twine cutting into my hands. It was like handling a string of sharp knives. With a growing south-westerly wind the lugger was slicing a deep groove through the water, rising and falling with the waves. The cold, wet air became increasingly blustery, tugging at our hair and beating hard, gusting blows against our backs, and more than once I caught a look on Rory's face that showed some concern at the fast disappearing land behind us.

Within a short time we reached Pooly Point – a crop of rocks a little more than a mile down the coast – and then we moved back in a little towards the shoreline again where we fed the net from the bow of the boat. The net was black cotton, coated with creosote to keep it from rotting and weighted to make it sink and sit low in the water. Cork floats hung along the surface, holding the net from running too deep. The herring were happy to flip-flop along the bottom during the day and then rise later to feed on the plankton. The task was to feed the nets into the water and allow them to drift on the tide and so catch the herring. A man could show his skill here. He had to know where the fish might be at any one time, and at what depth and if he got it right he might fill his net. On the other hand he might be entirely ignorant about the movement of the herring but stumble blindly into them, filling his net in the process.

163

The wind was still hard upon us and the net was all out, drifting, as Mr Harcourt intended, towards the shore. From the moment we had rounded the rocky outcrop that formed the point we had felt the full force of the gale and the driving rain, baring its teeth at us, lifting the ripped, whisked waves ever higher, pounding hard breaks against the boat and rolling it like a child's toy in a tin bath. At this stage, the child in me would have opted for dry land. Old Harcourt squatted at the back of the boat, head down against the rain and the spray off the waves catching in his beard. He was not alone in thinking they could only keep this up for so long. A beluga whale would have turned back by now. It was my feeling that we were not far off having to do the same, but there was no telling Mr Harcourt because he was in charge. I wrestled with ropes that slipped through my fingers and flapping sails that cracked against my ears. Rory was over the other side, slipping and falling around the deck, tugging on ropes like mine and hopelessly holding a hat tight against his head, strands of blonde hair hanging in long streaks beneath the rim.

At that point, it could not get any worse. Suddenly it did. Just as old Harcourt made the decision that they had to give it up and get back to shore, the net became snagged. The saltwater continued to crash against the side of the boat, cascading wave after wave across the deck. I never knew the sea held this much water. Duncan slipped and cursed as he grasped at a halyard that had broken free from its stay. He slid across the deck, on his back, his legs above his middle, like a rolled turtle, crashing like a curling stone against the other side of the boat. Harcourt remained at the helm keeping the bow pointed to the east, a worried look at Duncan who waved a reassuring hand back at him. I staggered to the bow, rolling with the undulations, gripped the net with frozen fingers and pulled for all I was worth. The net was clearly snagged on a rock, well down beneath the waterline. The rain whipped hard against our skin and then the waves slapped over us, and another swell swept and swamped the boat. We rolled again. And again. Still I tugged at the net, the rain coursing across my eyelids, down my cheeks in tight glazed rivers. I shook the wet from my face and pulled again on the net, leaning further over the bow of the boat, struggling to keep purchase with my soft, waterlogged boots. There was a risk that the net would be ripped and lost, but I knew I had to shift it from where it was caught, and if I did not achieve that we would have to give it up and we would lose the net altogether. Rory, broken by many falls, had been sheltering to the north side of old Harcourt but, in truth, there was no cover to be had anywhere. Suddenly, Rory rose again to his feet and surged forward to where I was at the bow, gripping the side with both hands. He leaned over to the left of me, slipped his fingers into the holes of the black net and pulled. Even in that thundering storm you could smell the salt, the kelp weed and the creosote. We pulled together, our hands icy pink in the ripping, grey water, our arms pushing and jostling, our faces wet and determined. In the midst of our endeavour, I glanced at him. Whether through guts or fear, he was working as hard as I was. His efforts pushed me harder. I pulled again from a different direction, felt the net cut through my hands, and took the strain across my shoulders and back. And then, there came a tidal disaster. Neither of us saw it arrive, focused as we were on releasing the net. The boat twisted to the starboard side and was caught by a wall of seawater. The vessel lifted and appeared almost clear and then crashed to the hollow formed by the waves. When I picked myself up, Rory's hands were no longer next to mine, they had slipped and gone from the net. He was over the side and already in the water ten or twelve feet away, waves crashing over the top of him, weighed down by his clothing, gulping for every breath like it were his last. Another wave like the first and he would be gone.

CHAPTER 30

I had the sense to throw off my sodden jacket before I lurched over the side. It was a challenge to get into the water, given the rise and fall of the boat, and I thought for a minute I would get no further than a little gentle crushing by the boat itself. Old Harcourt shook an arm at me and shouted words that I could not hear but I was over the side by then. I hit the water and immediately came the extreme chill of the water driven like nails into my bones. Every now and then I caught a sight of Rory across the tops of the waves and I swam as hard as I could in his direction. He was moving with the tide, as was I, but his head was bobbing very close to the water, disappearing under and then up again. Soon he would swallow a bellyful of water and the head would disappear for good. I kicked my legs and pushed to reach him. I saw the boat move further away as I flailed hopelessly in Rory's direction. I was struck on the head by something hard, floating in the water just above the surface, probably enough to cause a gash but I was still conscious. A piece of driftwood shaped like a pole revealed itself and, with my two hands, I pushed it hard towards Rory. It speared some way through the water.

I shouted at him but he seemed to be losing the fight. I went on, swimming towards him, slowly closing the gap. He was closer now and I could see his eyes were open and they were filled with a glazed terror. He clawed with his fingers and paddled with his arms like a human windmill. He kicked with his booted feet, the clothes he was wearing pulling at him, sapping his strength and sinking him. As I drew close, I put out my hands in an attempt to lift his head above the water. He raised his own hands, grabbed hold of the hair on my head and pulled me right under the water. All life blurred before my eyes and what was left began its slow, inexorable ebb from this place to the next. I struggled but how easy it would have been to let go. I was shivering as my metabolism slowed and my muscles were beginning to seize, making it harder to move my arms to save myself. I was entering the worst three or four minutes of my life.

He told me later he was thinking of his father, his dear dead father, who loved fruit chutney on his biscuits. He said he thought too of the old man's black-nailed fingers on a thick, green, glass bottle of Madeira, his tobacco in an oily pouch and his uncared for breath against his face. He kicked and drew himself nearer to the driftwood. I was almost done, exhausted, gasping, vision blurred to within a few feet, mental processes becoming weary and treacled. When his hands struck another time, hard against my head, I held on but I thought then that he had killed me.

When the tide is coming in under those conditions, it is like a sliding, unstoppable blob, dragged east across the seafloor, the moon pulling with a force we can only imagine. An incoming tide carries a person or anything in its grasp towards the shoreline with the same impossible grip. The struggle to close the small distance in the water between myself and Rory was far greater than the small effort exerted by the sea to drag us close to the rocks, but then disgorging us without ceremony onto a seaweed mulch, delivering us close to the shore. I could feel the reassuring rock and sand of the gently sloping beach underfoot. I gripped Rory's collar and dragged him towards the shore. We lay above the shallow water, too exhausted to move. My head was spinning. I felt light, dizzy and even moderately euphoric. My thoughts came back to me like I was reaching for the pages of a book. I was alive.

Mr Harcout, with steely, sunken eyes and fish-hunter's head, even through the thick buffeting of that storm had seen us, Rory and myself, hang by nothing but our fingernails to the railway sleeper that had clouted me on the back of the head. He then lost sight of us as he wrestled to keep the boat upright, battered by the relentless wind and spray. The net was lost on the rocks, still snagged below the waterline.

Mr Harcourt had guided the boat closer to the shoreline, but by that time the main sail was ripped and there was little control coming off the rudder and there was a real danger of splintering themselves against rocks that scraped the belly of the boat. Yet, still battered by the fierce wind, he was able to find some shelter in the lea side of the point and the gale there had eased enough to allow them to bale out some of the water sloshing like soup across the deck. They tightened up the main sail and, after a while, they limped home to the quayside.

Only then did Harcourt and his son allow themselves to think what had happened to us. Once they had dragged the boat up the beach and secured it to a mooring spot, they headed off on foot up the coast to the small stretch where Mr Harcourt was thinking we may have come ashore. He and his son knew it was not a given that we had come ashore at all.

They searched the coastline, threading like drunken weavers, up and down over the dunes, through the long rolled leaves of the wet marram grass, a seaside mile this way and that way. As they did so, the rain was still chucking down on them but the wind was blowing itself out. Shouting our names, scanning their eyes along the shore, Harcourt was tired by his efforts and was about to turn back again, but instead he walked towards the fields that cushioned the water's edge.

When Mr Harcourt approached the old barn, he had a sense that he would find us. Maybe the grey hair on the back of his weathered neck prickled up. He shouted out my name, like he had a hundred times already. When he did so, he was surprised to see me emerging from the top of a haystack, Rory right behind.

"You're alive then?" he said and spat a gob by the door.

"Just about," I said.

"What are you doing up there?"

"Trying to get warm."

"You cold then?"

"Yes."

Mr Harcourt stared back at me and then looked at the ground. He appeared embarrassed. "I suppose you would be. That's not surprising. You both okay then? Bit fuckin stupid jumping over?"

"I had no choice," I said, making my way down to ground level. When I reached him, he put his hand on my forearm and moved his mouth closer to my ear. "I was told you hated that boy," he said, raising his thumb towards Rory.

"I never hated anyone," I said. "Well, that's maybe not true."

"Best get going now," said Duncan, intent on steering his father out from the gloom of the shed.

"Is he okay then?" said Mr Harcourt, pointing at Rory who was still sat firm on the hay with his arms around his knees, pale and shivering and not speaking.

"I think so."

"You alright to look after him?"

"Yes," I said.

"Take care now," he said.

"You too Mr Harcourt."

"Net's fucked," he said. "Small price." He spat one last time before he headed out into the rain.

What I did not explain in any detail to Mr Harcourt about the haystack was its most useful property: heat. The haystack came to me from another book I had extracted from the farming section of Mr Shifner's library. It may have been catalogued incorrectly because it was not a book purely about farming. It was about five boys at a place called Williamstown in Massachusetts. There had been a violent thunderstorm and these boys took shelter on the lee side of a haystack. They were soaked through and shivering, so they got *inside* the haystack and the reason for getting inside the haystack was that they knew (for they were educated Americans) there was always heat in these places. The heart of a stack can get hot enough to start a fire and sometimes it does just that. Once they were warm they thanked God and were driven to become missionaries in Asia. Those missionaries gave birth to the *Haystack Movement*. They put up a twelve foot high granite monument in Massachusetts to celebrate the fact. It was with this little anecdote, culled from Mr Shifner's rosewood library (farming section),that I came to the view that I did. We had been on the beach a while, Rory and me. My head had taken a blow from the railway sleeper and was still spinning and pounding. I had likely been hypothermic, finding it hard to think. That is how the cold gets you: it slows down your brainpower and it becomes erratic and disconnected and you struggle to do even the smallest calculation. Rory was no better than me and was shaking and shivering and all folded up like he was going to die there and then, face as pale as the hair on his head. I knew we had to get warm but we had nothing for a fire. All we had was our wet clothes and it was hellish cold out there. Hellish cold. I dragged Rory along and up the beach with me, bent over, hunched up, trotting. We moved along the field to the old shed I had passed often enough, but a distance in from the shoreline. We got in under cover and I pulled a ladder away from the wall and leaned it against the stack of hay that sat inside. Rory climbed the ladder, struggling all the way, almost falling off the top rung, throwing himself down on the haystack. He pulled the broken bales of hay to one side and dropped himself into the hole. I followed him in. I was not too sure I would get my legs moving enough to get up the ladder after him. I did get up there and stood at the top and then placed myself in almost the same gap, splitting more hay and spreading it across us. For a second or two there was no noticeable difference and I began to have misgivings about those boys in Massachusetts. I was thinking maybe they were bogus and that granite monument may have been a waste of time and money. And granite. Monument to what exactly? Then suddenly, I felt the warmth seeping in and the chill began to ease out of my frozen bones.

We lay in the hay in the half-light until Mr Harcourt found us. Before that, I enjoyed a moment I will remember forever. Out of the stillness came Rory's voice. "Thanks."

"No problem at all," I said.

There was a moment's quiet, then he said: "You didn't have to come after me. In the water, I mean."

"I know."

"I would probably have made it okay on my own."

"Probably."

"I thought I was drowning," he said.

"You were."

"Then I thought I was dreaming that I was drowning."

"My friend, take it from me you were drowning."

He paused. "I saw my dad," he said. "I saw his chutney floating past me on a rye loaf."

"It was serious then," I said and the way he looked at me, I knew he was wondering if I was making a joke of it.

"It was bad enough."

"You didn't die," I said.

"Came close though."

"Maybe you did."

He said nothing for a while. Then, he raised his eyes at me and nodded. He did not have to say anything because I understood.

CHAPTER 31

Mr Harcourt had experienced a pleasant sense of relief when he found us, alive and well. He knew that in a different life he might have had two dead boys to bury. How would he have coped with that? He had buried Mrs Harcourt and that had been bad enough. He and his son, Duncan, left us and went straight back to the boat. They were worried that in their haste they had not secured it properly, but it was there, beaten but unbowed and none the worse for its ordeal, apart from the ripped sail. The tar used to fill the split bow was still holding good. They checked the boat ties and gathered up the belongings they intended to take back with them to the farm. Their clothes were still damp from the sea but they were warm enough from the work they were doing.

The horse called Ballymena was still tethered beneath the shed roof by the track, not too distant from the quayside. Ballymena cut a forlorn figure, his gut hanging low to the ground, one hindleg slightly raised and the tip of his hoof resting against the mud, like a petulant ballet dancer. His hindquarters poked out from the iron roof, wet through from the rain and he heralded their appearance with a shake of the head, as if to rebuke them. Duncan hitched Ballymena to the old carriage and then loaded their gear into the large chest that sat between the rear wheels. They wasted no time and minutes later they were making their way along the broken track, putting distance between them and the water, wheels sliding in the mud and heading towards home. All the while Mr Harcourt muttered and cursed.

At some point on their journey, Harcourt shouted at Duncan: "Bloody man!"

"Who?"

"Wilson!" he shouted. "None of this would have happened but for that fuck wit!" He whipped the horse. "We were a man down," he said.

"There's no harm done," said Duncan.

"There could have been," shouted his father. "There could have been two dead boys! Not to mention us!"

Harcourt cursed Wilson again as they cleared the crossing and followed the track up to the left. Who knows, with an extra man they might have manoeuvred the boat a little less close to the rocks, thought Mr Harcourt. They might not have snagged the net. They might have weathered the storm. They would have had an extra pair of hands to pull up the net when it did snag. They would have at least had a chance to get out of that situation. They might even have caught some bloody herring too! "Shit!" he said and spat from the corner of his mouth. Instead, they had nothing for their trouble but a boat washed out, a ripped sail, not so much as a tiddler caught and two boys half-dead in a haystack.

Wilson's farm was on the far side of Tullis. To have paid him a visit would have meant a round trip of less than thirty minutes. To Mr Harcourt's mind it would have been well worth the trouble. It was a minor deviation. He could get this thing off his chest. It would do no harm to drop by and let the man know he was an arse. Duncan said it might be better to let it lie, said as much in soothing noises, so far as he could against the clatter of Ballymena's hooves and the rumble of the wheels on the stone and through the mud. He said he had to let things settle down, but his father was beyond the point of listening. Old Mr Harcourt muttered something inaudible and pushed the horse a little faster, cracking both sides with his whip.

The sky was still grey and leaden, hanging like a slate cloud over the Wilson house. Balymena took the last bend at some speed, up a track heavy with mud between two chest-high walls, the coping wet through and covered with dull green moss. They pulled in at the front of the house and could see traces of black smoke leaking from the broken chimney cowl.

It so happened that Calum was standing at the window as Mr Harcourt drew his carriage up outside. He put down the watch chain he had been swinging through the air in front of him. "What's that old bastard want?" he said. "Looks like a drowned rat."
His wife joined him by the window. "Maybe he wants to sell you a fish," she said.
"Or a turkey," he grunted, pulling up his braces and looping them over his shoulders. He scratched each of his testicles in turn and then left the room.

Mr Harcourt was about to rap on the door when it swung open and Calum's face appeared. "Whoa!" he said. "Let's not ruin the beautiful paintwork."
"I'm not fussed about your fuckin' paint," Harcourt said. "I came close to losing my boat today because of you!"
"Maybe you chose the wrong weather, old fella!"
"I told you we needed more hands for that boat!"
"You need to calm down," he said. "Bad for the heart."

"What were you doing?"

"This and that, something came up."

"You should have been there, like you said."

"Yeah well," said Calum. "I had better things to do."
He stepped back a pace as if to close the door. "Is
there anything else I can do for you?" As he began to
close the door, Harcourt wedged his foot in the gap.

"Can't rely on pig-shit like you for anything."

"Is that so?"

"Those boys nearly drowned!" he yelled.

"Well, if they're still alive they've nothing much to
complain about, have they?" said Wilson, through the
gap.

"Rory Turner," said Harcourt.

"What of him?"

"He wouldn't be alive if it wasn't for Logan!"

Wilson opened up the door a little more. "Sean
Logan?" he asked. "The dumb one?"

"The one," said Harcourt, "who was here to get you
this morning."

"Oh that one. The cheeky fuck."

"He's not dumb either."

"I noticed that myself. He's a cocky shite."

"Speaks more sense than you ever did."

Calum opened the door fully and stepped forward
onto the step. He pushed his face very close to Mr
Harcourt's and breathed his lunch over him. Duncan,
who had been seated on the carriage throughout,
jumped down and moved towards them. He was
thinking he might kick Wilson and he and his dad
would run, before things got out of hand. Calum held
up his hand at Duncan but continued to press his face
into Mr Harcourt's. "Listen to me you old pisser! As
it happens I stayed at home today. I stayed at home

177

because I don't like your boring old ass. I don't like your manner either. Now get your shit out of my yard and don't take fuckin' liberties!"

"You're an arse," Harcourt said.

"And you've the nose for it."

Harcourt's face was puffed with fury and there were little red blisters raging on his cheeks. He did not say another word but his eyes spoke volumes. Duncan pulled him back towards the carriage and the two climbed on board, shook and slapped the reins and thundered out across the small stones, sliding along the dirt track towards Tullis, Mr Harcourt's face as dark as the track beneath them and thunderous as the clouds above.

Calum stood outside his door and laughed aloud. A dull day had turned out quite enjoyable. He laughed some more and showed his yellowing teeth. They were not so bad for a man who never cleaned them. "That old ass wouldn't like that, would he?"

"Why do you say that?" his wife said, appearing behind him. "He's just an old man."

"Thinks he's the only bastard who can fish that bit of coast." He turned towards her and stepped up close by the door.

"He's just an old man," she repeated. "He means no harm."

He stood before her and pulled the shoulder band off her blue smock, threading his thick hand inside her shirt and holding her nipple between his thumb and forefinger, like he was working a ball of clay into a narrow pipe. She had an idea he was going to squeeze it hard and crush the nipple. She sensed it

178

coming and she knew that it would be painful, but he did not squeeze. He ran the sole of his finger across the top of the nipple and then took away his hand, as if he were bored. He looked at her. "Do your own thing tonight," he said, "I'm not here." He turned for the boot room.

"You are going out in *this* weather?" She lowered her eyes when he turned back.

"I've some business in Cupar."

"What kind of business?" she said.

"The kind that can't wait."

"Are you coming back tonight?" she asked.

"I may have to go to Perth."

"That doesn't exactly answer my question."

"What do you think?" he said, moving back towards her. "What do you think?"

"It was just a question," she said.

"I told you I'm not here tonight."

"That's what you said."

"I think that's enough, don't you?"

"I suppose it'll have to be."

"That's right."

Later, after her husband had gone, after she had eaten some stale biscuits and the broken half of an old fruit cake; when she had drunk some warm, weak tea from a cup with a broken handle; when she had washed it down with a half glass of whisky; when she had applied some ointment to the heavy bruising around her eye where he had hit her on his way out; then she looked out of the window towards the Firth. It was enveloped now in a heavy, velvety darkness. She knew it was there but she could not see it. The rain was still on. She could hear the pattering drum of broken drops as they struck the slated roof. She knew

179

Tullis was there in the inky blackness, its people just down below, but there were no lights to betray its presence. She knew that that boy Logan was down there somewhere too. A strange boy, the way he had looked at her. Foolish to call him a boy. There was nothing of the boy about him. Saved the other one from drowning, old Harcourt had said. But who will save me from drowning? Who will pull me from the spinning, dark water that sucks me down and through the sluice? Those were her foremost thoughts.

CHAPTER 32

About the same time as I was experimenting with haystacks, my father was dying in his cell at Peterhead Prison. It was November, a month I hate anyway. Aunt Marion said he had given up and chosen not to live. I was not so sure it was as simple as that. Why would you serve seventeen years of a twenty-five year sentence and decide at that time, with the blue sky on the horizon, one foot tiptoeing out the cell door, the milk and the honey sliding into your peripheral vision, why would you decide then that you were ready for a more permanent incarceration, in another box, this one a little tighter and more attractively furnished in scots pine and ornate handles? It made no sense. Aunt Marion said she thought he simply turned his back on it, disappointed, like he had been given bad news about the weather. I could not fathom why he had not held on a while longer. Instead, he just gave up the ghost.

"Yes he gave up," said Aunt Marion. "But his past haunted him."

"Why would my father just give up like that?"

"People do."

"It seems cowardly," I said.

"He was never a coward," she said.

"He gave up," I said.

"Don't say he was a coward."

"Why didn't he keep going?" I persisted. She was annoyed at me, but I was annoyed more at him.

I was being harsh, I know that now. Sometimes you have to kick someone to save yourself. I think it was true that the assault on my mother hung like something rotten in my father's gut. It never quite escaped. It gassed up inside and leaked out in little poisonous bubbles all around him. His every step was shadowed by her death and the manner of her death. Every breath he took was yoked to that unspoken bitterness, an oozing, leaden bile in the pit of his stomach. What I heard is that sometimes in the prison they would be sent out into the Highlands in small teams to burn the heather. The purpose of doing so was to bring on the green buds, the new grass. Burn the heather, bring on the buds. They still burn the heather. New grass means bigger and fatter sheep. In the midst of all this, the men were herded by the guards around the fires. Surely, some would think of escape, a mad dash through the smoke? Then again, escape to where? Freedom? Fresh linen on the bed? The smell of the farm? The babble of the Bombo Burn at the end of the field that produced little more than prickly weeds? There was no place to go even if those prisoners had the strength to run, whether into the heat of the fire or away from the fire. They were hobbled. Even then, I could imagine my father staring deep into the yellow flames, nestled amongst the red embers, and he would never stop seeing her face. My mind tells me that that was what kept him going and paradoxically, in my view, it was the very thing that killed him. A small touch of pneumonia, if that is what it was, did not need to be the death of you.

Then again, there were times too when I could imagine my father would have sat back in his hard, grey Peterhead cell and he may have thought about the old wall at the front road to Logan farm, running his hand across the damp moss on the coping, and he would have seen himself looking down at the spray of sheep fanned out across the green, grizzled field.

Immediately he would have thought of her and the times they had had together, when they had sat upon the same wall, enjoyed the same view and shared the same pleasure at being together, there, then. Or else he might well have eaten something his sister Marion had left with him on one of her occasional visits and just a flavour of wild sage, just a taste would have done enough to bring back the sharp memory of his dear, lost wife, Tatiana. Her name itself was like the last breath escaping from a corpse.

Aunt Marion said he had never forgotten my mother. Her memory, she said, was sharp as bright midday sunlight, all the way to the end. Then again, I must confess my own view on that is a little different. Like a lawyer without a brief, I do not have any clear evidence for saying this, but the view I have come to is mine. I still cannot make sense of why my father died. When I think hard about it the truth pains me as much as I am sure it pained him. I have to ask myself, what if he was becoming aware that his memory of her was fading? What if he thought that he was actually forgetting her? What if he thought that was just one sheet of paper too many to bear? You can lose the thing you love the most, but how can you forget her altogether? How can you lose the memory? How can you drop the rope that tethers her to the shore and see her drift away like that? It is like she died twice. But then how can you keep any memory fresh? He should have asked himself that question. You cannot. You just cannot. Memory is no different from apples: over time, they lose the green skin and the water and the little seeds. A skinny old husk is all that remains; that is memory. He should have asked himself how anybody could hope to keep the picture from fading. You can beat this old boat with the weather for one season, maybe two, but eventually the mooring works loose and the memory drifts away or is swallowed up by the water. Memory, in the end, is no more than the shitty sludge that is left over once everything else is gone. And so, with regard to my father, I am more inclined to the belief that it was because the years were rubbing away the memory, like the gilt coming off a gold frame, that he decided that it was his time to go. Before the whole fucking thing disintegrated to dust in the bone of his hands. The spirit left him and he had no desire to keep it back. The detail of his memory was becoming so blurred I do not think he could reconcile losing the clarity in his mind. It was fading from memory, the clear shape of her ears and the deep green blackness of her eyes. He didn't like to see the dimple in her sallow cheeks fade away or lose from his mind's eye the neat precision of her Romany nose. In a sense, he was going blind. He was no longer certain of the accuracy of what he could see. He had worn her shawl against his skin every day of his life since that hated night, all through his prison years, but my belief is that he had begun to realise that there was nothing left of her in it now: no smell, no fragrance, nothing. It was no more than a rag you might wipe your stupid hands on. It was no longer her; if anything, it was him. I could imagine him wondering if his memory of her had in fact become a memory of somebody altogether different; did he worry that the person he remembered during the long, cold nights in his draughty Peterhead cell or out in the field damping down the fires, or even in his head, might never actually have existed? I believe now that he worried that the woman he remembered was not the woman he

184

had known. He could not live with that. It was like being unfaithful, promiscuous with another woman. He was coming to terms with the idea that memory, as it turned out, was little more than pure invention; nothing more than what is left when a man's disintegrating head has forgotten all the other shit that ever lived there.

These were the voices that crowded my own disintegrating head on the day they brought my father's body down from Peterhead. I knew a lot of this was conjecture, speculation and the rest but it made some sense to me and it made it easier for me as I opened the farm gate to let my father's body pass through. He was a long way dead and even with the lid hard down on a cold day there was still a chemical smell of formaldehyde in the air, preserving the tissues. After eighteen years his pale, grey, plugged body was once more come home to Logan farm. It had been a long time for my father and jail years must be the longest in any language. This was his farm and yet you could not help but feel that his ownership had been painfully brief. It had maybe skipped a generation.

Earlier, I tore off the lid and checked that he was there. We laid him out in the back room. He looked nice in that coffin, on the white sheet, so still, so ready to face all the shit that was coming. I had no memory of his face, barely having seen him. He was like a stranger in my house. Yet, I could see parts of me imbued within his features. We had some of the men and women from the village come by to pay their last respects. I looked at them but we shared few words. They took their own good advice and did not speak beyond formalities. Mr Fawcett came on in after he had locked up the shop for the day. He had taken off his apron and wore a black tie. His shoes were shiny brogue. I did not mind him coming too much but I took the opportunity to remind him that he had obligations not just to the dead, but to the living. He looked at me a little puzzled. He asked for an explanation and I said no, another time. I said to him: "Explanations will come later. What I want you to think about between now and when we lay my father in the ground, is where your responsibility lies." He looked uncomfortable and drank a large glass of gin.

"I don't understand," he said eventually.

"Don't worry," I said. "I can make you understand."

"But what do you mean?" said Mr Fawcett.

"There will be time to talk later," I said.

Others chose not to come, and they were wise. Forgiveness is not a bottomless pool. Once the formalities were over, the coffin was closed up once more and the body was put on the cart and wheeled to the cemetery in Tullis. Stupidly, I pulled out the nails and took a long, final look. I was not surprised to find him still dead and once more, I hammered down the lid. Aunt Marion put a hand on my shoulder and Lizzie took hold of my hand.

Initially I had some small issues with the minister. I think of the minister as a bad tooth that needs to be pulled or in some way anaesthetised. He was a man of forty or so years. He was known to smoke a clay pipe at the altar when he thought it was just him and God present, and he usually carried a liberal dash of breakfast egg on his cleric's bib. It was immediately apparent on our initial meeting that the minister was reluctant to undertake my father's burial. He gave me some meaningful shit about there being limited space in the cemetery, when I knew fine well the cunt's reservations were more to do with my father lowering the tone than causing subterranean congestion.

I had thought things over. I went back down to the church with the fish on the roof. The old boy was on his knees, declaring his transgressions to an empty altar. I sat at the back of the church and let him finish. He was there a long time so he must have had a lot to get through. Still, eventually he lowered his head and then turned back down the aisle. The lights were low in the church, a few small candles up there on the pillars at head height, and so my voice to him must have seemed at first disembodied, rising like smoke out of the darkness. Did he think that God was speaking to him?

"Evening, minister," I said.

"Who's that there?" he answered, craning a flat hand suspiciously to his brow to see me better, as if he had sun in his eyes. He held his other hand across his heart, as if to protect himself from celestial attack.

"It's me, Minister. Sean Logan."

"Oh," he said. "Sean Logan. What are you doing here? As I said before, I am sorry for your loss, Sean Logan."

"I want to consider the arrangements, Minister."

"Well, as I was telling you before…"

"Did you know my father?" I asked.

"I did not," he said. "He took his vacation before my arrival here. I knew of him though."

"He's up at the farm now," I said.

"Good."

"Looking splendid in his coffin."

"Oh yes, I'm sure he does."

"Looking forward to going into the ground."

"I see," said the minister.

"Likes the quiet, gets on with people. I'm sure you know the type. The cemetery here is ideal," I said.

"Well," said the minister. "I thought I had said, but there may be a difficulty there, see Sean."

"Why would that be? My mother is here already. He would want to join her."

"Well," he said, moving up the aisle towards me. "To put it plainly, he was a convicted murderer, Sean. Makes it difficult, you understand, to just put him in the cemetery, like any old Joe." He laughed lightly.

I sighed and folded my arms across my chest. "Maybe I am not being clear. For that I must apologise. For all my education and my having read your Bible from cover to cover, sometimes it's difficult to fully articulate my views."

"Yes..." he said.

"Would you like to sit down, minister?" I pulled him by the hem of his black gown. His knees caught against the front of the pew and he slumped like damp mud off a shovel down beside me. "Now, I should really explain. Understand this if you would: there's a man, my father, in my kitchen and he's lying happily enough in a box made of wood that is a little damp and rather too green. However, he's not uncomfortable. Two days from now I want him to be put in the ground to rest. He's been in the house too long already. It's a more permanent arrangement I'm looking for. The ground I want him in is here, right outside." I helpfully pointed at the entrance to the church. "Somewhere close to my mother's grave. He deserves that." I could hear the wind under the door. "What I am expecting are some words of condolence spoken over his body so that he might be remembered by those who wish to remember. I want him remembered as the good man he was, if possible. Do you understand, minister?"

"Well, as I have said…" I dug deep into my waist pocket, took out various items and placed three gold coins on the back of the pew in front of us. He looked at them. "There's three, which I consider ample. There will be a couple more when it's done. Now," I said. "Is that all settled, Minister? Can we go home and get on with the preparations?"

This minister had a nervous look about his face. He was leaning away from me and his eyebrows were raised in a frown atop his forehead. He still had his Bible gripped hard under the white knuckles of his freckled right hand. He got to his feet, and pulled away. "There won't be a problem," he said, quickly placing the Bible under his arm and scooping the coins into his hand. "But you know, there's no need to make threats." He walked away towards the small door to the side of the altar.

I looked down at my right hand. I had my father's fish knife with its curling head, gripped in my paw. I had taken it out when looking for the coins. I put the knife back in the sheath that hung from my waist. It was momentary inadvertence. I stood up and walked out of the large door at the rear of the church. I left by the same door and walked through the cemetery. I looked around and found the plot where soon my father would find his final place of rest.

CHAPTER 33

The minister was as good as his word. He put on an impressive show and the occasion did not lack dignity. Towards the end, he even spoke some Latin, something that in my opinion is rather unusual in a Church of Scotland ceremony. It may have been Gaelic, my mind was elsewhere. He wore spectacles to read the blessing. When we filed out I was aware of the troubled appearance he wore on his pale brow and it seemed to me every time I stepped near him he turned a shade paler and glistened like a honey nut with that evident coat of light sweat. When I was up close I could smell the pipe tobacco on his tongue. Yet, he had said good words. He had had the sense to tread lightly on the repentant sinner theme and I thanked him for that. I pulled my face close to his and squeezed his limp hand. I noticed the shine of the open pores on his nose. His eyes were too close together. He looked at me as if I was something sharp that could cut him badly. I delivered the promised coins into his open palm that he shuffled slyly into one of his many pockets.

There were people at the funeral service I had not expected. There were even faces I did not recognise. Who goes to funerals? Why do they go? If it is jokes you are looking for. Shelter? Maybe some seeking respite from the cold late November wind. Some to check the nails, make sure the lid was banged down nice and hard. Others, like a lot of those gassing women, would think it safe to turn up now and touch the coffin. The soldier-farmer and his gypsy wife were both dead after all. It seemed unlikely that my father was going to sit up now and bite them. I even

saw Joey and Tom, my old adversaries, lined up outside the Church gate like they had doubt about the wisdom of entering. Mr Shifner sat at the back of the Church, looking much older now, his sideburns streaked with grey. He shook my hand at the door of the Church as he left. "I've not had to buy another book since you left the school," he said.
"I am sorry to hear that, Mr Shifner," I said. "I have a decent library myself now."

My father was deep in the earth, already breaking down into his constituent parts. He was close enough to my mother's grave. Somebody could have made the kingdom of heaven easier to enter by making the ground a little softer. It took two men one and a half days to make a hole deep enough. The walls were like flint. Nevertheless, I did not begrudge the little extra I had to pay to have them dig a decent cavity. I was not of a mind to bury my father sideways just to save a farthing on the gravedigger.

When it was over, Aunt Marion stood by the church door and she too had her share of words with the minister. She said that at his next funeral he might wish to remove the egg from his cleric's bib. Lizzie meanwhile hung behind her and kicked small stones off the step. She was a plain girl, I thought, but then again, in the right light with just the right tilt of her head, she was pretty. Some people were like that; it depended on the light. I was still at the graveside when I became aware of Rory Turner hovering somewhere to my right. His fair hair was long now but he tucked each side back behind his wagging ears. He was wearing dark clothes, his sleeves were too long and the top button of his collarless shirt was tight against his neck. He wore no socks. He looked like he had been dressed by a psychotic blind man but seemed unaware of this fashion calamity. He coughed productively but today there were no graveside projectiles. I looked at him and he looked at me. We looked down at the coffin in the hole. They had not yet filled over with earth. The men would be along shortly with their shovels, beer and sandwiches. After a while, Rory stood tall and put the black hat back on his head. "My condolences," he said and in the same breath walked from the graveside, along the pathway between the slabs of stone. He then gobbed hard against the slim trunk of a rowan tree, his spittle flecking against the red-yellow, puckered berries.

"The tree upon which the devil hanged his mother," I muttered to myself because I had read that somewhere, and then looked back into the grave where my father lay, wedged inside his box.

CHAPTER 34

With my father gone, stiff and buried, to my surprise and with a little shame, my own anguine response was to shed my skin and regenerate myself with a new purpose and direction. I say shame because the last thing I wanted in my life was my father dead as stone in a freezing coffin, no good to no one, but undoubtedly, the effect of his dying was to galvanise me. I found a confidence I did not have before. I was like a man who began to understand what he wanted, who all of a sudden recognized his direction of travel. I have heard since that this is not so unusual when a parent dies; the death seems to remove a shadow and allows the light to filter in.

I set about reroofing the house. This involved stripping off the old Welsh slates, lining the timbers with sarking boards and relaying the restored slates across the top so that they fitted snugly together. The old wooden 'Snake' fences around the pasture field were pulled out and rebuilt. I cleared away the sandy scrub that wasted the earth of the field leading down to the Bombo Burn. I put in some Scottish Blackface sheep, partly to keep the weeds down, albeit typically they might have preferred a more hostile home than the hills of Fife. I supplemented their numbers with half a dozen gorse-eating feral goats who specked the field in their white socks and black charred necks. I then set about rebuilding the wall on the east side of the house with whinstone reclaimed from higher up the burn, in a spot some way before the soil turned to sand. I took a large sledgehammer to the soft stone that lined the west side of the byre, bagged up the chippings and shoveled them onto the track along by the burn. I took down the old gate that stood at the mouth of the farm; we all knew it had never served to keep anyone out, so I replaced it with one fashioned from old roof joists that I cut, sized and treated. The gate now released swung freely open, without a sound or a squeak of protest. I put a steel bolt lock on it. The invaders would have to come over the top and I would just have to shoot them. That's what an Enfield was for. I planted seed potatoes in the field to the east of the house, where I knew the soil was good, and stoned the track from the road to the house, sprinkling the surface with barrowloads of small chips and sand from the shore. Carriage wheels would no longer stick in the ruts. I pulled out the old fire that Aunt Marion had always cursed because it smoked so badly, rebuilt it and mended the cracks in the original chimney with shovels of wet lime. I glowed with pride when there was no trace of black woodsmoke leeching from the lining. Aunt Marion was appreciative; she looked at me as if I were the latest in a short line of deities. I took down the rotten ash trees over the other side of the burn, sawed them into lengths and split the logs. I stacked them in neat rows off the ground to lose their sap and moisture, where they would lie for another year. I laid hands on a Scots Grey cockerel and a posse of Scots Dumpy stumpy-legged hens and constructed a house out of rough wood and a run from torn fishing nets. We took more eggs off them than ever before. Omelettes were back on the menu! We had three horses now, two being good Clydesdale stock, heavy and massive with the plough, they could turn the earth all day. I found good work for these horses, miles around, running the plough through neighbouring fields and I earned a decent amount for it. I discovered in the process that money begets money. Finally, I had the blacksmith cut an iron fish from a steel sheet which he soldered to a stout bar to serve as a weathervane, and he attached it hard against the top of the front gable of the house. Often I would stand beneath it and enjoy the rusted fish as it turned in the freshening breeze, most times blowing south-westerly across the rooftop. The farm took on a prosperous appearance, giving it the kind of rude health that it had not seen for many years.

I was pleased with these achievements. It was good to wander around the farm and see it the way my father would have wanted it to be, its walls dark and solid, copings sharp along the top, its roof neatly tucked against the rafters, slates secure, free of draughts and leaks. The work had done me good physically: I already had my mother's dark, broody looks and these had not faded and I was leaner now than I had ever been. I had a back that was broad and straight.

With all these changes taking place you might assume that I would have moved on in my own mind, but there was much at the back of my thoughts that I suppose I was reluctant to confront. All the roofing and the fencing, the roadwork and the logging, pulling weeds out from gutters, none of it got rid of that need to know more. And when I knew more, I was beginning to recognise that I would have to do more. I would have to settle old scores. If I knew how and by whose hand my mother died, I could not put that to one side and carry on with a stubborn grip on the plough. I had come to recognise that fact. I may even have always known it. With knowledge comes responsibility. I had to take it on in the full knowledge that I knew what I was doing and what it would cost, not like some dumb fool stumbling into an open hole.

I have made reference already to that useful book misappropriated from Mr Shifner's rosewood library titled the *Nuttall Encyclopoedia*. This linen bound heavyweight provided a grand source of incendiary information for a young man entering his late teens with a passing interest in guns and small explosions. I enjoyed firing off the Snider-Enfield. The pleasure was such that I had worked my way through most of the "Boxer" cartridges. That is not to say I wasted any; I did not miss many targets because I was already intent on making sure that every bullet counted. It would be a lifelong philosophy. I shot a seal in the water off Pooly Point and Jacob Snider would have been proud of me, buried down there at Kensal Green Cemetery. It was a moving target after all, dipping in and out of the water, but I popped a steel ball straight between its ears as it craned its neck in search of a glistening mackerel or a tempting sea trout it would never enjoy. In ordinary company killing a seal for idle sport may well be considered by an average gentleman as *not quite cricket*, but I have to say that it was important to me to have some proper sense of what taking a life really meant beyond the abstract notion. Common killers rarely have any sense of what they are doing before they do it. When such a person takes a man's life or brutally rapes a woman or commits some other extremely vile felony some might very properly find that they have no capacity to withstand the effect on mental harmony of all that blood released so intensely in such close proximity. Worse than the mere physical discomfort there is always the unquantifiable complexity of guilt, that cloying excess of conscience. Of course, plenty others who undertake murder or other violence might just as well be snapping twigs off a log for all the feeling they have after their crimes. I felt it was only right that if I was going to kill somebody I had to do my research and discover what emotion I may someday have to deal with. Once aboard the assassin's boat, there are no liferafts and a killer must sink or swim. As it was, I did not feel much at all when I shot that seal. It sank and it was gone. So there was blood in the water. So what? God's peace go with you, dear departing semi-aquatic marine mammal. In my naivete, however, I concluded that my unresponsive conscience was not going to be an especial burden upon my enduring existence as a human being. This was in some ways a surprising and disappointing discovery; what marks us out as civilized human beings is our capacity to recognise guilt, regret and sadness for unconscionable acts. Shooting the seal told me that I had very little to fear in that department. To my mind, I had all the makings of an extremely cold fish: a killer with no conscience. More importantly for now, on a more practical level, I knew well enough that if I was to develop my aptitude for guns and minor explosions, I needed to get my hands on some new Boxer cartridges.

There was an old fellow with a red, purple-veined nose living in Tullis, somewhere near the cemetery. He was not yet in it, but his home was conveniently close. He had round shoulders and short, bandy legs, carried a little too much weight and often wore a blue felt hat with a green bandana. At the time, I did not exactly know where he lived but I knew that it was one of three or four houses near the Church. This man did not do much around the place and was often not seen for weeks at a time, but it was known that he drank a lot of wine, invariably red, which was delivered by horse-drawn coach from Alsace, a busy place to the east of France. Sometimes he had a small delivery of cheeses with his wine. Camembert and smoked Bavarian. He was a man with clear Franco-Prussian pretensions and a taste for wild boar – cured in an Alsace salt and cider mix, I believe, and then added to his despatch. As I came to discover, he did not mind telling you that he knew all there was to know about every little thing you did not even know existed. I realised very early on that if you told him you had three hairs growing out of a mole on the underside of your left buttock he was so sure of himself that he might very well correct you on that. He might say there were four, and you would be wise to check with a reflective glass that you had not miscounted. He represented himself as something close to a walking *Encyclopoedia*. He had a breadth of knowledge that would fill the shelves of old Mr Shifner's rosewood library. I figured that if he was just partly right about some of those things he would know where I might be able to get my hands on some new cartridges for the Enfield.

His name was Mr Hamilton. I found him one night in Tullis village, sat atop the cemetery wall, reflecting on the dead within, one of whom was by then my dear old father. I had circled round the village every afternoon and evening for a week before I stumbled upon him.
"Mr Hamilton? It is Mr Hamilton, isn't it?" I asked, to which he said nothing. "Sean Logan," I said and

198

put out my hand, but he only looked at it as if I had shown him something unpleasant and then turned his head to the side. Not to be discouraged, I sat down beside him. He looked back at me and then away again and I thought of something to say, to break the ice between us. "Can I ask you why you are looking at the cemetery stones with such great interest?"

He said nothing immediately, then wiped the top of his nose with a small finger. "I didn't know I had to ask permission to look at some old graves."

"Do you know *funus* is the Latin word for funeral?"

"Yes," he said.

"And do you know in Japan they pick out the Adam's Apple from the cremated bones?"

"Do they indeed?" he said.

"Yes, they put it inside the urn."

He looked away again as if wishing I were gone. Then his eyes drifted back to me. "Are you like me?" he said. "Do you find the dead an interesting subject?"

"Not really," I said.

"Are you frightened of it?"

"Not as a rule, no, but you can have too much."

"You mean your father?"

"My father, my mother."

Mr Hamilton considered this and then said: "Well, if you must know, I was calculating exactly how many bodies there are in this yard. Including your father and mother." I liked the disrespectful way he called it a *yard*. I could tell he had some wine in him but he was quite lucid. "You see, in this yard, it's easy to count each stone left to right, then count each row left to right, do the appropriate multiplication, then add in the nobodies at the end who have no stone at all."

"Well," I said, "That would give you seventy-nine bodies."

He looked at me with an eyebrow raised in a squiggle and then he smiled. "That may well be. You might cut yourself with all that speed." He tapped his unlit pipe against the wall and it made a clunking sound in the silence. It was wood, a briar pipe cut from the root burl, chosen for its extraordinary ability to absorb moisture and its resistance to fire. "Seventy-nine you say? The number seems a bit large," he said. "But in any event, are you not ignoring something?"

"I don't think so," I said. "It's not my habit to ignore things. Mr Shifner used to say I would be better off if I did because then I would have more time for what was really important. But I find detail around the outside every bit as important as the bit in the middle."

"Some of these bodies are layered," he continued. "You've got them double-stacked, you see. Could be treble-packed, I don't know. You don't know how many you've got underneath the ones on top. See what I mean? So how do you know how many bodies there are in here? Had you thought about that?" Mr Hamilton appeared satisfied with his logic.

"I allowed for double-layering," I said dispassionately, it seemed such a basic point. I moved my face towards him. I did so because I did not like the way he kept on looking away from me and I had learned that the quickest way to get someone's attention was to move yourself into their physical air space. This made them uncomfortable, submissive and receptive. However, Mr Hamilton did not appear uncomfortable or submissive and showed no signs of being at all receptive. "But they're not all double-layered. When I laid my father here to rest not long ago, I didn't want anybody shoving up from below."

Mr Hamilton gave me a look. "Go on," he said.

"So I checked it all out, you see, Mr Hamilton. Turns out there is some regulation about all this. Double-layers is fine. Trebling is not permitted under borough bye-laws. Therefore, the answer to your question is still seventy-nine."

He raised his eyebrows. "Well," he said. "If you're not pulling an old man's leg, I owe you an apology."

"I am not looking for apologies," I said.

"Good," he said and was quiet. "Well, what are you looking for?" he asked, screwing up his eyes.

"It is good that you ask me that," I said, staring straight back. "I am looking for advice."

"Advice? I doubt you need much advice from me."

"I can be more specific: I'm looking for Boxer cartridges and I'm looking for advice about where I might find them."

"What do you want them for?"

"My Enfield. No point having a gun if you're not going to work it."

"Do you like guns?" he asked.

"I like guns."

"Well it's true that you will do a gun no favours by locking it in a drawer," he said. "Enfield you say?"

"Yes."

"Snider-Enfield?"

"The very same," I said and there followed a long silence.

"The one that did Bobby, I suppose," he said very slowly, as if he was weighing out each of his words like they were individual baskets of heavy plums.

I looked at him. "Go on."

"What is it you want me to say?" he said.

"You said 'the one that did Bobby'."

"I may have done."

"You did."

"And if I did?"

"What do you mean by that? I should like to know," I said. The old man hesitated and looked at the briar pipe in his hands.

"Like to know what?" he asked. "Sean isn't it?" I nodded. "What would you like to know, Sean?"

"I've heard of a fellow by that name from my aunt Marion."

"Is that so?"

"She said my father talked about a man called Mad Bob."

"It's a common name," he said.

"Mad Bob or Bobby?"

"It's Bobby Weir she might be talking about," he said. "But his friends call him Mad Bob."

"Well?" I said. "That all fits. Do you happen to know where I might find Mad Bob?"

"It happens I do," he said. "Now, what about the Boxers? The cartridges? Are you not interested in them any more?"

"Of course," I said. "More than ever. I need new ones, you see. I will need a lot."

"I might be able to help you with that," he said. "It may turn out there are other things I can maybe do for you." I raised my eyebrows at him. He was looking at the pipe in his hands again. "You interested in guns then are you?"

"Well, put it this way. When I pull the trigger on an Enfield it's an enjoyable sensation. Something about the feel of the trigger when you squeeze it. And the smell off the barrel when it's fired. That's what I like."

"It's a good gun," he said. "But there are newer, better guns."

I waited for him to speak. Eventually I asked: "You said there were things you could help me with? What did you mean?"

"Oh yes," Mr Hamilton said, half tilting his head towards me. "I think I maybe can. It's probably time that someone did help you." He got to his feet. "It may be best if you come round to my house tomorrow." He walked away and then turned back. "You know my house?"

"Yes, I do," I lied, not wishing to betray my ignorance.

"I've got a lot to show you and some things to tell you," he said, as he looked back at the cemetery and pondered the bodies beneath. "Things that need to be told now." He walked away and disappeared from sight.

CHAPTER 35

Next day, I was around at his house at twelve minutes to ten in the morning, although I cannot be certain. It would have been earlier but I did not in fact know where it was. I had a good idea where it was but that is not quite the same thing. I got the wrong house and was chased from a fat lady's backyard because she thought I was stealing her hens' eggs or had threatened her chastity. The eggs was more likely. She swung her brush broom at me as if whatever threat I posed, it was a real one. I got down there early because I wanted to see Mr Hamilton before he had the chance to have his first glass of Vosges, but when I banged hard on the door, he opened up, already armed with a glass of red-brown Alsace in his right hand.

"You came then?" he said.

"Did I not say I would be coming?"

"You better come in, fella," he said, closing the door behind me.

It was a wide door but very low and I stooped my head to enter. It creaked on its hinges as it snuffed out the light behind me. He ushered me through the dark hallway, along a hard wood floor, into what seemed to be the main room of the house: it stretched from the front of the building to the back and was relatively bright, the morning sun filtering through the gaps between the shutters.

"This is my office," he said. "Do you have an office?"

"No, I don't," I said. "It's certainly big enough."

"I live in here, I suppose. It has to be big. It's my real space, where I have all my things." He waved his arm at the desk by the window. "Organised chaos."

It was indeed a surprisingly large room, dark walls and a wooden floor that echoed under your feet as you crossed it. There were oil painted pictures in large gold frames on the walls, depicting wild animals – leopards, elephants and stags. Behind the picture frames there was an old patterned paper. I had not seen that before except in books depicting the old French King Louis' palace at Versailles, before the revolution. Also some on the walls of the large royal palace in London. Big, thick, velvet, burgundy drapes hung at each side of the window, holding the light out and a little of the heat in, faded along the edges by years of occasional sun. Not that there was much heat in there on this occasion since the stove was out. "Sit down, sit down," he said impatiently as he flicked a cat from a wide cushioned stool in front of his desk. "Hate cats myself. You? Farmers always hate cats, don't they?"

"Not always. They keep the rats down, you see. They can be useful," I said. "Like most things, they have a good side and they have their bad side."

"I'm sure that's true. The *Rattus rattus* and the *Rattus norvegicus*."

"The black rat and the brown rat," I said.

"Did you know they only live a year and then they're dead. Very short, isn't it?"

"It is, if you're a rat," I ventured.

"Usually because they have gone from being the hunter to the hunted. There is a justice in that, when the hunter turns into the hunted. They normally end up as someone else's supper. Have you ever thought what it must be like to be the hunter and later, to have the tables turned on you, to become the hunted?"

"Not very pleasant, I imagine," I said.

"People don't think about these things, but they must. It's all about changing the perspective, seeing things from the opposite end. Like looking down a telescope – it's very different when you look down the wrong end."

"Yes, like the wrong end of a gun," I said.

"Yes."

"You can lose your head." I shifted in my chair. "Am I the hunted, Mr Hamilton?" I paused. "Or am I the hunter?"

"Things are never that clear," he answered, without answering. "And they change. Nothing stays the same."

"I would prefer to be the hunter."

"But, I promised that I could show you something more interesting than cartridges, did I not?" He spoke with a flowing intonation that pitched and fell. It was nearly musical.

"Yes, Mr Hamilton," I said. I sat with one hand on each knee. "It has given me a restless night to think what you were meaning when we last spoke."

"Well, let me show you something then that I have found very interesting and which may give you more restless nights before you are done." He took a large gulp from the glass he held in his left hand and placed it on the blue, leather inlay of the desktop. He lifted an intricately crafted key from his waistcoat pocket and unlocked the bottom drawer of the three-drawer Georgian desk with a mahogany inlaid top. He pulled open the drawer, and it squeaked as it came, as if the drawer was reluctant to release its contents. He took out what looked to be an old, oily cloth, but there was clearly something inside it. He moved his glass to one side and laid the cloth on the leather top of his desk. Carefully he peeled back each corner. Mr Hamilton looked at it affectionately. "You said you liked the Snider-Enfield," he said. "Know what this is?" I shook my head. "It's a close relation. One of the family. An Enfield Revolver." He picked up the gun and looked at it side on. "She's perfectly lovely, isn't she?"

CHAPTER 36

As it transpired, the Enfield Revolver was just the first of many. Each time he disappeared for a week or two, I knew Mr Hamilton would be back with an addition to the family. The strangest thing was, he did not want to keep them. He wanted me to have them and use them. He said there was no point him getting his hands on these beauties and hiding them away in a drawer. He wanted me to take them away up to the farm and make good use of them.

Another thing was the way the Vosges-drinking Mr Hamilton had what he called 'the office' for all his private things. After my visits became a little more regular, it got me thinking that it was high time I had an *office* of my own to house those private discoveries in my life that I was not inclined to share with others. To some degree I was already in a position to offer that level of desirable bureaucracy: I already had a big shed – what had once been a byre, the hay pens were still there, stinking at one end – a shed that I was gradually filling with those little pieces that were assuming importance in the overall direction of my life. This collection of guns was growing and I had to find a home for them. Somewhere I could take them apart and clean them properly and then store them the appropriate way. It was a collection that was growing for reasons I will explain, but first, I had purchased some timber from a merchant in Blairgowrie, and I bought off him an ample supply of screws, nails and other tools and bits of ironware. He delivered them to my door, having said he would be visiting the area anyway. I avoided Fawcett's shop for these supplies because he was a complication; I would be visiting him soon on other matters. For the present, armed with this equipment, I set about making an imposing wall cupboard. It was not difficult, not for a young farmer like myself used to putting iron and wood together and making them do something productive.

In that shed with the big double doors, I had a large table that was heavily topped in granite. The granite had been expensive but necessary to further my growing ballistic endeavours. It was not long before I had reached the evolutionary phase of my apprenticeship in weapons technology where it was not beyond me to cast my own personal bullets. This was not for reasons of pretension or because I had delusions of grandeur; it was simply to allow me to obtain the quantity I required and of the quality necessary for my overall purpose. To tell you the truth, I had no idea how many I would need, so I just kept on making them until I knew I had enough. It was also economical – that is once I had got the hang of it and had reduced the initial wastage. I needed nothing more than a fire, an iron pot and a heavy ladle. What I did was melt down the lead, skim off any crud and bubble it all into a pleasing, silvery texture. Mr Hamilton had quickly become an ardent supporter of my enterprise and was very useful in obtaining moulds for me, special shapes for individual firearms, no challenge was beyond him. I poured the liquid into the moulds and when it cooled the bullets dropped out, easy as that. Well maybe a little harder, but with a degree of learning, not too much harder. Of course, you needed to size and lubricate the bullets, but the whole process I found to be very satisfying. As a result I had more bullets and cartridges in my office than most cunts had wet dreams over.

The cupboard I was building to house my weaponry was supposed to be five feet wide and eight feet high. I paid a second visit to the woodshop in Blairgowrie to obtain more timber, screws and nails. He struck me as a strange sort of person: talked night and day about fishing in the loch and how he loved iroko wood, that all you could buy around here was spruce and elm. When the weaponry cupboard was finished it was easily ten feet wide by twelve feet high with a pine shelf along the top and bottom. I had a modest, wooden stepladder for reaching the top stuff. In the middle of the cupboard, sitting on two strong brackets and appearing like the sun around which the other planets rotated, was my father's Snider-Enfield. Circling it, as if following the numbers of a clock, at one I had the Enfield Revolver, being the first gun I received from Mr Hamilton, with its rugged, all-metal, large trigger look; its warm, cherry wood handle grip sat comfortably in the hand. You could hit your target at twenty-five yards, but with a little care it had a range of up to two hundred yards. I never hit a damn thing at that distance. At the two o' clock position I had to have another family member, the Lee-Enfield, a bolt-action rifle, one that was to become such a standard in the Great War that was coming sooner than we all knew (everybody said it would never happen. It did). With a range of two thousand yards and a ten round magazine, using the Lee-Enfield I could take the spot off a man's nose whilst resting a cup of Darjeeling tea on the barrel. Or nearly. Next I had a Mauser: a semi-automatic pistol, a classic with a pencil thin barrel and a broomhandle grip. At four o'clock I hung the Webley Bull Dog, a small but powerful revolver you could put in your pocket or, if you were a respectable lady with interests to protect, you might keep it in your handbag. The Webley had a revolving 6-round cylinder into which you just slotted the bullets and you could hold it very easily with just one hand. It was a pretty gun, primarily nickel with wooden grips, the type used once, I believe, to assassinate a President of the United States. Good credentials some might say. President Garland was his name - I do not know for sure, but that is what I read somewhere in a periodical newspaper in Mr Shiffner's library. Next I had the gun I have already described, the second that Mr Hamilton put me in possession of, a German four-barreled weapon known as the Reicher. The Reicher had to be for fun-loving aesthetes only; I did not see how you could kill anyone sensibly with it, not unless they were lined up in a row ten feet apart. It was the invention of a madman. Down at the bottom I had the classic Colt pocket revolver, although you would need long pockets to keep the barrel warm; it was the 1849 model with six chambers, and it used cap and ball ammunition, loaded from the front with loose blackpowder and a bare bullet. The underside of the gun body was angled down towards the dark wood grip, as sweet and comfortable in your hand as you could ever hope to hold. You had to cock the Colt each time you fired it and that could make your thumbs throb. You needed tough old paws like I do. It was heavy too. This was not one for the handbag. Going up the left side, I had a Cook & Brother Carbine, a dinosaur in this company with its muzzle-loading musket: for historic interest only. Then came the curvy Devisme revolver, a little nod to the

Frenchman who was actually far better known for all the military swords he used to make; this was a gun forged with elegance and gallic charm and an unusual octagonal barrel. You just had to look at it to know that it was French. You did not need to see the words *Devisme à Paris* engraved along the top flat of the barrel to know its provenance. Finally, a pair of the most brutal guns you ever saw, they never had a name that I could discover but they would strike fear into the toughest opponent: like a rifle, big trigger with a decent wood stock that tucked into the crease of your elbow; then a long breech and two very short barrels, one on top of the other. Big recoil but if you hit the target you would never see it again.

Those were my guns and I kept them in my brand new gun cupboard courtesy of the Blairgowrie timber mill, and I made more bullets and cartridges as the days went by until I had a stock big enough to start a third Afghan war. Of course, I was not the only young man to have had a profound interest in things that go bang. Alfred Nobel was still warm in his grave but luckily for me had spent the best part of his life since 1867 perfecting the invention that was to change the world forever: dynamite. I went to the library in Stirling and obtained a copy of *Pyrotechnia* by Vannoccio Biringuccio, a book that had been around for three hundred years but which contained the basic chemistry essential to a fledgling powdermonkey. I discovered that basic chemistry was still basic chemistry and there was easily enough there to keep me on the straight and narrow so far as bomb-making was concerned. As I mentioned, Mr Hamilton was the source of my growing armament collection. He said it gave him real pleasure to satisfy my curiosity on this subject and to provide me with ever more interesting and varied weaponry. Even books on the subject were not beyond him. So far as the bomb-making was concerned, he obtained some of the ingredients for me and, by trial and error, I put them together: three parts nitroglycerin, one part sawdust (although sometimes I used clay) and a small admixture of sodium carbonate. It goes without saying, it was important to obtain the correct mix: nitroglycerin is shock-sensitive, particularly when it is pure, and it blows up with very little encouragement. You tend to get messy results when you have an unplanned detonation. Once I had the correct mix I could shape it into short sticks and then wrap it in paper. The other thing you had to remember when you stored these sticks was that dynamite boxes have to be turned regularly, otherwise you get pooling when the nitroglycerin sweats. That, I very quickly learned, created a dangerous situation so far as involuntary and undesirable explosions was concerned.

"What are you doing in that shed?" Aunt Marion wanted to know, one day when I emerged blinking into the light after a five hour bullet-making session. "You're spending your life in an old shed," she said. "What's that all about?"
"Hobbies," I said.
"You don't need hobbies," she said.
"Just looking to the future."
"You need time out on the farm, getting the jobs done, fences mended, all that."
"I do all that," I said. "This farm is looking good."
"True but it could look better," she said.
"It's looking a lot better now than it ever did."

She paused before she continued. "That's a big lock and chain you put on the old shed door."

"There are bad people about."

"Nobody comes up here. What are you needing a lock on it for?"

"In the first place, to stop people from going in there."

"And why is that? What needs kept under lock and key?"

"Dangerous material," I said.

"Like what?" I did not answer. "What kind of hobby needs dangerous material?" she said.

"Just the stuff you need on a farm."

"We never used to."

"Times have changed."

"What's it for?"

"To keep us safe."

"To keep us safe?" she repeated. "That all?"

"I've got guns and I've got bullets, Aunt Marion."

"Oh?"

"Don't pretend you didn't know."

"Your business is your business," she said.

"And I intend to use them."

"I hope you know what you're doing."

"You think I don't?"

She hesitated. "I have to say, I'm scared for you," she said.

"Don't be."

"Let's get in for supper, it's cold out here."

The truth is that the work on the bullets and the dynamite and the growing collection of guns, these were the things that were keeping me going. Joey and his friends had always enjoyed teasing me about my jailbird father. They did not have to any more. My father had served more years in jail than I cared to remember. Of course, he never reached the end of that sentence. He was now dead as the dark hole he slept in, a slit in the ground behind the broken wall at the Tullis cemetery where Mr Hamilton combed the bones with his awkward mathematical estimates and calculations. Neither two farthings for his dreams nor a care in the world, I should not wonder. The threads of what had been his bumpy life were disappearing into the dust as fast as light fading at the end of a Michaelmas day. His time was well and truly served. On the other hand, I was twenty years old, I had some stubble on my cheeks and I had a shed housing an eclectic range of international weaponry as well as a selection of home-grown explosives boxed and wrapped in greasy paper. Add to all that, for the first time I had discovered I had a particular interest in a lady. True, she was married to a donkey brain but that did not make me desire her any the less. Marriage was not the same thing as ownership, or so I believed. The naivete of youth. In any event, my existence was surely ready to shake off the brown paper and explode into life. I did not know then that I was not the only dog in the pack with a thirst for revenge. Sometimes you have to learn the hard way.

CHAPTER 37

Sowing chitted potatoes in mid-March is not easy work. Backs are bowed, hands are cut, nails break, sweat drips and tempers fray. The fields are ploughed by horse, then ripped open with long trenches, each four to five inches deep. The base is padded with rich manure scooped from cows, horses, hens and any other livestock, mixed and turned. The chitted tubers are set into the trenches by hand, one at a time, six inches apart, being careful to keep their shoots intact and pointing upwards towards the prospective sunlight. The fields are packed with busy farmers, their bottoms in the air, cursing, laughing, sweating and sometimes fighting. The children are out there too, in their open shirts and brown pants, full of gaiety and noise, despite being roped in like the women, the infirm and the marginally lunatic and forced to work. There is the occasional flash of colour – yellow or even red – off somebody's clothing, and sporadic shouts or laughter carry down to the next field where others sometimes lift their heads to ask what the hell are they gawping at. There is the intermittent whiney of an awkward nag and the sound of a hoof scraping at the ground.

The Logan farm had three fields ploughed, turned and ready for sowing, each encased by an old hawthorn hedge along the boundary. The neighbours had fields of their own, all in varying states of readiness. Some, more work-shy or behind with their preparations, had stretches little more than half-ploughed or half-manured. Others looked fondly over their land, but they were so far behind in their preparations they could do nothing but daydream of when the ground might be good enough to take a flowering tuber. The truth was you could bury silver in some of that grassland and you would harvest nothing more than rust and a sore back. In their hearts these people knew that the earth of their barren fields would see another season without the bounty of a harvest. Nevertheless, come the first day of the third week in March, the families from all the farms would come together and, as a kind of unit or cooperative, would work their way round between the hawthorn hedges and the makeshift fencing, sowing the potatoes as they went. Any field not ready by the time they got to it would be passed by for another year. So it came about, that those from many miles around gathered at the Tullis village hall where they set about discussing which of the many fields were ready for sowing; and planning which to sow first, which to sow last and which ones they had not the slightest intention of sowing at all.

I attended the meeting. The village hall was an austere, wooden rectangular box with a leaky roof and rough timber cladding along one side. I sat there with Aunt Marion, rolling her eyes like a dizzy trout, something she did a lot these days, and somewhat clumsy Lizzie too on the other side of the table. There was the usual round of cursing and cynicism over which fields were ready and which were not. In the end it was agreed to take on the worst field first and that was to be found in a shady, sunken spot, penned by an old rope fence that the sheep took to eating. The field was flooded at one sloping corner by the heavy rain of several weeks before. It was because part of the field was still full of water that there was debate as to whether it could or should be sowed at all. It was owned by a one-time infantry soldier and his toothless wife. When she smiled it was like looking into an empty purse. He prided himself on his military service: three years in a canteen near Carnoustie and a dishonourable discharge for an incident with a small animal. The nearest he had come to a weapon of mass destruction had been the metal spoon he used to ladle the soup. This fact – which was common knowledge amongst the villagers – you would think might have lent a moderating effect to his frequent wartime nostalgia.

He begged them to sow his waterlogged field. "As a war hero, the least I deserve is a little support when the battle is done." His wife nodded her head and smiled gums like velvet curtains across the hall. "Yes," he said, "the field is flooded, but just one corner mind, and the rest is ploughed and ready!" He looked around him. "The rest is dry enough, soil's good enough. Boggy in places I grant you. Just a little. Not altogether pleasant, yes, but come on, fair's fair, just a little work!" He went on, "It's a small field – smaller than it would have been if it hadn't been flooded at one end." He ground his eyes into mine when I looked up at him. "I'm an old man," he said. "We're in this together, aren't we?" He stopped and gulped down the rest of his morning beer.

These protracted discussions meandered to their conclusion and, once resolved, the community separated into its constituent groups and launched themselves like swirls of hail upon the many fields. The sowing might take a week, depending on the weather, their state of readiness and their willingness to work. Their owners fought their cussed battles with one another along the way; one would be dissatisfied at the way in which the sowing was conducted and the amount of effort that was expended. Others would share those grumbles and make up a few more.

Keira was also at the village hall, but she wore a dark, hooded cloak and held herself at the far side where the light was poor and where people would have to come up close before they could know it was her. Her day had not started well. That morning, expecting her husband to join in for the sowing, she had been surprised to find him in the yard, mounted early on his grey horse just as the sun was rising. She stood by the front door, not yet dressed. She asked him where he was going.

"Business elsewhere," he said, leaning down and tightening the horse's girth.

"What about the sowing?" she said.

"What about the sowing?"

"We have fields here."

"I know we have fields here."

"They need to be sown."

"Oh," he said, picking at his teeth with a fingernail.

"With potatoes."

"I am familiar with the potato," he said.

"Well?" she said, but she knew what was coming.

"Well I have pressing business elsewhere."

"Who'll do our fields?"

"I can see your difficulty," he said, cupping his whiskered chin. "I can see your problem." He steered his horse down towards the gate. "But there is fuck-all I can do about it."

She had learnt during their short married life that her husband had shortcomings and she would work her way around them. That is what you did in a marriage.

219

You had to let him think he had his way and then just get to where you were going but by a different route. None of that had worked out. She reckoned there was injustice; the wrong she felt made her angry and went way beyond the usual politicking. She knew she should hold herself back and she knew he would probably beat her if she did not. She could not stop herself from shouting after him. "You have no right to leave me here!"

He turned his horse around and moved slowly back towards her until his shadow lay like a grey slab across her. With the low sun behind him she strained to see his features or even to gauge his reaction. She was not so deluded that she thought his face would appear warm and generous. The sun behind gave him a breath of hazy halo as he sat up there on that horse, bearing down upon her. She tried to keep her eyes on him. His horse moved side on to her. It was fat and over-grassed and there was mud caked down one side of his shaggy, unclipped hind leg. The horse was called Marty. Marty released wind as he stood there in front of her. The horse skitted nervously on the spot, at which point Calum swung his crop down across Keira's face. She had been around Calum long enough to learn that speed of reaction was sometimes critical. She was quick to pull her head back from the arc of his strike. It was just the very thin end of the black leather tip that struck the lower part of her cheek.

"There's something you ought to understand," he said, still on his horse, but leaning well forward in the saddle, pointing his crop at her. "Because we seem to be on the verge of something unpleasant here." She heard the leather creak under him. "I'll be there," he said. "When it suits me to be there. I don't need you telling me when. I don't need you telling me what I am and what I am not. I hope you're understanding me? I want no more of this nonsense. Is there anything unclear about what I just said?" He turned the horse and rode a short distance. "I'll be away for the week," he said.

"A week?" she repeated.

"Just depending on how things turn out." He cracked the riding crop against Marty's neck and the shaggy beast lurched heavily forward.

When Calum rode off, having lashed her face with the tip of his crop, Keira had to confess that her first thought was that those sodding potatoes could go mash themselves in a piss pot. It was his choice to do nothing. His choice if the field did not get sown. They would see how he felt about it when mid-winter came and the home spud was firmly off the menu. She enjoyed the thought of him regretting his decision. However, on reflexion, the adage that revenge was a dish best served cold did not appeal to her in the least: revenge was best served now, not some time in the future when the reasons why and what for were long since forgotten. Once she had cleared up the cups and plates she had hurled across the floor to assuage her anger after he had gone, she began to think more clearly. If she did not get the potatoes sown then nobody else would and there was only one person who would suffer when he manifested his fury. She thought to herself that she might as well go along and lend a hand and that way the fields would be done. She might just avoid a beating for which, come the day, she would be grateful. She was saddened by her own weakness, her inability to stand her ground against the brute.

Having rationalised her situation to such good effect, she pressed some ointment against her cheek to bring down the swelling and smeared some powder paste upon it to make it less obvious. She then set off, hooded, on foot, for the village hall. When she arrived, the place was busy and the meeting had already started. Seated in the gloom of the far wall, she listened to an old soldier, who most people laughed at, pressing his case to have them sow his field. When he finally sat down she hoped he would get his way. He saluted them with a deep slug from his beer pot. From her shadowed seat, she saw me there, close to the front, listening to what people had to say. A strong-looking boy with dark hair, she might have thought. At least I like to think so. Maybe she saw something good about this boy, this man. Yet, the more she looked the more it became apparent - at least I hope it did - that there was kindness and intelligence in my eyes; I suppose they were always quick, looking round, like dry sponges absorbing everything. She may have noticed the slightest hook to my nose, which I have to say, in the right light, is not so unattractive, and the long, dark hair against my collar. It would be almost black in that grey place.

Did she think back to the day I arrived at the house, when the fishing was foremost in my mind until I saw her naked leg through the window? Did she remember me then? Did she have any recollection at all? It seemed unlikely. She had known my story, surely, as everyone else did in these parts. She, of all people, could empathise with someone whose mother had been through that kind of hell.

We spewed out into the waiting fields and began the annual sowing. The sun rose in the sky and settled a little early Easter heat on our backs. In went the chitted potatoes and a light layer of soil to top them over. The process was repeated for many hours before we stopped for a bread and ham lunch and some flat, watery beer from one of the wooden flasks.

I will confess that I had seen Keira more than once across the field. The hood had dropped to her shoulders and the sight of the red bandana on her head had sent a flicker of heat through me. I had not seen her since that morning, some time ago, before the fishing that ended so disastrously. It occurred to me that whilst I had enjoyed the intimacy of her naked flesh that distant morning, I had never yet spoken a single word to her. It was a situation I would have to rectify. I wondered if she was alone or if her husband was out there too. I had not seen him since the day of the fishing trip, some time ago, but I knew too well that he was not the type to enjoy honest toil.

Towards the end of the day, with the light fading just a little, I wandered over to one of the sheep sheds at the bottom of the field nearest the track that wound up from the village. There was water there in a huge rusty basin. I took off my shirt and threw it over a wooden hayrack. I washed down my arms and hands with the cold water. My skin was refreshed and tingling. I drank from the flask and lifted my shirt from the hayrack. I put on the shirt and I used my fingers like a comb, running through my wet hair. I

223

made my way out of the shed and back up the field, avoiding the wet pools to one side.

Aunt Marion was waiting, Lizzie close by. "Where did you take off to?"
"Just having a wash," I said.
"He likes to keep clean," said Lizzie.
"I didn't know it was a crime," I said.
"The ladies like a clean boy," said Lizzie.
"Who said anything about ladies, Lizzie?"
Lizzie pointed at a girl with a red bandana down the field. My eyes followed hers.
"Don't be daft," I said, but I did not look away from the red bandana.
"If you've finished discussing your ablutions, we might as well go," said Aunt Marion. "I'm not spending the night out here just so you can smell pretty."

We walked from the field, through the creosoted gate, just me, Lizzie and my Aunt Marion. I looked up to the top field, searching for the red bandana, but saw none. I displayed my petulance by kicking a stone off the track that ricocheted into the green hawthorn. A bemused thrush leapt out startled with wild, flapping wings. Aunt Marion and Lizzie turned to look at me. Lizzie laughed and Aunt Marion cut me with a glacial look. Sometimes they seemed to forget that I was now a man, not the awkward schoolboy I used to be. I looked up at the darkening sky and began to jog down the broken track ahead of them.

CHAPTER 38

The next day came quickly enough. The same morning melee of jostling people, colour, children dashing between fields like leaves blown in a storm, dropping baskets, spilling tubers. I knew at some point, amongst all the coming and going, my path would likely cross with hers and I spent the day in anticipation of that moment. You would think I might have been better prepared. It was not until I was on my way to lunch that I more or less walked into her by the old stone wall that bordered the copse behind the increasingly muddy Tullis track. She seemed to be heading back to the fields, maybe having eaten already. She did not say anything, just lowered her head a little and I think she was going to walk right past me.

"Hello?"

"Yes?" I looked at her and admired the brightness in her eyes most of all. They had a clarity, a kind of purity; that is what I see looking back now.

"You don't remember me?"

"Your name is Logan."

"Sean. We have met before, I think."

"Have we?" she said. She was looking up at him. "I do remember a pushy fisherman."

"Better a pushy fisherman, I suppose, than not remembered at all," I said. "We weren't introduced."

"Were we not?"

"No." I thought I detected a trace of a smile at the corner of her mouth. Was she teasing me? There was a hint of that, but I have a good thick skin or I have a poor sense of humour, so I was not for giving up. "I remember you. I have a clear picture of you in my mind from that occasion."

"You have a picture in your mind?"

"Yes."

"Well, that's a good place for a picture. You have a good memory then?" she said.

"For the important things, I think I do."

"Important things?"

"Take butterflies, for instance."

"Butterflies?"

"Yes."

"What do you know about butterflies?"

"Do you know the three most beautiful butterflies ever to have existed?"

"No, I do not."

"You may need to know sometime."

"I'm very grateful," she said.

"The Blue Morpho, absolutely glossy and instantly mesmerizing, it has a wingspan of up to 8 inches."

"Yes?"

I wondered if I was boring her. "The Leopard Lacewing," I said. "Orange and yellow across the wings and the edges are like black boomerangs edged in white."

"Boomerangs? I don't think I have heard of such a thing," she said.

"It's a flat stick."

"A flat stick?" she repeated.

"It spins about an axis that is perpendicular to the direction of its flight. You throw it and it's supposed to come back to you."

"I see."

"It's not foolproof in my experience."

"You have your own?" she asked.

"Yes, I make boomerangs."

"Is that easy?"

"I am gaining expertise. The Egyptians made them first. Out of bones. They're not at all new. They've been around for a long time." I paused. How did I get on to boomerangs? It was all going wrong.

"Is it easy to remember these things?" she asked.

"Most things are easy when you turn your mind to them."

She was about to move on past him but she hesitated. I could see she was slim with a narrow, lovely waist.

"Three?" she said.

"Three what?"

"The three most beautiful butterflies that ever existed. What is the third?"

I looked into her eyes. "You," I said. "You are the third of the most beautiful butterflies."

She flushed a little when I said that, but I was not trying to cause any embarrassment and the words came out that way without me even thinking on them. I flushed around the ears and felt my own embarrassment.

"Thankyou Mr Logan. It's a nice thing to say."

"Sean Logan."

"Well, *Sean* Logan," she said, moving away. "Enjoy your boomerangs and your butterflies."

"Have you hurt your cheek?" I asked.

"It's a scratch," she said. She turned and walked away.

"You haven't told me your name," I called after her.

"It's Keira," she said, turning at the last moment. "I'm sure you knew that already."

"I'll be here tomorrow," I said. "There are other butterflies I wish to discuss."

"More beautiful than me?" she said.

"Oh no," I said. "Not even close!" I watched the back of her as it became smaller and disappeared from

227

view. Something had happened to me and I was not very sure what it was.

CHAPTER 39

Next day I saw her, but by design or chance, I was unable to find an excuse to speak to her. It was a pleasant, dry spring morning with some soft, uninteresting cloud overhead and a gentle, south-easterly breeze coming off the firth. Standing still, the air would have chilled you, but we were bent over the trenches, sowing and more sowing, and far from being cold, I would happily have removed my shirt. I worked through the morning on my own. Aunt Marion had stayed at home, complaining of flu that made her bones ache and her head spin. Lizzie remained to look after her but I knew Aunt Marion would not make an easy patient. Any nurse, even the 'lady with the lamp', would have struggled to contain her.

Late mid-morning, I bumped into Keira on her way back from one of the sowing fields. She had on a long, green woollen dress, partially covered by a white apron, with a white collar at the neck and a dull red cloak draped across her shoulders.
"I was thinking you were avoiding me today."
"Why would I avoid you?" she asked. "I don't know you well enough to avoid you."
"You've no reason," I said and she smiled. She was wearing nothing in her hair today. She had it in a simple bun but several dark lengths had fallen free and they dangled in front of her ears. I could just see her teeth when she smiled, and they were white and even. Her lips were light pink and as they met she occasionally pushed them together, almost like a pout.
"Are you thirsty?" I said.
"I have my own water," she answered.

"Would you like some of my water?"

"What is so special about your water?"

"Mine is taken from the Bombo Burn, water milked from the hills. There's no cleaner water for miles." She took the flask from me in her right hand. Her fingers were long and slim, but grey with earthlines from working the field, and the tips of our fingers touched as I passed it to her. She lifted the flask to her lips and tipped. I watched her throat move as she swallowed. The skin was white and intoxicating. I looked down her neck and I thought of everything that lay there. I will admit I had these thoughts but I tried hard to push them away. She lowered the flask and as she did so, the wind blew more strands of her hair forward. With one hand she pushed them back. The space between us was no wider than the width of her body. I imagined the gap like it was a ravine and I was looking for a bridge.

"What other butterflies are there?" she asked.

"There are many," I said. "Some don't even have names yet."

"Can you be a butterfly if you don't have a name?"

"If I can't see you, do you exist? You're clearly a philosopher."

"If I was a butterfly what would I be?"

"That's difficult," I said. I was close to her now and I could smell her scent. If it was a fruit, to my mind it was like blueberry. It had some subtlety, a light, sweet must, and I liked it more than I can say. "There's one with wings of orange, red, black, white and brown and it's called the *Painted Lady*."

"Is that what I am, Sean Logan? The painted lady?"

"Well, there is no doubting its beauty." I liked so much that she had spoken my name, I felt a warmth radiate from the words. "You can see them in

Australia all flying together, migrating south in huge numbers, all flying wing-to-wing, lighting up the sky."

"What else do you know about butterflies?" She asked.

"I know they are like women. They are not always what they seem."

"And I wonder what you mean, like women, you say."

"You cannot judge a butterfly by its colour."

"Why can you not? You have to judge it by something," she said.

"Because, for all their fantastic colour, their wings deceive you."

"In what way do they deceive?"

"They have no colour at all. They are transparent."

"But I have seen butterflies with coloured wings. Blue and gold."

"Ah, but they are transparent. The pigment of the wing absorbs the light, but the reflective structure of the wing splits the light into different colours. The wing itself has no colour." I thought maybe I had bored her to death, but she did not yawn, or laugh, or quietly pass away.

Softly, she said: "Is butterflies all you know about?"

"No," I said, enjoying the gentle laughter in her eyes. "I know about snails too."

"What do you know about snails that would interest me?"

"The thing about the humble gastropod is that it moves very slowly," I began.

"That is not very interesting."

"Well, that is not the *most* interesting thing."

"What *is* the most interesting thing?" she asked.

"The most interesting thing is the love dart," I said.

"The love dart?"

"Yes." I held up two imaginary snails. "Think of two perfectly sensible snails. They fall in love. The church has blessed their marriage and on their wedding night, with some eagerness they take to the bridal suite."

"I hope you are not going to make me blush," she said.

"There they are," I said. "Two snails circling the bed in all their slime, when suddenly, each of them shoots a dart into the other."

"What?"

"They shoot an arrow into each other. Across the bed."

"Why would they do that?"

"You have heard of *Cupid's arrow*?" I said.

"I thought that was to do with love."

"This is love," I said. "They are *in* love. When they go on to make actual love to each other the dart - or *Cupid's arrow*, whatever you wish to call it – the dart," I said, "serves to enhance the reproductive capabilities."

"To make baby snails?" she said. I nodded. She stood there in silence for a short while. "How do you know these things?"

"I read a lot. I subscribe to a snail journal."

"You're teasing me now."

"Maybe."

"Do you study?"

"I talk to people who know about snails."

"And you study snails?"

"I study snails minutely in their homes at night with a magnifying glass."

I looked right at her. I could see every hair on her head as it hung against her small, neat ears, above those eyes that were so big, so blue-green and round, shining out at me, still clear and sharp with a flinty hardness to them. Yet, it seemed to me what was hard could be fragile too. The look of fine china. Bang it down too harshly, maybe it would shatter into a hundred pieces.

"You're strange," she said.

"Fungus is strange. I'm not strange."

"Strange in a good way," she said.

"I will settle for that," I said. I looked into her eyes. "Maybe you know something about me but what do I know about you?"

"Not very much, I should think," she said, looking down at her feet. "There's not much to know."

"I think I know a little about who you are," I said, scrutinizing her.

"I doubt that," she said, looking away from me. "It's not in your books."

"Sometimes a person's eyes tell you as much as a book."

"You do eyes as well?" she said, now looking straight back at me.

"It's just an observation."

"You won't see much in my eyes."

"But I do," I said.

She was quiet for a moment. "You will see nothing but tears."

"That's sad," I said. "But I have seen through the tears."

She looked away from me. She *was* sad, even nervous, and she stepped back. "I think it is time I was going."

"Do you know snails are not so different from us?"

"That is another strange idea."

"It is well known that before they fire the dart they also do a small dance to get to know each other better. They circle around each other, sometimes for up to six hours, as long as it takes really."

"Why is that?" she asked.

"Because they want to touch, bite, to stroke and so on. You know the sort of thing. It's quite sensual."

"I see."

"I hope I'm not embarrassing you?"

"Not at all."

"All this happens," I said, "long before they fire the darts at each other."

"Do you think I'm a snail, Sean Logan?"

"I only mention it because you asked to know the most interesting thing about snails," I said.

"You are right, I did. I think you kept your promise," she said and smiled.

She began to walk away from me, but I held her in my gaze, and she answered my prayer by turning her face back towards me. "Do you like fish?" I asked.

"Still the fisherman?" she said.

"Not in the sea but with a rod and a line?"

"My brother used to fish a lot. I never did."

"You never liked it?"

"Not so much. I never learnt. It brought me bad memories."

"Well come with me tomorrow," I said. "I'll teach you properly."

"Don't you care what people think?"

I ignored her question. "It has to be very early. They won't miss us for a morning."

"They might," she said. "And people talk. How will you cope with that?"

"I'm asking you fishing, that's all. I do not plan to assault your virtue."

"Virtue?"

"I will knock on your door at six," I said. "I will guarantee you a trout."

"A trout?" she repeated.

"Guaranteed!"

"And the talk doesn't worry you?"

"It's only fishing."

"And my husband?" she said, the words like heavy frost.

"I'm not bothered about him," I answered.

"He may answer the door. What then?"

"It seems unlikely," I said, stepping closer towards her. "He's gone north, is what I heard."

"You've done some research then?"

"I was always a good student."

She nodded her head and smiled gently, pushed her hair behind her head and then moved away without a further glance.

CHAPTER 40

Sometimes I had a sense - I had done for a while - that I was being watched. It was like being caught in the fringes of a shadow that keeps changing the light, sparkling bright and dark, but every time you look up you cannot see it. It seemed as if it was always there, but search as I might, there was never any trace that it had been. I did not know who would wish to waste their time watching me or why. Not Calum Wilson, he knew nothing of me. Not those school goons, I had long since seen them off. My life was surely no more interesting than the perambulations of one of my dopey, skittish Blackface sheep. Sometimes less interesting I would say. On occasions, I might hear a noise, nothing much more than a twig breaking or a branch flicking or a flash of unusual light against a wall. Sometimes, I thought I heard stone crunching underfoot or the click of a shoe against a twig or a horse sending out a startled neigh. On one occasion I thought that someone had been looking in to my shed through one of the broken slats of the building. It seemed to me I could see some trace of a boot print in the mud where someone might have stood to peer through the broken timber. I filled the offending gap with a mix of black tar. Then again, there was no evidence to support this idle speculation. I had not seen a single person close by or hovering at my shoulder. Nobody seemed the least bit interested in either following me or looking at me. I had seen no suspicious behaviour whatever. There had been no gates left open, no locks tampered with, no hens flapping their flightless wings at the late night intruder, no signs at all to bring this man, me, to the conclusion that anyone was taking the least bit of interest in my day to day existence. Yet, that did not stop the niggling suspicion that someone was *on my tail.* Once bitten by paranoia, every shadow contains a shaft of menace. I looked over my shoulder many times through the day, like there was a bogey impersonating and mocking my every move. I took to peeking out of the keyhole on the shed door before I emerged, just in case there was somebody out there who bore me a modicum of ill will. I double-checked my guns and triple-counted my bullets before I turned in at night and same again the next morning. Yet there was nothing to indicate that anything was amiss and slowly, I lowered my guard.

This day in the second half of March, the sun was not yet fully risen but traces of yellow light already spilled like a gauze across the endless sky. As I skirted around Tullis on my young horse, a shoeless chestnut gelding called Master Henry, he skittered on the new macadam road that now stretched along the top path, his hooves unused to the altered sensation of the surface. I had chosen to take the longer route by the wider track in order to enjoy the freshness of the morning. Perhaps it was to ensure that I was not being followed; or perhaps at the back of my mind was the wish to put off my encounter, not through any lack of conviction on my part, but because I knew even then where it was likely to lead.

I had a decent rod with me, a single length maybe a little over six foot, made of a lightweight bamboo with a line made of horsehair. A lot of fishermen will tell you that when you fish for trout you need a rod with this kind of style or that sort of length and that these things are very important to a successful outing on the water. I do not believe any of it. Just give me a slice of whippy bamboo and a few lengths of horsehair. As for bait, worms would get you nowhere. For a fly, I fastened a piece of red wool with a couple of cock feathers taken from the coop. The trout would find it irresistible. I was largely self-taught in the fisheries department. I learnt all I needed to know about the subjects of rod, line and hook-making and the complexities of different flies employed for different times of year, from an afternoon poring over *The Treatyse on Fysshynge with an Angle* published at the time of the Tudors in 1496. Fish were timeless but I had depth to my learning for I had also read *The Practical Angler* by W.C. Stewart just before Christmas the previous year. Clearly I was the first - and may have been the best ever - armchair fisherman. However, as matters turned out, all this fine knowledge gleaned from the poorly lit library in Stirling and other repositories was to be so much wasted effort. In the first place, in spite of all my talent I rarely hooked anything particularly edible. In the second place, on this occasion, fishing was swiftly taken off the agenda.

By the time I reached the house it was half a breath more than ten minutes past six in the morning and the steadily increasing light now hung across the grey-slated rooftop. I sat there on Master Henry, close by a privet hedge swamped by a choking growth of holly, admiring the scene with a small shudder of anxiety never far from the surface. I had a premonition that something – everything – would happen, followed by a very real sense that absolutely nothing would occur. There was little change that I could see since the last time I had been here. The windows, the eaves, the walls all carried with them the same sense of broken decay and dissolution. There were no longer great pools of muddy water around the house but the windows were still smeared with grime and, as before, the insides were hidden from view. My route had brought me to the front of the house and I pressed my heels against Bob's heavily coated sides and he skittered forward.

There was no sign of life. There was no smoke coming from the chimney. There was no pink bunting on the porch. There was no criss-cross guard of honour. I dismounted and tied the reins to a metal hook sunk into the stone wall. I put the rod against the wall together with an old bag filled with hooks, flies, feathers, a fish-knife, cotton thread, scissors, lump of stale bread and other toolery of mass piscine destruction. What if Calum had returned? He was an unpredictable fellow. I patted Bob's neck with one hand and it was warm from the ride but not sweated. I let him nuzzle the palm of my left hand then rubbed the flash of white between his huge eyes. I walked towards the door and with each step I took, the golden sky above me seemed a little lighter. I stood facing the door and then knocked hard three times.

CHAPTER 41

I stood there, immovable as a deep-rooted tree. I had knocked three times, then another three, and then another three. Not a sound stirred except the heavy beat of my heart booming in my ears. I stepped back from the door and sidestepped over to the wall where Master Henry stood and shook his mane. I looked to the left and to the right and then untied the reins that tethered him.

I did not see her that day or the next. I tried not to look out for her but every time I looked up from working the field her image was in my mind and her voice was in my ears. The conversations we had had simply replayed themselves over and over. I thought maybe I had misread the situation. I knew I was capable of pursuing my own objectives with a single-mindedness that sometimes eclipsed the sensitivities of others. I could misperceive a situation, read in things that did not exist, leave out things that did. I could see steps along the path and I took them one at a time, no hesitation, because they would take me where I wanted to go. Once there was wind in my sails there was no stopping me. Other cunts would let me pass, they would stand aside, because I knew where I was going and I would mow straight through them if they did not shift.

On the third day I did see her. There was less work to do in the fields, the sowing was nearing the end. I put the saddle on Master Henry and rode over to the Wilson house. Maybe it was a stupid thing to do; I had not challenged too many brain cells over that decision. How was I going to explain myself to

Calum Wilson, should he have been there? Invite him fishing? That cut very little ice the last time, I remembered. Still, I was not for stopping, hesitating, reviewing or rethinking or any other sensible activity that might have stopped all this before it begun. I rode into the Wilson yard, tying Master Henry to the same iron ring as I had before. This time I stood at the door and was ready to beat it down, but as it happened, I did not have to wait long before it opened.

She had on a white cotton gown, very simple in its presentation, embroidered at the shoulders and belted tight around her waist. Her skin was smooth and her eyes sparkled beneath the dark hair that hung down against her shoulders. She wore no shoes and just a light pashmina shawl that covered the bottom half of her face, and draped its way across her shoulders.
"I came before," I said.
"I know."
I looked at her. "Are you hiding from me?" As if by way of answer, she lowered the pashmina from her face and I could see a blue cloud heavy across her cheek, spreading from her eyes. In the gloom I had not seen that both eyes were dark and heavily bruised.
"Good God," I said. "Who did this to you?" I asked.
"It was a wooden paddle," she said.
"Whose wooden paddle?"
"My own,"
"You did this to yourself?"
"With my husband's help. Don't worry for me. The worst is past."
"Is he here?" I said.
"No," she said. "He is not here."
"Where is he?"

241

"He came. He went."

"Why?"

"He didn't like what he saw."

"He's a fool."

"I won't argue."

"He's lucky he's not here."

"Would you beat him with a wooden paddle?" she said. "After all, it is the fashion."

"Was it because of me?"

"Oh no," she said. "He knows nothing of you. What is there to know?"

"Has he beaten you before?"

"It is not unheard of."

"Why? Why does he beat you?"

"He's got a thing about paddles."

"Does he not love you?"

"In his way," she said. "I'm his canoe."

I barely heard her. "A man who beats his wife has no love in his life."

"You say that, but you know about fruit?" she said.

"What do you mean?"

"Fruit is seldom rotten all the way through."

"Some fruit," I said, "is full of maggots."

By this time, I had crossed more than the threshold. I had entered the house and was close upon her. The moment came as if by design but it was spontaneous and unintended. In just one move, I had stepped forward and I had taken hold of her and held her in my arms. I pulled her tight against me and with the fingers of the other hand, gently I stroked and caressed the side of her face. Her eyes never left mine. I wanted to squeeze her but she needed gentleness. I brought my lips against hers and pressed them one upon the other, tasting the sweetness of her

242

mouth. I sensed her lips part and give way to mine. There seemed no need for words now, but there were words aplenty spinning round inside my head, a torrent of questions and ten sheets of empty answers. I pulled my head back from hers and looked close into her eyes. Without a word, she brought her lips back to mine once more and we never spoke another word about trout or line or fly or rod or Calum or whiskers or Master Henry in the yard or guns that kill or Mad Bob or sharks full of maggots. I kicked the door closed with the back of my scuffed, leather boot. The light dissipated against my back as she led me through the house.

If I had not been so consumed by what tender pleasures lay before me, I might have chanced another look behind. I might have seen a figure peering down at us from the track along which I had just travelled. I might have noticed some chance movement that would have signified an intruder or identified the silent recorder of these current events. I may have even seen the face of that person as he masticated a strip of loose leaf chewing tobacco, intermittently spitting a chunk of juice against the broken tufts of grass by his feet, his face insinuating itself between the boughs of a largely leafless, Rowan tree – the magical tree that according to mythology protects us all from the evil of malevolent beings. But I did not look back and I did not see the fat body rise.

CHAPTER 42

I went to interview Mr Fawcett – to find out what he could tell me. I had put off the moment long enough. It was early but the front steps to the shop had already been swept. I opened the door and that triggered a bell, somewhere in the gloom at the back. As I closed the door behind me, Mr Fawcett's face leaned out from the small room behind the counter. Seeing me, he called "With you in a minute," and disappeared back into the recess. When he emerged he was wearing his apron; black with a white stripe. "Morning to you Sean. What can I do for you?" he asked.

I approached the long counter, a series of planks spliced and glued together. I stood before Mr Fawcett, square on. "Customers in Buckhaven," I said.

He looked at me, puzzled, from the other side of the counter. "You'll have to explain," he said. "I don't know what you mean."

"You have customers in Buckhaven, don't you?"

"Well, yes," he said. "Not uniquely Buckhaven."

"Customers and the occasional acquaintance."

Mr Fawcett wiped his hands against his clean apron. "I'm sorry. Are you needing more nails?" he asked.

"Nails?" I said.

"Yes. Or wire. I have a new three-strand alloy wire. Very ductile."

"Your wire doesn't interest me today, Mr Fawcett."

"This is a hardware shop," he said. "If you don't want nails or wire, or anything else, then I don't know what you're doing here."

"I think I can help you there."

"Yes?"

"At my father's funeral I had to remind you that we all have responsibilities. Do you remember that?"

"Yes."

"Today I want you to think about your responsibilities."

"I don't understand," he said.

I walked to the end of the counter, casting an eye through the gap and into the recess. I could see a tall, green chair with a buttoned cushion and a high back. Mr Fawcett followed my eyes from his own position. "Is there something the matter?" he said.

I looked towards Mr Fawcett, leaving one hand on the counter. "We could talk for hours about this, but I don't have hours. Instead, I have a small experiment that I want to show you," I said. I extracted a package from the large, outside pocket of my jacket. I placed it on the counter.

"I have to get the shop ready. I'll be opening soon."

"This won't take long, Mr Fawcett," I said as I opened up the package. "We have things to talk about while I set this up for you." I pushed down the edges of the paper to reveal a large pile of what looked like tea.

"What is that?" he asked.

"A little while back, you had a visitor in your shop, Mr Fawcett."

"Did I?"

"You did. Must have been fifty years old or so. Something like that. Red hair but perhaps not a lot left. Thinning. That's what happens. He came into your shop, Mr Fawcett. He sat down in that tall, green chair through there," I indicated the recess. "He made himself comfortable."

"I don't know who you're talking about," he said.

"I'm told he came from Buckhaven?"

245

"I know many people from Buckhaven."

"I don't think you would have a man sit in your nice clean, green chair if you did not know who he was." His eyes moved to the left and then to the right, down at the counter, then back at me. I knew there was something he could say, something he could tell me, if I could only push him that far. I ran a trail of the tea from one end of the counter to the other.

Mr Fawcett looked unhappy with me. "What are you doing?"

"He may have had red hair. Is that jogging your memory, Mr Fawcett? He may of course be bald by now." I said. "You tell me." I looked at him. "Sitting in your recess. In the big, green chair. Who was he?"

"I don't know," he said.

"I think you do, Mr Fawcett," I said. "Had a chestnut mare, four white socks."

"Even if I did know, don't you think that's my business?"

"It's my business now," I said.

"Can you clear this up?" said Mr Fawcett, indicating the grey spillage on the counter. "I don't know what you're up to, but I don't like it."

I took a box from my pocket and extracted a long wooden match. These were luxury matches intended for a sophisticated gentry market. Designed for lighting candles in a big house. "Next thing I do is light one end," I said.

"What's the point of that," said Mr Fawcett. "It's only tea, isn't it?"

"Yes, it looks like tea," I said. "But it is actually China powder." I looked up at Mr Fawcett and he was sweating in spite of the early morning chill and the shop was still cold. "I make it myself out of saltpeter, which is essentially urine and a lot of old manure. I add some charcoal. And of course, there's a bit of sulfur. You have to have sulfur." I struck the match against my boot and I looked at the flame progressing slowly from the top and down the shaft. "I add water too," I said. "But not too much." I paused, hoping it would dawn on him. "And if you have all that," I said. "You have a good explosion."

"Explosion?" he said. "For God's sake Mr Logan!" He ducked and I lowered the match to the counter. "What are you doing with the match now?" he said, stealing a look above the counter.

"I hope not to do anything with the match, Mr Fawcett," I said helpfully. "But that very much depends on you." I met his eyes down at the end. "I want to know who the man was with the horse and the white socks. And the red hair. Not too much of it. Thinning perhaps. Sitting on your chair. I want to know now, because when I drop this match there," – I helpfully indicated the powder trail – "it will go all the way to there" – and again I pointed to the pile of powder at one end - "and then we will have the most wonderful explosion."

Mr Fawcett's eyes were riveted to the match. The flame was close to two-thirds down the shaft and the light shone yellow against my thumb. "I can't help you," he said, but without conviction.

"You've been here a long time," I said. "And this is a nice shop. And I have known you a long time. Let's not spoil it. Tell me what I need to know."

"Well," he said, twitching nervously. "Take the match away. I suppose someone should tell you anyway. I know why you are asking about this man. I can imagine why you wish to speak to him. That's not my business. But he's dangerous Mr Logan. You would not want to upset him." He moved a step towards me. "What happened to your father," he said unexpectedly. "And what happened to your mother too, of course. These were strange events and it was a strange time. I know all about that."

"So you know why I'm asking you about the man from Buckhaven?" I said.

"It's Buckstone you fool!"

"Buckstone?"

"Buckstone not Buckhaven. I can't say any more than that," he said. "You'd be better leaving it alone. These things happened a long time ago."

"It's fresh in my mind."

"He's not a friendly man," said Mr Fawcett.

"I'll take my chances," I said. "Shall I put the matches away?"

"I would appreciate that."

"What's his name?"

"Please Mr Logan, I don't want to tell you."

"You've got no choice, Mr Fawcett."

"I've known you since you were a boy," he said.

I brought the match closer to the powder. The flame was burning down, well into the last inch. "There's not much time," I said and I lowered the match still closer to the counter but kept my eyes fixed on him.

He hesitated for a moment, licked his lips nervously and blinked. "He will kill me."

"He may not be the only one. Now, speak up and tell me who this fellow is." Fawcett seemed unable to speak. "What's his name?"

"Traynor!" he said desperately, spitting out the word like it was hot in his mouth. "His name's Traynor. He lent me money when I needed it."

"You're in hock to him? That's not good."

"He took half of this place when I couldn't pay him back his money."

"Was he at the farm that night?" I asked.

Mr Fawcett hesitated. "He would kill me."

"Was he at the farm that night?"

"Yes."

"Where is he?"

"Buckstone."

"Where in Buckstone?"

"Don't go there Mr Logan."

"Where in Buckstone?" I repeated.

"Beyond the town. It's a farm. Decent house. Somewhere on the east side of the town, you follow the road out. I don't know exactly."

"On the east side of the town?"

"Yes, you can see the house from the road. You can't miss it. He lives with his mother, a mad old bitch."

"The thing about this stuff is that it is very volatile when exposed to heat," I said. "Stand back." I dropped the match on the powder trail. It zipped along the length of the counter, sparking all the way.

"I told you what you wanted to know, Mr Logan!" Mr Fawcett said, crouching down behind the counter, raising his arms to protect his head from the imminent explosion. The small flame ate up the trail of powder and reached the large mound at one end of the counter. "Watch!" I shouted. There was a large 'wooph' noise, like an explosion but wrapped in soft wool, and the powder ignited, creating a large cup of black smoke and a bright yellow flame ripping up the middle. There was a small pop and the smoke dissipated to the ceiling. All the while I was leaning on the counter, enjoying the extraordinary pyrotechnic spectacle.

I moved towards the door. "The thing to know about China powder is that it's a low explosive. You light this stuff and if you don't compress it somehow, then it just gives off this beautiful soft deflagration, a bit of smoke and a bright shaft of yellow/white flame in the cup. Quite beautiful, don't you think?" I laid my hand on the doorhandle. "Purely decorative of course, quite harmless. Like a firework." I opened the door. "Thankyou for your time Mr Fawcett," I said. "Good morning."

CHAPTER 43

After I had gone from the house, Keira told me she enjoyed the kind of euphoria, a sense of deep happiness, she had never known. It filled her and warmed every part of her. She had colour in her cheeks and a shine, approaching a dazzle, in her green eyes. It brought life back into her. She hummed as she went about her business. She found it hard to sit down. It was as if every sensation she had ever wanted or imagined was rushing through her veins all at once, keeping her in constant motion. She tried to stop her mind from thinking, from poring over that miraculous, overwhelming encounter. I say this not from arrogance but because she told me so herself. She said to me later that I had arrived in her arms and I was tender, smiling, twinkling in my eyes, so touched by her pain, her broken skin, her yellow-blue battered bones, before I wrapped myself around her, and kissed her with lips that she said took her to heaven. How she floated like air and bubbles and lightness. It had been so inevitable and so unstoppable, a rolling wave, there was nothing to impede its progress. The water was coming, she knew it was coming from the first time she set eyes on me, over her husband's shoulder, the day I stopped by for the fishing. Or so she said and who was I to argue? She remembered the embarrassment of that day. How Calum had spoken to me like I was nothing, uncouth and rough. She was right, I did not rise, I said my piece, I left. Just told him what was what. She said she liked that about me. At that moment, to her mind, I had won the battle – and it *was* a battle or at least a test of my resolve. She liked the look of a man who did not have fear. Most men she knew would not stand up to Calum. Most men took her husband for the thief and brute he was and they were not prepared to step in his way for fear he would turn on them with his fists or his guns. She knew I had no care for what ever he might do, maybe out of ignorance but she did not think so. I had that air of someone who did not care too much how you threatened him, I was not going to do anything that I did not want to do. She thought that I was a fatalist. I had youth on my side and the young fear nothing because they know nothing.

The very first time we had made love, it had been with a deep want, a visceral conviction of total need that came from somewhere neither of us had known before. When I entered her, I entered a world I had never experienced. I was no longer in my head, I was physically distanced from my head, and the electricity coiled round me and melted into her. It had happened so quickly. Later that morning, we shared our bodies with each other again, more slowly and with less intensity. The two of us experienced it all so deeply, I entered her again and again, it came easily and with a strength of entire commitment and purpose. Nevertheless, I knew she sensed within my lovemaking a measure of calculation that never quite escaped me. She noticed that I looked at her intently during the moments she was at her most vulnerable, when I was in her and she was fast approaching the release that her body told her would come. Later, she said I looked as if I were studying her biological reaction to my careful ministrations. I was studying her, that much was true, but not like some dubious laboratory experiment. That is not to say she thought I was *without* passion, just that there were times when we made love that I appeared to contain my emotion too well. It was as if I attempted to capture the moment like it was a scientific practical that I had to note down very carefully for fear of losing it altogether. Then again, to some extent, I confess: that was the man I was: my mind was everywhere in its complexity and hunger for new answers to old questions and it was little wonder that I would subject the manner in which we made love to the same analysis as every other thing I did. The experience was so insane for me, I could only take it one frame at a time. I would have exploded if I had not. In any event, she was astute enough to recognize that to rebuke me for cerebral analysis of what I was doing and experiencing was to call me to account for being Sean Logan.

She wondered if some might think, had they known, that she had an overly relaxed perspective on her predicament, but the danger inherent in our situation was neither lost on her nor was it something she ignored. She was aware of her husband's brutishness and the vengeance he would no doubt seek if he were to find out what she was embarked upon. She was not stupid either: she dodged the issue, but in her heart of hearts she was convinced he would in fact find out. There were ears and eyes all over the place, lurking behind each and every hedgerow, and sooner or later the news would leak like blue smoke from a cracked chimney and her husband would hear of it and when he heard of it, she had little doubt that he would respond with his own freakish demonstration of brutality.

Keira appreciated that they might have been more careful. They might have hidden away in the house on those days that Calum was not home, but love is a release from such restraints and concealments: she wanted to be in the open with me, run across the fields with linked arms, hold my big hand and let all those around know that she could not contain her love in a dark corner of that miserable marital home. Love cannot live in the shadows; it can only survive if it takes to the open ground and is allowed to grow. Love needs light to flourish; it has to be allowed to breathe out in the wide fields and beneath the limitless sky. Take that away and the leaves would curl and wither and there would be no fruit off the tree before the love was dead.

Yet that was not to ignore the fact that she feared her husband. Sean Logan might not, but she most definitely did. And that was not terribly surprising. If he found out – *when* he found out – his retribution would be truly awful. This coloured her days and made the highs so high and the lows – of which there were fewer - so crushing and breathtaking. She knew they had taken risks and were continuing to take risks – gambles that were sometimes foolish and occasionally reckless. I led her, she said. I encouraged her. We had lain on the damp grass up by the hills at Denton, where the view combed the pasture and stroked its way to the sea; where the Perth Blackface sheep bleated; where we could watch these beasts dragging their coarse wool backs across the fields; where we would hope that the two of us would be witnessed by nothing more than the silent wind and the open sky. Once, we had heard the voice of the passing shepherd just in time, talking to himself as you might expect, and we had lowered our heads to the ground to stay out of sight. He had walked on without seeing us, just a dozen feet away. It heightened the excitement. It made the two of us giggle like mischievous children. The worst part for Keira was that she never knew when Calum might return. He took himself off and she would never be sure if it was just a day or days that he would be gone from her. Sometimes it could be weeks, but there was no predicting. He might come home at any time to find this situation going on in his own house, under his roof, and they had to wonder: what would happen to them then?

When the truth broke, she knew before he told her he knew. He arrived home on his horse, Marty, and he had led the muddied, sweated beast straight over to the trough where there was water and a small bag of hay. He pulled off the bridle and threw it on the wall and he slung the strap of a halter around Marty's neck and buckled it just a little too tight. He undid the girth on one side, then removed the saddle and slung it astride the wall. He unbuckled the girth from the far side too and held it in his hand. There was something about his movement, a kind of quick impatience that betrayed the anger that was in him. He let the horse drink while the steam rose off his hindquarters, gathering around his flank and swirling in wispy tranches above and around his neck. He then took Marty to his stall and bolted the door with a sliding stab from left to right.

She saw the back of her husband from inside the house when he was dealing with the horse. She ran a hand through her hair and straightened her clothing.

She noticed the jerkiness of his movements as he approached but she did not know what he knew until she was close enough to see into his tight, little eyes. Only then could she see some trace of the rage that was consuming him, like red coals burning in the gorse. If there was fury, he still maintained the appearance of glacial calm and it made her think for little more than a moment that maybe she was mistaken. Could it be that there was nothing there to concern her, just the usual distance, the controlled angry hatred? He was not effusive but then he never had been. He approached her by the door, not three paces from the spot where I had first kissed her with my hungry lips, my breath in her mouth, melting the will to resist, before I took her inside and we took off our clothes and for the first time enjoyed our nakedness together. Her husband stepped in from the door and reached behind her head and stroked the brown hair with his hand.

"Any news from around here?" he asked.

"No," she said. "Just the usual things."

"You sure about that?" he said. "Just the usual things?"

She looked at him, wondered at the hard edge, tried to keep his eye. "I said, just the usual things."

His hand gripped the hair at the back of her head and in one move he was dragging her into the house like a dog on a leash.

CHAPTER 44

She screamed, tripped, stumbled and fell against the small table in the hall. He continued to pull her by the hair into the boot room. He banged her head off the upright jamb and blood quickly flowed from the wound. A picture fell off the wall. Once she was in, he slammed the door shut. He was still holding the leather girth. He folded its length in two and then beat her with it, repeated strikes against her body, until he had no strength left in him. The buckle gashed her sides like she was the horse for whom it was intended. She lay on the floor at his feet where she had fallen, blood leaking from her forehead in a steady trickle and a deep cut on her legs and her sides made each time the girth buckle caught hard against her skin. She felt sharp pain when she shifted her weight, may have broken a rib or two. She hurt all over from the heavy battering he had inflicted. She could see herself turning purple, yellow and blue, but she was still conscious and she understood that she was still alive when the beating was finally over. He slipped down the wall and sat next to her on the dirt, half-matted floor, amongst the sticks and the boots and the brushes and pans, the bloodied mat and the spilled rabbit snares, there were tears forming in his already reddened eyes.

He beat her again over the next few days, a couple of times, no more. Not so hard this time, but it was new bruises beaten on top of old bruises. She was scared of waking up in the morning. She was scared of not waking up in the morning. She was five shades of swollen, broken, layered, blue, purple and yellow. As the days unfolded, as he slumped in the kitchen chair with the broken wood frets or looked surly coming in from the outhouse, he stared at her with a steady, simmering, but unrelenting hatred. He threw the food she served back in her face and he put his boot on her back when she bent down to clean up the fallen plate and the broken egg. He struck her. He drank whisky for long parts of the day and night. He beat his fist hard against her cunt. He once tried to fuck her but his desire left him. He went out to drink and he became so incapacitated he had to lay across the horse's withers to get himself home, by which time he had vomited repeatedly down Marty's neck. Marty's sense of direction, however, could not be faulted, since he always got him home. All the while, in consciousness, Calum's mind turned over and picked at the events that had led to this. He dissected each and every moment of her betrayal, savouring each piece, like two juicy wings on a chicken. He consumed each and sucked the bones. The taste was good at first but lost something as he scratched for more. The trouble was that with each useless beating he was coming to recognise certain irrefutable truths. Whilst he beat her and despised her; whilst he tried harder than any man to hate all two hundred and six bones of her beautiful body; whilst he spat contemptuously at her that she was low, ugly and charmless; despite all of this the true, genuine hatred he was looking for and had expected just would not come. It was like squeezing drops of wine from an empty cask. The hellish truth of it was that he loved her as much as he had ever loved anybody. He loved her so much that all this torture was killing *him*, not her. None of this poison was coming out right or if it was coming out at all it was going straight back into him. No matter how hard he hit her with his boot or

258

his fist, she had her own way of hitting back, and her way was quicker, harsher and seemingly deeper than anything he could inflict. He knew he loved her and would always love her and to his mind it was a low, mean piece of feminine trickery that she should make him feel that way. She had no right to undermine the serious satisfaction he thought he had a god-given right to derive from dishing out a beating.

So it was, as the days passed he reached a point where he had to capitulate and concede that for all his raving, he was very much over the worst of his desire to batter her to a pulp. He just did not feel so bad towards her anymore. He sat down to eat his breakfast and told her that she should join him and she obeyed. He made her eat an egg and some fresh bread. He poured her a glass of milk and encouraged her to drink it. He said *you're not eating enough, girl. Your health is important now.* He put sweet jam on the bread and a thick dollop of cream and fed her the slice by his own hand. She ate it from him, albeit her eyes were twitching. She thought he might force the bread down her throat. Instead, he gently wiped the cream from the corners of her mouth and put the smear straight onto his own tongue. He struggled to understand the feelings that he still had for her, this woman he had married and who had done him the most terrible wrong. But he was not such a stupid man: he could see that this deep desire for her was not going to disappear. It was a stranger in the room and he had to find a seat for it and make it welcome.

"You may not see it now," he said. "But I still have a love for you that I can't control." She said nothing. "You may think I hate you because of the things I've done to you. The fact is, I don't know if I love you or if I hate you."

"That's a confusion," she said, but too late wishing she had not spoken.

He looked at her. "They may be two sides of the same coin for all I know. Whatever it is, I don't seem too good at letting it go." There was a moment of silence and he looked at her with real hurt in his eyes, a look that made her swallow like she had something putrid in her mouth.

"You almost killed me," she said.

"That is not a million miles from the truth."

"How can you call what you've done love?" she said eventually. "How can you strike with your own hand what you say you love?"

"That's the odd thing, isn't it?" he answered. "It's not so unusual to hate the thing that is dear to you. It stands to reason you would hate the thing you love."

"Why?" she said. "You hate me, you half kill me and yet you say you love me?"

"Love weakens us, that's the point."

"What of it?" she said.

"A man will always hate those things that make him weak."

"You make love and hate sound like the same thing," she said.

"They are," he said. "Love is sweet. Hate is sweeter still. One spoon or two, it's all the same damn sugar. They're two ends of the same fucking dog. It stands to reason, Keira. I'm beginning to understand this thing." He leaned towards her and for one brief moment she thought he was going to kiss her, but he just sat there looking at her with stupid, empty eyes above his whiskered face.

For ten days she had been a prisoner in her own house. He watched her like she was floating in a hall of mirrors, assuming the shape of every monster known to man and reflecting it back at him. Her presence was both a reminder and an accusation. Her body was the colour of an old cured ham left to hang for too long but, apart from the cut across her forehead, the bruising was largely confined to her trunk and her upper arms. With the right clothes you might not have known what a pitiful, broken creature lay beneath. Keira had become used to speaking to no one; Calum did not like company around the house. He said if he wanted intercourse he would use his wife. If he wanted stimulating conversation he was quite capable of going out and finding it. It did not need to come to him. For Keira, worse than being vilified by him was the desparate isolation. She could not speak to anyone about any of this. She could receive comfort from no one. He watched her from the moment she rose to the moment she lay down. Yet, in his earnest desire to hold her body and thought in the tightest grip, to pin her to the ground like a peg in the earth, a change had come over him once the initial fury had burned itself to nothing. She did not fully understand this change in him. At that time, she had little comprehension of his skewed perception of love and the strangely twisted feelings he bore towards her.

On the twelfth day, following many others during which he did little and said even less, he mounted his horse, Marty, and rode into Tullis. His face was still alive with a kind of hooded, brooding anger. He said he had people he needed to speak to, but did not elaborate. Perhaps this was the intellectual

261

conversation she was unable to provide. He said he would go to Perth for a number of days, then he would return. She did not believe him. She knew he was up to no good. She noticed that recently, more often than not, he had his rifle holstered by his saddle. She feared for what might happen, but she was powerless too. Keira watched him ride out of the yard, his hunched shoulders gently swaying upon the horse, disappearing slowly from sight. She sat on the bench by the front door and looked out over the potato field. She knew that he would follow the track down and if she waited several minutes she would see him turn the corner. She knew that if she did not see him turn in to the left, past the Rowan and the Hawthorn, then he was in all probability not heading for Tullis at all. Or even Perth. In which case it may have been a test, to see if she was going to run away, stay alone at home or take in a visitor, but if that was in his mind then he was more fool than bully: she waited and felt the minutes tick by, and then she saw Marty skitter in the distance, pulling irritably on the bit, twitching round the hedge, and she knew at least he was far enough away to allow her to sit back a little and ease some of the tension from her muscles. The sun squeezed out from between the grey-grit clouds and she felt the warmth against her face. She closed her eyes and enjoyed the relaxation wash over her, the first time in as many days, like she was starting to breathe all over again. The last thing she expected was to hear my voice.

She did not answer but she knew my voice and she leapt forward, covered the small distance between us and quickly buried her face against my chest. I stroked her hair with one hand and pulled her close with the other. I felt her legs press against me and sensed the warmth bleed into me.

"Have you been there long?" she asked.

"Since dawn," I said. "They say all hope begins in darkness but ends in dawn."

"What do you mean?"

"Never mind," I said.

"I do mind."

"It's the cold talking."

I held her in my arms for several minutes. Then, I lifted her chin with my hand and looked at her face. "I can tell you, it's not the first time I've been here, waiting for you."

"It's the first time I've been alone."

I squeezed her and I felt her flinch under my hand.

"Did he beat you?" I asked.

"Of course," she said.

"I hate to see you suffer."

"You reach a point when you don't care anymore."

"You should leave him," I said. "You shouldn't stand for it."

"Nothing's that simple."

"But it is simple. If he beat you, then you should leave him."

"But I knew he would beat me. I knew it from the second day we were married. Beating me changes nothing."

"Is he still?" I asked.

"Not now," she said. "He's moody though. He sits and broods." There was a deep silence, as if the cruelty had choked the dialogue between us.

"Does he know it's me?" I asked finally.

"What do you think?" she said, holding my eyes. "He beat me with his horse girth."

"I know."

"I didn't tell him," she said. "He knew already."

"I'll answer for it. I'm happy to."

"More fights and beatings?"

"As long as it's me and not you," I said.

"He'll come after you next. I know him."

"I'm not running," I said. "But I've got to go." She said nothing but raised her arms and put them around my neck. "What would you change?" I asked.

"You can't," she said. She kissed me on the lips. "Those are rules that don't apply."

"Change the rules," I said.

"You spend too much time reading books and studying snails."

"You throw that back at me," I said gently, her eyes close to mine.

"The real world has real rules," she said.

"You don't have to follow them." I put my hands on her waist, softly because I knew she hurt.

"Take care," she said. "He won't let it rest."

"I know. Let him come."

"There's nothing more he can do to me. He will come after you."

"Well, if he comes, he comes. But he had better come soon."

"Why?" she said.

"I have to go away for a while. I do not know how things will turn out."

"This is far better," she said unexpectedly. "I thought you would wish to bareknuckle fight him in the yard." I knew she was humouring me. "I am not waiting on him, but if he comes, he comes."

"And if your house is empty, he may just have to come home and beat me instead."

"You're almost right. It's me he wants now. Beating you will give him little pleasure."

"And now you abandon me?" she said with a hint of mockery.

"I do not abandon you," I said. "There are things I have to take care of. I pulled her close to me, kissed her on the lips and held my face against her cheek.

"Will you be gone long?"

"That depends if things go well."

"Will you come back for me?"

I looked at her, the green-blue glint of her eyes, the question left hanging. "I will," I said, knowing all too well that it was a promise that was never mine to give.

CHAPTER 45

Mad Bob had forgotten now why it was he had ever landed the name 'Mad Bob'. He just had become Mad Bob and everyone knew him as Mad Bob. He was not a crazy man, eating bird brains and child fingers. Nobody said they should put him in the mad house but it was true that his grandmother on his father's side had ended her days there – 'Bedlam' was what they called it then. The lunatic asylum. He was not a particularly angry man, someone who might have thrown his toys out of the pram when he was a boy or who might later pick stupid fights in a bar. He was none of these things. If you looked at him you might say, this man is skinny and his hair looks like baling twine and his nose is too large on a long face, like a handle in the middle of a plain door. He had a mirror on the wall just inside the front hall and he could see the reflection from the top of his head to half way down his chest. He wore a grey tunic shirt and a black waistcoat, black buttons too, just the one missing, two eyes from the top. He had a fuzzy stubble on his chin, half pepper grey and the rest black. Time had chiseled his features and left him with a permanent scowl. I suppose what he lacked was any colour about him, but colour represented joy and there was precious room for that in Mad Bob's existence.

As he brushed the hen shit off the porch outside his small wooden house, he heard his wife shout his name from upstairs. She was a woman with a heavy, round face, a mouth like a farthing coin and two eyes shaped like sharp, angry stab holes. She was bloated and fat and chewed catmint most of the day, whilst reclining against the Victorian headboard of a sagging bed, swaddled in its threadbare sheets and dusty spread. When the catmint was fully masticated she spat it into a clay bowl. It was three-quarters full already and Mad Bob should have emptied it by now. Mad Bob heard her shout his name again and this time he chose to ignore her. He brushed the hen shit onto a broken shovel. There was plenty. These hens had a free run over the place but, as a rule, he kept them out of the house. As he straightened and turned, a Scots grey hen scuttled under his feet and he kicked it hard with his leather boot, enjoying the flap of black and white wings, the angry squawks, the broken feathers, the panic and the alarm. Life can be precarious. He saw another piece of hen shit under the chair at the corner of the porch. Soft and lumpy, he scooped it onto the shovel. He heard his wife shout "Bob" from upstairs, the volume higher now and he could imagine the rising colour, the heavy beetroot bleed in her swollen face. The eyes would be popping like eggs in hot fat. He went into the house.

Mad Bob stood at the bottom of the stairs, as if deliberating on a very important decision. He was a little breathless and even small exertions such as brushing shit off the porch made him gasp. He had a dull pain in his lower gut. He had that pain so often it had become part of his life, part of his existence. If you took the pain away, he felt he would be a different person. She shouted his name again, but he hardly heard her. Bob, Bob, Bob. Bob. He dug a thumb and finger into his waistcoat and extracted a green pill. He flicked it into his mouth and crunched it between his teeth. The glucose syrup took away some of the bitterness. His tongue was dry and he swallowed three or four times before it went. When he was shot, he had caught a large part of it in his gut. That old bitch had shot him from about nine feet and it has to be said, it took him by surprise. True, he was not in her house for friendly reasons but getting shot by her was the last thing he had expected; he was less angry about it now. Had he not been the peacemaker? That is what he had told them at the trial but the truth was he was always going to fuck her. Maybe if she had been a little more welcoming, a little less trigger-happy, things would have turned out differently. Nobody pushed Bob too hard on that explanation: I came in peace, I came in peace, he cried, even when he had his pants over his ankles. Yet, that was no cause for putting a big hole in a man's stomach. Discharging a firearm was an incendiary action and once you lit that fuse God only knew where it was likely to end. In this case, a man had to live his life with only half a stomach, all because some gypsy girl got trigger-happy with her husband's rifle. Maybe she did suffer, thought Bob, but he suffered too. He was still suffering.

Mad Bob stood by the closed window. He still had the shit shovel in his hand. He looked out over the rough ground towards the green hill beyond. He thought of Mr Traynor. Traynor had been good to him at first. Traynor had encouraged others to see the facts a little differently. Show a little charity. It was all a matter of perspective. Policemen were not so interested: they had their man. They had him locked up in a cell the size of Bob's outside toilet. For a good while, it has to be said that Traynor looked after him, covered his back and kept him out of trouble. Traynor had the money of course, living on that big place, a good-sized farm, his mother only just alive but set fair financially. Traynor was a man who had never left home, had lived with his mother all his life. Mad Bob thought back to his own mother. Where the hell did she go? He could hardly picture her any more. He heard a noise from upstairs. Was it something being thrown at the door. Keep on throwing, dear. Keep on throwing.

Bob sat down on the chair by the window. He was looking out still but he was seeing nothing. He rested the shovel full of shit against the top of his leg. It was wrong to think he and Traynor were on a one-way street. That is what he had tried to tell Traynor the last time they met. The old guy did not take it too well, seemed to think Bob was acting ungrateful for a man who should have and could have been hung. That was not the way Mad Bob saw it. It was a long time ago, but they had both played their parts in the death of that young woman; that was something they had to answer for together. It could not be brushed under the carpet. The point was Traynor had to look after him now because it was a reciprocal arrangement they had. He did not have to keep his mouth shut, he could have blabbed all over. The point was he did not blab and that meant there had to be a better settlement between him and Mr Traynor. They were in this thing together, always had been.

Bob thought back again to that night at the Logan farm, as he often did even now. He had his regrets alright. Most of all he regretted the hole she put in his gut. He remembered the flash from the rifle's muzzle, how a lot of shot just went straight through the flesh and out the other side, hardly touching anything on its way. There was a medical man in Tullis and that man had saved his life. He was a national hero. It would be a mistake to call him a doctor because he was not in truth a doctor, but he had practiced surgery on Saddleback pigs and cattle, small children, the odd horse and a cat with a pile prolapse, and that to Mad Bob was a reasonable qualification. Gun shot was a new challenge for him. He dug most of the metal out, even if he did drink Bob's whisky to give him courage, from the first cut to the last stitch. Mad Bob reflected that his bowel was not too bad, all considered, even today. He could shit with the best of them. His lungs never got better; always out of breath, it made him think there must have been a piece up there somewhere. They did something to his bladder but he never did find out what; he could pee like a champion, but half a cup at a time. This meant that he had to pass urine three times per hour. That inclined Mrs Weir to joke that he was more Wet Bob than Mad Bob. As he thought of his wife, simultaneously he heard her voice call out his name from the upstairs room. Bob, Bob, Bob. A minute later she shouted his name again and ten minutes later there was a deeper, angrier tone to her voice. Bob! Bob!

Mad Bob rose to his feet and went through to the hall. He stepped towards the front door, turned the handle and pulled it open. He spat a gob onto the porch. He shut the door and turned towards the stair. His eyes followed the treads that slid one upon the other like heavy cards, all the way up to the top. He held the shovel in front of him, gripped the banister with his left hand and began the ascent.

CHAPTER 46

Farewells made, I was on my way to a destination in Montrose, a place I had never been to, but a good day's ride away, still on the east and not far from the coast. Against my better judgment, I had left the eccentric Reicher with Aunt Marion. The Reicher was the strangest kind of four-barrelled pistol you were ever likely to see. The product of a Germano-Austrian lunacy, but Aunt Marion had chosen it as her weapon of ultimate defence and I had failed to persuade her that the little old Webley was easier, prettier and more effective to discharge. The fact that it had been used to assassinate an American president counted for nothing with my inflexible aunt.

For myself, it was a sad time to leave. I had found a woman who excited and engaged me and yet, as if driven by a long-standing illness, I was leaving her too – at least for now. I had thought for the briefest of moments that perhaps she was the reason that I should lay down my arms and move my life away from its current circumlocution, its unerring pull towards a retribution for things past. Keira made me question my purpose in this quest that had consumed my being from the earliest days of my existence. Her arrival on the scene now forced me to question what was to come of this pursuit, this thirst for atonement. What if I should find that the holy grail of my endeavours turned out to be no more than an empty cup? Instead of quenching that destructive thirst, it might leave me with a salty mouth full of dry, unanswered longings? I thought of these issues and through sheer force of will I cast them to one side. I was far along the road to attain what my life's pursuit had always been. All the

271

gold in Jerusalem would have no power to turn me back.

I was conscious too that I was leaving Lizzie behind in all her clumsiness, her goodness too, her soup, her laughter.   Not to mention Aunt Marion: curtain-dresser, woman, eye-roller, mother of me when there was no other. I was leaving them all because the time had come to do what I had always intended, to follow the path to justice or retribution, call it what you will. I was going to settle some accounts and there was no guarantee that I would return to Tullis in one piece. I had my Webley and other useful weaponry, as well as heavy, greasy sticks of brown-papered dynamite retrieved from carefully turned wooden boxes, and a host of incendiary devices designed to bring down the heavens upon my enemy's head, wherever I might find him. I had my father's very own Snider-Enfield, Kipling's favourite, and nothing was going to stop me now.

Aunt Marion stood by the front door as I meandered away that morning, along the hedge-bordered track, between its damp, moss-topped walls, down the road to take me from the farm. Lizzie stood there by her side, her collar open, her skin white against her top. She had hugged me and patted my back with her freckled hands and there was moisture in her brown eyes at my departure. They both knew well enough where I was going, and for that reason, I presumed, Aunt Marion had kept her questions brief and to the point. Only once, did she ask me to think again about what I was embarked upon and what I intended to do when I got there, but she knew it was useless to seek to dissuade me from something that, like the turning tide, had been a draw against my entire life, that had asserted itself against me for as long as I could remember. We had our discussion earlier about which gun I should leave behind and, her explanation as to why she would have no need for it. I told her that I had enemies, that I was anxious that they be left alone, that I feared that anything I might do could leave them vulnerable.

"You're being over-protective," she said. "It's sweet, but it's unnecessary."

"We can usually look after ourselves," said Lizzie. "Worrying about us is not going to help."

"But a gun might," I said. "You're brave women," I began.

"Thankyou."

"But you're alone here."

"So, we're alone. We've nothing to be frightened of."

"I hope not."

"We'll be careful."

"Lock the door at night," I said. I took my aunt's hand in mine. "Don't take any chances."

"Alright," she said. "Now get out of here, if you're going."

"I'm not leaving you without a gun," I said. "Shoot rabbits with it if you like."

So it came about that I left her the Reicher, not because I thought it would be an appropriate protection for her and Lizzie but because it was the *only* protection she would accept. I pushed her again to take the Webley or even the Colt, but she said leave the Reicher, if you must, with all those barrels. And not to forget the bullets too.

"Because it kills four at a time?" I asked.

"No, because it looks so ridiculous whoever I aim it at will die laughing."

I had a feeling that there really was something to be frightened about. I did not know where that doom-laden sense might have come from. I recognized that I was setting out on a journey in the course of which I would probably upset one or two people, possibly making permanent changes to their life expectancy, depending where the trail led. I would shake a stick in dangerous places and whatever flew out of those dark holes might wish to attack me where I was vulnerable: I knew that home was the logical choice for my enemies, by bringing harm to those I loved. I had no idea where the attack would come from but I was jittery that it might happen.

Of course, it was not just the possibility of retribution from those I was intent upon confronting. That was enough to worry about, but I was still on edge about the times I had sensed that I was being followed or watched. I had identified nobody in but that knowledge did not render me any less anxious. It all served to fill me with trepidation, and when I had finished packing the final canvas bag onto Master Henry's back, I was still edgy that something would happen, not so much to me but to those I left behind. Yet I knew I had to go and I think Aunt Marion and Lizzie knew that too.

CHAPTER 47

The stair creaked under Mad Bob's scuffed leather boots. It was unusual for Bob to wear his footwear upstairs. It was one of her many rules that he did not wear his boots above ground level. She said the cracked soles were a repository for bugs. It seemed to him that she did not need to go looking at his boots for bugs; if she swept the crumbs, soiled pants, toenail clippings and clumps of head and pubic hair from under the bed, she would see what real bugs looked like. On this occasion he had no intention of abiding by his wife's rules. He had married her nineteen years ago because his mother told him that nobody wanted a skinny man with a long head, no money and holes in his gut that made him an incontinence risk. She had married him, so his mother had repeatedly told him, because she herself was grossly fat, short of body with very little neck and almost no distance between her shoulders and her waist, with few social skills and very little else for a husband to enjoy beyond the furry slit that housed her genitals. They both therefore came to marriage from a position of deficit. Any hope of maturing a thread of credit from the marriage was, as it turned out, well misplaced. It was very quickly apparent that his stomach cramps and the eternal passing of small cups of deep yellow urine were irksome to her. She made no secret of her ongoing belief that he was a useless wretch, less manly than a wilting dandelion, with little useful purpose in life other than to bring her food, empty her pots of masticated catmint and wipe her face with a cloth in the event of any mess during consumption. For two and a half years she had not felt it necessary to spend much time on the ground level of the house because the journey from downstairs to upstairs was an escalating challenge and mounting the stairs was a necessity she approached with a breathless, dwindling enthusiasm. The trouble with going down was that at some point she would have to go up, and so she attempted neither. She could recline on her Victorian bed and shout for Wet Bob and he would dribble up the stairs with food and other services. She could send him down for more, quite often beer in two-pint jugs was a desirable lubricant for the appalling food, and she liked him to restock the catmint for her to masticate through the flat tedium of daylight hours.

Mad Bob stood at the top of the dusty stair for almost six hundred seconds. On the wall there was a small picture of succulent fruit, a melon and two peaches and the feather of a pheasant. It was still light outside, but the grey shadows all around were lengthening. The repeated calling of his name had faded. He imagined she had fallen asleep. A permanent coma would have been too much to wish for. She would awake soon, angrier than ever by his failure to answer her calls. She would expect him to make the usual excuses, curse him for the wastefulness of his imperfect existence, swear at him and shout at him harshly to bring something tasty to kill these fucking tummy rumbles.

There was nothing unusual in all this. However, something had happened today inside the brain behind that long face. Mad Bob had decided this time would be different. Today, he had no intention of placating her. He gripped the wooden door handle in his hand and twisted slowly to the left. As he pushed and entered, he smelt the whiff of catmint from the chipped bowl by the bed. The fingers of his right hand were white and bloodless.

CHAPTER 48

Montrose is a flat old town, with only the smallest rise from the south to the north, occupying a position on a square basin that sits at the mouth of a river, known as the *Esk*. At that time, it had a population of about twelve thousand, so clearly the town had something going for it. I arrived after dusk the same day as I left Tullis, and followed the multiple houses, terrace after terrace, set gable to gable, along the length of the main street, past the unassuming statue of Joseph Hume, politician, doctor, freethinker, as far as the *Kingfisher*, a public house that bore a sign that offered the possibility of a room for the night.

The moment I entered the dark, fusty, low-beamed room, I thought to myself that had I been a dog seeking a new kennel with inbuilt quirky eccentricity I had walked in upon a worthy candidate. I could smell beer and damp clothing, unwashed bodies, fish, sperm, tobacco and fresh excrement. The floor was caked with grime. There were bound to be types present who would want to know who I was and where I was from and what my business meant to them, so I quickly passed through the shadows of the room, keeping my eyes focused on a skinny old man in a faded shirt, marshaling cups and liquids from behind the counter. I asked him for a room and he told me the rate.

"How many days?" he said, as if he was concierge at a famous London hotel.

"I will let you know," I said. "Probably just the one night, maybe two."

He looked at my muddied coat. "Would you mind settling up first please?"

"I'll pay you the first night," I said, putting a handful of coins down on the bar top. "Where do I go?"

He scooped the coins into his hand. "I'll show you," he said and at the same time stepped out from behind the counter.

I followed his curved back along a short passage, up a steep stair, banged my head on the crossbeam and swore under my breath. He smiled and said: "Mind your head, sir" and threw open the door to my room. It had a window, but for viewing purposes you needed a chair. It was definitely not Brown's of Mayfair.

"I have a horse outside," I said.

"My boy will take care of that. I'll tell him." He moved towards the door.

"Don't worry," I said. "I'll be down in a minute, I'll speak to him myself." I did not want anyone rummaging about in my saddlebags.

"He will want extra for the horse," he said and smiled for the second time. I chose not to smile and he closed the door gently behind him.

Later, I sucked up some meat-stained, oily water in the bar and chewed on a stale cut of bread that I dabbed and softened in the soupy mulch. It was surprisingly tasty. I grew used to the smell of my environment. I made a few discreet enquiries of the skinny man in the dirty shirt behind the bar, telling him that I was a cousin of Mr Weir who lived in these parts but that I had not seen him for many years and was not too sure where exactly his home was now. It was a tale as thin as the soup and initially the old man was cautious, wary of speaking to me about Mad Bob or even discussing the weather or time of day in any meaningful detail. A short while later, the room was quieter and I hoped to unlock any information by offering a drink at the bar. I could tell from the redness of his eyes and the rough, peeliness of his pale skin that he would find it hard to refuse. I was right. He drank a large whisky in three quick gulps, his hand trembling as he upended the glass. I bought him another that he drank more slowly and I consumed a beer myself and was surprised by the pleasant hopsy taste. By the end of the second drink he had told me where Mad Bob could be found. He lived on a small freeholding on the western side of the town, maybe three miles on from the last building. He said that if I kept riding I would find it no bother and I would probably hear Mrs Weir first.

"Confined to bed," he said. "The cunt's too fat to walk."

I said: "That sounds like a terrible hardship – for Bob I mean."

"Poor fella, I wouldn't trade places that's for sure."

I had not considered Mad Bob's marital status, that he might have a wife. I now considered that rather dull of me because, of course, his situation could have been almost anything. It might not have been just a corpulent wife I had to worry about. He might have had children too. Could I kill a man in front of his own wife and children? Would I flinch as I squeezed the trigger? It was not desirable, I knew that much. I ascertained that there were no children, but by this time the old man was looking at me with curiosity. In any event, my argument was not with her and certainly not with any children that might have existed, but she would be wise to keep out of the way. Nobody wanted collateral damage of that sort. I drained the weak froth at the lower end of my beer. I was not a big drinker, in fact it gave me an effect I was not altogether used to, so I thanked him for the conversation and walked out down the Montrose High Street, thinking about what tomorrow might bring. I would be up early in the morning. I needed to get down to Mad Bob's and survey the target in his lair.

I was over to the stable to look out Master Henry just after seven the next day, the sun rising in the cloud-filled sky behind my head. The boy, a thick-lipped, sideburned fellow, was asleep in the next bay to Master Henry, curled up on some straw against the wall. When he heard the stable door slam, he stirred and pulled his frayed braces over his shoulders. He said good morning and helped me saddle the horse and he pulled the bridle on over the horse's ears, feeding the bit between the teeth, he then pushed his knee hard against Master Henry's gut and pulled the girth tight. I spoke to him about the saddlebags. I would take one and leave the other two in his charge. I gave him a coin that he shuffled seamlessly into his pocket, sufficiently content with his reward to assist me onto my horse and then lead the pair of us out onto the High Street. I thanked him and walked past the front of the pub, but I was conscious that his eyes never left me throughout. I stopped Master Henry in his tracks and then half-walked, half-trotted slowly back.

I flicked the boy a second coin. "Just about the saddlebags," I said. "I don't want anyone sniffing around these bags. Keep them in a safe place, will you?"
The boy nodded. "Don't worry about the bags, sir," he said.
"What's your name?"

"Doug."

"Well, Doug. If I'm not back inside a week, the bags are yours anyway. Do with them what you like. If I am back, we'll sort something out for you." The boy smiled, unveiling a decent set of teeth between the heavy lips, a smile that transformed his face. I turned Master Henry around and we set off together at a brisk trot, sweeping through the morning greyness, until Doug could no longer see us.

Leaving the town, it was not long before we came upon the last building on the right, a solid, stone-built house with a slated roof and a broad black door. I kept on riding, trotting down between the hedges, breaking into the occasional canter. A mile from Montrose, the air cleared and lightened and the air seemed to fill with birds, the sound of herring gulls spilling tuneless honking from the shore. There were more houses, sporadically punctuating the green lane along which I rode. None of them seemed to match the house to which the old man had guided me. Eventually, I came upon the house that matched his description. It was more than three miles out, but to my mind less than four. Three miles and a further eight hundred and seventy-three horse paces and I came upon a bend in the track between two swathes of silver birch, clumped leafless together, and then down on the right, a scooped out hollow, a stepped up porch and a timber plank construction of some sort built over the top. I saw the hens first, strutting stupidly over the earth border in front of the house. I pulled into the side of the track, went amongst the trees and found a place to secure Master Henry. Once I had done so, he dropped his head and grazed. I ventured out thirty yards or so to see what more there was. I knelt down on the damp earth, peered out from behind the smooth trunk of an ash tree and looked down upon the house of Mad Bob Weir. The skinny old man behind the bar had said it was a house on its own, well beyond the town, with a porch and a green door – at least once upon a time it had been a green door and it might still be now, but you know, he said. Well, there was the door, closed against the outside elements, the colour of shit but I supposed it might have been green once.

My plan had been to wait, to work out when he came and went, who was there, what were their movements. I would then piece together the information and applying an intellect honed upon Mr Shifner's rosewood library at Tullis Board School, I would work out how best to respond. Yet, I was there, knees sinking into the damp earth, peering out from behind the heavy branches of the abundant trees, my father's Snider-Enfield laid across my thighs, and I had to ask myself what did I think I was waiting for. I knelt there for fifty-three minutes but I could not understand why I was holding back. Why was I waiting to concoct a carefully crafted plan when all I needed was to go in there, dip my hand into the justice bucket and loose off a few shots from the barrel of the Snider-Enfield? What was justice after all? The attainment of that which is just? Was that complicated? Was that any different from retributive justice? All I knew was that it was one way I could put right the wrong that had been done. Where I could inflict punishment for another man's wrongdoing. This man had done wrong and it was my intention that he would be forced to account. It made no difference that he never did wrong me directly; he had wronged my mother and my father and for that he was going to pay and I was going to enforce the payment. The thought that Mad Bob was down there in his house going about his business only served to heighten my growing fury, as if the proximity of the man was itself a further incendiary. I thought that I would have been cool and relatively calm when the object of my endeavours was placed in front of me. On the contrary, it fired me up with real anger.

In the fifty-fourth minute I made my decision. I took the saddlebag from Master Henry and slung it over my shoulder. My rifle was loaded and ready to fire. I walked down the green slope, my heels sinking into the mud, heading directly towards the house. Fifty yards short of the building, I tossed my rifle on its strap over my shoulder. I reached for one side of the saddlebag, pulled it open and extracted from the inside pocket two sticks of dynamite with beautiful thread-like fuses hanging off them. I closed the flap and tossed the bag once again over my shoulder. I struck a match against my boot, watched the phosphorous flare brighten and die down, protected it from any breeze and then lit the end of the first fuse. I looked at it as the fuse burnt down, held onto it too long if the truth be known, but then I hurled it overarm straight at the house. It had begun. It bounced on the edge of the porch, aired itself and clattered to a halt by the door. There were hens there strutting around the porch, scratching for a lone seed or something worth eating. They noted my arrival and then scattered as the action unfolded. The fuse burnt its way right down and, after a two second eerie silence, it created an explosion bigger and more powerful than I had ever experienced, even on the beach at Tullis. Too heavy on the nitroglycerin and too light on the sawdust. It blew the front door clean off its hinges, the smoke and dust hanging in the air. I saw a hen's leg fly up and crash against the window like a kindling twig. I saw two empty boots by the door, one of which was blown ten yards from the house, the other unmoved, smoking furiously. I could smell the explosive as I crossed the porch and entered Mad Bob's house with all the quiet rage I had nurtured these many years.

CHAPTER 49

When Mad Bob entered the room, he still hoped that
something, some inconsequential interception, would
divert him from his task. He had sailed down this
river a long time and he knew his chosen destination
lay ahead but it still filled him with some anxiety that
what he intended for his wife was something
irrevocable. He closed the door behind him without a
sound. Outside a dog barked, some Collie from a
neighbouring farm he would normally have yelled at
or in whose direction he would have loosed off a few
wild shots with his rifle. He could hear outside the
trees tossing their branches in a sudden breeze that
passed as quickly as it had come. Mad Bob stood by
the door and looked down the length of the bed. She
was half on the mattress and half out, the grey spread
draped against the bedend. She had a leg protruding
from beneath the sheet. She had on a camisole that
had ridden up against her thigh and he could see the
fat hanging off her protruding limb. He could hear
her breathing the late afternoon air, in through the
nose, steadily, rhythmically, out through the open
mouth. Like a pig. He heard the sound of air as it
squeezed out between her lips and the hypnotic rise
and fall of her chest beneath the covers. He stepped
forward, closer to the dusty, skin-scale, lumpy bed.
Her eyes were shut and her face was turned a little to
the right. There was a mark against her cheek made
by the indentation of piping on the cushion edge. He
took another step towards her. He was almost by her
side now and he could smell her sleepy breath. She
snorted. He could see one hand and the other secreted
beneath her thigh. Her lips were cracked and there
was a brown or orange tinge around her mouth. He

looked hard at the lips, that speaking thing that uttered such rotten waste. To him, it was a toilet hole, full of dead sludge and the source of all that rendered his life so worthless. Her chest continued to rise and fall, to show that it was still alive. She licked her lips and ran her free hand a glancing blow across her hair then let it slump by her side. Mad Bob still had the shovel in his left hand, containing a good quantity of chicken shit. He raised the shovel above the slack sheets, took hold of the handle with two hands and he rammed it hard against her mouth, splitting the lips at each end. The teeth disappeared into the shovel, her mouth widened and ripped into the comic look of a wide laugh, and he shoved deep in, his full weight behind the blow, with all the pent up hatred of the many years that had passed. He leaned on the slippery smooth handle and applied his entire body weight. The shovel slid further into her mouth, an open gash that was split now in a stretched tear from ear to ear. He threw himself onto the bed, brought his knees down hard against her arms and pinned them to her sides. He pushed harder on the shovel, then pulled it out, and it gulped and oozed a slurp. He thrust it back in again, her mouth flopping wider, gushing blood, and he tilted the shovel handle up the way and watched the hen shit slide down into the tunnel, into the open basin between her lips. Her eyes were wider now than he had ever seen them, filled with confusion, horror and resignation. She twitched and convulsed for what felt like minutes, but was less than fifty seconds, and then all movement was gone, her eyes as full now as they ever had been in life, yet vacant, staring, round and wide as thick pebbles in the river. For the first time in her life she had left without making a sound. He let go the shaft of the shovel and

287

slipped off the bed to the floor, his back to the Victorian spread where his wife lay dead.

CHAPTER 50

As I stood in the narrow hall, the smoking door still hung goonishly, tenuously, on its twisted steel hinges. Mad Bob appeared above me on the landing and squeezed a bullet from his rifle in my general direction. Good fortune took the shape of an open door on my left into which I had the quick sense to propel myself, moving with sufficient zip to avoid the bullet. From a prostrate position on the grubby bare wood floor, I poked the Snider-Enfield into the hall and pointed the barrel vaguely towards the landing, unleashing several shots of doubtful accuracy.

"What the hell do you want?" shouted the voice from the landing. "Who the fuck are you?" I was seeing red. All the anger and frustration, all the patient and considered waiting over many years had come to this. In my fury I remained silent. "Who are you?" he shouted again and fired another shot that ricocheted off the side wall.
"Logan," I said.
"Logan?" he shouted back. "I don't know any Logan."
"I think you do," I said.
"Where you from?" he yelled.
"Tullis," I said. The place went quiet. "Perhaps you remember now. In any event, it won't matter when you're dead."

Mad Bob fired a further shot, the bullet embedding itself in the wall by the front door. He fired another and then scurried backwards into one of the rooms behind. I heard a door slam. In the ensuing quiet, I pulled my knees up beneath me and hurled myself towards the staircase. There was no movement at the top of the stairs and I was pretty sure he was in the room up there and he had shut the door. I waited a little longer, then gradually pulled myself up and sprang two steps at a time. I could see the closed door he had entered - there was no other. I crouched before it, leaning in from one side, putting an ear close, but I could detect no movement nor sound. I stood back and released a shot from the Snider-Enfield, splintering the wood as it passed straight through the door panel and drilled its way into the room.

I followed the bullet in with a kick box against the door that took the heel off my boot. It was a room with a large bed against the opposite wall. There was paper on the walls, but old, scuffed and dirty. If there was a pattern it had lost its edge and instead it presented an overall strain of brown that I had not witnessed before. The floor was bare. To one side there was a dressing table with a chipped mirror above iron feet. The bed had an imposing wooden Victorian bedhead. Slumped against it was a woman with a large head. I looked at the sash window that was wide open, a light breeze blowing in, stirring the dust off the lace curtains. I heard noise and commotion and steered myself towards the window. There I could see a man kicking and beating a horse. I thought of Master Henry when I recognized the thump of hooves clattering along a grass track at breakneck speed. I moved closer to the window and saw the figure of Mad Bob clinging to the neck of an old pit pony, hammering hard across the ground, kicking up chunks of mud from the soft earth. I thought I saw him turn his face towards me, but he kept on going and was soon out of sight. I held my rifle at my side and watched him disappear, knowing that I had no hope in hell of shooting a moving target at that kind of distance. He had left his rifle leaned against the wall by the window.

I turned back to the fat woman in the bed. Curiously, her eyes were wide open and she had a large shovel clenched between her teeth and inside a lot of mud and possibly shit bunching up her cheeks. On closer inspection, it looked to me like hen shit. When I put my nose up close to her head, I knew it was hen shit. There was little expression on her face. I looked at her again. Surprise would have been appropriate. There was maybe just a touch of curiosity that she had ended her days with a mouth full of hen shit. She had a large hole in her forehead and I immediately thought well that is sod's own law: the bullet from my rifle could have ended up anywhere and it had to end up buried in this woman's head. I remembered my Kipling about *a Snider squibbed in the jungle, a big blue mark in his forehead, and the back blown out of his head.* For all the calm acceptance of her condition, the woman's eyes were crossed and between them the bullethole looked like a bindi, the mark of Kumkum. She would have plenty of time now for inner meditation and worship.

Mad Bob was well gone, carried away on a miniature retired pit pony, grey-white with black splashes and pink-edged eyes, leaving his dead wife behind, his possessions, and whatever shit had been his life. Something even told me I knew where he was going. I looked around the couple's home before I left. I went downstairs first. There was a sink full of dishes, a bag of abattoir meat knives, three cups and a stale loaf of bread. The dishes looked like they had been there for many days and the bread was hard and rough to the touch. There was fat and fungus floating on the oily water. There was a saddlebag in the hall but the pouches were stiff and empty. I looked inside the room into which I had propelled myself when Mad Bob loosened off his rifle from the landing. This room was tidy, little cotton-embroidered cushions gathering dust but puffed up, like nobody ever thought to sit upon them. I saw small traces of hen shit on the floor by the window, part flattened by somebody's shoe. In the corner, on the other side of the window, I found a decent sized hardwood desk. I pulled at the top drawer and found it locked. The second drawer flew open because I applied force, thinking it would be secured like the top one. I picked the drawer up off the floor. A small book with a cloth cover showed itself, some kind of log for purchasing timber and screws and the like. The bottom drawer I pulled gently. It had a handgun inside, looked old, the barrel blackened and no sign that it had been fired in recent times. The top drawer was annoying me, so I took the poker from the fireplace, jammed it into the crevice and levered the damned thing wide open like a dog's mouth. It split the wood facing but I was beyond worrying about the integrity of the interiors. There was a letter inside the drawer that I pulled from the recess and took over to the window. I read it in the grey light:

> *Well Bob, I am no great shakes with the pen but here's a letter anyway. Fucked if you need a personal appearance. We shared some business not so very long*

292

ago. You may remember. We both played our parts. The consequence of that party for me has not been good. You may have holes in your gut but my own father has disowned me. I won't see a farthing when he dies, or so he tells me. I recognise you got shot, but I am told that you live in some comfort and do not appear too stretched on the money side. I hear old fatboy is doing likewise. All very pleasing I'm sure, but I have nothing, have no prospect of anything and therefore I'm looking to you and fatboy for something. You understand? If you wish to keep the lid on this thing, you could do better than work something out with fat boy and arrange me a money transfer. Be warned, I am serious about this. It's only fair. I'm desperate and you got to look after yourself in that situation.

The letter was signed "Turner". Beneath was written an address. I had to read it twice because I was so convinced it could not be right. None of it made any sense. I shook my head. The handwriting was good and surprisingly legible. If it was not for the content you might have thought it had been written by a schoolteacher. I put the letter in my top pocket and buttoned down the flap. Something was not right. It was signed Turner but the man I was after was

Traynor. Who the hell was Turner? Traynor came from Buckstone – that was what Fawcett told me. Finally, Turner had written part of his address on this letter. It was marked Tullis? That made no sense.

As I passed through the front door, I dropped a small detonator with a black powder wrap. It was an interesting device that I had developed over two months in the old byre. It lay there on the floor as I stepped out into the light. Between fifteen and twenty seconds later, it exploded into a fireball, the blast carrying up and sideways in a mass of clearly defined orange, by which time I was already upon the hill retrieving my horse, Master Henry. I looked round to see a long plume of smoke and big tongues of flame licking out the front door. I climbed aboard Master Henry and I rode away from the scene as the sparks crackled through the air behind me. I was not entirely pleased with myself; the cool calculation of what I had planned for Mad Bob had imploded. Mrs Weir got her cremation without asking. Things had a habit of not working out quite the way you planned them. Still, that job was done and I was headed for Buckstone.

CHAPTER 51

On the old Braid Road, by the gated entrance to the Pentland Cemetery and on the east side of Buckstone itself, stands the *Buckstane* which is built into the existing wall. This is a march stone, about three feet high and one foot wide. It is a feudal relic, occupying a commanding site on another of General Wade's Hanoverian roads and it marks the spot where the buckhounds were released when the King of Scotland took to hunting the region. It will not surprise the astute reader to learn that it is from the *Buckstane* that the small town of Buckstone derived its name. I was several miles (four and a half) east of Buckstone when I was almost separated from Master Henry by some mad fool galloping his horse in the opposite direction. He looked at me like a wild man, frowning so hard his eyebrows almost knitted themselves into a woolly bandana; he muttered a profanity and watched me ride away with a look of some curiosity. I did not see why he was so mad at me; if anyone had a problem with equestrian skills it was him, but I soon forgot about that. Perhaps an hour later, I reached Buckstone itself. Earlier, I had felt some heat in Master Henry's fetlock, so I walked Master Henry as I approached this small conurbation, squeezed by its low, wet-drizzled, black-slated houses, its dry stone dykes, its twisted, red-berried hawthorn hedges spiking outward, and I sensed a place where hounds might well rip the throats from travellers foolish enough to stray too far off the Pentland Path.

Whatever reason I had for any sense of foreboding, the road transported me through the greyness of Buckstone itself, revealing one and a half storey houses to the left side, ivy-clad, patchy, plastered walls, chimneys smoking and bare ground with occasional shrubs, growth and trees on the other. A stubble-faced man stood in a doorway in a waistcoat, tweed tie and black trousers, drawing on a hand-rolled cigarette in his cupped hand. The chain off his fob watch hung from his waist. He looked at me out of the corner of his eye but there was something about him that made me look twice. I saw a woman through a downstairs window with a child against her bosom. Up a rough track off the main street I caught sight of a boy with a flat cap on his head, as he kicked a dog and I heard it howl. Further on were a number of shops, a man selling buckets and birch tree brushes and a barrow surrounded by more people, maybe just a few, buying bottles of ginger ale. The road was a broken track full of holes and puddles and I pulled Master Henry up outside a shop with a proud banner above its window: *Domenico Corrolla* it read. The door in was off a narrow wynd to the side of the shop. I hitched Master Henry to a small metal ring to one side of the wynd and stepped inside the shop. I sniffed around the shelves and then purchased a cup of beef soup and an oat biscuit off an Italian with a black moustache, part of the immigrant stream that was spreading north, beyond cities like Manchester and Glasgow, into the smaller towns of central Scotland.

I sat on a cushioned chair, a welcome change from the saddle, and consumed the soup. Some while later, I bought a further biscuit that I secreted in a handkerchief and inserted into my chest pocket. I asked the Italian if he knew where the Traynor house was.

"Gelati?" he said.

I said: "No gelati," and flapped the extended finger of my left hand sideways. "I am asking if you know a man whose name is Traynor?" I said, as if speaking to a deaf, sub-normal cretin. "Traynor?" I repeated.

"Traynor?" he said.

"Yes, Traynor?" I smiled back.

"Corrolla," he said with a heavy smile and twinkly eyes.

I stepped out of the shop consumed by thoughts of further enquiry, and then, as if struck by a thunderbolt, all the lights went out. My head entered into a deep, unrelenting blackness, punctuated by flashes of a bright, starlike quality, and I felt my chin hit the stone although I felt no pain as it did so. It was an interesting experience. I had in all probability been hit on the head with a fence post, a small tree or a sledgehammer. As I fell, I was aware that I was falling and I recognized the feel of stone as it scraped against my skin and the resounding thump as it hit the side of my face. I was aware of voices, grunting, rope and the spit off a man's tongue. Then I was inside a basket and it smelt of wet straw. My legs were crumpled beneath me and no matter how much I wished to move them they remained stubbornly unresponsive, as if the link between my brain and my body was uncoupled. I may have lost consciousness, but I was then aware of movement, a rumbling, jostling, vibration, as I was thrown from side to side. I assumed I was in a cart of some sort, moving at some speed, too groggy to know where I was going or even what direction I was headed. I forced myself to raise my hands above my head. I had a sense that there was a lid to my enclosure and if I only pushed I could break out into the light. I pressed with my hands in response to the voice inside my head and the basket top rose an inch or two above the rim. It was clear enough that I was indeed on the back of a horse-drawn cart, moving at speed, houses replaced by open fields, trees and fences and the splash and jolt of wet mud in the pot-holed road. Strangely, I could see Master Henry tethered to the back of the cart, eyes wide, breaking from a fast trot to a canter, his eyes catching mine as if unclear about my intentions. Then the lid rose up out of sight and a hammer or a mallet came down against my skull, just slow enough for me to see the hand that gripped its shaft. The fourth finger was missing. Once again, all was darkness.

CHAPTER 52

Once Mad Bob had split his wife's face open with the hen shit shovel, he had slumped to the floor. A great weight had been lifted from his shoulders and he intended to enjoy the moment. Without even articulating the thought, he proposed to luxuriate in the soothing balm of peace and feminine absence, and when he had finished luxuriating he intended to wash down his knives and get to work. Twelve years of his life had been spent doing what he considered to be his dream job, cutting up offal at Skene's abattoir. It was a place he could get away to, a place he could escape the whine of Mrs Weir and her incessant complaints, gripes and sporadic swipes of physical violence. He had been quickly promoted to boning at the abattoir and that was when they gave him his own butcher's knives. They were hung on a hook by the back door and he intended to polish and sharpen his knives before dismantling his dead wife's limbs. He had already dug a neat little hole, to a significant depth, beneath the new hen hutch for the purpose of housing Mrs Weir's bones. It was all prepared. These thoughts did not progress very much further because minutes later he heard an explosion that dispelled the need for such industry. His moment to luxuriate was over more quickly than he intended. He opened the bedroom door and tentatively stepped out onto the landing, leaning his head towards the stair and straining to see what had occurred. He could observe very quickly that the front door was hanging off its hinges and there was smoke and dust and broken plaster across the hall floor. He was momentarily stunned by what he saw and was unable to make sense of it. Instinctively, Mad Bob reached for the rifle he was in the habit of leaving outside his wife's bedroom door. Some might ask why you would leave a rifle on the landing, but Mad Bob figured that a rifle on the landing was the most accessible place from all points, upstairs and downstairs; it was the hub of the house and if he needed his rifle in a hurry, no matter where he was, he calculated that the nearest point would be on the landing. It was logical. Besides, it was not unusual for him to take up a position at the upstairs window and shoot the heads off foxes or rabbits. Sometimes, he would shoot at a distant neighbour's Collie dog if it was causing a nuisance. At the present time, there were no foxes, rabbits or dogs to take a shot at because no sooner was the rifle in his hands than he was looking down the barrel and firing at the figure of a stranger in the hallway. The damn fuck had just entered his line of sight by walking through the broken door like he had every right to be there. Later he would blame his eyes, his lack of practice, the dirty muzzle, the rusted bullet, the sweat on his fingers, the blocked toilet – almost anything but his own incompetence – for the fact that he missed his target and before he could release further fire, the man had rolled into the room off the hall and was firing back at him with extraordinary accuracy. Mad Bob cried out to him, who the fuck was he? What came back at him was like a long-forgotten tune. At first he could not make sense of it. He thought that name was in the past. He stayed away from Tullis, just for that reason. He had heard the name Logan. Logan? This man down there was Logan? Mad Bob lurched back into the bedroom, slamming the door behind him. He felt giddy and confused, like he had seen a ghost. He threw the window open. There was no way he was hanging around. He dragged his body out on to the corrugated lean-to beneath the window. Mid-dive he realized he had left the rifle by the wall inside the window. Too late now, but what would anybody think if he was shot by his own rifle? He would be a laughing-stock. He slid down the iron sheeting and found himself hanging off the guttering just a few feet from the ground. He dropped and ran round to the back of the house. He was panting heavily; that old lung was full of shit, he thought; that was the mad bitch when she shot me. The old pit pony was tethered there and Bob threw off the halter, jumped on his back and kicked his sides like his life depended on it. There was little time for pleasantries and the stumpy old pit pony reacted with unaccustomed shock, rocketing along the track, away from the back of the house, taking off as fast as its miner legs would safely carry him, hooves beating hard against the dry earth, propelling the two, man and beast, in a westerly direction. Bob's face formed itself into the shape of a grin. He looked back over his shoulder but could see nothing at the window, no gun, no face, nothing, just a wisp of smoke across the rooftop, dissipating gently in the breezeless air. Mrs Weir dead in her bed but maybe, he thought, this was a useful intrusion. After all, who else could be responsible for her death, other than that lunatic Logan?

CHAPTER 53

When I came to, I was wedged into an early bentwood Thonet rocker. Thonet had mastered the art of bending wood under the application of steam and he had succeeded in producing a lightweight rocking chair with a simple flowing form. The rattan seat of this rocker had been cut from the frame and my rear end had been forced down into the opening. My thighs were pressed hard against my chest in front of me. The wooden strut at the rear of the chair pressed hard against the small of my back, chaffing the skin and causing it to cut and bleed. My wrists were bound, tied in a greasy knot behind and below me. It was not a comfortable position in which to find oneself. I rocked gently, stupidly, in the stillness of the room.

When the rocking motion stopped, or some time afterwards, I opened my eyes and it seemed to me I was in a relatively dark room, full of shadows and unlit corners. My mouth was dry and my lips were cracked. I could make out a window and some white and rose-flowered curtains. I could see the edge of a round, cloth-topped table and three dark wood chairs with red velvet cushions. There was a fire to one end of the room with a white marble mantle and a green insert. The occasional flames puckered out from the cast iron grate and found themselves reflected in the brass coal bucket to the left of the fire. Above the mantle, and supported by it, was a gilt-framed mirror and in the corner, a small upright piano. Seated at the piano I could see the back of a man, and as I gathered my senses, I was able to hear the notes he played.

I have never professed to be a musician but in Mr Shifner's rosewood library there was a book of sheet piano music that I had often taken some pleasure in scrutinising. I quickly discovered that it was like learning a new language and I found that with a little application I was able to understand its fundamental vocabulary. It may have been the constant repetition of the main phrase, but it seemed to me I had some recognition of the notes the man was playing. It was a bagatelle – short, pleasant and not particularly demanding on the performer. Played in A minor and set in 3/8 time, the left hand begins with arpeggios alternating between A minor and E major, then C major and G major, before returning to the original theme. Another time I would have shown an interest in such things, I might even have named it, but in the circumstances I was short of things to say.

When he stopped playing, I said: "Your pedal technique is shit."
There was silence in the room as the pianist took in this observation, then a voice snarled from somewhere behind my head: "Turn the fucker round."

I felt myself spinning in the chair, awkwardly wedged, my rear end just inches above the floor. My sight took in the pianist to my left and two other men. I could not tell how old they were, but when I looked at them and heard them speak from the shadows, swallowed up by the gloom, I knew that they were not young men: they were middle-aged, tired-looking people, coughing twice, weak lungs, rough, rasping, uncouth, one bearded and the other two clean shaven. "Not pretty," said the big man, seated on a deep sofa.

"What did you expect?" said the pianist. "Bonnie Prince Charlie?"

Nobody laughed. The third man, leaning heavily against the wall by the door, never raised his head but when he moved towards me he appeared to grow in height. He swayed like a tall tree. "Nothin' bonnie there," he said. He had a thin, reedy voice.

"Your mother enjoyed that tune," said the big, balding man on the sofa. His arms were rested against the top of his large belly, crossed in front of him. They looked like they were too short and would only just reach. "Isn't that right, Jesse?"

"If memory serves me right," he answered, truculently banging the peddle.

"Are you Traynor?" I said.

He just looked at me. "Interesting question," he said.

The pianist turned on his chair, away from the keys, and looked to the middle of the room. "I thought they said he was a clever fuck."

"Are you Traynor?" I repeated to the fat man on the sofa.

He laughed. "Don't you know?"

"Obviously, I don't."

"You're like a bent, fucking compass."

"What do you mean by that?"

"It's a bit like a hunting dog. You set it loose and you tell it, go this way or go that way, and off it goes." He picked some skin off the top of his ear. "Meanwhile the fox has gone back to the hen house."

"You seem to know me," I said.

"I know of you," he said. "I was told you might be coming."

"Stupid thing to do," said the pianist.

"Are you surprised?" I said.

"By your stupidity?" he asked.

"How long will you be keeping me in this contraption?" I said, indicating the bentwood chair.

"Until we decide what to do with you," said the fat man, unfolding his arms.

"You can't keep me here," I said.

"Just watch us, fella."

"If you're short of space," said the pianist. "I can break your legs?"

"My legs are fine," I said. "But thankyou."

The lanky guy by the wall breezed over, a heavy black beard brushing through his fingers. As he approached, he swung his boot against my rear end. The pain was deep and bruising and brought tears to my eyes; I grunted loudly from the blow without screaming, without yelling. I knew what I was feeling and I did not plan to share it with them.

"Better now?" he said.

I grimaced. "Much better," I said. "Thankyou. Maybe a bit to the right if you could."

For a skinny man he was remarkably strong. He picked up the rocking chair in two hands and then simply shook me out onto the floor, like I was a fish in a holding net. Emerging at height, it was a hard landing. My hands remained tied behind me and I hit the floor with the side of my head for the second time that day. It was not doing me much good.

"Why are you here?" said the fat man.

I lifted my head from the floor. "Is your name Traynor?" I asked.

"Yes," said the fat man. "My name is Traynor and you're going to wish you'd never fucking heard of me."

CHAPTER 54

By the time Mad Bob was in through the large gate outside Buckstone, his little pit pony had nothing left to give. On four short legs, he had galloped the full distance from Montrose almost without a break and his light coat was wet with sweat and foam. His nostrils flared wildly as he drew in all the breath his lungs could take. Bob dismounted by the door, immediately adjacent to a large iron water trough. He crashed through the side door, ran past the kitchen and shouted down the hallway: "Hey? Anyone here?"

"Yeah, we're here," said the big man calmly, emerging from the room to one end of the hall. "What the fuck do you want?"

"We've got a problem, Traynor," he began, but then realized he too was panting like his pony and could hardly speak. He pulled a cloth from his pocket, wiped his mouth and then his forehead. "Some bloke," he said. "My place, came in…!"

"Whoa! You're making me giddy, you ass. What bloke?"

"There's a bloke, Jesus, at my house," he said. "Came to my place, in there waving his gun about. Blew the door in. Killed my wife. Not too sure but he left a bullet in her head. Place is on fire now. Guy a total nutcase. He said he was a… you're not going to believe this Traynor!"

"Said he was a what?"

"Said his name was Logan."

"Logan?"

"That's what he said."

"Is that all?" said the fat man.

Mad Bob looked confused. "What do you mean, is that all?"

306

"You said it was serious?" said Traynor.

"He killed my fucking wife!" said Mad Bob. "Are you not hearing me? He burnt my fucking house down! I think that is reasonably fucking serious!"

"He mention the Logan farm?"

"In a way, he kind of did. He said he was somebody Logan – I don't know who - and I got the feeling just by the way he blew in my front door that he wanted to kill me."

"Why would I be interested?" said Traynor, acting bored. "What's all this got to do with me anyway?"

"The clue is in the name," said Mad Bob.

"So, he's a Logan. So the fuck what?"

"If he knows about me, stands to reason he knows about you," said Mad Bob. "Let's face it, there's only one thing he would be interested in."

"I don't see the connection," he said. "In any event, he knows nothing about me. Unless maybe you've led him here. Is that what you've done, you fuckin' maggot? You led him here, have you?"

"He knew where I was."

"So?"

"I bet he knows where he can find you too."

"Plenty reasons why he wouldn't," said Traynor.

"Chances are he's coming here."

Traynor stood in front of Mad Bob and studied his face. He did not like what he was looking at, never had done. He had covered for him, partly to keep the constabulary away. Mad Bob was a bad case, he would spill his own guts if somebody nudged him. No more backbone than he had stomach. "He's coming after you, Bob," Traynor said. "Doesn't mean he's got any beef with me."

"Come on Mr Traynor. We're in this together, mate."

"Don't you mate me, you little shit," he said. "You wipe your own arse."

Mad Bob moved a fraction closer. "Sink or swim: we need to deal with this together," he said quietly, their faces so close that Mad Bob could identify each hair growing out of Traynor's bent nose. He wiped his own nostril with his fingers. He smelt hen shit. "Stupid not to," he added a little more calmly.

"It may be you've led him here, that's what I'm thinking. That would be a serious mistake."

"If I have, then I have," he said. "Tough. But whatever I have or have not done, he's now your problem as much as mine."

"Is that what you're thinking, you little cunt?"

"Look, Traynor, we need to deal with this maniac," said Mad Bob. "We can blame each other later, if that's what you want."

"I intend to do just that," said Traynor. "But I don't have your patience."

"The thing to know just now is that he's got guns and I think he's coming here. He tried to kill me. There's every reason to think he wants you too. Just think about that, Traynor."

"And you led him here, didn't you, Bob?" the big man shouted back. "Good old Mr Traynor, is that what you thought? He'll sort this boy Logan out! He'll sort him out for me."

"Maybe I did. I don't know. I didn't see him follow, but my guess is he was coming anyway."

"Billy!" A tall, bearded man stepped out of the shadows. "Give Bob some water. He looks so very thirsty." Billy stepped towards Bob and picked him up by the collar. He was light, all air and bone. "Give him a nice long drink, he's had a fuck of a ride."

308

A short time later, they climbed up onto the forward seat of the horse cart. The fat man, Traynor, cracked the frayed end of the whip against the horse's rear and the wheels turned with a creak and a jolt, the dust rose from the earth and the short, fat man on the left and the tall, skinny man on the right were away at speed along the track, heading rapidly down the road east, towards Buckstone and Montrose. The cart was unevenly balanced, leaning to the left. The pianist was already some distance ahead of them on a single chestnut horse, ridden at full stretch, with a rising wind pushing at his back, lifting his jacket tails to reveal a tan wool lining.

The town of Buckstone was their first stop but they did not intend to spend any time there. They figured that if this man Logan was coming they might as well get to him first. Not too much time had been wasted and they were already on the outskirts of Buckstone, when they spotted the pianist coming back towards them at a gallop, slapping his hat against his horse's neck. "I've seen him!" he shouted, as he drew up alongside the cart, his horse skittering anxiously. "Move fast, Traynor, he's in Buckstone. We can have him now."
"What are we waiting for?" said Traynor, wiping his lip, his thin hair wild and wispy across his crown. "Let's go get him!" he yelled and cracked the leather reins above the horse's back.

CHAPTER 55

It struck me that something was still not quite right. Whilst it seemed to me I had come and, to some extent, I had found what I was looking for, there was something missing. Some small piece of the puzzle was a bad fit. If I had got it right, all the pieces should fit neatly together, harmonious, no bumps, no rough edges. The first verse should ease into the second. The string section should fade and make way for the woodwind, the brass or the percussion, they should sound together as if they belonged together. Here, in my mind, the sections were playing the pieces without a conductor, breaking in early, leaving late. I was confused: the overall picture was not making sense. It seemed to me that there was a fat, balding man. His name was Traynor and lucky me, I had tracked him down. There was also a bearded, lanky man. And there was a pianist with a missing finger. To what extent they were involved and to what extent they had been involved, I did not know. I had the feeling that they were all involved in some way or another, all covering for each other, and probably had been over all these years since the day they arrived at the Logan farm. I did not detect any fondness for me or sympathy for my discomfort.

I turned over the pieces in my head. So, the fat man had a name: he was called Traynor. I did not know who the pianist was, but the missing finger on his left hand had not escaped my notice. I did not fancy his chances with a more complicated score. I recalled all too well that Aunt Marion had described a missing finger and most people in my experience had a full complement. My father had said one of them liked to

310

hum too but I had heard little evidence of that. Yet, a pianist might make a good hummer. There was also, it was reported, a tall fellow who played a part in events on the day. That was what we understood anyway. This man here was lanky as a hangman's noose with an ugly beard to boot. The fat man Traynor had an old lady in the house. Was it his mother? That was what the old man at the *Kingfisher* had told me. I did not get the best look at her from my contorted position in the bentwood Thonet rocker. She came in once they had started to drag the story out of me, but they were quick to push her out the door and I was not even sure she had seen me. I am not sure she knew exactly where she was.

"What the fuck are you doing here, Logan?" Traynor said eventually.
"You think you could just walk in here and shoot us?" said the lanky one, his voice high. "What were you planning to do?"
"A stick of dynamite in your pouch and a prehistoric rifle? Is that what you call a plan?" said Traynor. He stepped towards me and knelt down. They had beaten me already, whipped my face with hands, sticks and shoehorns. I think my nose was broken but whatever, there was blood and it was dripping out of my nostril onto the thin rug against the wood floor. These boys did not seem overly house-proud because the spillage on the soft furnishings made no discernible impression on them. "Look here, Logan. You are talking about things that happened a long time ago."
"Long since done and fucking dusted," said the lanky one.
"Shut up, Billy!" said Traynor. The lanky one stood back, leaned against the wall and stared up at the

ceiling. So, his name was Billy, another piece fell into place.

"Feels like yesterday to me," I said, my jaw creaking against the words.

"You weren't even there!" said Billy and Traynor again looked at him, irritated, but Billy was untroubled. "What do you know about it?"

"Oh, I was there," I said.

"Like hell you were!"

"Oh, I was there alright."

"You weren't even born," he said, moving back from the wall and approaching me. "Think you could come here, did you, take some revenge? Get your own back on those bad boys? For something you don't know nothing about?" He ran at me and kicked hard at the underside of my legs. "Revenge you piece of shit!" and he swung his boot at me again. "Look where it's got you."

The pianist sat down at the chair in front of the piano. "What we're going to do," he said, "is play some Schubert. What do you think, Logan? Maybe you're not in the mood for Schubert. I always play Schubert when things get a little tense," he said. "Or what about Beethoven? Let's play some Beethoven, shall we?" He played the notes from the *albumblatt*. It was Beethoven, of course it was. I knew it was Beethoven, even with the fourth finger missing. A minor, E major. C major, G major, and back again. Was this what he hummed when he killed her and I was there, just a heartbeat away? "Each time I hit this note," he said, helpfully playing a D major with his left hand, "the cunt gets a fucking kick. Okay Billy? Once the cunt has had his kick, he tells us everything. Everything about this vendetta he is on. If the tune stops or we stop kicking, then that will be it for today. Okay? Are the rules of the game clear, Logan?" I said nothing. Billy stepped back towards me. "Fine, let's begin. One-two-three," he counted, and so it went: with each D major, of which there were many, a boot connected with my shoulder, my back, my legs or wherever looked to be the most desirable fit. It was my first musical beating. The pianist had the skill to reappear seamlessly back at the beginning of the piece, many times over, and the blows rained down in blind musical obedience.

Some time later, I found myself breathing dust in a coal cellar. I thought I was dead, but after careful examination I discovered that I was not. I worked out it was a coal cellar by meticulous assessment of the available facts. It was a locked room. It was dark. It had a heavy door. There was a huge pile of coal. It smelled dusty. I did not remember how I came to be in there. My throat was dry and creaky. My lips were cut and my face felt puffy and sore. My ribs were layered in heavy bruises and some of those bones were probably broken. I had sat myself up and I was taking it all in and I was not impressed. I groaned each time I moved. I was grateful that my hands were no longer tied or the circulation would have gone completely. What time was it? What day was it? I had no idea how long I had been down there. I could hear no noise, no sounds, no wind, nothing, and I sat in silence for a long time. But it was relatively warm in this dusthole: warm, stuffy and I could smell spermaceti. For those with a limited understanding of liquid fuel development, spermaceti is a wax extracted from a sperm whale. Some people believe this wax is coagulated semen, and it may come as a disappointment to learn that spermaceti does in fact come from the whale's head not his sexual organs. It was also well known at the time as a useful domestic product. I felt along the floor, following my nose, and soon I came across its source: a huge vat of soft spermaceti, no doubt used for fuelling lamps and making candles. Well, spermaceti was about as much use to me now as an invitation to Queen Victoria's garden party. However, at the exact moment that I concluded my situation was so chillingly desperate, my eye caught something at the top of the room, where the ceiling might be. I thought I had fooled myself but I discovered I could only see it if I looked to one side and used my peripheral vision. The moment I looked directly up, it disappeared. Some things in life you have to come at from the side. I felt my way around the coal. I touched the walls. I felt pipes and what could have been a shovel. I worked out where the coal was and then I set about climbing up onto the pile. The difficulty was as I climbed, either I sank into it or it avalanched down and I made little progress. After a while, the coal pile was flattened out a good bit and I was able to feel the wall and I touched along the stonework to see what else lay there. It seemed important to me to find out what it was that I could see so faintly at the top of the wall to the store, but there was no obvious way to get there. As I moved along the wall, my knuckles clunked against another pipe. It was cast iron and appeared to run vertically from the ceiling down to the floor. It felt rough under my hands, like it had never been painted, was maybe rusted, but when I pulled on it to see that it was secure it did not move, it was quite solid. The rough surface meant that it was easier to grip. I worked out that if I climbed up the pipe, hopefully I would be able to reach whatever it was up there, close to the top wall of the store. The first two times I failed to get any purchase with my boots and I slipped heavily off the pipe and half way down the coal pile. I cursed myself, my life and all who had ever known me, but the third time, I managed to wedge the toe of my boot into the gap between the pipe and the wall. Eight minutes later I was at the top, where it remained gloomy but I could see that what I had been looking at was a wooden door or a hatch and there was a small amount of light leaking in around its edges. I pulled on the door and then pushed against it, but whilst there was some movement it seemed to me that in all likelihood it was bolted or latched from the outside. I needed something with which to prise it open. There was nothing else for it other than to descend back to the bottom and find something that would provide the necessary leverage – and hope that I could get back up again. I descended the pipe and scrambled over the coal pile. I felt around the room to see if there was anything I might use. There was nothing beyond the shovel I had found earlier. I wedged the coal shovel beneath my arm and dragged myself to the top of the coal pile. I then gripped the pipe and one inch at a time, moved on up, the shovel still gripped by my armpit. I reached the top of the pipe and the weak strip of rectangular light. I was pondering how I would manage to hold onto the pipe and at the same time apply the shovel to the gap. Despairingly and with very little hope, I ran my hand further up the pipe and to my astonishment, felt it turn at a ninety degree angle into the wall itself. At the underside of the turn, I found a sufficient gap to thread my arm through, beneath the pipe, and in doing so I was able to hook myself to the wall. I used my other arm to insert the shovel into the daylight gap, then wiggled it to and fro, repeatedly, in the hope that this small movement would tease out the securing screws. Little happened but, with increasing desparation, I pressed on. My other arm was taking all my weight and was agonizingly painful and tired. I was terrified that the shovel would break or bend and become of no further use, so I applied the leverage gently at first but soon realized that I was getting nowhere and was tiring fast. I had no choice but to apply further force and leverage and risk catastrophe. And then it began to rock. I could feel the hatch give just a little at first as it creaked under the pressure, and when it did so even more light seeped into the store. As the gap increased, I was able to grab a glimpse of the black hole in which I found myself. I resumed my work, pushed and pulled and as the opening widened I wedged the shovel further into the gap and continued with my effort. Suddenly, it was not the screws that came loose but the entire wood panel on the hatch split with a resounding crack. I stopped all movement, suspended from the pipe, the shovel still in place. Seconds later, I still could not hear any sound and I presumed therefore that I had not been heard by my captors. I edged the shovel in again and pushed upwards, forcing the wood to give way and splinter. I pulled the shovel out and felt for the latch. It was in fact a metal bolt and I was able to lift one side and slide its length away from the hoop that secured it. The hatch door opened and I could see that outside it was light. It looked to be early morning on a dull day but I could not be sure. What was clear to me was that the hatch I had broken through was the means by which coal could be dropped into the store from

316

outside without the need to enter the house. It was also my escape route, but first I would have to detach myself from the iron pipe and at the same time haul myself, using all the strength I had left in my other arm, through the opening above my head. It was a task I would not have enjoyed contemplating when I was fit and sound, but there is something about fear that feeds motivation, and with little hesitation I made the leap, releasing my right arm and hanging from the lintel by my left. With two hands on the ledge I pulled myself up, squeezing myself through the narrow opening and stretching out, breathless, on the grass beyond the hatch. I rolled onto my back and sucked in the clean air, caught my breath and then rose onto my knees. I was at the back of the house. The light was coming up but it was still the early part of the morning. There was a stretch of overgrown grass between where I lay and then there was the beginnings of a small wood, seemingly made up of spruce and birch, good cover for my escape. However, I noticed that to my right there was a small stone building, a kind of outhouse, and I decided to have a look. With my back pressed against the wall of the house, I moved towards the building. Now I could see the roof was sagging and the slates had slipped. The two doors to the building were open and inside, head tugging at a bag of dusty hay, was Master Henry in a makeshift stall. He appeared unconcerned by our predicament. I saw the saddle parked on the side panel of the stall; lying on the floor next to it was the bridle. I patted Master Henry on the neck and ruffled his dark mane; he snorted and chomped. I went back to the open gate and looked over to the house where I was glad to see nothing stirred. Returning to Master Henry, I re-entered the stall and

317

heaved the saddle onto his back and then taking the bridle from the floor, slipped the bit between his teeth and the leather strap over his ears. I reached under his belly and gripped the loose end of the girth that I pulled and then buckled. I led Master Henry out of the building, along the stretch of grass behind the house, his hooves quiet in the soft grass. There was a small stretch of green scrubland between me and the spread of trees that grew beyond. I knew that this was dangerous since I could be seen or heard at any moment from the house, but I had little alternative but to chance my luck and take the risk of being seen. I had nothing to defend myself with – no rifle, no bullets and no weaponry of any sort. It was now or never. I moved at speed towards the wood, leading Master Henry by the reins. I made it across the grassy stretch and, once in amongst the trees, again I stopped to listen, to see if I heard any sound that might indicate the alarm had been raised. There was no movement, no sign of life, no hint that I had been seen and that they were onto me. I put my foot into the iron stirrup and pulled myself up onto Master Henry's back. I rode further into the woods, threading my way between the clusters of silver birch and the ubiquitous spruce and occasional rowan trees. I ached from head to toe, but the movement seemed to have loosened some of my stiffness and I swayed in the saddle with the rhythm of my horse. I knew that I would not have long before my absence was discovered. I had to move and I had to make quick progress. I kicked him on and Master Henry jolted forward as if he understood my impatience. I had a sense that the sun was positioned forward of my right shoulder, what little I could see of it. That was east by my calculation and east was where I was headed.

CHAPTER 56

I arrived back at Montrose a little under three hours later. It seemed to be about lunchtime and I was not aware that anyone had followed me. In the distance I could see Joseph Hume, his formidable presence in statue form, appearing strong, resolute, even inspirational in the clear late morning light. Before I reached the statue I turned into the opening to my left side, arriving at the *Kingfisher* stable. The boy immediately stepped out and I could not miss the look of surprise upon his face when he saw me.

"Hello, Doug. Were you not expecting me?"

"No sir," he answered quietly.

"Has anybody been asking after me?"

"No sir," he said.

"Got the saddlebags?"

"Yes sir."

"Looked inside yet?"

"Not my place to, sir," he said.

"Sure about that?" I said.

"Yes, sir."

I patted Master Henry on the neck and nuzzled my palm against his nose. His breath was still hot and blowing from the long ride. "Some water, some feed and some hay. Okay?"

"You alright, sir?" Doug said. "Can I get you something?"

"A bath?" I said. I realised I must have looked an interesting sight: my face was blackened by coal dust and I was bruised, cut and bloodied by the heavy beatings and my clothing was filthy and torn. "I'm going in," I said.

"You're back then," said the old man, eyes yellow and greasy.

"I'll stay a night, if you don't mind," I said.

"Costs gone up," he answered.

"For what reason?" I asked.

"Recent circumstances," he said. "Recent events up the road here at Mr Weir's premises."

"I see. I still need a room and I want it at the front this time."

"It's extra for a room with a view," he said.

"Of Joseph Hume?" I enquired. "I was thinking it might be worth a discount."

"Take it or leave it," he said. Then he looked at me. "I'll throw in a bath for nothing."

I took the deal that was being offered, not because I coveted the bronzed view of Joseph Hume's backside; rather more because it offered a clear view of the road into Montrose and for obvious reasons I wished to be the first to know of any new arrivals. Still, I told him that for that price I expected to have my clothes washed and ironed. He told me to leave them outside my door and Doug would collect them. "I'll have them perfumed for sir," he said sarcastically, "free of charge."

Once in my room, I stripped off and examined my beaten body. Cuts, bruises, maybe a broken rib or two. The bath along the gloomy corridor was filled all of three inches with a brown tepid water that quickly turned black when I immersed myself. Later, the thick-lipped boy, Doug, delivered a ham sandwich and a glass of warm beer to my room. He came back later with a small parcel that he laid on the end of my bed. "Your clothes, sir."

"That was quick," I said. "Are they dry?"

"Of course."

I lay back against the bedend, feeling the sharp pain from my ribs as I did so. For once I was in the mood for talking. "What do you say about revenge, Doug?" I asked him.

"I don't know what you mean," he said.

"Revenge," I said. "You know, when someone kicks your arse and you want to kick him back but twice as hard."

"Doesn't seem much point," he answered.

"Why?" I said.

"Cos he'll only kick your arse again and he'll mean it this time."

"You might be right," I said. As he was about to close the door, I shouted out to him: "Have my horse ready at five, will you," I said as I closed my eyes. "I intend to get off early. And pack the saddlebags. I'm not sure if I'll be back here again."

I heard the door click as he left. I lay back with my eyes closed, but despite my tiredness my mind was busy and would not lie down. I thought of Keira, that image of her in a white cotton gown would never escape me, belted at the waist just enough to tempt me to discover what wonders lay beneath. Truth be told, things had already moved far beyond that temptation. That skin, so smooth, and those eyes twinkling like blue-green ice in a heavy frost, framed by her long dark hair. I had forgotten nothing, not a detail, not even the colour of the light as it filtered through the hall and across the tops of her shoulders. I thought we would make a fine pair now, with our blue, beaten faces. With my eyes closed, I sensed her lips against mine and I breathed in the fragrance that was Keira.

"Sir?" I was suddenly aware of being shaken from my sleep. "Sir?" the voice said again. "Wake up!"

"What is it?" I said groggily, for in my mind I had been far away. "Doug? What do you want?"

"Downstairs!" he whispered. "Men looking for you! Asking questions!"

"Who?" I said.

"Not seen before," he said. "Not round here."

"You sure they're after me?" I said.

"You've got to get out!" he said.

"Lanky bloke with a beard?"

"Yes," he said.

"One with a missing finger?"

"I can't say," he answered. "I didn't stay to shake hands."

I could see through the window that it was after dark. I must have fallen asleep for maybe four or even five hours. "Master Henry?" I said, then realised I was in my undershorts. "Clothes?"

"In the bag," he said.

"You had better be quick," said Doug. "They're downstairs now."

"Won't take them long to think of the stable," I said.

"Horse is ready," said Doug.

Doug led me along the corridor and down by a back stair that passed through the kitchen at the rear and led to a door that opened out to the stable. We entered the stable and I could see Master Henry was saddled and ready to go. "You did this?" I said.

"Best thing, I thought," Doug answered "Was to get horse ready."

Doug opened up the large stable doorway onto the High Street.

"You did well," I said. "Thanks."

"Where will you go?" he asked.

"Glad you asked. Back to where these boys come from."

"Where's that?"

"Buckstone," I said.

"They'll come after you, won't they?"

"That's what I'm hoping. Tell them that's where I've gone."

"They'll follow you."

"Let's hope so."

"Alright," Doug said. "If that's what you want." I swung myself up onto the horse.

"Before you go," he said. "Can I ask you?"

"Fire away."

"The revenge you were talking about. Revenge for what?"

"That's a good question. Revenge for what?" Once, I would have had a ready answer: it was what I had built my life upon. It was what Aunt Marion had inspired me to look for. But what was it for? Correcting the balance so that life could resume? A means of restoring proper functioning? "Life," I said. "I suppose it gives me life." I headed round the front of the building, quietly stepping away, down into the broken earth of the street, keeping close to the side and following the shadows, retracing my earlier route from Buckstone. I was naked on my horse, armed with a bagful of clothes and some decent leather saddlebags. Bloody cold it was too.

CHAPTER 57

I rode into Buckstone with my eyes shut. Master Henry seemed to know the way. Along the old Braid Road, past the Pentland Cemetery, some way further I came upon the small town itself. In the darkness, there was little light from the clustered, black-slated houses and there was no movement or sign of people in the street. I passed the shop *Domenico Corrolla* and was reminded of the reason for my raging headache. Closed now, not an Italian soul in sight. Master Henry walked on through the length of Buckstone and we reached the other side with no acknowledgement of our presence. A short time later and we came upon the house that had been the place of my incarceration and earlier beating. I sat there outside the open gate, shifting in my saddle. It was a clear night and for that reason a little cold but I could feel the heat from my horse beneath me. I had travelled in darkness for three hours and fifty-four minutes and my eyes had long since adjusted to the gloom. I could see the house itself, beyond the gate, detached, alone, foreboding.

I eschewed the idea of a front door entry, having had only modest recent success at the Weir house. I entered quietly through the side door by the kitchen and I was gratified to find on the dresser by the door, four or five oil lamps, ready for use. I could smell the spermaceti oil burn as I lit the nearest of the lamps, and then edged my way into a small kitchen with grey-white plates piled by the window and plain cups hanging off hooks. The place looked tidy enough almost like it was well looked after. I touched the kettle by the fire: it was still warm and there was hot ash in the grate and a large basket of dry wood close by. In the pale light, I made my way out of the kitchen, through to each of the other rooms on the ground floor. Every one of them was cloaked in darkness as I approached with the lamp, even the larger room where I had enjoyed a long period in the bentwood Thonet rocker whilst serenaded by the pianist and his boot-happy, lanky friend. Upstairs was all peace too and I was content with the belief that there was nobody there to worry about; the miscreants would be home all too soon. I guessed that I would have an hour over them. I had to get on with it. I had to be ready.

Having turned my back and begun a movement towards the stair, I heard a noise from behind a small door at the end of the corridor. I raised the barrel of my gun, one of two guns from my arsenal that bore no name but had a deadly pedigree. I felt the cold trigger against my finger as I moved the barrel towards the sound that I had heard. I came to the door and I strained to hear any other indication that someone else was present. I had been foolish not to check each and every one of the four doors, but for whatever reason I had left this one. I heard something scrape. I put the two barrels of the gun to within an inch of the wood panel, holding the rosewood stock tight in the crease of my elbow. I gripped the oil lamp a little tighter in my left hand, then looked to either side of me, as if unsure that I was alone, and I listened hard for another sound from inside the door. I could feel, almost hear, my heartbeat thump a little faster. I raised my foot and aimed the heel of my boot hard against the door lock. The door took the force and instantly flew open and as it did so my anxious finger made firm contact on the trigger and before I knew it I had released both barrels. Imagine my astonishment to find that not for the first time I had discharged my firearm and blown a hole in the cotton-covered headboard of another bed. It was habit-forming. These coincidences are not meant to happen. Next to the bed was an old lady, dressed in a white gown, looking as if she had been interrupted whilst preparing herself for bed. She was drinking from a glass of water.

"Oh dear," was all she said as she looked wide-eyed from the hole in the headboard to the man who filled the doorway. She had a small lace nightcap on her head.

"Oh dear," I said. I moved a step further into the room. "And who are you?" She hesitated and looked at me blankly. "Who are you?" I said a little louder. She did not answer and I immediately formed the view that she was either stupid, senile or simply deaf. What a lonely world that was, as I well knew, when one of your senses failed to function. Then, stranger and stranger: as I held out the light towards her it took a moment or two for it to dawn that I had seen her before. I realised who she was, unadorned, unclothed, hatless, even before she opened her mouth.

"Audrey Traynor," she said finally. "I'm Audrey Traynor. Who do you think I am?" I remembered an old lady (even then she was an old lady, at least she was to a young boy). "You'll have to forgive me. I don't hear too well." I looked at her again. Most of all I remembered the yellow dress and the big, flat, crinoline hat with the goose feathers. Those questions about The *New England Primer* and whether I had read that *A Dog will bite A thief at Night* and *The idle Fool Is whipped at School*.

"Why do you stare at me like that?" she said, bringing me back to the present. "You make me feel uncomfortable." Just as she had me feel, all those years ago in Mr Fawcett's shop, with my nails in a bag and my coarse wire purchase.

"You're going to be useful," I said.

"Am I?"

"Of course you are."

CHAPTER 58

Meanwhile, in Montrose, Doug was learning to swim. The visitors from Buckstone held his head in the water trough for longer than good sense permits for someone with no other means of breathing. When they pulled him from the cold water, he gasped and wheezed. He felt as if he had swallowed a small sea loch.

"I appreciate your reluctance to answer the question," said Mr Traynor. "But we have passed that point now, don't you think?"

Doug was tempted to agree, but said nothing. His stubbornness was made easier by Traynor's wretched fatness. The sight of this man was enough to make you wish your head was still in the trough. "So, let's try again. Where d'he go?" he asked.

"I don't know," said Doug, still breathing heavily from the last ducking. He knew he would tell them in the end, after all that was what he was meant to do. He had been *told* to do so. It was just a matter of picking the right time. They had found fresh dung in the stable and no horse in sight, so they quickly had him bent over the trough, throwing questions at him. By 'they,' young Doug would have described a lanky bloke with a wild beard and angry eyes; a small man who he now noticed did indeed have a sub-optimal complement of fingers, an irritating humming habit and who carried the stink of stale sweat; and a fat man, with slight wispy hair of an indeterminate colour. The easiest thing would be to speak now. Doug knew that too, but he was stubborn and he had a sense of pride in a job well done.

They ducked him in the water again. They held his head under longer this time, long enough for him to feel that if they persisted there was a real danger he would breathe the water just for the relief. When they pulled him out again, he gasped and spluttered and, his pride satisfied, he was ready to speak. The water was streaming down his face. "Buckstone!" he said. He caught his breath again. "Buckstone he said! Got on his horse. Buckstone!"

Mr Traynor was unsure. "Buckstone?" he said. "Why didn't you tell us before?"

"He told me not to."

"Why the fuck would he go to Buckstone?" None of it made any sense to Traynor. Why would the man flee from Buckstone and now choose to return there?

"He didn't... explain," said Doug.

"You sure about that? Buckstone?" said the lanky man.

"That's what he said."

"If you're lying," he said, his beard close to my ear. "I can kill you now or I can come back later."

"Later would be better," said Doug, his voice hoarse.

"Mama," Traynor muttered. "Mama!"

The three men ran out of the building, but by that time somebody had loosened the reins on the pianist's horse. Not just his horse but the horse-drawn cart too. They were in the field at the end of the village. By the time the three men had recovered the horse and dragged the cart out of the mud, Montrose was not their favourite town. Doug was toweling down with a horse blanket in the lobby and the old man was enjoying a small whisky in the bar, when they and a few remaining customers, moved en masse to the window, to witness the departure of the trio. The three men galloped down the road past the pub, in a direction away from Montrose. There was a loud cheer from inside the smoke-filled fug as Traynor and the other two pulled past the window, eyes fixed, ahead.

In Traynor's own eyes, not all they said of him was true. Yes, he was cruel, vindictive, took things that did not belong, kicked the dog, broke things, hit things, hurt his mama by being so much less than his father and never read poetry or even Dostoyevsky's *Crime and Punishment*. Yes, he did prostitutes or they did him and ate more bad food than was good. All that was true, but to Traynor's eyes, there were two sides to everything. We were living in a three-dimensional world. Not everything came in flat, uncomplicated shades of black or white. Yes, he would admit freely to himself that he raped a woman; it was not pretty, he drank too much, he lost control and yes, he raped her. Strangely, in that moment he had become someone else. He would admit he ruined another man's life. He had no hesitation in saying that he had felt some real shame and it never left him until well into the following day. Nevertheless, guilt and shame were awkward concepts. He had killed a man in a fight with an ash-can and a brick and an iron bar and it was true that as a rule he chose to steal rather than work. But shame? Not really. He saw no reason why another man should hold onto his possessions just because he had toiled long and hard in the field in order to acquire them. He was going to work hard to unacquire them. He recognized that he was a fat man with short arms, no cultural preferences, and a lot of grey-black hair on his back and shoulders that did not sit comfortably with the thin, colourless lines on his head. All this was true, that was certain. He was self-aware. He reflected on this as he rode back to Buckstone to find this man

Logan who was going about being an almighty fucking nuisance, all over something that happened a shitload of years ago. Traynor believed that if you put a body in the ground it should stay there. If a dog digs it up, you have to kill the dog too, and that was what he would do to Logan. He would kill the fucking dog.

Traynor looked across at the piano man, cantering steadily to his left. Not the first musician to lose a finger and yet Jesse could play most tunes you threw at him. Like Traynor, he had spun a kind of life according to his own moral code, even when it fucked up other peoples' lives. He could have played a different tune, been a proper musician. He killed people instead and never got the chance to enhance his skill on the piano. To Traynor's right, teeth set against the cold, eyes flashing with his usual anger, the skin stretched tight across the bones, lanky-limbed almost to the ground, Billy Keefe, a man he had known all his life, a rapist, bigamist, sadist, thief, tobacco-smoking killer; but he had a bad side too – he slurped his soup. Anyway, to Traynor's mind, he was in fine company, the kind of company that demanded respect.

Traynor plumped his lips and looked straight ahead of him. He considered their present predicament. He accepted that between them they had cumulatively done bad things. In such circumstances, who could blame a man for seeking retribution? Yet, he considered it a harsh judgement to conclude that they were all bad as human beings. He himself was a rapist, he could not deny the truth. Yet, he had refused to take a wife so that he could look after his dear mama. She had always enjoyed his total devotion ever since his father died. Even during that illness that nearly killed her. She had smallpox - blisters everywhere, down your throat, up your throat, choking her to death. But he kept mama alive through that. He had diphtheria himself as a boy, so he knew how to cope with sickness. They had a house together, he made it nice for her, right down to the white and red rose curtains. No marriage, no children, of course. He fucked whores if he had the desire.

Jesse was cut from a different cloth. Jesse had a wife and child, and he lived a very different life from Traynor – or so Traynor thought because it was often unwise to enquire. Jesse's wife was from Alloa but you would never know and again it was best not to ask. She was able to play the piano herself. Jesse was teaching his son, Alex, to play; sometimes he wondered who had the missing finger. Jesse had some sheep and hens, was not averse to honest work, but honest work never kept out the draughts, so he was always involved in Traynor's capers. Jesse had become his right hand man and he was trusted to kill people for him should that become necessary.

Billy on the other hand did not have a cultured dimple in his body. He had three wives but had lost touch with the first two. Each of them thought they were the first, but they soon learned from Billy that he was the only one who ever came first. He married Shona because she had an infectious smile that made even he, Billy Keefe, the wild man, feel that he could be a million times better than he was. Shona made the mistake of spreading her smiles too widely and Billy did not like that, which may have contributed to the fact that one day she was found bobbing below the waterline, literally, and never surfaced again. There was no evidence of anything untoward occurring but people did talk. Second wife was pretty too, but soon they fought, they drank, she lost her looks, and he beat her so hard with his rifle strap she lived three years with *Made in the British Isles* tattooed on her cheek. Like the first wife, she disappeared and nobody asked Billy where she had gone because questions like that were unlikely to be good for one's health. There was evidence that his third wife was still alive but she was rarely seen. Traynor knew nothing about her, other than that she had tried to commit suicide after being delivered of her third child in under three years. Her mother and father-in-law had moved into one of the cottages immediately adjacent to Billy's house. The father-in-law appeared to have some personal issues with Billy but was wise enough to keep his grievances private. He drank a lot of a grey-sweet drink called cider but he was a drunk who surrendered peacefully rather than fight the world. Still, the local police sergeant had been called in more than once to defuse arguments between Billy's wife and her family. Traynor did not understand Billy to have taken any part in the family disputes and with the local police sergeant becoming involved it was just as well. Before long Mrs Billy Keefe was drinking her husband's beer and some said she had gone from being a sober woman to a wife with a drink problem. It could be said that it was to Billy's credit that his three children were never left to starve, they always had a roof over their heads and had a wider than usual network of family support; it was also quite likely that they would grow up to be every bit as cruel, bullying and vindictive as he was.

334

The one thing Traynor was not too stupid to recognize was that for the three of them their destiny, their lives, their purpose and their survival had all been shaped and forged by that one event at the Logan farm, so many years ago. It was their turning point, their life-changer and every step that followed fell in the shadow of that event.

It was well after ten o' clock at night when the three men slowed their horses as they passed through Buckstone. It had been a long, hard hack through the cold, evening darkness. They were tired, sore and aggressively sober. They did not share words as they passed the shopfront of *Domenico Corolla* and they did not discuss what they planned to do when they got to the house. That depended in no small part on what they found there.

"We should be careful when we go in," said Jesse. "We don't know much about this fella."

"We know he's on his own," said Billy. "Three against one is decent odds."

"But Jesse's right, Billy," said Traynor. "We need to take a little care. He slipped away last time, you remember." They did not much wish to remember. Logan was unconscious, nearer dead than living. It never occurred to any of them that he would be able to get out of that coal cellar. They had locked people in there before, days at a time. No trouble. They once had an old fool die in there. No problem, leastways no problem till this time.

Traynor was quiet as they moved through the village and emerged on the other side, following the road, ten minutes from home he guessed, but he was worried about his mama. He left her in the house alone because when they discovered that shit Logan had escaped, they had to get after him and there was no time for tea and cookies with mama. He did not like to leave her on her own. She was confused these days. She did not seem to share the same points of reference. She wandered in and out of rooms, stumbling into his business dealings, interrupting orders he had given and generally getting in the way. She did not seem to know what was going on. Conversations with her were on a two minute loop – things she spoke of at the beginning of the loop were repeated again at the end of the loop. Life did not progress, it just ticked on in endless two minute replays. They say the memory of a goldfish is just ten seconds. Traynor had heard it from a man in a bar and he did not understand how anyone could ever know this. If true, it was a bit like reincarnation six times a minute. Mama had much in common with the goldfish, only her reincarnation was every two minutes.

They arrived at the bend in the road, close to where the track ran in a muddy thread down to the house. You could see the clear outline of it from where they stood, even in the darkness. To the left was a dark copse, full of spruce and birch, ready to cut for the fires. The wood stretched back over a mile and Traynor expected it to provide him with some basic necessities over the next twenty years. The more extravagant and unusual expenses, of course, had to be paid for by crime but in the future he planned less crime, more trees. Next to the copse was the house itself and a small spread of green to the side, more grass to the front, trees, shrubs, wild growth nobody ever trimmed back. It was a beautiful house and he had lived here all his life; he intended to die here. Then he noticed, with some alarm, that the front door was open and from where they were positioned they could see light spilling out from the hall onto the front step.

"What the hell?" said Traynor. "What is this?" He took off his hat and scratched his scalp through the thin hair. "What's he doing?" To Traynor, a lamp burning in the hall and the door wide open, did not bode well.

"This Logan," said Billy, towering in the darkness. "We finish the job this time?"

"We do," said Traynor.

"Old wounds," said Jesse, thinking aloud.

"You lick wounds, Jesse. This guy decided to open them."

"Let's go open some more."

"Think he's in there?" said Billy, sounding anxious.

"Does a dog shit? Course he is."

"Are we going?" asked Jesse. "Or are we going to chat about it all day?"

"Billy?" said Traynor. "Work your way round the back. Jesse and I'll go in the front door." Billy climbed down from the cart and pulled the handgun from his pocket. "Remember Mama's in there. Don't want bullets flying around the place, her getting hurt and so on." Billy moved off towards the copse. Traynor and Jesse stood side by side; they clicked the firing caps of their guns and then moved forward together towards the house. In a second, all three had melted silently into the darkness.

CHAPTER 59

In 1856 Karl August von Steinheil and Léon Foucault discovered the process of depositing a thin layer of silver on the front surface of a piece of glass, thereby making the first optical quality mirrors. Either Traynor was a very vain man or he was simply a man at the forefront of scientific discovery and development, but he had a number of these highly polished mirrors distributed around the house. I took two off the wall in the living room, wood-framed. I upended a Georgian full-length dressing mirror known as a *cheval* from the draped window in the bedroom. I set them up in the front room, the scene of my recent beating. I had a growing trepidation, a feeling this could all be a mistake but in the end I figured that Traynor was a man who liked to use his own front door; he was not going to mess around with the side entrance. He would be straight in, all barrels blazing, shouting "boo-hoo, mama, what have you done with mama?" Well, there was some retribution even in that small victory, even if nothing else came off. I dragged one chair into the hall and I positioned it adjacent to the door to the living room. I adjusted, sat down, got up, readjusted, and so on. Precision is always important. I steered Mrs Traynor towards the chair and placed an oil lamp on each of the two tables nearest the chair. I said to her she must sit in it and she must not move.

"Why must I not move? Why on earth shouldn't I move?"

"Your son is coming home tonight," I said. "He wants to see you there in that chair."

"Where has he gone?"

"Montrose," I said. "Just a short trip."

"Montrose?"

"He's coming home now, let's focus on that. He wants to come up the track and find you there. It is very important that he finds you in the chair."

"I see," she said.

"So once you're in the chair, that's it."

"That's it?" she said.

"Yes."

"What do we do?"

"I'll tell you when you're in the chair," I said.

She sat down in the chair and looked surprisingly regal. "Where will you be?"

"I will be in the living room."

"Where are you going?"

"I've got things to do first."

Before going down to the basement, I stoked up the fire in the kitchen with a steel poker, threw on some dry wood and pulled the big cauldron off the table and hung it over the fire. I stood there for several minutes, looking into the flames and watching them flicker, redden and glow. Before I left the room I put my hand against the metal rim, pleased to find it was already warm to the touch. I went out into the hall and found the door down to the basement. I took the steps quickly and came across the open entrance to a room that was familiar to me. I smelled the spermaceti before I saw it. This time I had light and I could see there was a reasonable quantity. What other substance would allow you to light a lamp or a candle or allow itself to be turned into a bar of soap? Just a pity you had to mince a whale's head to get there. I filled a small bucket with spermaceti, took it up to the kitchen and tipped it into the cauldron. I repeated the trip six times and the level in the cauldron was up to within an inch of the top. The heat was rising off the fire as the flames gripped hold of the logs and licked the pan. The spermaceti began to melt. My only concern was that it would all happen far too late.

I went out to the back where Master Henry was standing motionless, like he wanted nothing to do with me. He had hay but he needed water. I grabbed a bucket and stepped out to the water trough. I was about to submerge it when I took two quick steps back and almost yelled with shock, like I had seen a ghost. Something came out of my throat, I do not know what. I felt sick from the pit of my stomach and I could feel an urge to retch, pushing up inside me. In the water, his nose just proud of the surface, knees bobbing stiffly, lay Mad Bob, dead as stone, offal-cutting days buried forever.

A life on the farm had clearly desensitized me to the point that very quickly I had recovered my composure and I was able to drag the body out of the water. It sat their stiffly leaning like a thick plank against the trough; rigor mortis had set in and it was difficult to bend the body but it was not impossible. With a little effort I figured I could bend the legs. I knew that rigor mortis was at its peak between twelve and twenty-four hours post-death then it dissipated. That meant Mad Bob had probably died more than twenty-four hours ago.

I recovered my composure and went back to Master Henry who still had no water. This time I filled the bucket from the trough and he gulped at the water without too much concern about its overall quality or provenance. I took the saddlebags off his back, which

I had the strong sense was likely to endear me to him, and then dragged them over my shoulder and into the side door of the house. The bags were heavy and by the time I had hauled them upstairs I was sweating, my shirt was damp from perspiration and from dragging Mad Bob out of the trough, and my head was pounding like a hammer against stone. I carefully removed the pasted dynamite sticks, three parts nitroglycerine to one part diatomite sand. I plugged a blasting-cap into the end of the stick and neatly trailed a fuse to the living room. I repeated the process and positioned the dynamite sticks, smoothly wrapped in their waxed paper, in the position I had chosen for maximum effect. I no longer questioned what I was doing. I was set upon the course I had embarked upon; if you followed the trail no doubt it would lead back to a time before I could walk. There was no more likelihood of me letting go now than there was of the moon landing in the front garden here at Buckstone. As I worked, Mrs Traynor sat upon the hall chair and studied my movements with an air of superior curiosity, as if telling me she knew exactly what I was up to, but did not wish to discuss any aspect of it. She assumed a pose of regal superiority. When I dragged Mad Bob into the house, she turned in her chair towards me.

"Who is that?" she said.

"I thought you would recognise him."

"It looks like Mad Bob. Has he been drinking?

"Mainly water," I said.

"Has he been swimming?"

"He may have been, but he's not any more."

Before I had finished running the fusewire out of the upstairs window, she said that she was feeling the cold and was it absolutely necessary to have the front door open. I gave her a blanket from the bedroom which she took reluctantly, as if it might carry an unpleasant infection, and then spread it neatly across her knees. I smashed the downstairs window and fed the wire through.

I went back to the kitchen to check the cauldron. The heat off the fire was working the spermaceti into a heavy liquid. I took a stick from the fireside and poked it into the mixture. As I stirred, the odour rose off the liquid and clung to the air about me. Five minutes later, the spermaceti was the consistency of clear soup. I had searched the cluttered kitchen, the stable and a store room at the back of the house and had managed to find half a dozen buckets or pots of various sizes. I filled each of them and took the individual receptacles to their designated spots, the sharp, unpleasant aroma now permeating all corners of the building, upstairs and downstairs. I looked out of the upstairs window. Maybe they were out there, biding their time. Let them come, I thought. I checked my pocket for the phosphorus matches, a small comb that I scraped with the tips of my fingers, and then made my way downstairs, past Mrs Traynor, still seated in her chair in the hall.

"What do we do now?" she asked.

"We wait."

"Who for?" she said, her eyebrows arched.

"Your son. When he arrives he will ask for me."

"Will he?"

"Yes. Tell him I am upstairs."

"I see," she said. "Is this a game or something?"

"Yes," I said. "It's a game. Just tell him I am upstairs."

CHAPTER 60

Traynor and Jesse moved slowly towards the front of the house while Billy took the covered route through the copse. It was a clear night, stars bright in the sky as far as the eye could see, but it was dark enough to hide them from sight as they approached. They moved slowly, taking care to ensure that Billy had sufficient time to travel the extra distance to the side door. He stood in the grounds of his own house, unseen and unheard. On the journey back from Montrose he had had time to think some more about all this; time to think over what it was that he was coming back to face. In particular, he was thinking about those events that had coloured his life and led him to this point. In some ways, he considered that everybody was a victim, one way or the other. Every damn one of us. Even the perpetrator can be a victim because when events take hold they grip so tightly they dictate what will happen; the dumb fool who could not keep his trousers buttoned, he has to be a victim too. This thing happened and it changed everything. The conversation he had had in his head earlier kept repeating itself. Yes, he raped the bitch. So what? Move on with it. Yes, he should have known better. Maybe he should have had a father to tell him what was right and wrong, instead of always thinking for himself and always making the wrong choices. He was a victim too, because something changed in him, and for him, that day. They all changed that day. They all became something they had never been. They all did something they had never done. They lost their humanity just for a short while but they never got it back again, not properly. The whole shit train came off the tracks. Yes, guilty, but there was something that led to all this. Traynor could still smell the gypsy, that perfume permeating so deep into his soul he could remember it today like it was fresh off the petal. Above her on the kitchen table, yes, but she took the wrong turn when she shot a hole in Mad Bob. Still, God knows the little creep deserved it. There was one guy, Mad Bob, who would be no trouble to anybody from now on. He had proved to be a poor swimmer. As for the woman, she had taken the wrong turn. The situation had been inflammatory but she did nothing to take out the heat. It was like she had lit a match and started a conflagration. She set in train a series of events and they were all stuck with the consequences. Yes, he was on the table and he was on her and, yes, he was fucking her. He remembered her skin, a sheet of pale silk, already prophetically corpse-like, a face that had seen too little sun in this northern climate. He had bitten on his lip, bloodless, dry in the evening light. He had been a big man, even then, how many years ago? Twenty? Twenty-five? Who the fuck cares? He had been heavy even then, heavy on his knees, he could feel the wood off the kitchen table grate the skin as he slugged between her thighs, grinding like two oversized pegs. It was like yesterday. He had her skirt off by then, of course he did: it lay somewhere crushed, discarded on the floor. There was a jagged line of sweat off his temples like tiny, liquid jewels, glistening in the yellowing, murky light. It had never been a solitary effort. They held each of her limbs, but she had no more strength to kick than say a prayer. Poor girl, you could feel sorry for her. He could see her lips were dry, stretched, cut, bruised. They should have stopped but how could they? How could they? When she shouted that she would cut off Traynor's balls, one man with thick, bristly hair on the backs of his hands and a flat, wool hat on his head had stuffed a rag into her mouth. It must have tasted of linseed oil and grit and stale sweat and Mad Bob's blood. She retched. Traynor was annoyed that Billy had beaten her face; truth be told he wanted to hear her shout, he wanted to feel she was there. Her anger told him she was alive. Nobody wants to fuck the dead. They should have stopped if they knew right from wrong. Traynor pictured himself hanging over her, as she would have seen him, like a bag of ripe plums. He kept on. He did not hear much or see much. He just kept on plugging away. Jesse was humming a tune. Traynor knew it was Jesse because he was holding down the woman's arm and he could see the missing finger. He wondered if you could actually *see* a missing finger. It did not make sense. It sounded grammatically and technically wrong. Traynor interrupted his thoughts by glancing at the silver fob hung on a short chain off his waistcoat pocket. It had belonged to his father. With the motion of the cart he could not clearly see the face of the clock but he was sure it was after nine. He had always worn this fob and chain. He hated his father but always wore his fob and chain. It was another of the contradictions that he lived with. Even that night at the Logan farm he had it tucked in his waistcoat pocket. Traynor remembered Jesse still humming. Jesse did not stop humming until Traynor was done, all this being a good time after Mad Bob was fully ventilated, whilst the old boy, silly fool, husband, lay out there on the porch, clubbed half to death. He might have been better dead than rotting his life away in a cell. At his side Mercer, sliced like a fish. Later, when the dust had settled, Traynor had got his pigs - they were no

346

use to him dead. The woman never gave up, of course. Eastern blood, thought Traynor. Kept fighting she did, but Billy or someone, one of them slapped her mouth and broke her jaw. He thought he had heard a click or a crack as it broke. There was blood by this time. She must have thought she would drown in it as the bright light, the shiny sparks, exploded behind her eyes. To die, drowning in your own blood. Traynor had not been totally happy when Billy broke her jaw; as if by doing so, Billy had diminished Traynor's pleasure. Her eyes had flickered and he knew then she would probably be dead before he finished. He knew they should have stopped but he was beyond stopping. He pushed with short, quickening stabs like he was punching a goose pillow, until eventually the desire left him altogether. He climbed off the table, red-faced, fumbling with his buttons.

Was it because she was so far into her pregnancy that he lost his desire? He would never know. Her fullness had excited him, her enlarged breasts intoxicated him, yet when it came down to it she had rendered him impotent, had stolen his sexual desire, had embarrassed him and stripped him of self-worth. She had made him look a fool, weak, impotent. The wind outside the door had risen and squealed through the house and died. The tall man climbed onto the woman, still humming, still smiling, as Traynor had slipped out the door.

Traynor and Jesse were close enough now to see that the large door to the house really was wide open. He could see bright light and he could see his mother strangely seated in her lace nightcap, a blanket pulled across her legs.   As he approached the door, she looked at him and he looked at her.   He launched himself through the door and noticed nothing unusual, other than the fact she was seated in the hall, her lace nightcap upon her head.

"Mama?" he said. "What's going on? Why the hell are you sitting there?"

"Upstairs," she said. "He wants to see you upstairs."

CHAPTER 61

How often do you get caught in rain whilst the sun is still shining? Plenty I would say. How often do the best things happen after you are dead? If you have ever heard the sound of a baby's first cry, it can make a flint wall squeeze out a tear. There is joy at the long awaited delivery and, with it, the naive optimism of what lies ahead. It is the sound of roots going down and spring buds bursting. Plugs in the golden earth. As if someone reset the old Whitelaw clock, with its fish scale frets and cornucopia drop handles, and time was allowed to begin again. A birth confirms that there is a future and even if we are not there to enjoy it ourselves, we have left something that will survive and resonate with a beating heart strong as a ticking clock, long after the white orchids on our graves have withered and powdered. A birth is the nearest thing to immortality.

As I sat there, I knew that the phosphor of conflagration was just a heartbeat away. Out there were the men who would seek to end my life with the same violence with which they witnessed my beginning. I recognized who I was. I was Horatio's baby son. I was born of Tatiana. I thought now of the fact that I came into this world on the same rising sun that saw her depart. The truth was that I had shared my first breath with my mother's last. Where was her revenge for the life they had stolen? Where was the justice for stealing not just her life but mine too? Was this it?

As Traynor and his men drew closer, I sat in the chair to one end of the living room, the pieces osmosing and melting into place. When the men had gone, my father, Horatio, the man who walked from Afghanistan, had lain there on the Logan farm porch, long after creeping darkness had spilled its tendrils across the bloody scene. His head in a kaleidoscopic whirl, his tongue thick with blood and his thoughts groggy, like a boxer drifting in and out of consciousness, feeling blindly for his opponent. He may have met the Iranian Pashtun woman in his galloping dreams, she who fed him all the healing weeds she had brownly beaten by laying a spoon against his tongue. Did he see a horse with no head, just blood spurting through a wound like an open pipe? He had tasted his own blood or somebody's blood and it zipped on his tongue like metal. Eventually, Horatio was stirred by the scrape of the front door, caught by a breeze, banging, banging, repeatedly against the jamb. He was unsure in the half-light where he was and his sight was still blurred, as if grease had been smeared across his eyeballs. The door had slipped in and out of focus. How long had he lain there on the ground? It was impossible to know. Maybe he awoke, looked up, saw Mercer there with his gaping back, stiff in death and the cool of night. My thoughts shifted. They would be here soon. It would be settled. But moons past, Mercer lay dead and no doubt my father would wake to see the movement of bugs as they began to hover and dig plots in the wound. Through this curious befuddlement, his recollection would have pieced itself together. He would call out her name and his voice would be met by a horrible silence.

Later, my father would have clumsily climbed to his feet and he would have noticed he had no boots.

Walking with a sideways, crouching motion towards the house, the door still swinging and snapping in the breeze. Blood down the outside wall where it looked as if a body might have slid like the wipe of a wet sponge. Would he have pictured a man with a hole in his belly? His hand on the door handle, he would have entered the house. My mother Tatiana lying broken on the wooden floor, on her side, a shadow behind the kitchen table. Her face swollen, puffy and beaten different shades of blue. As if looking at her through a cobalt blue pigment glass. Her front tooth broken, split half way up, blood caked down one side of her face, a dry run from her nose along the side of her mouth. Her gums coated poppy red, I could easily imagine, and her tongue lolling like a sunflower from side to side. I could imagine her jaw, grey and twisted, and the top teeth no longer matching the bottom. Her black aubergine hair matted and sticky. Was her arm broken? Or her leg? Her left leg would look wrong. Was she still alive? Yes, she was alive and my father, broken-hearted, would have found a cup and trickled water between her lips. Did she cough hard on the first dribble? She would have shivered in his arms as he cradled her; a stiff kind of shaking that would appear to come from the shoulders up. Her eyelids, thick as gorging leeches, would never open, would never see the light again. Did he hold her in his arms? Did she shiver and shake right to the end? Her breath would have whistled inside her lungs and he would have sensed she and her life were departing.

As I sat close by the window, consumed by the sweep of total blackness, the curtain slightly billowed by the breeze, that much was understood by me. The worst

351

thing was knowing so little. In the hall I heard Traynor speak, an echo of gruff hostility, and then I heard the creak as he placed his boot on the stair.

CHAPTER 62

Traynor did not like to leave his mama there in the hall. It seemed wrong; she looked pale and old, like she was lost in the woods. Jesse stood behind him, his gun cocked and his good finger itchy on the trigger. He looked at Traynor's mother but did not acknowledge her: the woman was a fruitcake. Traynor put his leather boot on the stair and heard it creak beneath his weight. He raised his gun above his head and edged on up to the next step, and then the next. He would shoot holes in the fool. He had every justification. Logan was in his house and he did not recall having issued an invitation.

Upstairs, the bedroom door was open. There was an oil lamp on the corner table that spilled light across the darkened room. Traynor could see a figure seated in the high chair by the window. He looked at Jesse and moved his head in the direction of the door. They took up positions on either side and Traynor leaned in to take a look. They could see him seated in the chair by the window, seemed to be smoking a cigarette, probably one of his own, stolen from the desk drawer downstairs, no doubt looking out into the blackness, hoping to see Traynor and his men arrive. Well, they had arrived, thought Traynor, and they were taking no prisoners.

"You better hold it right there, Logan," he said, stepping further into the room with a lightness of foot unexpected of such a big man. "Don't do anything stupid. I've been using this gun a long time, so I'm good at it." Traynor edged his way deeper across the bare floor of the room, his gun aimed at the back of

353

the chair. There was six feet between him and Jesse close by and both had their eyes trained on the smoking figure in the chair.

"Better raise your arms," Jesse said. "Nice and slow." The man in the chair continued to smoke. He wore a hat and he stared out of the window, his head set back on the chair, staring as if all he wanted was to be somewhere out there. Traynor considered that with two guns aimed at your head, you could be forgiven for wishing you were somewhere else. He wanted to wrap up this business now. He had had a long ride, chasing this Logan bastard all the way to Montrose and back again and he was angry and tired. They had locked Logan in the coal cellar after Billy had shown him generous hospitality with the boot leather. The bastard had escaped, God only knew how, like some fucking bird or wall lizard, out through the top. Well, the bird was home now and he had made his last flight. Logan had broken into his house, had disturbed mama and no doubt helped himself to food in the kitchen and cigarettes from the desk in the living room. He may have had his hands on the wine too. It was time to close him down and put an end to the past. If it was revenge he was after he would learn that revenge was a very questionable aspiration.

"Are you deaf? Put your arms in the air!" Traynor said. He sat there, motionless, and showed no intention of raising his arms. Traynor waved his gun at him again. "You can put your hands in the air and you can turn around," he said, "or I can put a bullet in the back of your fuckin' head."

At that point, Jesse, a man of lesser patience, took the view he had waited long enough already. The middle finger of his right hand squeezed the trigger and the gun released two bullets in voluble quick succession. They struck him in the back of the neck, one bullet passing straight through the chair itself. He rolled to one side as if he was about to be sick down the arm.

"What the fuck are you doing, Jesse? Did I say shoot him?"

Jesse lowered the gun to his side. "Quit stressing, will you? He broke into your house for fuck's sake! You're entitled to kill him!"

"Maybe," said Traynor, "but why the rush?" He stepped forward and pulled the hat off the dead man's head. He leaned down and looked closely at the figure in the chair. "Holy fuck!" he said, at which point the spark of fusewire caught his peripheral vision, as it snaked its light through the broken window pane, down the wooden panel and into a treble row of brown-wrapped sticks in greasy paper. The dynamite was positioned inside a small box of wood logs taken from the fireplace, on top of which sat a large bucket. Traynor did not have the time to ascertain what was in the wood bucket. He did not see the other buckets dotted around the room, filled to the brim with spermaceti. He did not have time to turn away from the full blast of the dynamite. He did not have time to tell Jesse what he had seen when he took the hat off the dead man, that the face of the man he had shot was none other than Mad Bob – which was impossible since Mad Bob had been snuffed out earlier. Jesse had just shot a dead man. It made little sense. Although Jesse did not learn this unexpected detail, he was nevertheless quicker on the turn and was halfway to the door when the explosion came. As is sometimes the way with these things, the reverberations from the exploding dynamite and the detonated bucket of spermaceti had different effects on the two men still alive in that room. For Jesse, he was halfway to the door when the force hit him, ripping off his left leg somewhere round about the groove between the groin and the thigh, and in the luminous flash of the explosion he was able to watch the leg as it flew over his head, entirely separated from his body. He watched it land uncannily upright against the painted wall, like a gymnast landing off the bars, strangely like a prosphetic limb waiting for its owner to collect. Except he was still conscious and he could see the leg, part of his torn trouser still hanging off the knee, standing there with one small piece of scrotum still attached at the top end. Meanwhile, his blood was running out of him like a river through a sluice.

In some sense - I do not know what sense - Traynor fared a little better. He was closer to the blast than Jesse had been, but although blown to the floor, spread-eagled like an overgrown turtle, he had the good fortune to keep his limbs. He felt as if he had been sledgehammered with a large bat, a blow that had sucked the wind out of him, squeezing the oxygen from his brain and knocking him senseless to the floor, his head bobbing against the wood like a heavy ball. However, there was a problem for Traynor: he was on fire. The explosion of the spermaceti had scattered a wet sheet of fire across the room, and all that it fell upon was quickly ablaze, including Traynor. In its midst, he recovered consciousness and felt the heat on his back as the flames burned through the black coat and came into direct contact with his flesh. He saw the flames licking off his head as his hair exploded into a glowing halo of fire. He struggled to raise himself to his feet, wobbled and crashed against the doorway, rolled into the hall, beating himself with his hands in a vain attempt to extinguish the flames. His cuffs and the sleeves of his coat were now on fire and his only thought was to escape downstairs, away from the heat and the flames. He fell from the top landing, rolling in a ball of flame to the bottom. His mama looked at him then, rigid, confused, unable to do anything for him. He regained his feet and ran out into the darkness beyond, a bright wash of fire moving away from the house, falling, a mobile firework entirely consumed by the flames.

The explosion was well beyond my unholy expectations. Half the roof was lying in the garden, the black slates scattered like broken packs of cards. Some of the floor was spread in smokey pieces across the downstairs room. I was still seated in my Victorian wing armchair by the window, where I had lit the fusewire that had sparked its way through the window to the upper floor, combusting the dynamite and the raindrop spermaceti to such spectacular effect. I looked like a ghost, having been showered in plaster from the devastated ceiling, and there were tiny splashes of spermaceti on my coat that for some reason had failed to ignite. Nevertheless, the room was partially illuminated by a number of small fires scattered between myself and the doorway. I looked up and noticed a man in the doorway, the lanky bastard Billy who had kicked my ribs inside out, swaying ever so slightly, the nose of his gun elevated to a level that would have taken off each of my toes. Billy did not know what had happened. One second he was pushing open the side door, edging his way through the house from the kitchen, wondering what the hell the smell was, his gun out and his face looking mean below the sway of hair and the ragged beard. Then the explosion that shook the house to its foundations. He had seen Traynor – at least he thought it was Traynor – roll past and out into the night, the burning man with his hands aloft, his hair crackling, stinking, with a wash of fire. He stepped beyond the stair and into the room adjacent to the hall, his gun still raised. He looked hard in the gloom, across liquid pools of light released by the small puddles of fire. He saw what he no doubt thought was the wildest spirit he had ever seen, coated white as Banquo's ghost, mad eyes wide and staring. Billy was not the type to hesitate so he fired his gun straight at the point he perceived me to be; his preference was to shoot the shit out of me first and ask questions later. When the first bullet shattered the image of me, tinkling harshly in the cold darkness, Billy was not too sure what had happened. Which is why he chose to release another bullet in the same place, but this time my face was gone, there was nothing to aim at, just the sound of glass breaking once more.

I once said you needed long pockets to keep the Colt pocket revolver warm, such was the length of its barrel. Yes, it was the 1849 model so it had been around for a while, but with six chambers, using cap and ball ammunition, loaded from the front with loose blackpowder and six bullets, with a grip in your hand as warm, comfortable almost maternal as you could wish for. I never even took the barrel from my pocket. It was cocked and I had my hand in there on the trigger. I just squeezed.

The skull is made up of twenty-two bones of which fourteen form the face. Most of these bones are fused together by joints that lock the bones, like pieces in a puzzle, to form a rigid structure. The bullet from my Colt revolver hit Billy just to the lower left side of the nose, blowing a clean hole in the maxilla. Its trajectory then took it through the zygoma, deviating the bullet's path into the cranial roof, where it lodged and slowly cooled. One way or another the effect of the bullet had been to break down the facial jigsaw, such that as he lay there on the floor, Billy's face seemed to have collapsed into its constituent parts. The boney joints had dissolved and his face simply fell apart. I was surprised at the outcome because my faith in the mirrors had been rooted more in hope than in confidence. I had set up the three mirrors, stretched along the space between the door and my wing chair by the window, with two mirrors on the left side and one on the right. Standing in the doorway and looking at the first mirror on the left, Billy would have seen my face and that was what he was shooting at. Trouble is the image on the first mirror was only a projection from the third mirror. By careful positioning of the first mirror from the chair, I was able to project my image onto the first mirror which was then reflected onto the second mirror before ending up on the third. My face on the third mirror was seen by Billy and, not surprisingly, that was where he aimed his gun, causing him to fire at the image whilst leaving me unscathed.

You would think that I might have had a sense of gratitude, as I rode the cart away from Buckstone, Master Henry tied to the back by a rope and halter collar, trotting hard behind. After all, here was some atonement for the wrongs suffered by those closest to me, the innocent victims you might say. But it was an empty sensation because the proof was that it changed nothing. It brought nothing back. It had wiped the slate but it did not restore the chalky picture that had once existed. It would take a man cleverer than me to realise that it never could.

I mused to myself, as the cold air cut past me, the wheels thundering down between the hedgerows, that this night had been a long time coming. Since I was born. Since my father delivered me that fateful day, on the cusp of a blood-soaked dawn. Of course, my father had done lambs, calves, piglets, cats, dogs, cows and horse foals in his time. He had a good record when it came to delivering live goods. He had pulled plenty out on the hills and in the hollows, when it was too late to bring the animals in or when the snow was so deep he had no choice than to do it there and do it then. A little human being was no more than a life, a precious life, and you did it just the same as a Blackface or a Galloway or even a Clydesdale foal. As he set about the task, Tatiana was in all likelihood still alive with just the faintest twitch of a pulse. It was easy to tell that he knew what he was doing. He would know he had to be patient: patient but firm. When it was coming, you had to pull and then give it a turn if that was what it needed, just to make the journey a little easier. My father would have known that he did not give life; he was a facilitator of life. Facilitating life was what a farmer did. He would have eased the passage between that world inside the mother and this world out here, open to the knocks and throws of life. When I slopped out from the hold, like any lamb he had ever pulled, he must have held me in his arms, pink and mottled, messy, sweet, beautiful and tiny as a gilded toy.

As the night bore on and I edged closer to Fife, the sky lightened, and in the distance I could see the North Sea as it turned down towards the Firth of Forth. My mind went back again to where it had all begun for me. It sounds simple but in fact my father had taken great care. He had wiped the blood from the kitchen table and then laid two wool blankets, one upon the other. Aunt Marion had told me this; whether she knew from my father himself or from what she put together later, I do not know. He had lifted Tatiana off the floor and laid her on the wooden table. He was not a stupid man, he knew she had been raped and it looked like the table was where it most likely happened. Then, of course, he had no choice: there was nothing else to put her on. He had taken the kettle from the stove and filled a pot with water, still warm from the night before. Diluted with a little cold from a large drum by the back door. He would have picked a cloth rag off the floor, not knowing its provenance, and dabbed it deep into the pot of warm water. He would have gently wiped her face from the forehead down. He changed the beetroot-coloured water more than once and he would have washed her body, end to end. It was a body he loved and it was a deep tightening anguish that filled his heart as he looked upon the cuts and wounds, the bruises, the broken, twisted bones and the orgy of defilement. Still, I dare lay a bet she said nothing, but her eyes may have opened a sliver and they would have stared up at him like they were slits in a blacked-out window. Did he know if she saw him? There would be no focus, searching somewhere beyond him, where she would go alone. He would touch the mound of her stomach, bringing his eyes and ears close to her skin, as if to see or hear whether the baby could still be alive. No beating heart, no kicking feet? But he was a farmer and he would recognize how hard life must fight to be given its chance. Touching her again and the sense of something, something small beating inside her. She was as close to dead as anyone could be but could she have been in labour? Would doubt set in? Did he think he might be foolish to harbor such thoughts? Would he have touched her again to reassure himself there was something in there. Something was coming. Would either she or the baby see this through? Just before seven in the morning, on the gored kitchen oak, the premature, blotchy, pink baby was delivered. Tatiana would be barely alive at the delivery. Did she see her son? Did she register the life with her eyes? Did she look, catch her breath and die?

That was how I pictured her, as the cart jolted down the track. Tatiana's skin pale as ivory and the salted sweat dry upon it; the flesh cold to the touch and tighter in death. No hate in her expression; as if being dead had closed her eyes to the horror of what had occurred. Horatio, my father, bare-chested, with the baby, slippery in his white arms, wrapped warmly in his coarse, cotton shirt. His face softer now, the anger gone. Love, confusion, sorrow and elation all washing back and forth across his features. In his eyes, however, a deep, broken hurt and over time, slowly etched in each line of his face as he slumped in the chair by the stove. Did he sit in that awful silence, bluebottle flies already hovering over the blood inside and outside the house, his body shaking in steady, rhythmic convulsions, and the small baby pressed against his chest?

He called me Sean, a nod to his Irish roots. Tatiana would have expected that. And two middle names, Andrei and Grigore, after Tatiana's father and grandfather. He would have whispered in my ear and hugged me to his chest. The father I never had.

Outside, the sun would rise as it always does, bathing the Logan farm in its fresh morning light, and he would have heard the gate open and a single voice breaking the stillness.

"Come on out Logan," is what he would have heard, followed by an icy pause. "Don't try anything funny or it's a bullet in the arse."

CHAPTER 63

As if the rape and murder of my mother was not enough, my father had to suffer the consequences of his own attempt to stop the carnage. For the death of Ben Mercer, he was sentenced to twenty-five years. His entrée was six years at Inveraray prison followed by an uncomfortable departure in a cold, horse-drawn, springless coach to the new Peterhead Prison in Inverness. Each of the six years behind those massive rough hewn, red, stone walls at Inveraray was hard to bear. My father was a man used to the open air, the wide, windy spaces. He had crossed many borders, worked his way through the barren desert of northern Iran and skirted the mountains south of the Caspian Sea. He was accustomed to decent air in his lungs. Inveraray prison had no tik-tik flies or Pashtun women but precious little else going for it. At Inveraray he walked the yard just once a day, three small circuits, after which he was jerked back to the cell with the barred but broken window on the third floor. The years that followed at Peterhead brought the pleasurable relief of change, but an eight foot by six foot box was still a box, irrespective of geography. When you are a prisoner that long, any change is welcome but there comes a point when you have served so much time that you do not like change at all. Better the devil you know or something like that. After six years he had not yet reached that small crisis but he was perilously close to it.

At Peterhead he was despatched to Stirlinghill Quarry to break granite with a pickaxe. He went from doing very little at Inveraray, confined to his cell for most of the day, to the rough reality of hard physical labour.

There were fights, open warfare, disputes over the slightest trivialities, and there were petty tensions and issues that made life extraordinarily dangerous. Still, if they were not breaking granite they were locked up fourteen hours of the day and it was not always easy to make trouble even if you had a taste for it. My father, Horatio, sat in a filthy cell with more fleas per square inch than even the Tullis cockerels suffered in the coop, and he thought of that distant place, the Logan farm, for much of the day and most of the night. The mind is a great channel to the wide open spaces.

My father's sister Marion had felt the pain of her brother's torment in every turn of his head, every movement of his eye. She had some serious metal in her water. She was there for the trial and she was there for the sentence. She was someone who could take punches. She had long ago acquired a talent for making what she called *the necessary adjustment*. Any big thing, to her mind, could be taken care of, so long as you made the necessary adjustment. When they took Horatio away, she said simply, "I'll take care of things here." And the rest is history.

So it was that Aunt Marion, and her fifteen year old daughter Lizzie moved from their cottage in Glenfarg to Tullis and their new home on the Logan farm. "I will give you a better life than you might have been expecting," she had said to me.

"I will give you milk," said Lizzie, holding a bottle up to my face. "A sight more bloody useful."

My mind was full of such thoughts as we entered Tullis in a dead man's cart. The events of the night had made me tired. I longed for home, for Aunt Marion and Lizzie, for the arms of Keira. The revenge I had sought had left four men and a fat woman dead and a deep hollow inside me.

CHAPTER 64

As I stood there by the gate, I knew my brain must have shrunk in the night. I recognized now what a mistake it was to leave the Lee-Enfield holstered on the other side of my grass-munching horse, Master Henry. I stood there, my fingers brushing the splintery surface of the gate, and I could see Lizzie and behind her Aunt Marion standing just proud of the door, frozen on the step, like stills from a photograph, faces skewed by the sight of three men holding Colt army handguns aimed at the back of my head. Even at that distance, they looked pale. I had heard the three clicks as they cocked their guns and my face had also blanched.

"I was hoping you would drop by," said Calum Wilson. "You disappearing off like that had me worried."

Even though I had not heard it that often, there was no mistake about the voice, the sneer that ran right through it, that filled my ears. "What do you want?" I said and I could hear the sound of irritation or tiredness in my own voice.

Calum moved closer in behind me and the other boys followed suit. "Oh, plenty of time for all that," he said.

I turned round, holding in my mind the thought that I would just tell him where to go, but I had revolved only ninety-seven degrees when he whacked me in the face with his fist, still clenching the gun. It was a miracle he did not blow my nose off. I got back off the ground, aware of the jarred pain in my neck and the throb in my jaw, but I said nothing this time.

"Who's she?" He was pointing at the old lady in the cart.

"Mrs Traynor."

"Who is she?"

"I'm looking after her."

"What's she doing here?"

"She's on a tour of east Fife," I said.

"I don't find you funny, Logan."

"Then feel free to leave."

He looked me straight in the eyes. He turned his mouth downwards, as if he had eaten something that did not taste right. "The problem with you, Logan, is you take things."

"I take, I don't steal. Men like you steal."

"Where did you take the old woman from?"

"For your information, I didn't take Mrs Traynor," I said.

"You're always taking things that don't belong, Logan."

"I don't think so."

"I don't like what you do."

"What don't you like exactly?"

"People like you."

"People like me?"

"People like you messing with my wife."

"If she's your wife," I said. "You should have treated her like a wife," I said, looking him straight in the eye. I had had a long week.

"Is that so?" he said. "Don't you think if it's my wife, I can treat her the way I want to?"

"Keira doesn't belong to you," I said.

"Well, that's your perspective."

"People don't belong to anybody," I said.

He adopted a look of great concern. "What? I remember the vows. To have and to hold from this day forward. You know, till death do us part? That's all fucking bullshit?"

I looked back at him and studied his face. A man with whiskers bushing in every direction, little clumps of pale hair in his ears, shorter than you might expect, eyes bagged and something yellow and liverish in the whites. "Where did it say in your vows you could beat her with a paddle?"

"My wife," he said. "is my business."

"I've made it *my* business."

"Where did you get the right to do that?"

"We all have that right," I said.

"To interfere in my marriage?"

"You left an open invite when you beat her."

"Do you know anything about women, Logan?" His eyes were sparkling. I stared back at him.

"I know they turn blue when you hit them."

"Keira likes to be hit with the paddle," he said. "Did you think of that?"

"She likes to be hit?" I said, scratching my head. "She *likes* to be hit?"

"Did you not learn anything at school?"

"No," I said. "There was nothing in my class about beating women. Nothing about raping them or killing them for that matter."

"Don't you understand?" he said, like I was very, very stupid. "Keira likes the paddle because the paddle tells her when she is out of line."

"Oh," I said, tapping the side of my head with a finger. "I see now. Keeps her on the straight and narrow."

"Yes it does."

"Like a minefield. You stand on a mine and it blows your leg off?"

"Exactly."

369

"But at least next time you know how far you can go."

"That's right," he said. "It's a route map."

"Well," I answered. "Thanks for the message. Now put your guns away and fuck off out of here, will you?"

There was the shortest silence and I wondered if I had pushed him a little too far and all this was going to end badly. Yet I hoped, in my boyish naivete, that having allowed him the opportunity to discuss – and perhaps justify – his marital violence, he might now leave us in peace.

"We'll go when we are good and ready," said Joey, speaking for the first time. Tom stood by him, holding the other gun, casting a wide eye over at Joey, smiling like a puppy. Calum's hooded eyes moved away from me only briefly, as if Joey was intruding on personal grief. Joey failed to register or simply ignored that look from Calum and continued: "In the meantime, don't you think it would be nice to take advantage of the facilities you have here."

"What are you on about?" said Calum, finally showing his irritation.

Joey licked his thin moustache, looking with heavy slitted eyes at Lizzie by the step to the house. Tom laughed and his gun wobbled in his hand. "Hello, Lizzie," he shouted over and raised a wave with his left hand.

Calum laughed gently. "You can't blame him, Sean. Like yourself, he's got needs."

"Keep him away from the livestock."

"It's only natural. People do this sort of thing."

"What is it they do, Wilson?"

"It seems they go around taking things that don't belong to them. You said so yourself," said Calum.

"I'm bored," said Joey. "There are better things to do round here." He looked at Lizzie.

I followed his line of sight. "Lay a finger on Lizzie and I'll have your neck," I said without emotion.

"That's what we all want," said Calum, wagging his head. "Some kind of retribution. We all want to avenge something."

"Some have cause."

"I agree," he said. "I feel the same about my wife. Vengeance is a two way street."

"You earn vengeance," I said. "There has to be something that deserves to be avenged."

"You make my point for me," he said.

"You're missing the point."

We were facing each other straight on but I assumed a look of calm even there was none beneath my skin, one arm raised and resting casually on the cross bar of the gate. "You have to earn vengeance," I said. "You can't just do what you like and dress it up as vengeance."

"Well?" he said. "Haven't I paid enough already? Haven't I paid with my wife? Don't I get your blood for that?"

"Keira is her own person. She can answer for herself."

"You fucked her," he said, pulling closer, his gun pressing in against me. "That means you made me very angry."

"It doesn't work like that," I said.

"It does."

"Who says I wronged her?"

"I do."

"If you were right to be aggrieved, you lost it when you beat her."

"That's not how I see it," he said.

"You're a man with no eyes."

"The way I see it, you took something."

"I took nothing."

"You took it and it was mine." He pushed his face closer to mine. The whites of his eyes were liverish. "My right," he said, "is to come after you with everything I've got."

Who knows where this philosophical dialogue was going to lead – nowhere good, that was for sure. However, Aunt Marion, who had never fully emerged from the house, had slipped back inside, shielded by Lizzie, and at that moment she reappeared. She gave no warning or necessary introduction, but was holding in her hands the Austrian Reicher and we discovered very quickly that this time it was fully loaded. Oh my God, I had wanted to see that gun fired! She pulled the trigger and four Logan farm bullets released simultaneously from four barrels of the same gun. What madness was this? What deafening noise it created! Almost each and every man present hit the ground with the pointed end of their faces whilst the bullets whizzed and ricocheted around our ears. The trajectory of each bullet was an issue of some debate. One hit the world's most unlucky hen and removed its head but the message was slow to reach its brain, its thin legs pumping round the yard, oblivious to its changed circumstances. The second bullet went straight up in the air over our heads; just God and a few startled Blackface sheep would know where it landed. The third hit the wooden gatepost and, if it had not deflected, I fear I might have ended up in the same headless territory as the hen. The fourth hit the side of Traynor's cart, off which it pinged, slowed and distorted by the impact, and thereafter whirred in the direction of Tom and Joey, before choosing the bigger target - Tom's fleshy arse - in which to sink its nickel neck. As it impacted, the smile came off his face quicker than bacon off a pig. Meanwhile, in my singularity, I did not fall on my face, but for a tired, bruised, out-of-sorts lowland farmer, I did well enough to throw myself to the back of dead Traynor's cart, roll under Master Henry and whip the Lee-Enfield from the holster before anyone fully registered my acrobatics.

"What the fuck?" said Calum, getting off the ground, his sight still trained on the retreat of Lizzie and Aunt Marion who had hurled themselves back into the house, followed by three slugs from Calum's gun, embedded in the post by the door. Tom was still lying on the ground, on his side, his rear end hoisted, screaming and moaning, wildly grimacing because he objected to having an extra hole in his buttocks. Joey was off the floor now and pointing his gun at me. I had my Lee-Enfield pointed at Calum. This had the hallmarks of an impasse.
"I'm going to shoot your women," said Calum with virtuoso clarity. "But me and Joey are going to rape them first."
"I know who I'm going to shoot," said Joey, looking straight down his gun at me.
"Do you want me to shoot *you* Calum?" I said. "I've got you in my sights and it's not a difficult shot." Calum looked at me out of the corner of his eye, a sneaky fox-like look that told you more about him than any words could. I looked over at Joey. "Not so

easy for you, Joey. You might shoot my horse first."
I took my left hand off the barrel of the rifle and
stroked Master Henry's withers.
"I might," he said.
"You got something against horses?"
"Take it easy," said Calum, to me or more likely to
Joey. "Nobody needs to get shot here. Least of all,
me."

At that point came the sound of a thunderous
commotion on the track behind us, mud thrown up
behind the wheels of a small, black, one-pony hansom
cab. We all turned in its direction, as much as we
dared without taking aim away from our intended
targets. The horse-drawn cab was galloping towards
the house and gave the impression it was going to
crash into the lot of us as we stood there transfixed in
a coagulative impasse by the gate. Joey's gun had
been pointing at me. My gun had been pointing at
Calum. Calum's Colt army hand gun .44 caliber cap
and ball had been pointing at Aunt Marion and Lizzie,
but they were back inside the house, so he waved it
threateningly in the direction of the window, looking
like he might fire for the hell of it. Tom was still on
the ground, wimpering, with a hand fixed against the
new hole in his arse.

It took me a second or two to realise who the velvet-
coated figure was driving the cart straight at us, but
during that time Joey had moved his gun marginally
away from me and now fully released a shot directly
towards the oncoming cab, followed by another. The
horsecart did not deviate initially and it appeared that
the driver was unharmed, largely because a skill-free
idiot like Joey was hardly likely to hit a moving target

374

with a handgun. However, in a sense I was very wrong about that. The shots came nowhere near the man in the driver's seat but instead spooked the horse pulling the cart. Suddenly, the thundering beast deviated to the left, looked as if he might jump the wall, but in fact galloped along the rough verge of the track. The cart bounced on its thin wheels behind the horse, crashing from side to side, forward and back, cuffing hard against the rocks, the earth and everything else that stood in its path. I had the impression it was going to gallop on past, some distance to our left, and in all probability pull up at the corner of the field. If it tried to jump the wall, God knows what would have happened. In the event, the horse, still spooked out of its mind by Joey's gunshots, bailed out of turning left and, knowing its limitations, refused to take on the wall. Its only course was to whip round to the right and swing the cab in our general direction. The trouble was that, by this time, the far wheel had buckled, its spokes twisting and cracking, and the cart was half way to toppling over. It came ever closer towards us and we were scattering to avoid the impact, other than Tom who was still on the ground, clutching his wounded arse and not really knowing what sort of further danger he might be facing. At that moment, the broken wheel caught itself against a large rock, stopped in its tracks and the whole cart went over on its side, dragging the horse with it, tethered like a chicken on a hot spit. The driver was thrown from the cart, his velvet tail floating high in the air, impacting with his full weight against the overturned cart.

Like the rest of them, I was reacting to events. I was down on the ground but I pulled myself up with the intention of getting across to help him, when Calum fired a shot from his handgun that popped near my left ear and deafened me as the bullet shrieked too close to the crown of my head. I crawled round to the back of the cart and from there I could see Mr Hamilton, his florid face looking out, defeated, from the broken lean of the stone wall. Nearby, the harnessed horse was still kicking its hooves to free itself from the twisted wreckage, yet unable to escape. I ran across the gap between myself and Hamilton, expecting to be picked off by a shot at any moment. I was halfway when a bullet pounded off the ground just an arm's length from my foot. Incentivised, I kept moving. Then, I heard a repeat of the extraordinary explosive noise created by the Reicher. Aunt Marion must have reloaded, for the bullets were crashing around the yard, albeit nobody's life was seriously threatened by a direct hit.

I threw myself down at Hamilton's side and I knew straightaway that his situation was far from reassuring. He was already drifting in and out of consciousness.

"Mr Hamilton?" I said his name a number of times before he opened his eyes and looked at me. He looked puzzled and then appeared to recognise who I was.

"Sean? Thought you might need some support," he wheezed and then coughed, light droplets of blood spraying thinly against his chest. He wore a waistcoat and a bottle green velvet jacket – not blue as I had thought. He was sweating and I loosened the collar on his shirt.

"How did you know I was here?" I said. There was then a blast of three or four shots, causing us instinctively to duck. However, the shots were not aimed at us and they hit the ground in front of Calum and Joey.

"I'll shoot you if I have to." He was stood on the roof of my old barn and he had one of those American Winchester rifles pointed down at us. These rifles I had read about: they had a lever action which meant you could load a magazine full of bullets and fire up to fifteen shots before you had to reload. He spat a large gob from the side of his mouth that ricocheted off the lower part of the roof. It was hard for those on the ground to see him, because there was strong light coming from behind that gave him a holy messianistic appearance, but when it dawned on Joey that the man on the roof was Rory, you could see the smile creep across his face like a wide crease. Joey began a slow, triumphant walk towards the gate, basking in his mastery of the moment.

"Nice to see you, Rory," said Joey. "I knew you'd come through for us."

"That's far enough, Joey," said Rory. "Put your gun on the ground."

"What?"

"I said put your gun on the ground. You too, Wilson. I want to see the fucking guns down on the ground in front of you." They did not appear to move fast enough for Rory and that compelled him to fire another two shots into the grass in front of them. "Do it!" he shouted. The effect was to galvanise Joey and Calum to drop their guns right where they stood.

"Come on, Rory. Don't be an ass! You're one of us," shouted Joey.

"I got bored with your bullshit a long time ago," he shouted back, the blond hair falling off his ear and hanging across his brow.

"You better be careful what you say," said Joey.

"I've got a gun," said Rory. "I don't need to be careful."

"Why are you with him? There's no need. We were always against him."

"I don't know what good it did."

"We faced things together. That's what we did."

"I don't know what the point of it was," said Rory.

"There didn't need to be a point."

"Bullshit, Joey. Bullshit."

"You're making an enemy of me, that's the point," said Joey.

"I can live with that," said Rory.

"Don't count on it."

"Besides, he saved my life."

"Hurrah."

"Logan saved my life and I appreciate that."

"Hurrah again."

"You never would have done that, Joey. You would let your own mother drown if it meant you kept your feet dry."

"This is a mistake, Rory."

"We'll see."

"I'll fucking kill you."

"That's nice."

"Think on it."

"I have," said Rory. "I'm bored now. I'm going to give you all thirty seconds. If I can still see you by then, I'll start shooting at you with my Winchester."

"Come on," said Joey.

"Sorry, those are the rules. As an old friend, trust me."

"This is dumb."

"Clock starts now," said Rory. "Thirty seconds."

Tom had heard enough to get to his feet. It was not easy but he was well motivated. He did not fancy a second bullet. Once up, clutching his rear with both hands, he was the first to turn and stagger off down the track, pulling as fast as his legs would carry him, away from the rooftop firearm. Joey stepped back a few nervous paces, waved a grubby finger at Rory and then he too turned and ran.

"It's been lovely, but don't feel you have to stay, Mr Wilson," said Rory. Calum needed no reminder and moved away from the farm, just intermittently glancing back over his shoulder to see how serious the situation was. At the end of thirty seconds, true to his word, Rory fired over their heads and enjoyed the reward of a quicker pace.

I turned back to speak to Mr Hamilton. He was still conscious. "What do you think of the rifle?" he said. I did not answer. "Winchester '73. Repeat action. Fifteen -"

"Shots to every magazine," I finished. "A repeater rifle with a single barrel."

"You had a good teacher," he said weakly.

"You okay?" I asked. "The fun seems to be over now. We can get you inside. Aunt Marion will help you with the gunshot."

"It's not... It's not a... gunshot wound," he said.

"No?" I said.

"No."

"What is it then?" I looked down at him and noticed from the way he was lying that his front seemed to be bowed out. I twisted my head to look beneath him and because he was slightly turned to the side, I could see the wooden spoke from the wheel sticking up from the ground, deep into his back. There was a lot of blood pooling under him. I looked back at him and it was easy for him to register my alarm.

"See what I mean?" he said.

"We'll get you to the house."

"I'm not going anywhere," he said. "Oh God, I feel cold."

I took off my coat and laid it over him. "Is that better?"

"Thankyou," he said quietly. After a second or two, he said: "Where've you been then?"

"Why?"

"You don't look good."

"*I* don't look good?"

"I'm older than you. I'm entitled to look my age," he said. He winced as he twisted his body on the spoke embedded in his back. He was like a butterfly pinned to a silk board. I did not say anything. I was thinking whether I should tell him where I had been. "Are they dead?" he asked suddenly, as if reading my mind.

"Are who dead?"

"Look," he said. "You know I'm dying here. I know it too. So, we could sit and chat about the weather or crop rotation or hat pins but I haven't got time for that." He swallowed. "I'm moving on. You understand that?"

"Yes, I do."

"Did you kill them?"

I looked straight at him. "Tell me, by 'them' who do you mean?"

"Christ, Sean, I know you went there." He was wheezing like he was speaking in a funnel. "And I know people in Montrose. I want to know if you killed them."

"There were a number of casualties," I said.

"Is that the same as dead people?" he asked and winced again. His face was yellow-pale as old milk and a damp mist floated over him in a cold sweat.

"How much do you know?"

"Oh," he said. "Some. Quite a lot actually."

"How?"

"Because," he paused, catching his breath. "Put it this way: in a sense I was there." I did not quite understand what he was saying. He was there?

"You were where?"

"Up here, just where I am now. Except it's worse than that." There was a clear film of sweat on his forehead now but he was cold and he was beginning to shiver. He had blood on his teeth, like he had just eaten a particularly bloody piece of steak.

"You don't have to talk," I said.

"I do," he said. "I was there. The night."

Aunt Marion and Lizzie had come out from the house and were standing behind me. Aunt Mario overheard.

"That's not true," she said. "How could you have been? You would have been recognized."

"Is that a woman's voice?" he asked. "You know things are bad when you can't tell the men from the women."

"It's Aunt Marion," I said.

"Ah, well. Anyway, I was here, in a sense I was here. That's why," he said, catching his breath, "that's why, it's worse. That's why you should hate me. There's no other reason."

"I'm not hating you," I said.

He paused. "Well maybe you should." He closed his eyes. "I wasn't here, myself, no. But my son was."

I said nothing at first. Eventually, I said, "You have a son?"

"I did." He broke into a fit of coughing that saw a heavier stream of blood drip from his mouth and down his chin. "He's dead now."

"I didn't know that," I said. "You never mentioned it."

"No, I didn't."

"What was his name?" I said, not thinking too carefully why I had asked.

"His name was Turner," he said. "He was a young boy, stupid with it." He coughed again. "Fell in with those bastards. A bad crowd. Always in trouble. I could never seem to get him out from under them."

"He was here that night?"

"He was." Hamilton kept on talking, his eyes barely open and his voice weakening. "I tried to stop him, but he was a big lad, bigger than me. He did what he wanted. He didn't need to ask me. I couldn't have stopped him. I couldn't have stopped any of them from coming up here that night."

"If that's true, you could have spoken at the trial," I said.

"What for?" he said. "What for?"

"You might have kept my father out of jail."

"Don't think so," he said. "He was always going to jail. They fixed it that way."

"Who fixed it that way?" I asked. "How could anyone fix it?"

"Traynor was well connected. He had money behind him. You've seen his house. Nice house? Not the poor house anyway."

"They fixed the trial?"

"Not exactly, but they moved it in the direction they wanted. They knew enough people to do that."

"Which was what?"

"Only your father would see jail."

"Couldn't you have stopped them, if you knew all this?"

"What did I know? I'd seen nothing. I wasn't there. I just knew, that's all." He breathed quickly through his nose. "He was my son."

"I already knew of him," I said. "I just could not work out how he fitted in."

"He fitted in alright."

"But you knew all this and you did nothing?"

"There was nothing..." He paused. "Well, who knows. Anyway, I was a coward too," he said. "I realised there was no stopping them. My boy, Turner, was tied up in all that. He was in on it and I couldn't stop him or any of them. I just hoped it would come to nothing."

"What happened?" I asked.

"I drank," he said. "Makes it easier to deal with. Everything begins to look the same colour when you drink."

"What happened that night?"

"They came up here, you know that already. Never occurred to me they would rape your mother. I never thought they would physically attack any one." He swallowed hard. "Never thought that, not once. Rough words, yes. Waving sticks at your old father, maybe. But that kind of violence, no. Don't ask me why it happened. There was a madness around. I don't know why. It made no sense."

"Where is your son, Turner, now?" I said.

"Oh, dead," he answered absently. "Long gone." He paused, blinked, and then he said: "I shot him with the last gun I gave you, the Devisme revolver." He registered the look on my face. "What else could I do?" He shifted against the spoke and winced at the spasm of pain that shot through him.

"He wrote to Mad Bob," I said. "I found his letter. I think he felt they had been unsupportive."

"He stayed out of jail, that should have been enough."

"Why did you shoot him? He was your son, no matter what he had done."

"I killed him because he was an animal, even if he was my son. I had to kill him and I didn't want to kill him. But I knew I had to. I knew I just had to."

"How did it happen?"

"I drank. I drank a lot. I got myself so I could hardly walk let alone fire a shot at him. But he tried to take the gun off me, the Devisme, you know?" I nodded. "Well, the gun just went off and there he was, room spinning around my head, a big red hole in his chest." His eye were full of tears. "Anyway, no road back from there. Sat with him all night. Just staring at his dead body on the floor."

"Where is he now?"

"I found a place," he said. "I said goodbye."

"Is that why you gave me the guns?"

"I had to do something."

"You knew I would come to you sometime?"

"I thought you would," he said. "Everything told me you would come. Tom Shifner always told me you had the kind of curiosity that would never leave this thing alone."

"He never spoke to me about it," I said.

"He would never want to know about it. Schoolteacher for God's sake! But I knew you would have to find these men and deal with them." He clenched his teeth and waited for the pain to pass. "He died," he said. "My son died and so they had to die. These men had to die. It was only right that they should die. They should have died long ago for what they did."

384

"So, you used me to get to them?"

"Yes," he said, placing his hand on my arm. "If you want to look at it that way."

"You used me?"

"I did, but don't tell me our paths were not heading in the same direction?" I looked away. "I had to do something," he said. "The worst thing is doing nothing."

"But, you killed him? You killed your own son?"

"I did. But he was ruined. They ruined your life too. Call it revenge if you like," he said. "For both of us. For all three of us."

"For my father and mother too. Revenge for all that shit."

"It was revenge. That's what it was and there isn't much point in dressing it up as something pretty. A pig is still a pig, even when it smiles," he said. He coughed blood against the back of his hand. "Bad as it was," he said. "Your parents were not the only ones to suffer. We suffered too."

"You taught me all about the guns, you encouraged me." I looked at him. "My God, you played me very well, didn't you?"

"You didn't need much encouragement, Sean. If you remember, you came looking for me. Not the other way round."

"You knew I was coming. You knew where I was going. You knew why. You'd thought it all through."

"Well…"

"You knew what to say to me. So when the time came I would do it."

"I knew you would kill them," he said. "I knew you wanted that as much as me."

I pointed up at Mrs Traynor, still seated in the cart, looking ahead blankly, her hands crossed in her lap. "What about her?"

Following, the fire bomb in Buckstone, I had taken the dead Traynor's cart, sat his mother up there on the bench with me, blanket across her legs, and I brought her back to Tullis. She did not say much and I had not been in the mood for talking. I had to bring her with me. There had been nothing else I could do. How could I leave her in the wreckage of that house in Buckstone, amongst the smoke, the roof all over the garden and the fires and all that stinking spermaceti? Not to mention her son quietly carbonized, smoking dead like the tail end of a camp fire. She was half-demented already. She had little real idea of what was going on. I had to bring her back with me, but the miracle was she had sat up there in the cart, looking down at us, and not once had she said anything. All these bullets buzzing around like a plague of midgies and carts tipping over and more shots being fired than she ever knew, and she just sat there watching it all, like she was bored with all this noise.

"Who is she?" he asked. "I'm not seeing too good."

"Traynor's mother, " I said. "I think he was at the front when they attacked the farm."

"The mother?" he said. "You don't need her. The old bitch. Any event, there was only one leader. My son. He was the front man, the fool. And he's dead for his trouble."

"He's dead, that's true. What I mean is, she's lost a son too."

"Her son wasn't the main trouble."

"You don't know that."

386

"Whatever," he said.

"I heard one of them crept away. Slipped out the back."

"Not Turner," he said. "Turner wasn't like that. Turner was a beast. He would have just taken what he wanted. Just like the rest." He opened his eyes again and stared up at the sky. "They were just six idiots who lost control."

"Yes, but just the one who took off, who didn't rape or kill anybody. We don't know who that was."

He sighed and swallowed. "We'll never know, but someone is carrying a heavy secret out there," he said. "But in the end, you got your revenge." He coughed up more blood across the back of my coat. "And in the end, I got mine."

"In the end, it tastes of shit. It tastes of nothing," I said.

"Maybe now it does, but it may be a taste that gets better with time," he said. "Like a fine wine," he added.

"I'm not sure about that. Today it tastes worse than shit."

"True it never brings people back."

"You should have told me."

"I'm telling you now," he said, "before I die."

Hamilton lay there for a little longer, cold but covered by my coat. Gradually, he stopped talking. He drifted into hallucination, spoke of Dutch windmills, apples, open windows, an old Spanish horse, one white sock, called George. The words petered out, becoming monosyllabic, punctuated by grunts and occasional light curses. Finally, he grew quiet again, looked straight ahead of him and then he closed his eyes and let go of the rope. He died, as if he had said all he wished to say and was ready to leave.

On my knees, I closed his eyes. I pulled the coat up across his face. I stood and hugged Aunt Marion and Lizzie to me. We had reached a milestone. Rory, satisfied that Tom, Jo and Calum were indeed gone, delivered a final spit and then climbed down off the roof where he had been patiently waiting. He lifted the coat from Hamilton's face, looked at him hard for a moment and then put the cloth back. I shook his hand.
"Did he give you the Winchester?" I asked.
"He insisted," said Rory. "He hardly knew me."
"He knew you well enough," I said. "Well enough to judge your character."

I helped Mrs Traynor down off the cart. "Are we there yet?" she asked.
"Yes," I answered.
"Where are we?"
"This is my home."
"I don't think I have been here before, have I?" she asked.
"Let's go inside."
"Am I staying?" she asked, something sad in her look.
"As long as you like," I said. "You can stay as long as you like." I took her hand and helped her off the box seat.

Aunt Marion put her arm around my waist. Lizzie squeezed my hand. In the right light she was truly beautiful. We walked towards the open door of the house.